KING OF THE ANGLO SAXONS

Millie Thom

SONS OF KINGS:
BOOK FOUR

To Mike,
   With best wishes
      from
   Millie Thom .

Copyright © 2020 by Millie Thom

The moral right of Millie Thom to be identified as the author of this work has been asserted in accordance with the Copyright, Designs and Patents Act 1988.

All rights reserved. No part of this publication may be reproduced, stored in a retrieval system, or transmitted, in any form or by any means, electronic, mechanical, photocopying, recording or otherwise without the prior consent of the publisher.

Sincere thanks for the excellent cover design and internal formatting to Alan Cooper Design
www.alancooperdesign.co.uk

Contents

Dedication	5
About the Book	6
Main Characters	9
Maps	13
One	19
Two	45
Three	63
Four	77
Five	100
Six	111
Seven	128
Eight	142
Nine	150
Ten	168
Eleven	176
Twelve	189
Thirteen	216
Fourteen	222
Fifteen	235
Sixteen	254
Seventeen	272
Eighteen	288
Nineteen	305
Twenty	317
Twenty One	332
Twenty Two	352

Twenty Three	367
Twenty Four	376
Twenty Five	394
Twenty Six	410
Twenty Seven	423
Twenty Eight	433
Twenty Nine	445
Thirty	452
A Note to the Reader	465
Reviews of Books 1-3	466
About Millie Thom	469
The Alfred Jewel	470

Dedication

To my daughter, Louise, who has always been there to bounce ideas off during the writing of my books.

About the Book

King of the Anglo Saxons is the fourth and final book in the *Sons of Kings* series and it brings the stories of the real-like King Alfred and the fictional Eadwulf to a close. It's been a long journey. The four books cover a period of forty-eight years, from AD851 to AD899.

It is odd to think that I originally set out to write a single book about Alfred's childhood and the events in the Kingdom of Wessex until he was crowned king in 871. The one book gradually evolved into two when I decided to add a second protagonist. I felt that Eadwulf's story, especially his life as a thrall in the Danish lands, added another perspective to the Danish invasions of the Anglo-Saxon kingdoms that start in earnest in 865 (Book 2: *Pit of Vipers*).

The stories of the various characters continued to expand until I had a trilogy but even then, I felt that Alfred's story in particular, was not completely finished and, surprisingly, Book 4 ended up being the longest one of the series!

In Books 3 and 4, Alfred continues the long struggle to keep Wessex free from Danish control while, consecutively, Eadwulf's complicated life and his overwhelming desire for revenge continues. That Alfred and Eadwulf should eventually meet (Book 3) seems destined from the start, considering their shared links with family members – notably King Burgred of

Mercia and Alfred's only sister, Aethelswith. Book 3 covers the most gruelling period of Alfred's life when he comes head-to-head with the devious Guthrum, who so nearly brings about Alfred's downfall. It is from these encounters with Guthrum that Alfred learns how to become a great king, one that his people respect and gladly follow.

Book 4 begins in 883, where Book 3 left off, five years after the final conflict with Guthrum at the Battle of Edington in 878. Alfred has reached the first real period of peace in his twelve-year reign. Yet at best, it is a tentative peace, and Alfred can never be certain that another horde of Danes will not invade. Random raids occur, particularly around his coasts, and once again, he determines to increase and improve his naval fleet.

Alfred's tireless work to fortify his major towns, strengthen his highly mobile armies and build up an effective navy never ceases, and before long his new defences are put to the test. The defeat of a large raiding party attacking Rochester does much to ensure Alfred that his new system can both withstand and repel Danish attack. It also encourages him to continue the work – which proves to be invaluable during his struggle against the devious and relentless Dane, Hastein, in his later years.

Nor does Alfred's desperate quest for knowledge and the desire to bring learning back to his people falter. To help him in this, he seeks out scholars from across the Anglo-Saxon kingdoms and even further afield. One such scholar is Asser, a monk (later abbot and bishop) from Saint David's monastery in the Welsh kingdom of Dyfed. Asser becomes one of Alfred's most trusted friends and advisors, best known today as the man who wrote the book, *Asser's Life of King Alfred the Great*.

Asser's book gives us so much detail about the king to whom, centuries later, was awarded the epithet of 'The Great'. Alfred is also remembered as the king responsible for the union of two kingdoms, Wessex and West Mercia, which became known as the Kingdom of the Anglo Saxons (hence Alfred's new title, and that of Book 4). It was Alfred's grandson, Aethelstan, who eventually reinforced the union and brought the other kingdoms into it to form Angle/Engle-land – and the birth of England.

Since *King of the Anglo Saxons* is the final book in the series, I have tried to draw together the threads of the various groups of characters – and there are quite a few of them – in order to bring the story to a satisfying end. I'll certainly miss having both Alfred and Eadwulf in my thoughts for some time to come.

Main Characters

In Wessex:

King Alfred

Ealhswith: Alfred's wife

Aethelflaed, Edward, Aethelgifu, Aelfthryth, Aethelweard: their children

Garth: former fenman in Somerset, now one of Alfred's thegns

Wessex Ealdormen:

Radulf of Hampshire

Raulf and Uhtric: his sons

Aethelnoth of Somerset

Aethelhelm of Wiltshire

Aethelbold of Kent

Odda of Devon

Paega of Berkshire

Aelfric of Surrey

Scholars and Clerics at Alfred's Court:

Abbot Asser / Bishop of Sherborne: formerly abbot at Saint David's Monastery in Dyfed, Wales

Werferth: Bishop of Worcester

Plegmund: former hermit from Chester, later Archbishop of Canterbury

Werwulf and Aethelstan: mass priests

Grimbald: monk and priest, formerly of Saint Bertin, Francia

John the Old Saxon: Alfred's choice for abbot at his new monastery at Athelney

In Mercia

Aethelred: son of Eadwulf and Ealdorman of Mercia, known as 'Lord of the Mercians'

Aethelflaed: his wife and Alfred's daughter

Aelfwynn: their daughter

Leofwynn: Eadwulf's daughter and Aethelred's sister, married to Oswin and living in Farndon, East Mercia

Aethelnoth: Eadwulf's lifelong friend, still living at Elston, East Mercia

Odella: his wife

In the Danish Lands:

Eadwulf: son of Beorhtwulf, deceased King of Mercia and one-time thrall at Aros

Freydis: Eadwulf's second wife, former wife of Hastein and sister of Bjorn

Thora: young daughter of Eadwulf and Freydis

Yrsa: Eadwulf's half-sister and Freydis' 'adopted' daughter

Ameena: daughter of Beorhtwulf, and Eadwulf's half-sister, born in al-Andalus

Hamid: Beorhtwulf's adopted son and half-brother of Ameena, born in al-Andalus

Basím: young slave boy from al-Andalus now a free man living with Eadwulf in Aros

Bjorn: son of Ragnar Lothbrok, jarl at Aros and formerly Eadwulf's master

Kata: his wife

Hrolf: Bjorn's eldest son

Leif: Bjorn's old steersman and friend

Hastein: Bjorn's cousin, first husband of Freydis, notorious raider

Dainn and Aguti: sons of Hastein and Freydis

Greta: second wife of Hastein

Raud, Davyn and Inga: children of Hastein and Greta

In al-Andalus

Sumayl: ageing stonemason and one-time associate and friend of Hamid

Galiba and Rani: one-time friends of Ameena

Al Mundhir / Rajiv: hated emir in al-Andalus

Rivers and towns involved in engagements in Book 4

Danelaw boundary after 886

Wessex shires

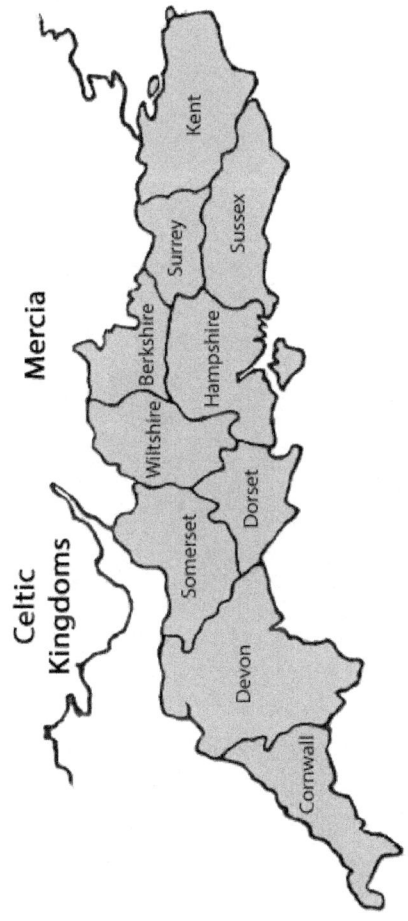

Francia rivers and towns in Book 4

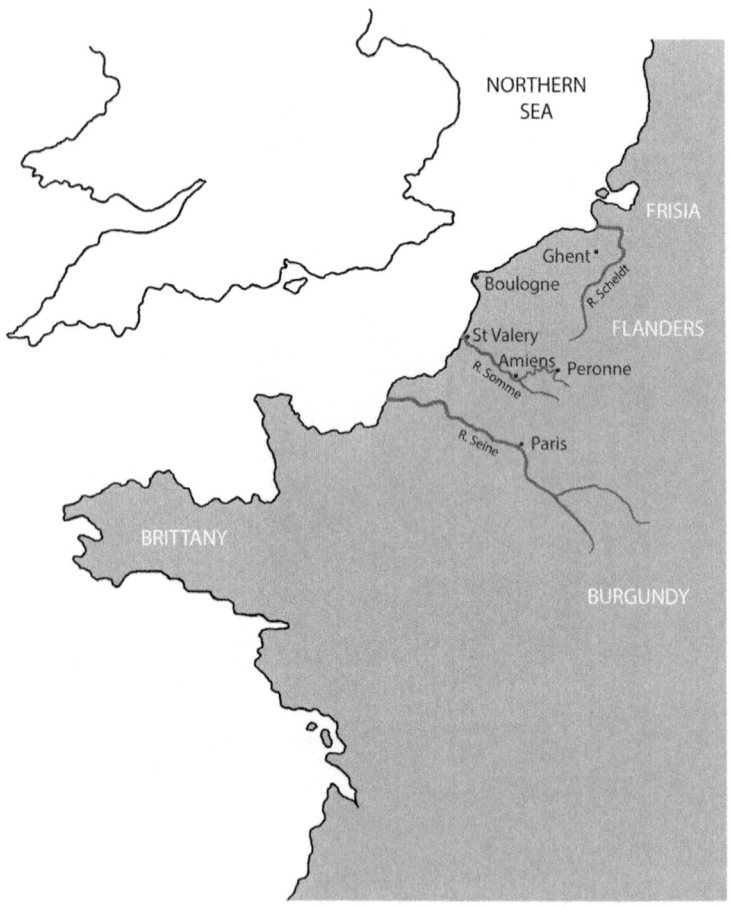

Divisions and towns in the Iberian Peninsula, late 9th century

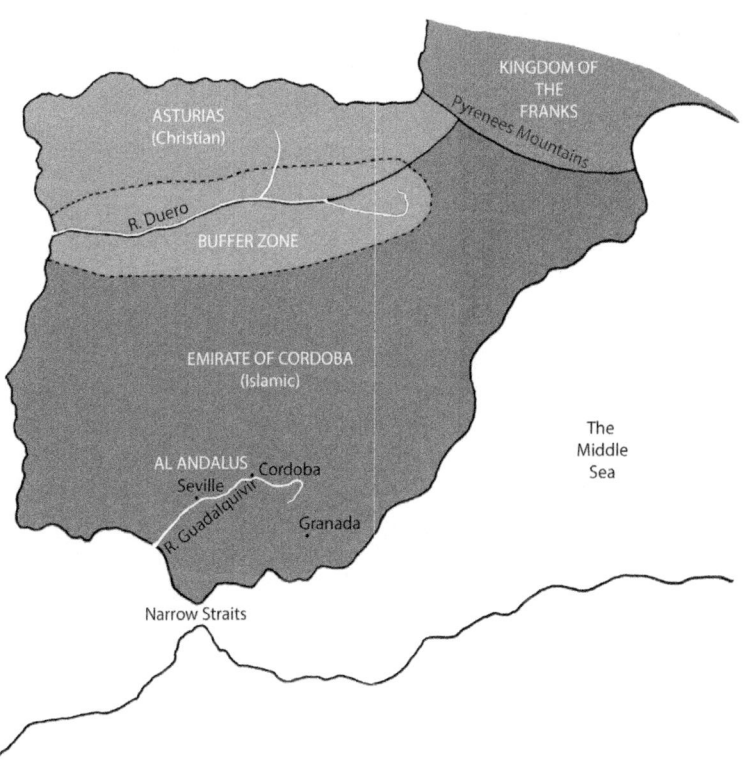

One

Winchester, Wessex: August - mid-October 883

An uneasy silence fell over the Winchester hall. Alfred glared at Sigebert, barely able to believe his ears. 'He said *what?*'

Before the red-faced messenger could reply, the Wessex king pushed on. 'Didn't you think to persuade him of the folly of disobeying me?'

Sigebert gestured at his two fellow messengers. 'We stayed at the monastery for three days, trying to do just that, lord. But every time we approached the monk, he gave us the same answer: he would not come to Wessex.' He paused, staring down at the newly laid rushes on the earthen floor. 'I will tell you the actual words the monk said, but I beg you to remember that these are his words and not ours.'

Alfred scowled, knowing he wouldn't like what he was about to hear, and nodded for Sigebert to continue.

'Lord Asser listened well enough to what we had to say whenever we gained audience with him, though his face told us he didn't like what we were requesting. But as soon as we finished, he just repeated the same thing…'

'Which was…?'

Sigebert glanced at his two companions and took a breath. 'He said, "I have no intention of leaving my monastery for any pretentious king in the kingdoms of Britain!"'

'Did he, by heaven? Doesn't he know that the people of Dyfed entrusted the safeguard of their kingdom to me?'

'He does, lord. We made that clear to him but it made no difference. He simply said that as the recently elected abbot, the responsibility of ensuring the continuing growth and success of his abbey was too great to leave to anyone else at this time.'

Alfred heaved a sigh. Having failed to realise that Asser was now the monastery's abbot, he could not deny the burden of responsibility felt by all leaders, especially when newly appointed. Yet one part of Sigebert's message sparked a ray of hope.

His probing gaze moved between the three messengers. 'You are sure the monk…the abbot…actually said "at this time"?'

'We're certain, lord,' Sigebert confirmed as the men nodded. 'We even talked about what he meant by it as we rode home. To have questioned him further would have seemed disrespectful and we could see he had no intentions of continuing the discussion.'

'Then I thank the three of you for your efforts. It seems that all the good abbot needs is some time in his new role. I'll give him a year or two and perhaps once he's come to terms with running a monastic community, he might be willing to spend time in Wessex.'

*

Over the next few weeks events at court kept Alfred busy, his prime concern to ensure that at least some clerics responded to his summons. The need for the revival of learning in his kingdom filled his days as he sent messengers out to various known scholars, each of clerical calling.

One

The first two of these arrived at Winchester on a bright, crisp morning in the third week of October. Werferth was the scholarly bishop of Worcester; and Plegmund, who hailed from a small hamlet three miles north-east of Chester, was a hermit of middle years famed for his wisdom and piety. Alfred's hearty welcome reflected his joy at having such learned men at his court, and within days they were scrutinising scrolls and manuscripts together with relish.

A couple of weeks later, two more Mercians rode into Winchester. Aethelstan and Werwulf were both mass-priests, skilled in the translation of Latin scripts.

'You have no idea how pleased I am to have the four of you here,' Alfred said as the clerics seated themselves at a trestle and servants scurried in with refreshments. Introductions were made then Alfred allowed the men time to drink their ale and eat the warm bread and cheese provided.

'Since you are all Mercians, I'm sure you'll have plenty to talk about,' Alfred eventually resumed. 'I'm also certain you have much to teach me. The destruction of so many of our precious scrolls by the Danes has grieved me these past few years and my knowledge of Latin is minimal.' He gestured to a corner trestle where the dozens of scrolls were heaped. 'I alone could not translate the surviving texts.'

He smiled at the questioning faces of the two new arrivals, knowing they'd be wondering why the son of a king was so lacking in education. 'The many upheavals in Wessex during my childhood left little time for tuition,' he said, by way of explanation. 'That I never learned to read and write Latin grieves me to this day, especially as I see the love of learning absent among our people – and I include nobles as well as villagers here. The translation of these scripts into our Saxon tongue is vital if we are to educate our people, and it is men like you I need with me at court in order to do this.

'Our two kingdoms are presently enjoying a period of peace,' he continued, 'and I can only hope it lasts many more years. But nothing is ever certain, and in the event of a further invasion we must be prepared.'

Werferth nodded. 'Over the past two weeks, Plegmund and I have realised how much work you've already done in rebuilding and fortifying many of the towns across our lands. And since the Norsemen retreated to the Danelaw and you took control of Western Mercia, you've worked tirelessly in an effort to unify our two kingdoms.'

'Indeed lord,' Plegmund agreed, 'and we admire how well you work with Lord Aethelred. His leadership of the Mercian people in your name has proved a perfect balance for harmony between us.'

Alfred laughed. 'Aethelred is so like his father, whom I came to know and admire as a dear and trusted friend. But Aethelred's a deserving leader in his own right, and a great warrior. I put my trust in him to keep not only the Welsh from raiding Mercia again but for the control of our Wessex borders along the Danelaw. I've had no complaints from him, or complaints about him, from either Mercian or Wessex nobles. He has a way of leading that inspires trust and I commend him for that.

'But I'll say no more about Aethelred – *Lord of the Mercians*, as he's become known. You've met him on many an occasion, I know, Werferth. Not surprising, since you both live in Worcester.'

The bishop smiled. 'I've come to know Aethelred well, lord, and often enjoyed a meal at his hall. I can only agree with everything you say of him. For one so young he has a wise head on his shoulders, as well as being a proven warrior. Though I often feel he misses his family. His father, Ealdorman Eadwulf, and the rest of his family have visited on occasion and I've been fortunate enough to meet them. They're a closely-knit group, and I can understand why Aethelred would feel lonely once they've left.'

Alfred knew that was true. Aethelred had said as much to Aethelflaed the last time he'd come to London. 'Aethelred will be here next week, so you can meet him then,' he said, his gaze moving between the other three clerics. 'I've decided to make one of my most loyal warriors a thegn, and since he and Aethelred are friends, I invited him to be present. It's a simple enough ceremony, and a hearty meal will be served afterwards.'

He raised his ale mug in salute. 'But until then, I'll give you two new arrivals time to settle in. Familiarise yourselves with the texts and select those you deem needful to work on first. Werferth and Plegmund have already made progress with some, but there are so many of them we need an army of scholars to get through them all. But don't worry,' he added with a grin. 'I'm not expecting you to work yourselves into the ground. You'll have time to walk or ride outdoors each day, or simply rest in here. We have plenty of sleeping spaces in this hall, but we've also built a useful guest house for occasions when we have a number of people here at the same time. I'm not expecting too many more clerics at this time of year, but next spring we will, hopefully, be entertaining guests for a while.'

Aethelstan and Werwulf again looked puzzled and a grin creased Bishop Werferth's face. 'If God wills it, King Alfred will be welcoming his sixth child into the world next April, and intends to invite numerous guests to celebrate the birth. Lady Ealhswith is feeling a little indisposed at present, unfortunately, and food is not the delight of her life.'

Alfred laughed out loud. 'Well put, Werferth. That sounded much more polite than saying my wife spends most of her days feeling sick as a dog.'

*

The heavy oak door was firmly shut against the driving November rain and Aethelflaed paced back and forth before it, unable to conceal her excitement at Aethelred's imminent arrival. Edward shoved past her, shaking his head and tutting, and Ealhswith knew he'd had enough of his sister's impatient pacing and exasperated comments.

'And just where does he think he's going in this weather?' Aethelflaed demanded, spinning round to face her mother, who'd been telling Aethelgifu and Aelfthryth one of Aesop's fables about a fox and a crow while the nurse kept little Aethelweard amused. 'Poor Aethelred will be soaked to the skin when he gets here.'

The two little girls giggled about the antics of the clever fox and silly, vain crow while Ealhswith focused on Aethelflaed, the eldest of her five children. By the time her sixth babe was born

One

Aethelflaed would be close to her sixteenth year and had long since shed the appearance of a child. 'Edward's probably gone to the forge to see what your father and Garth are doing,' she said, swallowing down the waves of nausea plaguing her innards. It was almost noon but the sickness showed no sign of abating. 'They only went to order a helmet for our new thegn but they must have stopped to gossip or they'd have been back by now...

'I hope Edward doesn't let slip about the sword. He's not too good at keeping things to himself and it won't be much of a surprise if Garth knows about it before the ceremony.'

Aethelflaed's interest was piqued and she came to sit with them at the trestle along the side wall. 'Have you seen this sword, Mother? Papa wouldn't let me anywhere near it, but he said that Isen had done himself proud. It's pattern-welded, and has a decorative hilt.'

Ealhswith smiled. 'We're fortunate to have such a clever ironsmith. Isen has made some beautiful swords in the past. But no, I haven't seen it. I told your father that the rest of us ought not to so it would be a nice surprise on the day. I'm sure we can all wait another two days. Besides, Garth's family won't be here until tomorrow and it wouldn't be fair if we'd all seen it and they hadn't.'

'I'm so looking forward to the ceremony, and the meal afterwards,' Aethelflaed chirped. 'I like Garth and he'll make a good thegn. I'm not surprised he and Aethelred are such good friends; they're so alike in many ways, both liking fishing, for a start–'

The voices outside brought a momentary silence to the hall. Then Aethelflaed charged to heave back the door. 'Aethelred's here!' she yelled.

*

Alfred hurried from the forge to welcome his guest, with Edward and Garth on his heels. It was several months since the ealdorman's last visit.

'You weren't blessed with good weather for your journey,' he remarked as they greeted each other, the warm hugs between Aethelred and Garth making him smile. 'Let's hope it improves before you ride back, but if it doesn't oblige, you're welcome to stay here as long as you wish.' He gestured to a large, wood-planked building filling what was once a substantial space between the hall and stables. 'That's our new guest house, which consists of four bed-chambers suitable for families to share, around a central hall, which itself has sleeping places around the walls. So, as you see, we've ample space for you and your half-dozen men.'

'Thank you, lord,' Aethelred said, 'but I'm hoping we won't need to impose on your hospitality for too long. I know you already have a number of scholars staying with you, and I'm praying the rain will stop before it turns to snow. It's been cold enough for it these past two days.'

Alfred just nodded; snow was a curse to travellers, but was always a possibility at this time of year.

'We allowed ourselves four days for the journey here,' Aethelred continued. 'One hundred and five miles is a fair distance and riding more than thirty miles a day in this weather would be a trial for both riders and horses. I arranged for us to be housed in the halls of Mercian thegns for the first three nights, so at least we had a hot meal and a warm bed and, of course, stabling and feed for our horses. We also managed to dry our clothes off overnight – just to get them soaked again the next day!'

They shared a grimace and Alfred led them to the hall door, leaving grooms to deal with the horses. 'I've only managed to find four scholars so far, by the way, although I remain hopeful of others arriving once winter's done. They've already made a start on a number of texts, for which I'm grateful. I believe you know one of these men, as you'll soon see.

'Now come and greet the others and later you can tell me how everyone at Elston is doing.'

Servants relieved the travellers of their wet cloaks, hanging them to dry around the walls before scuttling off to fetch refreshments. Introductions and renewals of friendship were made, after which the four clerics returned to their table to resume their work on the scrolls. Alfred led the new arrivals to a trestle tactfully positioned by the central hearth, knowing what bliss it was for winter travellers to eventually be indoors, where the warmth of a glowing hearthfire would seep through damp clothing and allow tense muscles to relax. He mouthed his thanks to Ealhswith as she steered the children to their side table, the promise of honey cakes enough to keep them quiet while the men were engaged in their discussions.

Alfred waited, amused to see how quickly the pottage and warm bread were devoured. But the travellers' hunger was understandable. Aethelred had said their morning meal had been a soggy affair, eaten beneath the leafless boughs of a tall beech.

'It seems Anarawd's still keeping to the treaty,' he said, addressing Aethelred as he and his men sipped their ale, warm mugs cradled in their hands.

'The Welshman's quiet enough at present, although his brothers, Cadell and Merfyn, compete with each other for control of Powys and Ceredigion.'

Alfred nodded, having received word of unrest in those kingdoms himself. 'Until recently I'd assumed Anarawd held Powys as well as Gwynedd.'

'He holds some parts of Powys, lord, but Cadell holds numerous estates there, just as Merfyn holds many in Ceredigion. From what we hear, Anarawd's content with Gwynedd – at least for the moment – and leaves his brothers to sort things out between themselves regarding the other two kingdoms.'

'Well, Aethelred, we both know it won't be to our advantage if Cadell and Merfyn declare war on each other, and I doubt Anarawd wants disharmony between the three of them. Let's hope he can talk sense into the pair before things get that far.' He paused for a moment, considering things. 'But when all's said and done, I'm not wholly convinced we can trust Anarawd. The threat of battles between the brothers could well be a ploy to lure our armies into North Wales to keep the peace. None of us have forgotten how good the Welsh are at laying ambush.' He shook his head at the memory. 'But we'll talk about such matters another time. We have a ceremony to look forward to first.'

Garth shuffled on the bench and put down his ale mug, his face unusually solemn. 'King Alfred does me great honour in making me a thegn,' he said, his dark-eyed gaze alternating between Aethelred at his side and Alfred opposite, though his words were aimed at Aethelred. 'It's more than a man of my lowly status could ever have foreseen and words can't describe

One

how grateful I feel. I'm a fenman, born and bred, and I've been honoured to serve Wessex and my king.'

'I can't tell you how happy I am for you,' Aethelred said, giving Garth a friendly punch on the arm. 'I know how loyally you've served King Alfred and any man would be proud to have you at his side in battle, and as his friend. Just think, I'd never have learned to fish properly if not for you.'

The two young men laughed, Garth's dark head next to Aethelred's red, and Alfred's thoughts momentarily returned to the time they'd spent on the Isle of Athelney in the heart of the Somerset Fens. It had been the start of what promised to be a lifelong friendship between these two. 'Aethelred's right,' he said, focusing on the fenman. 'No man could have served me more loyally than you, and making you one of my thegns will show everyone how much I value such loyalty.'

'Will there be many at the ceremony, lord? I'm unsure about what I've to do.'

Alfred gave a reassuring smile, knowing Garth to be naturally modest and unassuming. Subjecting him to the prolonged scrutiny of others, particularly those of noble birth, would cause him some discomfort. 'Just remember, Garth, thegnship is not only the right of the noble-born who often simply inherit it. As the Wessex king, I can bestow the status upon any man I believe has earned it. Some of our ceorls fortunate enough to increase their land ownership to five hides, which boasts a kitchen, a church and a bell house, are entitled to seek that status. Then there are those who serve Wessex with selfless devotion – as you have done.'

Alfred leaned across the table and grasped Garth's wrist to

congratulate him. 'You've been more than deserving of this honour since we were on Athelney five years ago and I doubt any of my existing nobles would dispute that. As for the actual ceremony, there's little to explain, but it's really nothing to worry about. It will be fairly brief and straightforward, and you'll be required to say little, other than to make your oath to me and thank me in appropriate places. I'll give you a wink when the oath is expected.'

Garth smiled at that and Alfred jested, 'It will be me doing all the talking – something I've become used to over the years – so everyone will just have to put up with that while you simply stand before me and listen for most of the time. And the number of guests will be minimal. As well as your family and mine, there will be Aethelred here, our four scholars, whom you've just met, and two ealdormen, Radulf of Hampshire and Aethelnoth from your home shire of Somerset. So there won't be anyone you don't know. And I'm sure Aethelred would be happy to hear you recite the oath of loyalty later, though I don't doubt you already know the words well.'

'I do, lord. I just hope they leave my lips in the same order I hold them in my head.'

'Don't worry on that score, Garth,' Alfred said once the laughter had died down. 'If you say the wrong words, Aethelred will be at your side to remind you of the correct ones.'

'He will...? Why, lord?'

Alfred smirked and shook his head. 'Oh no, my friend, you'll find that out at the ceremony and not before. You'll also have Ealdorman Aethelnoth flanking your other side and he will be saying a brief word about you.'

One

Servants refilled their ale mugs as they brought each other up to date with their news. Alfred had little to report of Norse activity and spoke of his rebuilding schemes and the odd additions of ships to his naval force. Aethelred reported of his recent tour of Mercian halls and villages, the need for regular checking of the fyrd's state of readiness for battle. Only a small portion of West Mercia was included in Alfred's network of burhs and standing armies, most of the ealdormen further north still relying on the old system of calling up the fyrds only when the need arose.

The late November day darkened into an early evening and servants hastened to light more oil lamps and candles, illuminating the corners of the hall as shadows encroached. Alfred fixed his attentions on Aethelred. 'How is everyone at Elston? It's two and a half years since we all met in this hall. I imagine Eadwulf's still entertaining his Danish guests. Didn't you say Bjorn will be returning next spring to take him and a few others back to the Danish lands?'

Aethelred nodded. 'Bjorn should arrive sometime in May, and I can't say Leofwynn and I are looking forward to our father leaving Mercia. I'm thankful that Aethelnoth and his family will still be staying. But I know my father will be happy to be back in Aros. He loves Freydis dearly and wants to spend the rest of his life making up for all the years they lost. They were married in the little church in Elston soon after Freydis arrived last year, and I'm happy to say that I haven't seen him smile so much since... since my mother died.'

'Unfortunately, the rigours of childbirth take too many of our women, Aethelred, and I know from Eadwulf how hard it was for you all to lose Leoflaed. Although I never met her, I believe she was a loving wife and mother.' He glanced at Ealhswith, hoping she was too engrossed in her game with the children to have heard his words. Yet knowing the perils of childbirth, how could he help worrying when she was due to give birth again in a mere few months? 'But I'm glad to hear of Eadwulf's happiness and I know how proud he is of his children. No doubt he'll miss you both as much as you'll miss him, and I'm sure he'll be visiting you often.

'On a different note, I'm surprised to hear that either Eadwulf or Freydis agreed to be married in a Christian church – although I do recall your father telling me that he and Leoflaed were married in that church.'

'They were, lord, but my father's feelings about religion are odd, to say the least. He's confessed to me many times that he and Aethelnoth don't believe in any god at all. As for Freydis, she is a true believer in the Norse gods and worships her goddess, Freya. But she agreed to the wedding to stop the local folks gossiping about her being Eadwulf's concubine.' He chuckled at the memory. 'The poor lady was quite embarrassed to learn that someone had actually suggested that. The wedding put them both at ease, and they intend to have a second ceremony when they're back in Aros – a true, Viking one.'

Alfred smiled as he thought of how typical of Eadwulf that sounded. 'None of us is getting any younger, Aethelred, and I believe your father deserves to be happy as he ages. After all, his early years were far from easy. He must be eight years my senior…?'

Aethelred's face noticeably brightened. 'He is, lord. He's

One

reached his forty-second year, and already thinks he's an old man! Freydis will reach her forty-first year at the beginning of December. Oh, I almost forgot to tell you… Leofwynn gave birth to her first child just three weeks since – a fine son. She and Oswin are delighted and I'm trying to get used to the idea that I'm now an uncle.'

'Then on your return to Mercia, you must take a gift from my family to your sister with our hearty congratulations on the birth. I hope Leofwynn and her husband have many happy years ahead to enjoy being together. As for Eadwulf and Freydis, I will pray that being in Aros with Bjorn brings them the contentment they've sought for so long. From what I've heard of Freydis' brother, he's an honourable man… for a Dane.'

The men chuckled and settled into general conversation that continued until the evening meal was ready to serve.

*

By the day of the ceremony the rain had stopped and the watery November sun peeped out from behind ragged clouds. In another three days it would be December and the Christmastide season would be upon them, followed by the gift-giving on the sixth day of the new year. Alfred could only wonder at the speed with which the present year had flown.

Garth's parents and younger brother had arrived the previous day. Alfred welcomed them as old friends and would ensure they did not return to their fenland isle empty-handed. Since the start of Garth's periods of service at court, Alfred had sent coin and a variety of foods, woollen cloth and household goods back with him each time he returned home. He knew that anything they didn't need themselves would be shared with fellow islanders. The Fen Folk always took care of each other. And Alfred would never forget how much he owed them all for the survival of his little group of exiles during their earliest days on Athelney.

The hall had a celebratory feel, as Alfred had hoped it would. Sometimes, these ceremonies could be a little too formal, and he knew that Garth would feel even more uncomfortable placed in such a situation. And for Alfred, the knowledge that his hall was well guarded outside by his and Aethelred's men, enabled him to enjoy the ceremony without fear of an attack taking them unawares. Peacetime or not, he couldn't risk another incident like the one at Chippenham – which resulted in him losing his kingship for several months and to be hidden away in the Somerset Fens.

He stood at the far end of the long hall with the high table to his rear, regally dressed in a tunic of deepest blue, with a circlet of gold adorned with sapphires upon his head. To his right, as representative of their Christian faith, Bishop Werferth waited in his ceremonial robes, as the occasion merited. To Alfred's left was Radulf, who had been the ealdorman of Hampshire since King Aethelwulf's reign.

Before them stood Garth, tall and proud in his dark green tunic and black hose. His thick, dark hair and beard had been neatly trimmed and though his body looked calm and relaxed, the odd flash of unease in his eyes did not escape Alfred's notice. Flanking Garth's right was Aethelred and to his left was Ealdorman Aethelnoth of Somerset.

One

The guests gathered round at a respectful distance, Alfred's own family amongst them, chatting amiably until he held up his hand. Bishop Werferth stepped forward, his long, clerical vestments sweeping the rushes as he opened the ceremony with a short prayer of thanks: the harvest had been a bountiful one and the people had enjoyed another year of peace in their kingdom. He concluded by asking the small congregation to dwell for a moment on all that was good in their lives.

After some moments, the bishop silently moved back and Alfred swept the onlookers with an intense gaze. 'Before me stands my faithful subject, Garth, son of Wilgard and Githa and older brother of Edwy,' he started, gesturing to each in turn. 'But today, this man will become much more to his kingdom and her king than the warrior and friend he has been for some time. From this day on, Garth will be recognised in the rank he truly deserves: that of a thegn, answerable only to me and Ealdorman Aethelnoth of Somerset.'

He smiled reassuringly at Garth. 'The foremost duty of a thegn is to serve his king loyally and obey his ealdorman's call to rally the local fyrd when our kingdom is threatened. But, if the ceorls are to accept his authority and obey his call to arms, a thegn must ensure that his estate – which should be the minimum of five hides – provides his ceorls with a home and a good livelihood. They are free men after all, entitled to such necessities. If the estate should fail to provide sufficient for their needs, the thegn will very soon lose his ceorls' loyalty and respect.'

Alfred acknowledged the nods of agreement with a raised hand. 'So, it is evident that the role of a thegn requires effort on his behalf if his estate is to continue to flourish. This effort includes performing certain services – demanded by me, I must add, though of necessity, overseen by your shire's ealdorman – such as managing his land carefully, keeping his roads and bridges in good condition and settling any disputes that arise amongst the ceorls. And let's not forget, by keeping his own estate in good order a thegn is doing service for me, and contributing to the ongoing well-being and prosperity of Wessex.'

He paused, allowing them time to digest what he'd just said before continuing, 'As you must realise, I choose my new thegns carefully, and there is no doubt in either my mind or Ealdorman Aethelnoth's that Garth is capable of performing these duties efficiently.'

'You'll hear no doubts of Garth's abilities from my lips, lord,' Aethelnoth said as Alfred gestured to him. 'I've known him since he was a lad, and can think of no man better suited to this role.'

Alfred nodded his thanks to the Somerset ealdorman, his gaze moving again to sweep those gathered. 'You may wonder from where this position for a new thegn has arisen. Perhaps you'll guess if I repeat something that we all know only too well: life is short and we all meet our Maker in the end. But unlike life, responsibilities must go on. New thegns, new ealdormen, kings, or indeed, holy bishops and abbots, must step forward now and then to replace those whom death has claimed. When a thegn passes away, for whatever reason – illness, battle or simply old age – the thegnship may well pass to his eldest son, with my approval, of course. But, if the deceased has no sons, then another man must be found. And this was the situation in which we found ourselves recently.'

Garth's face displayed his interest and Alfred knew he'd have to explain further before he moved on to the actual oath-making.

'Thegn Osmon of Somerset died less than a month ago, leaving a wife and two daughters. Since both young women are married and living in their husbands' halls, Osmon's widow will be only too pleased to reside with the elder of the two at Somerton. I assure you, Garth, it's a fine hall and thriving estate close to Glastonbury, so it's not too far from your family's fenland home. I hope you will be prepared to move to your new hall next spring?'

Garth nodded, as though in a dream, and Alfred went on, 'Lady Ardith has requested to remain there until the warm weather returns but she would be happy to accommodate you at any time over the winter, should you wish to familiarise yourself with the place, provided the weather permits. Most of the servants and retainers, other than the lady's personal attendants, will remain at the hall when she leaves, so you have no need to gather new ones straight away.

'Is all this agreeable to you…?'

Garth's beaming smile was mirrored in Aethelred's. 'My lord, it is more than I could have ever dreamt of in a lifetime.'

'Then we'll proceed with the most integral part of the ceremony.'

Alfred gave an almost imperceptible wink, as promised, and the Somerset fenman sank to his knees and responded with his oath:

'My king, I thank you for the great honour you have bestowed upon me this day. In the name of Christ Our Saviour and before my gathered kin, I pledge my loyalty to you. I vow never to cause you harm and to fight to the death on the battlefield. I will perform my duties diligently and care for the people on my estate justly for as long as I live.'

Alfred pulled Garth to his feet to clasp him in a congratulatory embrace. The delighted onlookers applauded loudly. 'Knowing you as I do, Garth, I would expect nothing less. Your devotion to me and our kingdom cannot be disputed.'

He stepped back to his former position and gestured to Aethelred, who moved sideways to halt beside a small table on which a crimson blanket covered the new sword on a rectangular cushion, thus hiding it from Garth's view. Alfred was determined to keep that part of the ceremony as a surprise for his new thegn. Aethelred picked up the cushion and came to stand beside his friend.

'This is my token of thanks to you, Garth,' Alfred said. 'I will always be grateful to the Somerset youth who did so much for us on Athelney – including teaching Aethelred to fish.'

Again, everyone laughed and Aethelred proffered the cushion to Alfred, who peeled back the bright red cover and lofted the sword high for all to see. Reflected rays from the hearthfire bounced from the jewelled hilt; Garth's awe-stricken gasp as he stared at it drowned by those from the onlookers around the room.

'I present this sword to you, Garth, in the knowledge that you will continue to serve your kingdom loyally. A pattern-welded sword is strong and not easily snapped, and is a treasured item to all noblemen. I am confident you will use

One

this weapon with skill in times of need and never with malice in everyday dealings.'

'My lord, I will treasure this gift until my dying day and swear that its only use will be in the name of Wessex and my king.'

*

Winchester: Early March 884

Muffled sounds of servants starting their first chores of the day beyond the bedchamber told Ealhswith it must be dawn. She knew she should rise to oversee their work but after a night of fitful slumbers as the babe inside her rotund belly refused to still, she kept her gritty eyes closed, needing the darkness and warmth beneath the furs. Perhaps sleep would embrace her just a little while longer.

Beside her, Alfred's breathing was steady as he slept. It had been well past midnight when he'd crept into their chamber, trying so hard not to disturb her. How could she speak and admit she had not yet slept herself when she knew he'd been working for hours with his clerics, sorting through more Latin texts? He needed his sleep to cope with the enormous workload of his daily life. New batches of scrolls had been arriving weekly, from one religious house or another, and it was beginning to seem like a never-ending task.

With a small, resigned sigh, Ealhswith heaved her cumbersome form into a sitting position, taking care not to rouse her husband. She smiled down at the outline of his face, hoping his dreams were peaceful. It was only a week since he'd recovered from another bout of his illness, and the gruelling pains and diarrhoea always left him weak for several days afterward.

The new day had barely begun and the grey light squeezing through the shutters created oddly shaped shadows around the room. The air felt chill now that the brazier had burned down and she tried not to shiver as she stepped out of their bed to don her tunic and over-gown before entering the hall. A sharp pain shot across her lower back as she bent to pull on her boots and she almost cried out with the intensity of it, admitting to herself that this pregnancy had not been a good one. It had been many months before the sickness had abated, and now, with still another four weeks to go, the frequency of these pains over the past couple of days had started to trouble her.

Rubbing her aching back and praying that this pregnancy would be her last, she gritted her teeth and headed to the hall.

*

Aethelflaed was worried about her mother. Ealhswith hadn't looked well for months and for the last few days it was obvious from the sudden small gasps and the tensing of her body that she was experiencing some painful twinges. Yet no physician had been called and Aethelflaed wondered why her father hadn't insisted on doing that. Perhaps he was just too busy working to notice his wife's anxiety.

As the eldest child, Aethelflaed felt it her duty to have a word in her mother's ear. But it was never easy to catch Ealhswith alone and Aethelflaed hovered around the hall until

One

Agnes hustled the three younger children off to their beds, two-year-old Aethelweard's objections still ringing clear from his chamber.

Relieved of the burden of entertaining the young ones further, Ealhswith sank into a cushioned chair, leaning back and closing her eyes. 'Isn't it time you told us what's causing you so much pain?' Aethelflaed whispered, pulling up a stool and perching beside her. 'I've noticed you wincing and rubbing your back a few times recently. Could you have jarred it, perhaps, by lifting something heavy, or just bending down and rising up a little too quickly? It can't be easy doing anything carrying a big lump like that around all day.'

Ealhswith chuckled and Aethelflaed was glad that she'd at least succeeded in cheering her mother up.

'This "big lump", as you call it, happens to be your new brother or sister. But between you and me, I'll be glad when the weight can be carried around by others as well as me. And I'm also hoping this babe enjoys being in the crib a lot more than you did.'

Aethelflaed hadn't missed the way her mother had cleverly avoided answering her question, and she had no intention of letting her off that lightly. 'Tell me honestly, is there something wrong with your back? If there is, *I'll* ask Papa to call our physician, even if *you* won't!'

Ealhswith pulled a face of mock indignation. 'You're becoming quite a bully, daughter, but in all seriousness, I don't want to pester your father while he's so busy. Alfred spends hours sorting through piles of texts, as well as seeking out the names and whereabouts of possible new scribes and sending men out to recruit them. On top of all that, he's still planning new rebuilding works and naval projects for the year. All in all, he has enough to think about without worrying about my aches and pains.'

Knowing her father's workload in recent weeks to be little different to that of any other time, Aethelflaed refused to accept that excuse. She reached out and took her mother's hand. 'Then tell me what *you* think is wrong with your back. If you say it's quite normal at this stage in your term then I'll say no more. It's just that I don't remember seeing you in pain before you'd even reached eight months during your last two pregnancies.'

'No, you wouldn't have, because these back pains have never started before the onset of labour in the past. Of course, I can speak only of how things occurred with me. Pregnancy and birth affect all women differently. But with me, the frontal cramps that followed were always the most powerful – and painful …' She smiled at Aethelflaed's grimace and gently stroked her cheek. 'Unfortunately, sweet one, new life rarely enters this world without pain, but think how worthwhile it is in the end. So, as you may have guessed, I'm worried that the pains are telling me labour is about to start… and that this babe may be born far too early.'

'Then we *must* tell Papa! He'll be grieved to know you've been in pain without telling him. And if you believe the birthing will be soon, the midwives need to be summoned, and our physician – and the priest.'

Ealhswith let out a resigned sigh. 'You're right, and I know your father would chide me for not telling him of my worries.' She smiled at Aethelflaed and squeezed her hand. 'If I promise

One

to speak with him before I retire, will that stop you worrying?' Aethelflaed nodded, knowing the nod to be a lie.

'Good,' Ealhswith said, pushing herself up with an ungainly wobble. 'No doubt he'll have the midwives and physician here by tomorrow.'

*

Ealhswith was delivered of a third son the following evening after a long and painful labour that had started before daylight relieved the land of its gloom. The pains in her back became a constant nagging ache which continued throughout the hours of gruelling cramps across her swollen belly. Weak and exhausted by late afternoon, she thanked God when, at last she was able to push the child from her body to greet the world.

'He's so tiny and looks a little yellow,' she croaked when the midwife placed the babe in her arms. 'And he hasn't a hair on his head.'

The midwife gave a small smile. 'He could have done with those final four weeks to grow a little more, that's for sure, and I've rarely seen a newborn come this early with any hair. I just hope he feeds well.'

'But he *will* grow, just like any other babe, won't he, Mildrithe... if he takes his milk, I mean?'

'Much depends on that, my lady, but he hasn't had a good start in life. He certainly has some catching up to do, and as you say, he looks a little sickly. I'd also feel happier if his cry was a little more forceful. But we'll take good care of him and you've never had problems producing plenty of milk for your other babes. So, shall we see if we can get him to suckle now?'

Ealhswith nodded and put the sleepy babe to her breast, but to little avail. Worried now, she looked to Mildrithe for help.

The midwife took the child and handed him to her assistant, Hild, who took him off to be bathed. 'No need to go fretting, my lady. I've seen many a newborn too sleepy to suckle. We'll try again soon. He should be more than ready to feed after a nice warm bath. Until then, let's get you clean and comfortable before the king arrives. Young Aethelflaed took the message of your safe delivery to him a few moments ago.'

Ealhswith nodded, unable to put her troubled mind to rest. The child had simply been born too early, and she realised the folly of comparing his appearance to his brothers and sisters at birth. Mildrithe was right, the babe had a lot of catching up to do and only time would tell whether he would soon be as robust as the rest. But until then she could not help fearing the worst, and as soon as Alfred arrived, she would ask him to send in Father Eldwyn and have their tiny son christened.

Two

Danish Lands: late-May 884 - February 885

A brisk south-westerly pounded the red-and-white striped sail, driving the *Sea Eagle* across the Northern Sea. Eadwulf savoured the respite from rowing, warm sunshine caressing his cheeks as he gazed across the blue-grey water and contemplated what he was doing.

At his usual place at the prow, Bjorn was scanning the open waters, while close to Leif at his steering oar in the stern, Freydis and Yrsa were engaged in cheerful conversation with Hamid and Ameena. Eadwulf was with so many people he loved and knew he should be content, but he was not. Leaving his two children and lifelong friend behind in Mercia was one of the hardest things he'd ever done.

After dreaming of returning to Aros for years, he now wondered for the umpteenth time at the sense of this move, and having Hamid and Ameena's futures to consider only added to his worries. He just hoped Bjorn's people would accept them all and they could work alongside each other contentedly.

Freydis was suddenly at his side, her voice cutting through his thoughts. 'Still unsure about this?'

He shook his head and squeezed her hand. Now wasn't the time to worry her with his brooding. 'Just thinking what a surprise Aguti will get when he sees us at his door. Bjorn hadn't planned on coming to Ribe when he set out, after all. But it's a good idea, especially for you and Yrsa. It's been a while since you both saw Aguti. And as far as our move to Aros goes, I'm sure we'll make a good life for ourselves there. You love the place, and being close to Bjorn and his family can only be good. Besides,' he ploughed on, as much to convince himself as Freydis, 'there'll be plenty of work for me and Hamid to do, building us somewhere to live, for a start. And we've got the summer ahead to do it.'

Freydis smiled, her blue eyes sparkling in the sunshine. Eadwulf knew he'd be happy living anywhere as long as she was with him. 'Bjorn's promised to find others to help you,' she assured him, 'so it won't be left to just you and Hamid. And he's told me many times that we're welcome to stay in his hall until our own is ready.'

'I know, and I'm grateful for it. The novelty of sleeping under the stars would probably wear off after a while.'

In the early evening of their third day at sea, the lookout's cry of 'Landfall!' had them all gaping eastward, where the low Danish coastline was emerging on the horizon. Crewmen burst into their usual, joyful songs of homecoming and, at the stern behind, Leif joined in. The ageing Dane would never lose his love of his homeland or his role as Bjorn's steersman. Soon they'd be heading into the estuary of the River Ribea and Leif's skills with the steering oar would be needed.

Eadwulf recalled the times he'd sailed up that river in the past, often just to visit Hastein at his hall, sometimes on their return from raids or trading trips to the Low Countries. But Eadwulf's first time here was over thirty years ago, when he was too deeply sunk in grief and despair at the loss of his parents and home, to remember in any detail – except that he was with

Two

his kindly and learned tutor, Sigehelm. To this day, that visit was one he'd always preferred to forget.

*

The Ribean hall was unusually quiet when the travellers from Mercia arrived in the gathering twilight. On this occasion, it seemed that no one had spotted their approach across the water meadows from the river and Freydis decided that most folk would be indoors, busy with preparations for the evening meal. As she stepped inside, beyond the great oak door, she eagerly sought out the familiar frame of her younger son, only to find that he wasn't there. But meal preparations were well underway and she guessed he'd be here before too long. Aguti had never been one to be late for a meal.

A stooped, white-headed thrall, who had served in this hall since before Hastein became jarl twenty-six years ago, placed the hefty log he was holding on the hearthfire and ambled over, ushering them to a trestle to await refreshments. Two serving girls scurried off to the kitchens and Yrsa followed after them. Freydis smiled at her retreating back, knowing that the ever thoughtful Yrsa would be ensuring they catered for all of Bjorn's crew and not just the immediate family.

'Skoli, are you telling us that Aguti's gone chasing around the Low Countries to look for Dainn…? But why? And where is Frida?'

The old thrall took a hesitant breath, as though uncertain of which question to answer first. 'My lady, in late March, Aguti had news that Dainn was still enjoying himself and gaining boundless plunder, so has decided to stay in the Low Countries for another year or two. He was with a raiding band somewhere near Ghent, although it seemed they'd be moving south into Francia before winter set in… somewhere near a place called Amiens. To our surprise, our jarl made the sudden decision to get some plunder for himself and at the beginning of April, he sailed off in the *Jormungand* to join his brother. But he hoped to find Dainn before then and be back here by the autumn.'

Freydis frowned, able to believe that her eldest son could relish such a life, but not Aguti. Like her son's father, Hastein, Dainn had an adventurous spirit, but Aguti had always preferred the comforts of home. 'What did Frida say about the idea?'

'She'd probably be glad to see Aguti go,' Yrsa cut in, returning to her seat next to Freydis and lowering her voice to a whisper lest Frida should suddenly appear. 'Having full control of the hall would suit her calculating nature.'

Skoli shook his head. 'Frida is no longer Aguti's wife. He divorced her not long after you and Lady Freydis left for Mercia last year. He was relieved to be rid of her – as were all of us,' he added, gesturing at the servants around the room. 'The lady had a way of causing trouble for everyone, and we all work too hard to be constantly chastised.'

Yrsa patted the old man's arm. 'I know that only too well, Skoli. She tried everything in her power to make Aguti hate me and throw me out. Thankfully, Aguti and I had been friends for too long for her to succeed.'

'Well then,' Bjorn said, speaking for the first time since entering the hall, 'as Aguti isn't here, we'll just stay overnight and

Two

continue on to Aros tomorrow. But as soon as Aguti returns, I expect to hear of it. Is that clear?' The old man nodded. 'If it isn't too late in the year we'll sail here, otherwise we'll risk a journey overland. Lady Freydis will want to see her son.'

There seemed little more to be said on the subject. The meal was duly served and soon after dawn the following day, they were back on the *Sea Eagle* heading north for the Limfjord and the Kattegat Strait, and eventually, Aros.

*

Throughout the next few weeks, the small party from Elston worked hard to fit into the way of life at Aros. For Freydis, Yrsa, and even Eadwulf, that wasn't difficult, and Eadwulf soon felt that the twenty-five years since he was last here had just melted away. Work on their new house and byre was quickly underway, and although Bjorn's hospitality in his hall was boundless, Eadwulf did not wish to impose on it for longer than necessary. He also sensed that Hamid and Ameena felt the same.

Aros still looked much the same as he remembered, nestling on the drier ground at the foot of the low hills, away from the water meadows flanking the river. On the gentle, lower slopes, villagers grew their crops, while on the steeper rise higher up, woodland took over: a valued source of building materials, as well small game, fruits and berries, and logs for the hearthfire. Eadwulf shuddered when he recalled the copse of huge, gnarled oaks along the crest of the rise, the place where the yearly sacrifices to Odin were made. Memories of Cendred's cruel end on that fateful, October morning would never be erased. No matter what his crime, the outspoken thrall had not deserved such a death.

The tall imposing hall with its magnificently carved doorway, surrounded by storage sheds, a long stable, barns and a byre looked unchanged by the years, and servants and thralls still worked in the fields or were busy with food preparation and other chores around the village. The sight of the little vegetable garden he'd worked in so often with Thora still flourished, scents of aromatic herbs drifting around the yard encouraged by the warm, summer sunshine. Eadwulf absently wondered whether Bjorn's wife, Kata, delved into herb lore as Thora and Freydis had once done. He smiled, wondering if Freydis would create her own herb garden close to their new hall.

Other than a few new reed-thatched roofs around the place, little at Aros had changed, and memories flooded readily back. He thought often of his old tutor, Sigehelm, and how he'd helped Eadwulf through some of his darkest times when they were first captured and brought here. He strove to focus on the good things but, inevitably, memories of harrowing events crept in now and then. To Eadwulf, the absence of Jarl Ragnar was noticeable, as was that of his sharp-tongued wife, Aslanga, and their two vindictive sons Ivar and Halfdan. Much had happened since then, and so many people were now dead. The hall had been Bjorn's for many years now, and he and Kata ran it smoothly and fairly and the village folk loved them for it.

They had arrived in Aros on the first day of June and by the end of July, Eadwulf's hall was finished. Located on an uninhabited stretch of Bjorn's domain, it had perfect access to

Two

the river and plenty of open land on which to grow their crops and rear their animals. The laborious work was tackled with relish by Eadwulf and Hamid, the thought of creating their new home keeping a spring in their steps. After felling enough trees and cutting the wider boles into sturdy planks, the work of constructing the framework on which to nail the planks had begun. Kata helped Freydis, Yrsa and Ameena to create thick tapestries to cover the inside walls, something they'd need once the bitter winter winds swept through the Aros valley.

All they needed now were some household goods and storage chests, plus some breeding stock and seed to start off the farm – all of which could only be attained from a market.

'How do you feel about sailing down to Hedeby?' Bjorn asked as they shared a mid-morning meal in his hall. 'I realise it won't have happy memories for you, Ulf, but we'll keep away from the slave stalls and focus on what we're looking for. We'll take the *Sea Eagle* and three knarrs, so we should have enough storage space for any livestock you buy. The trip will be good experience for Hamid and Ameena, if they'd like to come – and I'm sure Freydis and Yrsa won't decline the chance of a trip, either.'

Eadwulf would never cease to be amazed by Bjorn's generosity. 'I already owe you so much,' he replied, 'but I'd be grateful for the chance to buy our goods.'

Bjorn nodded. 'That's settled, then. We leave a week from today, which gives me plenty of time to get our crews and supplies together. And once we get back and you've organised your new home, we'll make plans for your wedding.' He suddenly gave a mischievous wink. 'Freydis is determined to have it as soon as possible… something about not being able to fit into a suitable tunic if we left it much longer.'

*

Rays of the rising sun glinted on the blue-green waters of the river as the *Sea Eagle* and three sturdy trading ships pushed away from their moorings at Aros. On reaching the open sea, they veered south, steering a course that hugged the eastern coast of the Danish lands, so avoiding the many islands that dotted the narrow sea, and continued on the journey of over a hundred miles to the opening into the Schlei Fjord. The wind was favourable for most of the day and sailing was good. By late evening they had covered the near twenty-five miles of the fjord and the broader expanse of the lake-like Haddeby Noor to moor along the jetties of Hedeby, one of the most important markets in the Viking lands.

Leaving the crew to guard the ships, they found suitable lodgings and enjoyed a hearty meal before retiring for the night.

A day of browsing and buying goods around the bustling market was enjoyed by all. The constant buzz of many conversations and haggling at the stalls mingled with the row of honking geese, lowing cattle, yapping stray dogs and the interminable screeching of the seabirds wheeling overhead. Aromas of roasting meats and baking breads did much to disguise the stench of animal dung and rotting waste that sat in piles around the site. Delicacies both savoury and sweet sated their rumbling bellies as the buying continued.

The women selected crate-loads of household goods while

Two

Eadwulf, Hamid and Bjorn purchased a selection of seeds and breeding stock that would, hopefully, be the start of their new farm over the coming years. How many livestock they could buy was limited by the space in the holds of three knarrs, but as long as they purchased a healthy young bull, stallion, ram and cockerel to start with, Bjorn assured Eadwulf he'd be able to buy female stock from local villages.

It was a busy visit and Eadwulf had little time to dwell on the day he'd become a thrall of Bjorn's father, the notorious Ragnar Lothbrok, at this very market. But before they made their final trip back to their ships something drew him to the slave stalls. And it seemed that Hamid was equally intrigued.

Eadwulf could barely stop himself from yelling at the sight of the remaining captives, pitilessly trussed along the stalls. By this late in the day most would have been standing for hours, some denied as much as a sip of water. Memories of Sigehelm, Aethelnoth and himself being in this very situation crashed into his head – of his legs giving way and being dragged to his feet, just as Ragnar reared into view before him…

Freydis took his hand, aiming to turn him away, but the anguished cry from one of the captives as he felt the sting of the slavemaster's lash, caused him to break away and yank the whip from the brute's hands. Eadwulf glowered down at the man, on the verge of using the lash on him, when Bjorn and Hamid stayed his hand.

The young thrall fell to his knees, speaking rapidly in words Eadwulf didn't understand, though he recognised the Arabic tones he'd heard in al-Andalus. He stared at the pleading dark eyes, identifying with the desperation reflected there. He took in the olive skin and straight dark hair, the smooth skin of his face shadowed by the first sprouting of beard. Eadwulf pulled him to his feet, his mind working fast – but the young man suddenly swung his attention to Hamid, standing at Eadwulf's side, staring at him as though recognising a fellow countryman.

Hamid glanced at Eadwulf and reeled off words in Arabic, which the young man responded to, frequently gesturing to the slave master behind, now standing back, glaring at Eadwulf.

'His name is Básim; he's almost eighteen and is from a small village near Seville. He says that raiders from the northern lands sailed along the Guadalquivir, turning back once they'd done their trading in Cordoba to raid and pillage settlements along their route downstream. They took a few dozen captives, both men and women, and even some that hadn't yet left childhood behind.'

Eadwulf nodded. It was a familiar tale, and to his everlasting shame, an activity he'd once taken part in himself. He'd spent years trying to put his barbaric actions in Francia behind him, though they often returned to haunt his dreams. 'How much?' he asked the scowling stall holder, gesturing at Básim.

'Three gold coins.'

'We could buy three slaves for that!' Hamid cut in. 'One coin at the most.'

The stallholder's scowl deepened. 'He's young and healthy, with years of work in him. You'll get nothing as good elsewhere.'

Bjorn thrust a finger at the tip of the man's nose. 'Nice try, my friend, but we all know that if you haven't sold your wares by this time of day you might as well pack up and go

Two

home. Take the coin my comrade offered and be glad you got anything at all.'

The stallholder's wide-eyed attention shifted between the three of them, seeming to weigh up his chances if he refused. He took the coin from Eadwulf's hand and shoved the lad at him. 'He's all yours.'

*

On a glorious day in the first week of September, Eadwulf and Freydis made their marriage vows for the second time. The sun still held its warmth and a gentle breeze rustled the gold-tipped leaves in the little woodland glade on the hillside behind Aros. To Eadwulf, Freydis looked as fresh and lovely as she had done in the days when they first loved each other. Her pale blue over-gown, simply decorated with colourful appliqué around the hem, set off her pale complexion and bright blue eyes. Only the few streaks of silver amidst her fair hair indicated that Freydis was no longer young. Eadwulf sent a silent prayer of thanks to the gods he didn't believe in for returning her to him after all these years.

Their child would be born in late February, just in time to welcome the spring. Despite the concerns he felt over Freydis giving birth in her forty-second year, Eadwulf could not contain his joy at the thought of fathering a child with the woman who meant more to him than life itself.

The whole village gathered for the ceremony. It was a relatively simple affair, since both Eadwulf and Freydis had been married before, but a joyful one, especially for all who had known the bride and groom for some years. The sacrifice of a goat to Thor, a boar to Frey and a sow to Freya were just the same as Eadwulf recalled from both Bjorn's wedding to Kata and Freydis' wedding to Hastein all those years ago. The exchange of rings and treasured swords and the recital of marriage vows beside a little altar were also the same. And once they were married, although the bridal run back to the hall was omitted, Eadwulf did carry Freydis over the threshold of their new home. To live under the shadow of a bad omen should she trip and fall in the portal between worlds, was not something anyone was prepared to risk. Finally, before heading to the Aros hall to enjoy the sumptuous feast Bjorn had provided, Eadwulf thrust his sword into the supporting pillar of his home. He smiled to himself as he remembered Bjorn doing the same at Kata's family home on the island of Bornholm. He stood back while Bjorn, Leif and a few others examined the scar.

Leif turned to face him, grinning from ear to ear. 'Looking at the depth of this scar, I think it's safe to say that you and Freydis can expect more luck in your marriage than you could possibly use. You could even afford to share some of it with us all and still have the blessings of the gods.'

Laughter erupted, and on that happy note, they made their way over to the Aros hall to feast and make merry for the duration of the honeymoon.

'Happy?' Eadwulf asked his glowing wife as they savoured the delicious foods that Bjorn had generously provided in his hall.

'Blissfully,' she replied, before averting her eyes.

Two

Eadwulf didn't need to ask what she was trying to hide; he felt the same way, too. 'To have had all our children here would have made our day perfect,' he whispered. 'And I know how worried you've been over not hearing from Aguti. But don't give up hope just yet. The seas are often calm enough for sailing until mid-October, if not later.'

'I haven't entirely given up hope of that, Eadwulf, or in hoping that Aguti will have news of Dainn when he does get here. It's just the not knowing I find so hard. I know Bjorn's offered to sail down to Ghent to look for them in the spring if Aguti still isn't back by then, but I can't bear the thought of spending the long winter months in ignorance.' She reached up and touched his cheek, the love she felt for him bright in her eyes. 'I have our baby to consider for a start and I want to enjoy feeling the child grow without constantly fretting over…'

Eadwulf squeezed her hand. 'I understand, but today is our wedding day – well, our second wedding day,' he amended, with a grin – 'and we owe it to the family and friends we *do* have with us to make it as enjoyable as we can.' He glanced at their little family group, easy in each other's company and laughing at some jest of Bjorn's. A smile creased his face as he focused on Yrsa and Hamid, sitting next to each other and constantly sharing coy looks.

'I've had my eye on those two for some time and they make me smile, too,' Freydis admitted. 'They've become so close. And I'll tell you something else: Hrolf and Ameena are also fond of each other's company.'

Eadwulf's jaw dropped. 'You're sure?' Freydis nodded. 'You don't miss much, do you?'

'Is that so surprising, considering the family I was brought up in? A second pair of eyes would have been useful with Ivar and Halfdan around.'

Eadwulf shuddered, needing no reminder of her brothers' evil ways. He'd put the past behind him and had no intention of dwelling on his treatment as a slave all those years ago. He'd come a long way since then and exacted his revenge on at least some of those who had brought his family so low. But his days as a warrior were over, and he had no need to prove his courage again. All he wanted now was to take care of his family and farm his land.

But despite his consolatory words to Freydis, he had a strong feeling that, come next spring, he'd be with Bjorn and his crew once again and sailing down to northern Francia.

*

The winter months passed quietly at Eadwulf and Freydis' new home. Freydis, Yrsa and Ameena spent their days cooking and doing other household chores, including weaving winter cloaks, tunics and blankets. Eadwulf, Hamid and Básim set to work building a barn and a few storage huts and fences, all with timber they'd cut from the nearby woods. Nor was it long before Hamid turned again to his carpentry and, unbeknown to Freydis, he soon set to work on a rocking cradle, ready for the arrival of the new babe. Básim proved to be a capable boy who did not shy away from hard work. He spent much of his time with Hamid, who refused to chat in Arabic. As a result, the lad became increasingly fluent in the Danish tongue.

Two

Eadwulf set Bjorn's shipbuilders to work building him a sturdy knarr, so that he and his family could sail down to Hedeby or up to Aalborg to trade without feeling reliant on his wife's brother. Though he knew Bjorn would never refuse to take them in the *Sea Eagle*, Eadwulf felt happier knowing he had no need to repeatedly play on Bjorn's goodwill.

The Aros jarl and his family were frequent visitors to Eadwulf and Freydis' new longhouse, and they shared many a meal in each other's homes, generally catching up with news and enjoying each other's company. The celebrations of the Yule came and went, spent entirely in Bjorn's hall, and the cold, icy weeks that followed dragged by as everyone longed for spring to arrive.

By the last week of February, Freydis was at the end of her term and though she never complained, Eadwulf could see how tired she was. The birthing pains started in the late afternoon, increasing in intensity as the evening wore on, and by the time the first rays of the rising sun crept over the horizon, a healthy, newly washed daughter was placed in Freydis' arms.

'She's beautiful,' Freydis cooed, 'and her voice seems to be working perfectly. She obviously doesn't like being bathed.'

Yrsa giggled. Having helped the midwives with the birthing, she now shared Freydis' relief that all had gone well and the babe was whole and hearty. 'Eadwulf will be pleased when he sees that hair,' she remarked, her finger stroking the silky swathe of red covering the tiny head. 'And your mother would be pleased to know you named your little girl after her.'

'She would, and I can tell you it was Eadwulf who chose the name. If the babe had been another son, it would have been Jorund. He knew you would have liked that.'

Yrsa nodded. 'I would have, and Jorund would be happy to know he was still in our thoughts. But, right now, I think the proud father will be waiting to greet his new daughter.'

'He will, and as soon the little one gets over her indignation at being rudely dumped in water, we can send for him.'

'Not before we get you looking respectable,' Yrsa retorted, taking the babe from Freydis and laying her in her beautifully carved new cradle. She set the rocking in motion, her fingers moving across the delicate designs on the cradle's hood. 'I'm amazed at Hamid's skills with those carpentry tools of his; everything he creates is a work of art.'

Freydis smiled but said nothing. Yrsa was smitten with everything about Hamid and from what Eadwulf had told her, Hamid felt the same way about Yrsa.

'A good wash down and a clean robe and you'll look as good as new, even if you don't feel it yet,' Yrsa remarked, heading across the room to pour a jugful of warm water into a large pot bowl. 'Then I'll go and tell the new father that his wife and daughter are ready to see him.'

Eadwulf gazed lovingly at the babe in his arms as thoughts of his stillborn son all those years ago inadvertently returned. The boy would have been fourteen by now. 'Another redhead,' he said with a grin, 'although little Thora's much prettier than me. I'm guessing she'll grow up looking like her beautiful mother, and her lovely grandmother, of course.'

Freydis chuckled. 'Except for the red hair… but as you know, I love red hair. At present Thora's eyes look blue, but they may soon turn as green as yours and Bjorn's, and Hrolf

Two

and Ameena's, too.'

The babe began to chunter and Eadwulf pulled a face that made Freydis laugh. He promptly handed the child to the waiting nurse and came to sit beside her. 'Bjorn wants to sail down to Francia sometime in April to look for Dainn and Aguti. We'll head up the River Somme to Amiens and if the band we think Dainn's with is still pillaging around there it shouldn't be hard to locate. If they've moved on, the locals might have some idea of where they were heading.'

Freydis said nothing, news of her sons' raiding evidently the last thing she needed to hear right now, but she needed to know what her brother had planned. 'Hamid and Basím will stay here, partly to keep our home safe but also to run things outdoors. They're both happy with that as Hamid's keen to keep his carpentry work going. Bjorn's sons won't be coming with us either,' he added. 'They'll be there for Kata as well as taking overall responsibility around Aros. 'So, if we aren't leaving until April, it gives us a few weeks for Thora to settle before I leave you to cope alone.'

'Cope alone…? That's never going to happen with Yrsa and Ameena here, and Kata not far away – not to mention the servants. I doubt I'll ever be alone for a moment. Besides,' Freydis added, smiling as she took Eadwulf's hand, 'you know as well as I that your fussing over Thora is likely to be more hindrance than help. For a start, you can't feed her, can you?' Eadwulf grinned and shook his head. 'And I'm quite sure that by April you'll be more than happy to get away so you can catch up on some sleep.'

Having no arguments to counter her points, Eadwulf

simply smiled. 'I admit my failings, but knowing all you said to be true won't stop me from missing you while we're gone. But if we can find Aguti, at least we'll have good news to bring back to you.'

Three

It took four days for the *Sea Eagle* to reach the smooth, sandy coastline of northern Francia, a sharp contrast to the rugged, island-strewn coast of Frisia further north. Eadwulf savoured being back in a longship, warm wind on his face and briny air filling his nostrils as they headed to places unknown. It was fourteen years since they'd set out for Cordoba in search of Beorhtwulf and once again they were in search of well-loved family members.

The increasing warmth of the late April sun as they journeyed south brought back memories of Jorund when they'd sailed to al-Andalus and, inevitably, to Eadwulf's grief on losing him at the battle of Edington seven years later. It had taken him so long to come to terms with his younger brother's death, but now he was able to dwell on memories of the happy times they had spent together.

It was a tiring journey, despite having spent the first night on one of the small islands in the Limfjord. Since then, Bjorn had insisted they keep moving and as the wind had rarely been in their favour, they'd faced long periods of rowing. Crewmen slept in rotation, a few hours at a time, and by now all were in need of a long night's sleep away from their oar ports.

The longship veered east towards the bay-flanked mouth of the River Somme and Eadwulf focused on Bjorn as he moved along the central aisle to stand beside the sturdy central mast.

'We'll follow the river for the next day or so,' the ship's master started, yelling to make his voice heard over the harsh keening of seabirds circling above. 'From what I remember there are a few settlements along the way and, with any luck, some of the people there might know of the whereabouts of bands of Norsemen. Hopefully Dainn will be with one of those bands – and if Thor really smiles on us, Aguti will be with him. Today we're sailing only as far as the first settlement we come to... which, if I recall, is named after some Christian saint or other and is pretty much at the river mouth. Leif...?'

'I believe it's called Saint Valery,' the old steersman supplied as he manoeuvred the great steering oar at the helm, 'and I've heard it's grown a lot since we were last here ten years ago.'

'Then we should find everything we need for our first night on dry land, including a good brothel or two for anyone so inclined.'

Hoots of laughter erupted and Bjorn held up his hand for quiet. 'I want to be sailing again by noon tomorrow, so some of us will deal with the business of restocking food supplies, while the rest of you enjoy yourselves in town. A few unfortunate wretches will stay here to watch the ship. I'll do a rota for that so no one misses out on a bit of fun – and I hope I don't need to remind you all that violence is out on this trip. Anyone starting a rumpus, causing injury to locals or damage to property, will be answerable to me. We're here to find Dainn and Aguti and nothing else. Keep your ears open for news of any raiding bands hereabouts but be careful how you ask questions. I don't want people thinking we're looking to join them. That could put us in the awkward position of being set upon.'

Bjorn made his way back to the prow, throwing over his

Three

shoulder, 'And make sure you're sober before heading back to the ship!'

As Bjorn had expected, the people of Saint Valery viewed them with a mix of fear and mistrust, and the crew was wary of splitting up or finding lodgings for the night. They restocked food rations and returned to the ship, rowing a few miles upstream in order to find a suitable place to camp for the night. By early morning the following day a steady breeze was propelling the *Sea Eagle* south-east along the Somme. Bjorn's aim was to cover the forty miles to the town of Amiens by noon, which would give them plenty of time to look around and ask a few questions before sailing further upstream if need be.

'It's understandable the people of Saint Valery are suspicious of strangers, especially Norsemen,' Bjorn said to Eadwulf as they walked along the quayside after mooring at Amiens. 'The village has been plundered by several bands in recent years, the one Dainn joined probably among them – and most raiding parties would have continued inland. And I wouldn't be surprised if we get a similar reception here. It's not going to be easy trying to convince these people we're only here to find my nephews. And pray the gods, we *will* find them. Freydis will never stop fretting until she knows they're safe.'

'And if we find they aren't...?'

Bjorn shook his head. 'That's a possibility I don't want to think about, Ulf, so we go about this search in the belief that the gods have kept an eye on the two.'

The crew split into pairs in order not to raise alarm and spent the rest of the day looking around the sizable settlement which spread out around a bridge across the Somme. It also soon became clear that no Norse bands still occupied the town.

Eadwulf stayed with Bjorn as he bought a few provisions at the busy market while making discreet enquiries cleverly disguised as casual conversation.

'A tribe of Gauls called the Ambriani were the first people to settle here hundreds of years ago,' a swarthy stallholder replied to Bjorn's remark about the impressive size of town. 'They called the place Samarobriva, or Somme Bridge, because they'd built the first bridge across the river. When the Romans came, they called the place Ambrianus – after the Ambriani, you understand – which became Amiens over the years.' He handed over several loaves and cheeses in exchange for Bjorn's silver, evidently pleased to have strangers admiring his town. 'Amiens has become the largest and most important settlement in this region. It's a nice place to live and our people work hard to keep it that way. We get a lot of visitors; some sail up the river to trade, but others come here only to take what is not theirs.'

Eadwulf and Bjorn shared a glance, which wasn't missed by the eagle-eyed vendor. 'Oh, yes, we've been plundered many times and until only a few weeks ago a large band had been camped less than half a mile away. Not a happy time for us, I can tell you, but at least they only harmed those who refused to give them coin or food and they did little damage to property. But they took most of our horses.'

'And you say this raiding party isn't here now?'

The stallholder's dark eyes narrowed. 'Why do you want to know? Are you hoping to join them?'

Bjorn flashed a jovial smile. 'We aren't, my friend. We're looking for my nephews – two young lads who left home in

Three

search of a life of adventure a few years' back. We'd heard they'd joined a band that sailed up the Scheldt and spent some time raiding around Ghent. Last thing we heard they'd moved further south and headed up the Somme.'

'That's how most traders – or raiders – get here, just as you have done. And once they've finished with Saint Valery and Amiens, some sail up to Corbie, or south towards Montdidier. Others just head back down the Somme.'

'What of the band recently plaguing you?' Eadwulf asked. 'Which way did they head? If you could help us locate them, it would be worth a couple more pieces of silver. The two lads we seek aren't only my comrade's nephews but sons of a woman I recently wed. To be able to put her mind at rest means much to me.'

Eyes glinting at the mention of more silver, the vendor licked his lips. 'And you'll not come back for the silver if it turns out your lads aren't with them?'

'We don't reward helpfulness with theft,' Eadwulf retorted. 'Tell us where we can find this band so we can check it out and two silver coins are yours. It won't be the first raiding party we've come across,' he lied, 'and we're getting desperate to find these lads. My wife's happiness depends on it.'

'We'd heard they sailed on towards Péronne, though whether they'll be staying there, I couldn't say. It's a fair-sized town so perhaps they're intending to pillage around there next.'

'You have our thanks,' Bjorn said, as Eadwulf took two shiny coins from the small leather bag attached to his belt. 'It seems Péronne will be our next stop.'

'If you head upstream for a couple of miles you'll come

to a fork in the river. Take the left-hand branch that heads north-east. Sail on past Corbie and pretty soon the river will start to wiggle about like a snake in agony. At a guess I'd say those bends make it a good seventy miles or so form Amiens to Péronne.

*

The stallholder's information proved correct. A large encampment came into view as the *Sea Eagle* rounded a bend in the river when they'd been sailing for almost seventy miles. Longships lined the banks and Bjorn ordered his crew to moor alongside.

Daylight was beginning to fade as they headed across the meadow to the camp. Smoke from the cooking fires rose in the still evening air, the meaty aromas making Eadwulf's stomach growl. People hovered close by and it soon became apparent that this raiding party had women and children amongst them. But before they could get closer than fifty paces a group of armed men spread out to block their way.

The Eagle's crew needed no telling to halt and Bjorn stepped a few paces forward. 'We're not here to cause trouble,' he yelled to the menacing line.

'You'd be unlucky if you were,' a voice yelled back. 'In case you hadn't noticed, you're more than a bit outnumbered.'

'We're looking for two men…'

Laughter rippled along the line and Eadwulf couldn't help smiling at Bjorn's words. There must have been well over two hundred men in this band. 'They're my nephews,' Bjorn continued, 'and we'd heard they'd joined a group that had been raiding along the Scheldt a couple of years ago. Are you part of that company?'

A young man with gingery hair shoved through the human barricade. 'Bjorn! What in Odin's name are you doing here? Has something happened at home?' His gaze ranged the men in Bjorn's crew. 'Is that Leif with you… and Ulf?'

A broad grin creased Bjorn's face, 'Good to see you too, Dainn, and if your comrades see fit to invite us into your camp, I'll tell you why we're here.'

The armed men shuffled back to their cooking pots and Dainn led Bjorn and his crew through the expansive camp towards his tent. Bjorn motioned to his crew to sit and wait a short distance away and gestured to Eadwulf and Leif to come with him.

A cauldron of pottage simmered over a glowing fire outside Dainn's tent and close by Eadwulf was surprised to see two young ginger-headed boys – twins by the look of them – enjoying bowls of pottage beside a young woman.

Bjorn tilted his head at the trio. 'Your lads…? They have your colouring.'

The woman giggled, and Dainn pulled a face. 'Not exactly…'

'Thor's bollocks, Dainn! What does *that* mean?'

'It means the lads are… um…*related* to me, but they aren't my spawn.'

Bjorn scratched his head, nonplussed. 'They can't be Aguti's because he only left Ribe just over a year ago. Besides, I don't yet know if he's here with you….' Dainn's gaze flicked to the tent flap but he said nothing. 'And I'd guess these two lads are nearing their fourth year, so I think you'd better explain.'

The tent flap moved and Eadwulf prayed that Aguti would step out. But when the figure made an appearance, he felt his jaw drop.

'Papa!' one of the lads squealed as they jumped up to hug a leg apiece. 'Strange men are here.'

'I can see we have visitors,' their father said, 'but I wouldn't say they're all that strange. We're actually all well acquainted, so eat your food and show them how well-mannered you are while we talk.'

Bjorn stared at the familiar face then shot a scathing look at his nephew. 'Frey's prick, Dainn, you told us he was dead!'

'I almost was,' Hastein replied, relieving Dainn of an explanation, 'and Dainn believed I was, too. That Frankish ambush saw the death of many of our band, and those who didn't manage to flee only survived by playing dead. Luckily, I had nothing worth looting so I was overlooked. Even my helm and shield landed several feet from me when I went down, and I was wearing no mail byrnie that day – the reason the damned Frankish sword found its way through my jerkin.'

Bjorn was still staring at him. 'Why were you so poorly armoured for a raid?'

'We were only raiding a monastery, just a couple of miles from where we'd been camped at Ghent. As you well know, monks rarely put up much of a fight so few of us bothered with our byrnies – and we had no idea Frankish warriors were on our trail. I took a wide gash, and though it wasn't deep I'm convinced the amount of blood helped convince the Franks I was dead.'

Three

Bjorn suddenly clutched the cousin he'd believed dead for the past four years in a bear-hug embrace. 'I should have known you were still alive; you always had a knack of coming through dangerous situations unscathed. But how come Dainn's with you again?'

'I met Jarl Logmar's band again in Ribe, about to set sail,' Dainn explained, gesturing at the extensive camp. 'They were a mere four shiploads at the time, though numbers have more than trebled since then. I sailed with them up the Scheldt, raiding first around Antwerp before sailing on to Ghent. While we were in Antwerp, Logmar was killed and our raiding band was without a leader for a time. We came across Hastein at an inn in Ghent. It was sheer luck, and I was as surprised as you to see him alive…'

Hastein nodded. 'Most of the men in the band I'd been with were dead, and I was biding my time with Greta by then. She'd taken pity on me as I'd crawled into town and took me to her room at the inn where she was a serving girl. If not for her, I wouldn't have survived.' Hastein smiled wanly at his cousin and friend, as though embarrassed to relate how low he had fallen. 'Once I was strong enough, I spent a few days a week earning my keep by pouring ale and keeping the inn orderly while Greta served at the benches. So, when Dainn walked in with some of his leaderless shipmates, it was Greta who persuaded me to sail with them and take her with me.

'And there's something else you need to know… Now's probably a good time to show yourself,' he said moving back as the flap was pulled to one side.

Bjorn laughed out loud and Eadwulf and Leif couldn't help

joining in. 'Well, well, why aren't I surprised? It seems you've been enjoying a little family gathering without inviting us!'

Aguti grinned. 'I imagine you're here because of Freydis?' The three of them nodded. 'I knew she'd be worried when I didn't get back last year, and I'm sorry for that. I'd only just met up with Dainn and Hastein by then and I wanted to spend some time with them here. I had intended to go home, but found I enjoyed being part of the band.'

'And now…? Will you be staying with them?'

'Let's all sit, and we'll talk things over while we eat,' Hastein said, preventing Aguti from answering. 'We have enough pottage to share with you three but, unfortunately, not for your crew.'

'That's not a problem,' Leif assured him. 'We have plenty of food aboard ship, so I'll head back there with the lads while you sort out your family business.'

Hastein smiled. 'Thanks, old friend. We'll catch up with each other later.'

Little was said while the meal was enjoyed, the hot pottage a welcome change for Eadwulf and Bjorn after the cold food they'd had while sailing. Though keen to hear Hastein's story, Eadwulf was glad to have his grumbling belly pacified first.

Hastein swept his sleeve across greasy lips, his earnest gaze catching their attention. 'I took Greta as my wife soon after we'd met. She nursed me back to life and has made me a family man again.' He held out his hand and Greta came to sit at his side. Eadwulf smiled to himself as he realised how similar she looked to Freydis as a young woman. Fair-headed and dimple-cheeked, Greta made Hastein a pretty wife.

Three

'Our twins, Raud and Davyn are almost four.'

'They are fine boys,' Bjorn said, sincerely. 'To know you're not only alive but happy and thriving means much to all of us.'

Hastein smiled, his gaze shifting from Bjorn to Eadwulf. 'I hope you and Freydis are happy, Ulf. You waited a long time to be together. No,' he said, raising a hand as Eadwulf made to speak, 'I need no apology or explanation regarding your marriage. I knew soon after Freydis and I were wed it wasn't me she loved. She called out your name so often in her sleep. I lived a lie for far too long, every year hoping she'd forgotten you and now loved me instead.'

'Hastein,' Eadwulf eventually got in, 'Freydis loved you and would never have done anything to hurt you.'

'I never doubted that, Ulf, but she loved me like a brother rather than a husband. Freydis was always a dutiful and caring wife and mother, but it grieved me to see her struggling to keep memories of you at bay. At night while she slept, those memories played at will. That she called out to you told me that.'

For a few moments no one spoke, though Eadwulf sensed Hastein hadn't finished. Greta kissed her husband's cheek and headed back to her boys, her hand against the small of her back.

Hastein's fond gaze followed her. 'But it's in the past and we've all moved on,' he said, nodding as he thought. 'I've found happiness with Greta. She's a good wife and doesn't shy at the constant travel or living in a camp. I tell her she should rest more, but you know women – turn a deaf ear when it suits them.' They all chuckled, nodding in agreement. 'And to have my two grown sons seek me out has served to strengthen my bonds with them. That they willingly accepted Raud and

Davyn as their brothers fills me not only with relief, but with gratitude and pride.'

Bjorn grinned. 'To have sired four strong sons does you proud, cousin, and who knows what the future holds? Greta is young and you may well add a few more to your brood in future years. You might have a daughter next.'

Hastein stared at Bjorn, his lips twitching. 'You always had a perceptive eye – or did you just guess?'

'The aching back was one thing, but I also spotted a rounded belly when Greta's tunic pulled tight as she rose. I'd say a new babe could be entertaining you with bawls and sleepless nights in a mere few months.'

'Three,' Hastein said, 'and we'll probably be far to the east of here by then. And as to your question to Aguti, Bjorn, all I know is that Dainn wants to stay with the band, but Aguti is torn. I'm as keen as you to hear his answer.'

Aguti shuffled beneath questioning eyes. 'I love it out here,' he said, gazing across the camp. 'This is a lifestyle I enjoy and I love seeing all the different places but…' He hesitated and Eadwulf guessed what he was about to say. 'I'm not cut out for raiding. Father's band will be raiding and pillaging around Péronne over the summer, and I haven't the stomach for it.'

Aguti focused on Hastein. 'You gave me the hall at Ribe seven years ago, and that is where my responsibilities lie. Much as I love you and Dainn and will miss being with you, I'll travel back with Bjorn – if he'll have me aboard. The estate will be in need of its jarl. And you have your band to organise.'

'*Your* band!' Bjorn spluttered, gaping at his cousin. 'These men are under your command?'

Three

'They are – well, over half of them. As Dainn said, the band lost its leader in Antwerp, and many of the men had heard of me.' Hastein grinned and gave a one-sided shrug. 'I should say, they'd heard of *both* of us, Bjorn. It seems our adventures in Paris and the Mediterranean all those years ago are still the stuff of campfire tales.'

Bjorn chuckled. 'I have fond memories of both of those ventures, as well as some I'd rather forget. And I'm sure Ulf could say the same about our time along the Seine. But you were telling us about the rest of the men here with you.'

'They're a completely separate group and I have no say in what they do or where they go.' Hastein shrugged, his hazel gaze moving between Bjorn and Eadwulf. 'They only arrived in Amiens a few days before we were due to leave and their leader's a moody, ill-tempered sod. But he asked if we could join up for the summer raids and I couldn't think of a reason to say no at the time. Together our numbers are impressive, though I can see us coming to blows if we can't take enough plunder to go around us all.'

Bjorn nodded. 'I'd say the sooner you break away the better.'

'I agree, cousin. Sven's band joined us on the understanding they'd stay with us only until next spring, by which time we'll have bled this region dry and be ready to move on elsewhere. Fortunately, we each have different plans regarding where that will be.'

'Which are…?' Eadwulf asked, inadvertently drawn into the exciting life of raiding.

'Sven intends to head back to the Saxon kingdoms. He's

livid that the large numbers of our countrymen in the East Anglian lands refused to join him in taking on Wessex six years ago and he wants to try again – but with more warriors than last time. It seems a band they met raiding in Frisia earlier this year claim they'll have enough men to join him by next spring, so they've planned to meet somewhere along the Frisian coast in late April next year and sail for Wessex together.'

Eadwulf felt Bjorn's eyes boring into the top of his head, but he refused to make eye contact. His thoughts were in turmoil, jumping between Alfred, and what another incursion into Wessex would mean to him, or to his own son. Aethelred would likely be leading a Mercian army to assist the Wessex king.

'Eadwulf,' Bjorn said, coming to his side, 'you can't fight Alfred's battles for ever. You've left the Saxon and Anglian kingdoms and must trust that people you love will come through unscathed. And I can understand what worries are going through your head about your son.'

'I hope someone fills me in later on what you two are talking about,' Hastein said rising to his feet and focusing on Eadwulf. 'I've evidently said something to upset you, my friend, so I'm sorry for that.'

'It's nothing you've done, Hastein, so it's me who should be saying sorry for holding up what you were telling us about your plans.'

Hastein nodded and went on, 'There's not much more I can say about what I intend to do in the future. My band will be sailing out of the Somme in late March next year and heading south to the Seine estuary.' He looked levelly at Bjorn's gaping face and grinned. 'Yes, cousin, I intend to attack Paris again.'

Four

Winchester, Wessex: late March 885

'The meal is all cooked, Papa,' Aethelflaed said, coming to stand by Alfred's side. 'I've already told the scribes, so I'll instruct the women to serve, shall I?' She smiled at the three messengers. 'They've prepared three extra places for our guests.'

Alfred grinned at his sixteen-year-old daughter, not for the first time thinking how much she resembled Ealhswith at that age. Her gold-brown hair flowed down her back and her blue-green eyes twinkled in the glow from the oil lamps and candles. 'Is your mother joining us tonight?'

Aethelflaed shook her head, her face suddenly downcast. 'She's only just left the chapel and says she isn't hungry, but I'll have some sent to her anyway once we've finished in here. I'll let the servants know I need a helping of everything keeping back.'

Alfred kissed his daughter's forehead. 'If you instruct the servants, I'll take the meal to her myself. I need to tell her about tomorrow. Don't worry,' he added at her puzzled look, 'I'll be telling the rest of you during the meal.'

Alfred entered the bedchamber followed by one of the serving women carrying a tray of hot food. Expecting to see Ealhswith sitting in the wicker chair where she'd spent most of her waking hours in the past few weeks, he was surprised to see her curled up in bed, seemingly asleep.

'Just put the tray on the table, Nelda,' he whispered, 'and I'll take over from here.'

The woman smiled, casting a concerned glance at her mistress. 'My lady really should eat something, lord,' she whispered back. 'She's had nothing at all yet today and has been sitting in that cold chapel for most of it.'

'I know, and we're all worried about her. But I can't force her to eat or come into the hall.'

Once the door closed behind the kindly woman, Alfred sat on the edge of the marital bed and stroked Ealhswith's gaunt cheek. Her eyes opened in surprise. 'I didn't hear you come in. Have I been asleep?'

Alfred nodded. 'But now it's time to eat something before you waste away.' His attempt at light-heartedness did not provoke a response from Ealhswith, but she glanced at the table and the steaming food.

'I could probably manage a little soup and some of that bread, but I'm not sure about the meat. My appetite seems to have deserted me.'

Alfred felt his pent-up emotions rise; the sadness of it all and the uselessness he felt to put things right again. 'Shall I bring the soup to you, or will you come to the table?'

Ealhswith seemed to think about that, then pulled herself up and climbed out of bed. 'I don't want to spill soup all over the furs, so I'll come to the table.'

Alfred sat opposite her as she sipped the soup from a wooden spoon. 'Aethelflaed tells me you've been in the chapel most of the day. It must be cold out there now.'

'I have my cloak, and I don't notice the cold while I pray.'

'But you don't need all day to pray and the hall is always nice and warm.' Alfred felt tears stinging his eyes and walked across the room to light another candle before she noticed.

'I want you to come back to us, Ealhswith. I love you… we all love you… and miss you in the hall. Our children keep asking whether you're well again yet, and Agnes has had a hard time stopping the younger three fretting for you.'

Ealhswith stayed silent, as though she had heard nothing, so Alfred went on. 'It's been two months since Winfrith died. We all mourned his loss, especially as you tried so hard to keep him strong. That he lived for as long as ten months is because of your constant care and devotion and the hours you spent trying to get milk into him. But, as both the midwife and our physician told us, being born too early left him very weak and his reluctance to feed meant he never grew any stronger.'

'I know that, Alfred, and I don't want to go over it all again. In my heart I know his death was God's punishment for something I've done. Perhaps I should have been a better wife and mother, or a better daughter to my parents, or not teased my brother so much. Perhaps I should have spent more time in prayer when I was younger… I don't know what I did that was so wrong! But losing babes before they had chance to be born was so hard to bear – though even that was not as grievous as losing one I'd come to know and love. I'll never forget Winfrith's little smile.'

Tears coursed down Ealhswith's cheeks and Alfred pulled her up to him, holding her close as she sobbed. 'No man could ask for a better wife and mother than you,' he whispered, 'and your parents and brother love you dearly for the kind and caring person you are. I can't tell you why some babes never manage to be born, or why innocent infants and small children sometimes fall ill and die. I only know that if it's God's will, we must accept it and move on. God would not want us to spend our days continually blaming ourselves…

'Come back to us, Ealhswith, and be the loving wife and mother again. We've all mourned the loss of Winfrith but now we grieve the loss of you. You've borne your sorrows alone for long enough and we miss your smiling face more than I can say.'

At Alfred's soothing words of reassurance, Ealhswith's sobs gradually ceased. She lifted her head to look into his eyes and he kissed her tear-streaked cheek. 'You're right,' she said, 'I have no right to ignore you all, or to believe I'm the only one to be grieving. Give me tonight to pray and tomorrow I'll come to the hall and smile as though all is well. The children deserve that from me. And so do you.

'But Alfred, I'm scared.'

Alfred frowned, wondering if someone had already told her they'd be spending the Eastertide in Sussex. 'I knew you'd feel a little anxious, but you have to return to normality sooner or later. I would have told you sooner, but I only had the news from Ealdorman Unwine today.'

'Told me what?'

'About tomorrow, but you've evidently heard already.'

Ealhswith shook her head. 'I've heard nothing. Are we to have guests?'

'The court will leave for our manor at West Dene tomorrow and will stay until early May. Eastertide is barely two weeks away, and our devotions will be made in Chichester Cathedral, with Bishop Aylmer leading the services.' Ealhswith nodded and Alfred was pleased to note she didn't look worried about

Four

the thought of travelling the forty miles to Dene. 'You haven't been to our Sussex manor for a few years, and it's a pleasant place to be in the spring. Though I confess, I also have another reason for wanting to visit Dene at this time. It seems the Welsh abbot, Asser, will be in nearby Chichester, visiting the good bishop, and I intend to invite them both to spend a day or two at our hall.'

Ealhswith gave a wan smile. 'I'll ask Agnes to organise the servants in packing our travel boxes first thing tomorrow morning. There are a lot of us to pack for, even without dear Winfrith.'

*

Dene, Sussex: April 885

Asser, Abbot of Saint David's monastery in the Welsh kingdom of Dyfed, entered the royal hall and bowed to Alfred. Beside him, Aylmer, the robust Bishop of Chichester, did likewise, and together they walked forward to stand before the king, who had purposely chosen to look regal for the occasion. After the blatant snub from the abbot two years ago, he was determined not to appear overly friendly until he felt the man deserved it. Sitting tall and straight in his high-backed chair on the low dais, Alfred had donned an impressive deep blue, velvet tunic trimmed with colourful braid. To his right, his first-born son, Edward, sported a tunic of crimson linen, and to his left, Unwine of Sussex, who had been one of Alfred's strongest supporters since the battle at Ashdown fourteen years ago, was garbed in a tunic of dark ochre, which contrasted well with his coppery hair and beard.

Stony-faced, Alfred inclined his head at his guests, the circlet of gold around his wheaten hair glinting in the glow from the hearthfire and accentuating the hue of his owl-like eyes.

'I confess to being surprised by your invitation, lord,' Asser said, 'though I cannot deny feeling honoured at the opportunity to meet you and your delightful family.' He gestured to Ealhswith and the five children, a momentary frown creasing his face as Aelfthryth giggled. 'I look forward to speaking with them all personally over the next few days… during periods when we three aren't engaged in conversation, naturally. I imagine it was Lord Unwine who notified you of my presence in Chichester?'

Alfred rose and stepped down from the dais, taking in the appearance of a man of similar age to himself with a tonsured head and garbed in the simple, brown travelling garments of a monk. Nothing about his appearance suggested the air of arrogance or pomposity that Alfred had noted in others of such an elevated status as abbot. The small smile plucking at the corners of Asser's lips suddenly made Alfred feel ridiculous for his incivility and attempt to appear grandiose and haughty.

In turn he grasped the forearms of his two guests in greeting, choosing to answer Asser's question indirectly. 'Welcome to our hall, my lords. It is many months since my court has resided here, and it occurred to me that it would be a perfect place to spend the Eastertide this year, particularly as I had a few matters of state to discuss with Unwine. But for now, I suggest you sit and take refreshment before we talk and become better acquainted.'

Four

The guests savoured the welcomed ale as the searing silence of the past moments was gradually filled by the hum of chattering voices and servants at their work. Trestles were being set up for the evening meal while tantalising aromas of meats roasting on the hearthfire wafted around the high-ceilinged room.

Alfred could not help noticing how the giggles and squeals of his younger children at play continued to draw the abbot's attention, and he wondered whether Asser had had an unhappy childhood or, maybe, a lonely one. Of course, the man could simply feel uncomfortable in the presence of little ones. Perhaps, one day Asser would feel enough at ease in the company of the Wessex court to tell him. But, for now, Alfred needed to break the frosty barrier that had settled between them, and chided himself for his childish display of incivility and pomp.

The following day, Bishop Aylmer returned to Chichester to resume preparations for the Eastertide services in the cathedral. Holy Week was almost upon them and he needed to ensure that the choirboys were sufficiently practised in their hymns to do the cathedral proud in front of the Wessex king. But Asser would remain at Dene for another three days, and Alfred was determined to make full use of that time. To exact some kind of promise from the abbot regarding coming to Winchester was foremost on Alfred's mind.

*

Ealhswith slowly warmed towards the abbot. At first she found him distant, a man loath to give too much away about himself. On the occasions when he'd wandered over to speak to her and the children, he was happy to ask questions about them, but his answers to their questions about him were brief and often evasive.

'Are you from a big family, too, Lord Asser?' Aethelgifu asked when he'd joined them for the mid-morning meal on the second day of his visit. Alfred, Aethelflaed and Edward were out on their morning ride with Unwine, and the three younger children continued to eat their fill of the meaty pottage with Ealhswith.

Asser seemed taken aback by the ten-year-old's question and noticing his face, Ealhswith said quickly, 'I'm sure the abbot doesn't wish to be constantly bothered with such unimportant issues, child. My apologies, Abbot. Sometimes children can seem a little forthright, though generally they are simply inquisitive.'

Aethelgifu frowned, fingering the head veil she always wore. But if the abbot thought such a garment covering the hair of a child unusual, Ealhswith was pleased he did not remark on it.

'I didn't think people's families *were* unimportant, Mama,' Aethelgifu said. 'Everyone has a family and you're always telling us we must love each other. I'm sorry, Abbot,' she added, facing him again. 'I didn't mean to be rude.'

Asser gave her a warm smile. 'I'm sure you did not, Aethelgifu. My hesitation in answering such questions is something I need to deal with, and speaking with this family is the first time in many years I have needed to face the truth of my own childhood.'

Ealhswith reached across the table and patted Asser's arm. 'My lord abbot, you have no need to divulge anything further.

Four

I have no intention of making you feel obliged to speak of things you would sooner forget.' Her gaze swept the bemused faces of the three children. 'There will be no more questions from any of you for today. Understood?'

'But we can still *speak* with the abbot, can't we, Mama? I like him… well, I like him when he smiles.'

Asser laughed out loud at Aelfthryth's remark, although Ealhswith squirmed with embarrassment. 'Again, I apologise, Abbot. The child is barely six and has yet to learn the art of being tactful.'

'No, Lady Ealhswith, it is I who must apologise. I've fended off personal questions for far too long. The truth is,' he went on, his warm brown gaze sweeping the three earnest faces, 'I never knew my family. You see, when I was barely a few weeks old, I was found by a passing lay brother from a small monastery in Dyfed. I was inside an old wooden crate in a hut in a village that had recently succumbed to Danish raids. The monks who reared me thought my parents probably hid me to save my life. If that lay brother had not heard me cry, I would likely have died of starvation, or else been eaten by wild animals.'

The children stared, open-mouthed, and Ealhswith felt compelled to speak. 'We are honoured you felt able to explain this to us, Abbot, though you really had no need.'

Asser smiled. 'But I think I did, my lady. I'd sooner explain than leave here tomorrow thinking you all considered me cold and unreachable. It's simply that I find it hard adjusting to family life. I never had brothers and sisters, you see, and could only guess what it was like to play games, or even laugh and chatter.

'Oh, I'm not complaining,' he added, glancing at Ealhswith's concerned face. 'I've had a good life, with food to eat each day and the opportunity to study from a very young age. I soon found that learning filled me with joy, as did sharing my skills and knowledge with those who sought them. Guiding others has become my role in life and if I can help them understand a little more about God, and the writings and teachings of our forefathers, I feel fulfilled.'

*

By the time Alfred and the others returned, the Abbot was sitting on a stool in the midst of Ealhswith, Agnes and the three young ones, telling them the story of David and Goliath. The story was by no means new to any of them, but Asser had a way of embellishing it with fine detail and colour that brought it vividly to life. The four of them stood, statue-still in the doorway, becoming as rapt in the story as they.

'It seems the abbot is not as cold and aloof as you thought, Papa,' Aethelflaed whispered. 'Or perhaps, he just enjoys being with a family.'

Alfred smiled at her and nodded, hoping that this carefree little gathering would ease the way into his own earnest talks with Asser later today.

The morning of Asser's departure came all too soon. The abbot made his fond farewells to Ealhswith and the children and reaffirmed the promise he'd made to Alfred. He would remain at Saint David's for the next six months, ensuring his monastic community could cope without him. Someone who could assume leadership during his absence would need to be elected, a process which could take some time. But the arrangement wasn't altogether to Alfred's liking. Asser insisted he'd be unable to stay at Alfred's court on a permanent basis. His monastery still needed his guidance, he'd said. Consequently, he would only agree to spend six months of every year in Wessex. During that time, he would help Alfred with his understanding and translation of Latin and in restoring the love of learning in the Saxon people. Asser would also be willing to assist with updating the laws of Wessex and other clerical work as deemed necessary.

Alfred watched the abbot's wagon pulling away, thinking that at least, this was not an outright refusal on Asser's behalf as it had been two years ago. Nor was Asser a stranger to him. Things had moved on, and perhaps after a few years, Saint David's would be in a position to cope indefinitely without the esteemed Asser.

*

Winchester, Hampshire: November 885

The sound of unfamiliar voices in his hall requesting immediate audience with the king sent a shudder of alarm through Alfred's chest, and he wondered what could be so urgent at this late hour. The November dusk was falling early after what had been a miserably cloudy day and servants were already setting up the trestles for the evening meal.

He shoved the missive he'd been reading aside, realising

there was nothing he could do about the recent turn of events in Dyfed. It saddened him to know that Asser had been one of the many people stricken by some kind of raging pestilence that caused angry red pocks to cover the body and a high fever that took them to their beds. Yet the fact that the abbot's stay in Wessex was delayed, yet again, exasperated Alfred. It would now be at least next spring before Asser would be well enough to leave his monastery, and Alfred had set his heart on spending the winter months getting to grips with his understanding of Latin.

He rose from amidst his group of clerics in the candlelit corner of the hall and came to meet the visitors, Garth and another of his thegns moving to his sides, ever the diligent bodyguards. The news the three men carried was the last thing Alfred wanted to hear.

'Rochester is under attack! What... now?'

'Yes, lord,' the spokesman for the group continued, evidently thrown by the king's sceptical outburst. 'A large fleet of longships sailed into the Medway in mid-afternoon three days ago, carrying almost three hundred warriors, we reckoned. They began the attack on the town as soon as they'd moored.'

Alfred's first thought was that at least Rochester had been one of the Wessex towns to have its defences strengthened and a contingent of his new-style army constantly based there in readiness for times such as this. He just hoped the town would withstand the assault until reinforcements got there.

'Then we've no time to lose. You two,' he said, jabbing a finger in the direction of another two of his thegns, 'inform our troops to make ready. We head for Kent at first light.'

Four

The two sped from the hall and Alfred turned again to the messengers.

'The fighting was still fierce when you left?'

'The attacks had been on and off all the following morning but, thankfully, by the time we managed to leave around noon, little damage had been done to the fortified walls. There are also some formidable archers amongst your warriors – and the townsfolk themselves – who kept driving the Danes back. It was thanks to them that we and other riders managed to get out.'

Alfred nodded, the scene playing in his head as he listened. 'You and other riders…?'

'Yes, lord. Ealdorman Aethelbold sent the three of us to you, and others to instruct the standing armies of Kent to be waiting to join your troops when they got there. They'll muster at the old Roman town of Dartford, which is less than fourteen miles from Rochester. Aethelbold reckons it's far enough away so as not to alert the Danes.'

'I owe Aethelbold my thanks for that. Together we'll be an impressively large army and the Danes won't know what hit them. But until then, we must pray our men in the town hold the Danes off.

'You've done well to cover the hundred miles from Rochester in two and a half days. You must have ridden like the Furies, and be dog-tired and famished. Fortunately, it smells like the food will soon be ready and after that you need a night's sleep before we move out at dawn.'

Explaining to Ealhswith that he was leaving to do battle with the Danes was not something Alfred relished. Although it had been almost six months since his wife had ceased isolating herself in her bed chamber, she was still not completely back to being her usual self. She was still highly emotional, and tears would fall at the first signs of her being upset. Nor was she as tolerant with the children as in the past, and spent increasingly less time with the younger three. Agnes was finding it difficult to cope. More often than not, Aethelflaed was called upon to deal with little Aethelweard's pining to see his mother.

The most worrying thing to Alfred was the way his wife continued to push him away, choosing to spend most of her nights in the women's bower, leaving him alone in their marital bed. He knew he would be within his rights to demand she put an end to this strange behaviour and return to their bedchamber, yet instead he chose to be kind and give her the time she needed to return to him. But as the weeks passed, his patience was wearing thin.

'I'm leaving with a contingent of our troops tomorrow and riding to Rochester,' he said bluntly, seeing little point in dragging things out. He gestured at a small trestle along the side of the hall, where they could speak privately, away from the servants busy with the cooking and the children at play while they waited to eat.

'But why…? Is this something to do with Aethelstan? Has he broken his word after all this time?'

'As far as I know, Aethelstan has nothing to do with it, and I intend to make sure he doesn't get the chance to do so. But Rochester is being attacked by raiding Danes and in need of our aid.'

'Do you have to go yourself? Can't the standing armies in Kent provide the reinforcements?'

Four

Alfred took her hand and led her to sit beside him on a bench. 'This is a substantial army we're talking about, Ealhswith, not on the scale of those of Halfdan or Guthrum, thank God, but still big enough to cause alarm. I can't risk them taking Rochester and I'm hoping the new walls hold firm and the number of warriors inside is enough to repel them until we get there. If these Danes take the town, they'll have clear passage up the Medway and into the heart of Kent.' He shook his head at the prospect. 'If that happens, I can see some of the East Anglian Danes being tempted to join them – plus others from across the sea who want to try their luck in our lands again. No, the larger the force we hit them with, the better.'

'Oh Alfred, I've prayed so often that Wessex would see no more raids. Will it never end?'

'No matter how many invaders arrive over the coming years, I'm confident we've done enough in strengthening many of our towns and creating a regular army to repel any would-be raiders – or at least, make it difficult for them to gain a foothold here. We still have many more towns to fortify, and that will be an ongoing task. We also have a good number of ships in our fleet, with enough skilled crewmen to challenge incoming raiders.'

'Knowing all this doesn't ease my mind about the danger you'll be facing at Rochester. Why can't the cursed Danes just leave us alone?'

Alfred shrugged, not wishing to go over all that again, but his wife's concern for his welfare did much to assure him she still cared for him. 'I'll be leaving at first light, and I know the hall will be in good hands with you in charge of its running.

Radulf will be here by noon tomorrow with another group of the Hampshire army. Some of them will remain here, so you have no need to fear that Winchester will be left unguarded.'

There seemed little left to say and, relieved that Ealhswith had understood the need for him to leave, Alfred left her to oversee the final touches to the meal before serving it. But tonight, while Alfred made ready to leave for Rochester, he knew that Ealhswith would be back in the women's bower, settling in her solitary bed, just as she had done on most nights since Winfrith died.

*

Alfred's Hampshire army passed by the large Surrey village of Guildford in the mid-afternoon, continuing for another ten miles before sharing the campfires of one of the shire's standing armies for the night. They had covered almost fifty miles and both horses and riders were in need of food and rest. Though cold, the November night was dry and frost-free, and the dog-tired men succumbed to a few restful hours on their bedrolls before setting off at daybreak on the forty-mile ride to Dartford. Riding with them were the thirty men from Surrey.

The sight of the sizeable army waiting for him outside the old Roman ruins at Dartford filled Alfred with pride. Together with his eighty Hampshire men and the thirty who'd joined them in Surrey, he estimated a force close on five hundred strong.

At his side, Garth gave a low whistle. 'We couldn't have asked for a better response from Kent, lord. So many men…'

Four

'And if what we've heard is true, the Danes are a couple of hundred fewer. I'd say the odds are now doubly in our favour. We have an army to be proud of and we'll be taking the Danes by surprise.'

Garth nodded. 'There'll be many among them who've experienced the failings of our old-style fyrds and won't be expecting things to have changed. Hopefully, they won't have planned to be looking out for reinforcements for at least another week.'

Alfred grinned. 'I'm relying on it!'

He turned and ordered his men to dismount before urging his tall white stallion, Pegasus, over to the crumbling ruins where the Kentish armies had gathered to watch his arrival. 'Men of Kent,' he yelled, his voice echoing around the crumbling ruins, 'my heart swells with pride at the sight of you, and your loyalty will not be forgotten. Tomorrow, Saxons from East and West will fight together to rid our kingdom of marauders from across the sea. Together, we will repel them!' Their cheers brought a lump to his throat.

'Rochester is but fourteen miles away,' he continued, 'a distance we could cover in less than a couple of hours. But the day is already fading and our horses have come over forty miles at a steady trot. It would not be wise to push them further, only to arrive in darkness and unable to assess the site we are to attack. So, although I might wish otherwise, we'll set up our campfires and bedrolls amongst you and gain some much-needed rest for the night. Before dawn we'll be riding to the aid of our beleaguered town of Rochester.'

*

The eastern skies were paling as Alfred's impressive army headed along the old Roman road toward Rochester, and by the time they crossed the bridge over the Medway the crisp November morning had dawned fine and bright. No sounds as yet carried from the town, but as they drew closer, a series of newly constructed circular ditches and earthen embankments came into view just beyond the sturdy main gates. Inside those earthworks the Danes had made their camp.

Alfred raised his arm, halting the army behind, while at his sides Garth and the three messengers sent by Aethelbold reined in. 'Looks like they've already laid siege to the place,' he murmured, 'which tells me the town's defences and the skills of its archers have given them something to think about.'

'They'll be planning to try every now and then, though,' Garth said, 'working on the idea that repeated attacks will eventually wear down the gates, if not the walls.'

'Saxons attacking!' a voice rang out, cutting off further appraisal.

'Now!' Alfred yelled, heeling Pegasus to a gallop.

Five hundred mounted Saxons surged to the camp, a loud cheer rising from the town at the sight of astonished Danes scattering like sheep assailed by a pack of wolves. Almost half made it to their ships, abandoning slaves they'd taken and horses brought with them from Francia. The other half threw themselves at Alfred's mercy.

Alfred cursed as the ships pushed away, heading down the Medway towards the Northern Sea, probably intent on returning to the Low Countries. At this moment, he had no way of stopping them.

Four

'Get the captives inside the town,' he yelled. 'Once they're securely held I'll decide what to do with them.' He turned to the group of ashen-faced men, knowing some would be anticipating death. 'Whether I have the lot of you killed depends on how well you respond to my orders. I'll leave you to think about that until tomorrow morning. If you all keep quiet and cause us no trouble, I may allow food and drink to be brought to you later on.'

The captives spent the night split into four groups in the region of thirty men, each held inside a securely locked and well-guarded storage hut. Ealdorman Aethelbold drew up a rota for the guards, ensuring that none had to endure the cold November night for more than a couple of hours.

'You have my sincere thanks for organising the defence of the town, Aethelbold,' Alfred said, addressing the red-headed ealdorman once their evening meal was over. 'You've served Wessex well and your quick actions won't be forgotten – nor those of your four messengers. To have ridden over a hundred miles in little over two days is quite an achievement.'

'They're loyal men, lord, and like all of us, they didn't want to see the Danes rampaging in Kent – which the bastards would have done if they'd managed to take Rochester. And we all know why they targeted this town first! Word of our churches' wealth seems to have spread far and wide. We've had many a traveller arriving here just to ogle at the silver on display – though, as yet, we've had only a few robberies, and those by unscrupulous Saxons!'

Alfred grinned at the look of indignation on the ealdorman's ruddy face. He was evidently a man of honour, and a pious one at that. But he was right, Rochester's reputation as a wealthy ecclesiastical centre was as well-known as its importance as a seaport since Roman times.

'We thanked God for the strengthened walls and gates,' Aethelbold continued, 'not to mention the troop of men stationed here. We already had some decent archers amongst the townsfolk, but I think some of the standing army must have spent time practising with a bow. We reckon the Danes lost close on thirty men to well-aimed arrows.'

Alfred downed a mouthful of ale and replaced his mug on the trestle. 'That's good to hear and I long for the day when all our major towns are as well reinforced and manned. But for now, I'm content that Rochester held out as well as it did. And let's not forget, without the swift response of our standing army, camped across the countryside ready for such a call, the town's defences would have been even more sorely tested. It's the combination of these two I'm relying on for the future safety of Wessex.'

The Kentish ealdorman could only agree and the conversation gradually dwindled as wide yawns took over.

*

Soon after daybreak the following day, the group of dishevelled, sour-faced Danes were led from their makeshift prisons to face the Wessex king, strategically surrounded by the rest of the Saxon army. Straight-backed and solemn astride his placid white stallion, with Garth and Aethelbold at his sides, Alfred scrutinised the prisoners, his keen amber gaze moving slowly

Four

from one side of the group to the other. 'Is there anyone who can speak for all of you?'

Men hung their heads or shuffled their feet, but for some moments no one spoke.

Alfred scowled, his patience wearing thin. 'I've no doubt there are one or two leaders amongst you. Stand forward so we can see you.'

Two men made their way to the front, one tall and wiry with dirty-blond braids and beard, the other shorter though more muscular, his darker hair and beard straggling about his neck.

'Names and titles,' Alfred demanded.

'Skari,' the wiry man replied. 'I'm a jarl from –'

'We're not interested in where you're from,' Alfred snapped as Pegasus snorted. He jabbed a finger in the brawny warrior's direction. 'You?'

'I am Gorm, a jarl, also.'

'So, *jarls*, I'll explain what I've decided to do with you all, after which you two will have a task to do for me. Step back to your men.'

Alfred waited as the two jarls did as told and the murmurs died down. 'I'm prepared to be lenient,' he declared, his intense gaze ranging the suddenly hopeful faces. 'By that I mean I'm willing to allow you to leave in peace – that is, *most* of you may leave. Some of you will remain as my hostages until I'm certain the rest of you won't be raiding elsewhere in my kingdom. But if you should succumb to such temptation those hostages can be certain of one thing: they will die.'

Again Alfred waited, this time for the buzz of worried voices to quieten, and pointed at the two jarls. 'It's time for you to do that task I mentioned.'

The two jarls shared a glance and nodded slowly. 'First,' Alfred started, 'are there are any other leaders in your company?'

The two Danes looked behind them for some moments and spoke quietly to each other before nodding agreement and Gorm replied, 'We think there are two others,'

'Step out, now!' Alfred yelled, annoyed that these men had ignored his initial order.

The two pushed their way through their group, one a grizzled veteran who glared brazenly at Alfred; the other no more than a gangly, clean- shaven youth.

'Can we take it that Gorm and Skari are correct and you are both jarls?' The old warrior nodded but the youth's brow creased in evident confusion. 'You are young to hold a position of such trust and authority,' Alfred remarked, hoping to spur the lad to speech. 'Perhaps your comrades were mistaken in picking you?'

'They weren't wrong, exactly, lord, but I don't know yet if I *am* jarl. Your archers killed my father, and I won't know until we get back to Zealand whether our people will accept me as jarl in his place.'

'Re-join your comrades.' Alfred ordered, waiting for the lad to do as bidden before continuing. 'So, we have three jarls, and each of you will now call out two of your best fighting men.'

Ashen-faced, the three did as requested and, at length, nine men were lined up along the front of their comrades.

'These men are now my hostages,' Alfred yelled to the rest of the Danes, 'and as from today, how long they continue to live will depend on your actions.' He paused, allowing time for that thought sink in. 'Once you've all sworn oaths never to plunder my kingdom again, you will leave these lands and never return. Four of your ships are still in the port, and I'll expect you to be sailing by mid-afternoon.'

Five

The standing army of Kent returned to their posts ready to resume the regular training necessary in the event of future attacks on their shire. Alfred and his army headed back to Winchester, the thirty men of Surrey riding with them as far as Guildford. All had received praise and grateful thanks from their king.

As they rode Alfred had much on his mind. Foremost was the problem of where he'd place the hostages. Whereas in the past, when individuals were held on the estates of trusted noblemen, on this occasion he decided it would be wiser to keep them together at Winchester, at least for the first few months. For their sakes he prayed their comrades would honour the oaths made in the names of their gods. If they did not, he would have no other option than to kill them all.

Alfred was also keen to return to work with his scholars. He longed to be able to read and translate the Latin texts himself and knew he must spend more time at his studies in order to do that. And always, at the back of his mind, hovered his concerns for Ealhswith. He hoped that being in the hall with their children had enabled her to rise from the deep pit of melancholy into which she had fallen since the death of their baby son.

As things turned out, Alfred had been back in Winchester barely two weeks when, once again, messengers from Aethelbold arrived. The Danes who had so recently been permitted to leave Rochester had not sailed away as they'd vowed, but

Five

were now plundering the Kentish lands south of the Thames. And it seems they'd had help from another dozen, unknown shiploads of Northmen. Aethelbold had already begun the task of the assembling the Kentish fyrd.

'How could I have been so stupid?' he raged once the messengers had gone to stable their horses before sharing the mid-morning meal. 'After all I learnt while dealing with Halfdan and Guthrum!' Garth and the rest of his thegns stayed mute, waiting for him to stop pacing the room and his rage to abate. 'I swear this will be the last time I trust a treacherous Northman! By all that is holy, deep down I knew they'd dishonour their oaths. And heaven alone knows where these other twelve ships came from, but we now have another large force to deal with.'

'Does this mean we must kill those eight men, lord?' Garth's face paled at the thought.

Alfred heaved a sigh. 'I can see no other way. I made the threat in front of all in Rochester and if I don't carry it through, I'll be seen as a weak, ineffectual fool. It's clear the treacherous dogs had no intentions of leaving Kent and evidently care nothing for the lives of the hostages. But I see no need for undue suffering and I'll ensure their deaths are quick.'

'When and where will you do this, my lord?' Having stayed silent since the messengers arrived, Ealhswith's voice came as a surprise, and all eyes turned her way. 'I need to make sure the children are kept well away, so I'd be grateful if no mention is made of it once they return for the meal. I'm relieved none of them are here at this moment.'

Alfred nodded, ashamed to admit to himself he hadn't

checked whether they were in the hall or not before his outburst. 'Where are they now?

'Aethelflaed and Edward are out riding – and before you ask, yes, they have a group of our men as escort. The younger three are with Agnes in the hall of the guest house. They've started decorating greenery and pine cones in preparation for the Advent. The Christmastide season will be upon us in a week.'

Alfred smiled kindly at his wife, her pinched cheeks causing a wave of sadness to wash over him. Ealhswith was recovering from her mourning, though it seemed heartbreakingly slow to Alfred. 'It will be done soon after noon, so I'll insist the three older children spend time at their studies with our good clerics if you wish, and Agnes can continue decorating pine cones or some such thing with Aelfthryth and Aethelweard.'

Ealhswith nodded and Alfred went on, 'As soon as my men appear, the hostages will likely guess what fate lies ahead of them. I'll make it clear that their deaths are not of my choosing; their dishonourable comrades broke their oaths in full knowledge of the dire consequences of doing so. They will be bound and taken to the woods beyond the meadow where their throats will be slit; death will be instant and they'll be buried in the woods. It all has to be done today as we ride for Southampton at dawn tomorrow.'

'We aren't going straight back to Kent, lord?'

'We are, Garth, but this time we're taking our ships. My messengers will ride for Radulf's hall in Southampton this afternoon and by the time our army reaches there tomorrow I'm hoping he'll have the ships ready for sailing. By the time we reach Dover, Aethelbold should be there with the Kentish standing army waiting for us.

*

Radulf had wasted no time in alerting the crews of the dozen Wessex ships moored at Southampton and Alfred was heartened by their speedy response: they would be ready for sailing by dawn tomorrow. As Alfred had ordered, Radulf had also sent riders to notify the portreeves in Hastings, Folkestone and Dover, where extra Wessex ships were moored. They were to be ready for sailing on the king's arrival.

'I can tell you little more than that, Radulf,' Alfred replied to the ealdorman's question as they strolled along the Southampton wharf amidst the scurry of men around the ships. Food and watered ale were being stored in sea chests while other men checked the rigging and overall seaworthiness of each vessel. 'All we know is that the lying scum broke their vows, yet again, and are now raiding in northern Kent as far inland as Canterbury, aided by a far larger group than their own. Estimates put the total number of raiders in the region of five hundred, which is almost four hundred more than the band that made their deceitful vows to me. As for the number of ships they'll have, with the four that left Rochester, my guess is that there are likely to be fifteen or more. I've no intention of being caught outnumbered, so we'll take as many of our ships as we can. With the twelve from here and others we join as we sail, by the time we reach Dover I'm hoping for a good two dozen.'

Radulf nodded as he digested the information, and Alfred added, 'But what we don't yet know is where these extra Danes came from. Aethelbold's messengers left Kent as soon as they landed.'

'Perhaps it's another band from Francia trying their luck in Wessex?'

'It could be, and in many ways, I'm hoping that's exactly what it is. The alternative isn't something I want to contemplate right now. But we won't know until we get there.'

Radulf shot him a quizzical look but Alfred was already lost to his thoughts.

*

Kentish forces were waiting when Alfred reached Dover with his score of ships. He was keen to hear news of the raiders' movements and where their fleet was moored, and after checking his five extra ships already at the port, he and a small group of his men headed over to meet with Ealdorman Aethelbold.

'At first it was just the group that made oaths in Rochester,' Aethelbold affirmed, shoving his red hair from his face as a strong gust of wind swept in from the sea. 'They sailed along the north coast of Kent and raided any small settlement they came across. I'd barely begun gathering our standing army to confront them when they were joined by a much larger force and their raids moved further inland. At that point I sent messengers to you, knowing you'd bring extra forces.

'At first we had no idea where this new band had come from,' the ealdorman continued at Alfred's nod, 'although

Five

the Low Countries seemed the most likely place. There were a dozen or so shiploads of men and our biggest fear was that there'd be more on the way. But it turned out it was a renegade group of East Anglian Danes who'd sailed across the estuary from Benfleet in Essex –'

'So that's where the bastards came from! I've been praying that wouldn't be the case but, renegade group or not, it's Aethelstan's job to keep his people in order, an issue I'll confront once this band is dealt with. So where are they now?'

Aethelbold shrugged. 'Last information we got three days ago had them raiding along the north coast of Kent, their ships moored near the Isle of Sheppey. But they could be anywhere by now – perhaps back in East Anglian lands or even in the Low Countries.'

'Then we head north around the coast at dawn tomorrow. Pick suitable men from your army to fill our ships, Aethelbold. I want as large a force as the two dozen ships can safely hold. The rest of the men can head north along the coast, just in case the enemy attempts to engage us in battle inland.'

As Alfred's fleet prepared to sail next morning, four of Aethelbold's men rode in to report that the Danes had sailed across the estuary back to Benfleet.

'There's something else, lord,' Edgar the spokesman added. 'Aethelbold's had some of his spies in Benfleet for some time now and they keep us up to date with things in King Aethelstan's lands.' Alfred glanced at the ealdorman, who confirmed that with a nod, and urged Edgar to continue.

'The two groups of Danes arrived in the Essex town two days ago, lord, but before a day had passed disagreements had broken out between them over how they would confront your ships.'

'They'll have got wind of our arrival,' Alfred said, as his ealdormen and thegns murmured agreement. 'What's the situation now?'

'As far as our spies could tell, the four ships from Rochester left Benfleet and sailed off across the Northern Sea, likely to join their old shipmates in Francia. Last thing we heard, the East Anglian band had also left Benfleet and sailed north from the Thames. Could be anywhere by now.'

'Then the Anglian coast is where we'll head. We'll give these bastard Danes a lesson they won't soon forget. We'll raid settlements without mercy and take anything of value. Aethelstan might realise there'll be consequences if he just sits by and allows his people to break our treaty.'

Little after noon the twenty-five Wessex ships neared the mouth of the River Stour on the East Anglian coast. They had sailed almost eighty miles with the wind in their sails, and made good time. 'Time to do what we came here for,' Alfred yelled. 'The Stour's as good a river as any to head into.'

But as they veered west into the river, it became clear there'd be no raiding just yet. Strung out across the estuary not more than a hundred yards away, sixteen Danish ships were waiting. Alfred knew instinctively that these were the East Angles from Benfleet. He also realised that the Danes were greatly outnumbered – a situation he intended to put to good use.

'Swing alongside and prepare to board,' he yelled, his orders instantly echoed by masters of the rest of his fleet as the Norsemen's oars dug into the brine, propelling the longships

Five

straight at them. 'The ships from Dover, circle out behind them and attack from the rear. Spare none of the bastards!'

Ships crashed, the screeching and scraping of wooden strakes ringing out, and opposing crews spilled onto each other's ships. Fighting raged for almost two hours, fierce and bloody as swords, seaxes and battle axes struck out, while overhead seabirds circled and wailed. The dead fell to the decks or overboard to a watery grave. Some would be washed out to sea with the river's fast flow, many to be returned with the incoming tide.

'No quarter!' Alfred reminded them as the outnumbered Danes fell like flies. 'And I want their ships with whatever plunder they carry.'

Cheers rang out from Saxon crews as the last few Danes were tossed overboard to feed the creatures of the deep. But their jubilation was short-lived as the realisation sank in that many of their friends and comrades had also been lost. Alfred shared their grief, knowing only too well that no battle could ever be won without losses on both sides. But he had the Danes' sixteen ships and their hoards of loot, which would be towed behind them back to Dover.

From the helm of the *Wyvern*, Alfred led his victorious fleet out of the Stour, veering south and intending to raid a few East Anglian coastal settlements before setting course back to Dover.

Radulf's sudden cry of 'Norsemen to the rear!' sent a wave of panic through the crews.

Alfred cursed as he took in the large fleet of Norse ships rapidly closing in on them. He estimated more than fifty ships – more than double the number of his own – and they were already less than two hundred yards away.

'Turn and face them,' he yelled. 'It's too late to flee!'

Unskilled in such manoeuvres, turning was a clumsy affair, losing the Saxons the time and momentum needed to meet the Danes effectively head-on. Before their rowing could pick up speed, the enemy had surrounded them.

'Offer no resistance!' Alfred's order was again echoed across his fleet. 'Drop all weapons and yield.'

'You speak wisely, King Alfred,' a voice rang out from amidst the Northmen spreading across the Wyvern's decks. 'A good leader knows when he can't win, and that lives *may* be saved if he surrenders.'

A tall, well-muscled man of middle years with braided, light brown hair, emerged from between the parting Danes, his pleasant features marred by the ugly sneer he assumed. Alfred remained silent, realising the prudence of doing so while the Dane said his piece.

'Now we have the problem of what we should do with you,' the Dane went on. 'We could kill you all, as you did with our comrades back there. But, alas, that would put the East Anglian king in a very bad mood and consequences to our crew would not be pleasant if we returned to his kingdom. He's already ranting about the men who sailed from Benfleet to raid in Kent, but since they're now all dead, the punishments he had in mind won't be forthcoming.'

'If you're all from East Anglia, you're right in thinking Aethelstan would not turn a blind eye to you breaking the treaty between us. He is too honourable.'

The Dane threw back his head and roared, while around him, his men sniggered. 'How little you know of Guthrum,

Five

King Alfred! Beneath the Christian façade he displays to you, my uncle is still the same devious sod that left our homeland years ago. He's simply grown too old for fighting and wants an easy life – which you kindly handed to him.'

Alfred nodded, admitting to himself that this man spoke the truth. Deep down, he'd always known that a wolf does not change its clothing. 'You may be right,' he admitted, 'but it doesn't change the fact that Guthr… Aethelstan has kept the treaty, and those who have recently broken it are rebels.'

The Norseman grunted. 'True enough, and I confess that many of us here are East Anglian rebels, including me. We've been behaving ourselves for too long and wanted some action in our lives. So, we thought we'd try our luck at raiding again. After all, the treaty is Aethelstan's problem, not ours.' His arm swept round to encompass his large company of men. 'Besides, we aren't planning to return to Anglia, at least, not until my uncle's in his Christian grave. From what I've seen of him lately, a few more years and he'll be gone. So, as soon as we've dealt with you, we'll be sailing to Francia with these men who've recently joined us from there.'

Alfred glanced round the silent, grim-faced Danes, then at Garth, whose face mirrored his own anxieties. He swallowed hard. Their hopes of survival were scant if the threat of Aethelstan's anger held no weight with these men.

'Does family honour mean nothing to you? You would disobey and desert your uncle and king?'

The Dane glowered, stepping close enough to Alfred to touch the tip of his sword to his throat. 'You ask too many questions for someone facing possible death!'

Alfred's stomach lurched as he anticipated the order to kill them all, but the Dane's rage diminished as suddenly as it had flared. 'I was named Guthrum after my uncle,' he said. 'He is my mother's younger brother and she doted on him, though I could never do anything to please the man. Perhaps he saw me as a threat to his leadership…' He gave a one-shouldered shrug. 'But from now on Aethelstan is not our concern. As I said, Francia holds better prospects for us than East Anglia.'

His lips curved into a self-satisfied smirk. 'No need for undue concern, Alfred. If you do exactly as I say there will be no further bloodshed today. But if any of your men make a wrong move, by Thor I swear that none of you will see another day. Is that clear?' Alfred nodded. 'Then I suggest you relay that message to them all.'

In the unnerving silence Alfred shouted, 'No one move, or we're all dead,' to be instantly echoed by Radulf in the *Hampshire* and masters of all Wessex ships.

Guthrum's nephew grinned, displaying a set of perfect white teeth. 'Good. Now, we're almost ready to take our leave – just as soon as we've relieved you of those ships you just took. They are, after all, rightly ours, and the booty will serve us well until we can rely on Frankish generosity.'

Alfred watched the Danish fleet sail off across the Northern Sea with the sixteen ships in tow, thanking God that no more lives had been lost in this encounter. Yet the bitter taste of defeat would not abate, along with the knowledge that no matter how well his new armies were organised and his new burhs constructed, the Northmen would always be masters of the sea.

Six

Winchester, Hampshire: March 886

Winter frosts and snows gradually took Wessex in their grip and or the next few months life at the Winchester court revolved around the usual cold-weather routines. Christmastide and gift-giving were celebrated in jovial fashion and for Alfred they seemed doubly happy. Since Ealhswith's return to the hall her pinched cheeks had begun to fill out, and the anguish in her dark-rimmed eyes was gradually lessening. She fussed over their children again and claimed back many responsibilities that had been allocated to Aethelflaed in her absence.

Alfred thanked God for bringing Ealhswith back to them, although his total joy in that was marred by the fact that the wife he adored had not yet welcomed him back into their marital bed, despite the fact that they still shared it. As soon as they entered the chamber, the once loving and passionate woman turned cold, distancing herself from him by curling up on her own side of their bed, not even responding to his questions regarding what he could do to help.

But tonight, it was Ealhswith who wanted to talk.

'I'm so sorry,' she said, rolling over and reaching out for him. 'I know my neglect of you is unfair and how much you are hurting. I want so much to be a good and loving wife, the wife you deserve. It's just that...' She broke down in heartbroken sobs and Alfred held her until they subsided.

'No need for explanations tonight,' he said, kissing the top of her head. 'I know how you suffered over the loss of our son and I thank God that you're slowly healing.'

Ealhswith pulled herself back a little, lifting her hand to caress his cheek. 'It's true, the pain of loss diminishes with each passing week, but I'm still so very scared.'

Alfred drew breath to ask what she meant but Ealhswith shook her head, touching her fingers to his lips to silence him.

'I know that pushing you away is not wifely behaviour, Alfred, and sometimes I yearn to feel the warmth of your body next to mine. I miss our closeness and the tenderness we've always shared. I'm so lonely without you, my love, but–'

Realisation hit, and Alfred pulled her close as she softly wept. 'I understand,' he whispered into her hair. 'The death of a child is a heavy burden to bear and your fear of it happening again is only to be expected. But you must promise me never to keep your fears away from me in future. I can't help you in your distress if I don't know the cause of it. Telling me has also erased my own fears.'

'Yes, I know you have grieved over Winfrith's death, too, and –'

'I have, but dealing with so much around our kingdom has helped to stop me dwelling on it. My biggest fear in recent weeks has been that I was losing you… that you had stopped loving me. If you'd told me how you felt, I could have reassured you that I'd never force myself upon you.'

Ealhswith raised her head, her glistening turquoise eyes meeting Alfred's amber. 'I could never find the right time to tell you. I knew how much stress you were under with the Danes raiding in Kent and to burden you with my worries was the last

Six

thing you needed. I'm sorry I've been so cold and unreachable in our bed. I was afraid that if we so much as touched it would lead to more, and I could soon be with child again.'

A choked sob escaped from Ealhswith's throat, and Alfred continued to hold her in silence, certain she had more to say.

'The fear that another of our babes could die has possessed me, Alfred, and I don't know how to make it go away. I tell myself that many infants grow to adulthood, and I give thanks to God that we've had five healthy children. But the thought of watching another child growing weaker and weaker until he simply fades away, won't leave my head.'

Alfred smiled down at her. 'Then we wait for time to do its work. Fear, like grief, can lessen with the passing of days. Until then, just having you in my arms again will be enough. No one knows what the future holds, Ealhswith, but if God intends us to have another child, we must face things together, whatever happens. Just remember, the chances of another babe being fit and healthy far outweigh those of another weak and sickly one like Winfrith.'

No more words seemed necessary and Alfred pulled Ealhswith down beneath the furs to snuggle beside him. Sleep would come easier now that the bond between them had been restored.

*

Alfred had been anticipating notice of Asser's intended arrival at some stage during the spring but as the end of March neared, further word of the abbot's continuing ill-heath reached Winchester. He wondered if the man was deliberately forestalling his move to Wessex… then chided himself for such uncharitable and unreasonable thoughts. Whatever pestilence had stricken so many people in Dyfed, it must have been a virulent one. There had been news of many deaths, not only amongst the frail, the old and very young, but indiscriminately across the population.

He put the matter from his head. Right now, he had more pressing matters to deal with concerning the future of his kingdom, for himself and his descendants in years to come.

A little over a week later, Alfred met with five of his ealdormen in the Winchester hall. His aim was to discuss a course of action he'd often considered over the past few years, and following the attacks in Kent the previous November, his decision was firmly made and needed putting into action.

Riding cloaks were hung around the walls to dry and they settled at a trestle close to the hearthfire to enjoy warm ale and honey cakes before the meeting began. To Alfred's right sat Aethelhelm of Wiltshire, to Alfred's left was Aethelred of Mercia, and opposite them were Paega of Berkshire, Aelfric of Surrey and Radulf of Hampshire. Their faces displayed puzzlement at being summoned when a gathering of the entire witan was due in little over a month. Alfred did not keep them in suspense for long.

'I'm taking control of London.' His blunt ultimatum caused a few sharp intakes of breath but Alfred had no intention of hearing thoughts or objections until he'd said his piece, and he pushed on. 'The recent raids on Rochester proved, yet again, the ease with which the Danes can sail into the Thames and

Six

not only continue up to London but on into the very heart of Wessex. Halfdan and Guthrum's attempts to conquer our kingdom made us all too aware of our vulnerability in this respect and the desperate need for us to fortify our major towns.'

He paused, observing the nods of agreement before continuing. 'So far, we've been successful in strengthening the defences of many of our towns and ports, as well as creating a standing army now proven to be effective and a great improvement on our old-style fyrds. Yet no matter how well our inland armies and newly built burhs counter any attacks, our major problem still lies in the fact that the cursed Norsemen can still *get into* our kingdom in the first place!

'I've asked three of you to be here because the Thames flows through or borders your shires.' He gestured to Paega, Aelfric and Aethelhelm, before turning his attention to Aethelred of Mercia. The young man's red hair and green eyes triggered a fleeting thought of Eadwulf and the little group who had meant so much to them all on Athelney. 'I asked you to attend, Aethelred, in your role as Ealdorman of Mercia. As such, you are entitled to hear my plans for a town that has been a part of Mercia for generations, but I'm also hoping you'll agree to play an active role in the manoeuvre.'

Aethelred nodded and Alfred took a swig from his ale mug before focusing on the Hampshire ealdorman. 'Although the Thames neither flows through nor borders our shire, Radulf, I've included it since it's the Hampshire army I call on first when I'm in Winchester. It can be readily summoned, which we found during the raids on Rochester last year. I intend to lead a contingent of our men, while you will strike from a different angle, if need be – which I'll explain more fully soon.'

Radulf didn't question further. 'Taking London makes sense to me,' he said instead. 'It needs to come under the control of one leader, and you're the best one for that in my book. Once the town's part of Wessex, we can ensure that visiting traders and townsfolk alike appreciate the consequence of falling foul of our laws. And, as you say, we've done a good job in fortifying many Wessex towns but, so far, London's been overlooked.'

Aethelred shuffled, and Alfred invited him to speak, knowing he'd have something to say about a town that had been Mercian for generations and hoping he'd raise no objections to his plans.

'I've been concerned about London for some time, lord,' Aethelred admitted. 'It's always been a whirlwind of activity for traders and such like from countries near and far as well as for local people, but since your treaty with Aethelstan and the division of Mercia with the Danelaw boundary, the town's become an open house for a mix of peoples. I realise your intention was to leave London as a place where Mercians, Saxons and East Anglian Danes could mingle and trade, but things have got out of hand.'

'I'd heard as much… Is it as bad as they say?'

'It is. Brawls and thefts are frequent in the old Mercian area of Lundenwic, and the Roman walled city of Londinium on its eastern side is heaving with Danes. Most arrive there simply to overwinter, but many have chosen to settle. There are over two hundred of them there now, and they've already had a few run-ins with ceorls in nearby villages. Folks are worried they'll

Six

soon turn to full-scale raiding and, if that happens, we'll have a job confronting them, especially once they're back behind those ruins. It would take a huge army to do that. To make matters worse, the old defences along the river banks are crumbling, and pretty useless for keeping new arrivals out. Danish ships moored at London's jetties is a sight our people have had to get used to, but they don't like it one bit. There are often between fifteen and twenty longships there.'

Alfred nodded, relieved to hear no objections but embarrassed at hearing the results of his lack of forethought being voiced. 'Exactly the reasons why London must be brought under my control, Aethelred, and I'll have contingents of the standing armies from Hampshire, Berkshire, Wiltshire and Surrey to do it. So yes, our army will be big.' He heaved a sigh and held out his hands. 'I admit, I made a mistake in leaving the town as an "open house" – to use your words. But let's not forget, like Rochester, London has been one of the greatest ports and markets in our lands for many years and leaving it open for all to trade seemed the fairest thing to do for everyone concerned, including Aethelstan's Danes. I confess, I overlooked the fact that it could result in the place becoming a magnet to Norsemen raiding in Francia, and right now, news of Aethelstan's Danes breaking free of East Anglia to raid in Kent will be an incentive to even more of them to sail over and join them.'

A short silence followed while the men considered the facts laid before them and, at length, Paega raised a finger to speak. Alfred simply tilted his head in anticipation. Like Radulf, the Berkshire ealdorman was one of Alfred's oldest and most trusted advisors, his hair now more grey than dark, his kindly face lined and heavily jowled.

'I agree you should take the town, lord. As you said, the ease of access to London poses a threat to the whole of Wessex; few of us in Berkshire have forgotten Halfdan and Guthrum's occupation of Reading.'

'Paega's right,' Aethelhelm added. 'The people of Wiltshire haven't forgotten the destruction of Wilton and the battles that claimed so many of our fyrd. And I believe that having contingents of our troops permanently stationed in London could also answer some of the problems of disorder that Aethelred mentioned.'

Paega nodded. 'The presence of troops would make a lot of difference, but we also need to consider improving the old defences along the embankments.'

'From what I've seen of Lundenwic in recent years, it needs more doing to it than simply the rebuilding of riverbank defences.' Aelfric of Surrey tweaked his bushy brown beard as he thought. 'Most of the dwellings in the town are no more than hovels, including those inside the Roman ruins. As Aethelred said, the whole place seems to attract people who revel in brawls, or worse.'

'You're both right,' Aethelred agreed, glancing from Aelfric to Paega. 'Lundenwic's a filthy place, overrun with rats, and the streets wind about all over place, little more than muddy alleyways in winter. Cut-throats and thieves can be hidden from sight before anyone has chance to see which way they went. Thankfully, as yet the town's spread little across the river into Surrey, but it's growing rapidly along the northern bank.'

Six

Alfred took in the earnest faces around him, relieved to hear these men not only supporting his plans for taking London but avidly suggesting schemes for the town's overall improvement. 'You all seem to be telling me that London needs a completely new layout and a lot of rebuilding,' he said, smiling round at them. 'I've no doubt that can be done, in time, once it's under my control.'

'Since we all agree that London must be taken, lord,' Radulf said, taking Alfred's words as his cue, 'all we need now is for you to explain how and when you intend the manoeuvre to be made – especially considering that we have two different areas to deal with.'

'The "when" is easy to answer, Radulf. It's a case of the sooner the better. Who knows how many more Danes will sail into the Thames come spring? I had the second week of April in mind, and if we make it the twelfth day of the month, it gives us nine days from tomorrow to gather our armies and move them into position. The men are trained to be permanently ready to move out, so that's no problem, but it could take a few days for them all to reach your mustering points. Be sure to gather at locations close enough to London so you can reach there early on the day, but far enough away so as not to be seen by any scouts.'

Alfred noted the affirmatory nods. 'As to the "how", Radulf's right, we have two distinct areas to deal with: the walled city of Londinium and the area of Lundenwic to its west, where most of the original Mercian settlement focused. With that in mind, Aethelred's own Mercian force should be sufficient for driving out any Danes, or any known thugs or troublemakers, while your Surrey warriors, Aelfric, will line the banks on your side of the river to ensure that no one from the town manage to get into Surrey by sailing across.'

No one spoke as Alfred gathered his thoughts to continue. 'The rest of us will take Londinium from different sides, and one thing I want to make absolutely clear is that the strike must be a coordinated one. As soon as the sun arcs on the horizon we hit them hard.'

'The best place my Berkshire army can attack is from the north,' Paega said, acknowledging Alfred's nod and turning to Aethelred. 'We'll need to ford the Thames at Wallingford and ride across Mercia in order to do that.'

Aethelred nodded. 'That shouldn't be a problem, Paega, and the settlements along your route are unlikely to offer resistance. But don't forget, you'll have to cross the old defensive ditch in order to get to any part of London.'

Alfred flashed the young Mercian a grateful smile. 'We'll all have to cross Mercian lands, Aethelred, so it might be wise to warn your villagers to expect quite an army passing through. But I want no word of our intentions regarding London leaking out, or the Danes could well be waiting to welcome us, either along the way or inside those ruins. Our attack *must* be a surprise one. As for the ditch, my memory tells me it has barely any water in it nowadays and presents little barrier to would-be raiders – as is the case with all the old earthworks around London.'

'My small Hampshire force will join your Wiltshire army at Wallingford, Aethelhelm, along with Paega's,' Alfred went on, focusing on his nephew. 'It will be a good seventy-mile ride for

Six

you from Wilton, so it would make sense to allow yourselves two days for the journey. But it would be useful to have our three armies joining up there and riding to London together. That way, we can ensure a coordinated strike.

'So, that just leaves you, Radulf.' Alfred grinned at the Hampshireman. 'I imagine you've already guessed what role in this I want you to play.'

Radulf returned the grin. 'Commanding the ships, I reckon.'

'Exactly. There's over a score of our vessels berthed at Southampton, which you'll man with our usual crew. Head round the south coast and into the Thames and be sure to have the fleet blocking the river just upstream of Londinium by dawn. We'll be driving the Danes towards the river and I want those who make it to their ships unceremoniously escorted out of the Thames. It would also be of help to Aelfric if you position several ships along the south bank of the Thames so that the Danes realise that heading for Surrey would not be a good idea.'

Alfred heaved a resigned sigh. 'I don't think I need to remind any of you here that no lenience will be shown to Danes who offer resistance. If they refuse to leave the place, we cut then down. That's the message I want Aethelstan to get. Let's hope it will remind him to keep a tighter rein on his people in future.'

There was little left to discuss and Alfred drew the meeting to a close. By tomorrow these men would be riding back to their shires to start mustering their armies. The twelfth day of April suddenly sounded very close.

It seemed a long time since Aethelred had visited Winchester and Aethelflaed was keen to talk with him again and catch up with news of his family. Once the evening meal was over and she'd helped her mother to pour the mead, she watched as the visiting ealdormen continued their conversations with her father, and realised she wouldn't get chance to speak with Aethelred on this occasion. Disappointed, she headed to the back of the hall to sit with Edward and their two young sisters, Aethelgifu and Aelfthryth. Agnes had already taken four-year-old Aethelweard off to bed and Ealhswith would soon follow to read him a final story, the surest way of getting him to nod off.

Edward had been in a grumpy mood since early afternoon and visibly sulked as he ignored the happy babble of the two young girls. But it took little time for Aethelflaed to prise the reason for his ill temper out of him.

'Father's forbidden me to take any part in the raid on London. He wouldn't even let me sit with them when they were planning it earlier.' Edward sounded so peevish that Aethelflaed laughed out loud, only to annoy him further. 'It's not funny!' he threw at her, shoving his dark hair back from his face. 'Father usually involves me in these things – at least, he allows me to listen to any meetings regarding the ruling of the kingdom. He keeps saying it's important to learn how things are done because I'll be king one day, but this time he wouldn't let me anywhere near.'

Aethelflaed shrugged. 'Probably because he didn't want you interrupting while he explained what he wanted each of

Six

his ealdormen to do. I've heard you butting in a few times and Father usually humours you. But this time, he'd already decided what he was going to do and wouldn't want you questioning things – or even trying to worm your way into riding with the Hampshire army.'

Edward sighed. 'I admit I would have asked to go with them. I think I'm old enough, and I have to learn what happens on a raid.'

'Give it another few years, Edward.'

Aethelflaed spun round, pleased to see Aethelred standing behind them. 'King Alfred's right, fifteen's a little too young to take part in a raid,' he added. 'I was seventeen when Eadwulf allowed me to ride out from Athelney with your father's raiding band. Sitting in on meetings and learning how things are done is the best thing you could do at present.'

Edward nodded, seeming appeased by Aethelred's advice, and said nothing more.

'Has Father asked you to play any particular role in his taking of London, Aethelred?'

The directness of her question seemed to throw Aethelred and he looked momentarily crestfallen. 'I'm sorry,' she said, realising she'd hit a sensitive spot and standing to lay an apologetic hand on his arm. 'I imagine it must be a tug of loyalties for you. London's been Mercian for so long, yet I thought I'd heard you support Father's plan to take it this afternoon.'

'I did… and still do support it. If more Danes keep coming to London, Aethelflaed, we could end up with full-scale battles on our hands, so we need to toss the lot of them out before things get that far. King Alfred's already in control of western

Mercia so I see no reason why London shouldn't be his, too. Besides, he's far better able to raise an army large enough to do it than I am.'

Aethelred flashed her a smile, causing her cheeks to burn. 'While King Alfred and his armies deal with Londinium, I'll be taking a force of Mercians into Lundenwic to drive out Danes and troublemakers who have settled there. My spies keep me informed of who and where they are, so it shouldn't be hard to locate most of them. There are always a good many Norsemen in the town, come to trade at the market or just carouse at the inns. My men will make sure they leave the city or else end up dead at the hands of my warriors.'

Aethelflaed nodded, that usual feeling of anxiety engulfing her. Although her father had been facing battles for as long as she could remember, she could never bear the thought of it without fearing he might never come home again. And suddenly she felt that same sense of dread for Aethelred. 'So, tomorrow you all go back to your halls and start gathering your troops. Where will you start in Mercia?'

'For the force I need – which is between a hundred and fifty to two hundred men – I shouldn't have to look much further than fifty miles north-west of London. I'll already have my regular company of thirty trained warriors with me, and between Buckingham and Oxford there are two contingents of the Mercian standing army, set in place when your father had those two towns fortified a few years ago.'

'Then my mother and I will pray for you all to return safely, which is all any woman can do in times of armed conflict.'

'Not quite *all* women, Aethelflaed. Didn't your tutor ever

tell you the story of a certain warrior queen if the Iceni?'

'Of course he did! Boudicca was my favourite person in the stories about the Romans in these lands. But that was hundreds of years ago and Saxon women aren't permitted to do such things – not even the wives of kings.'

Aethelred shrugged. '*That,* Aethelflaed, would probably depend on the will of the wife in question.'

*

In the midst of preparations for the taking of London, quite unexpectedly, Asser arrived at Winchester.

'I am heartily glad to see you here at last – fit and well, I hope,' Alfred said, his hands held out to support the Abbot of Saint David's down from the wagon. 'Come inside out of this wind and warm yourself. At least the rain held off today.'

Asser climbed unsteadily down from the back of his covered wagon, taking Alfred's hand and grimacing as a sharp gust of wind hit him. 'I confess I'm relieved to have reached the end of this journey, my lord. It has taken us five days to get here and the constant wet weather has caused more than a little discomfort.' He gestured to the dozen men in his escort. 'And these good brothers have yet to make their return. This is the first day since we left that the rain has, indeed, held off – as you put it.'

The two men held each other's gaze and Asser chuckled, a low throaty sound that caught Alfred unawares. 'Forgive me, King Alfred, I meant no insult to you, or your concerns for my welfare. Whatever the weather had delivered, the journey would have been a trial for me. But here I am, still in one piece, and happy to be here for the next six months, in case you were wondering. I am satisfied that my replacement at Saint David's is a capable cleric and worthy of the position of abbot until my return.'

Alfred took in the abbot's pale face and the frailness of stature that spoke of long-lasting illness and lack of good food, and realised that Asser had suffered much at the hands of the pestilence that had swept through Dyfed.

'Then we'll enter the hall and allow you to rest for as long as you please before you undertake any work for me. I also need to explain that I'll only be at Winchester for the next few days, then I'm likely to be away for some weeks. But I assure you, good abbot, you'll be made most welcome by my wife and family, as well as the other clerics in my hall.' He gestured to the men seated around the corner trestle, working diligently amidst the mound of scrolls.' If you feel able to join them at some point during my absence, I would be eternally grateful.'

Alfred suddenly smiled as he noticed Aethelgifu creeping closer, listening to what they were saying. 'I must warn you though, that my daughter here will probably pester you with questions about life in a monastery. She seems to have taken a keen interest in the subject in recent months.'

'Then I'd be more than happy to talk to you about my life at Saint David's, child,' Asser said to the blushing girl, favouring her with a broad smile. 'It would probably do us both good to talk.'

Aethelgifu's face lit up and she called a quick, 'Thank you, my lord!' as she headed back to join the rest of her family.

Six

Alfred turned to the men in the abbot's escort, each garbed in the brown robes of a monk. 'Good brothers, you are all welcome to share our hall and food for a day or two before you head back. And when you do, our cooks will ensure you have enough food and ale for such a long trek.'

Seven

London and Winchester: early April - Mid June 886

Alfred spent a relatively comfortable few hours sleeping under the stars close to the ford at Wallingford. The night was dry and mild for early April, and like the rest of his eighty Hampshiremen, after the long ride from Winchester he was tired enough to sleep in the saddle if he had to.

Heartened by the number of Wiltshire and Berkshire troops that had joined him, Alfred's anticipation of an easy encounter in Londinium heightened, and as the sun rose to greet the new day, they were heading south-east on another forty-mile ride that would take them to within ten miles of the north-western curve of the old city walls. By late-afternoon they were setting up camp for the night and eating a meal of bread, cold meats and cheeses from their saddle packs. Come tomorrow's dawn the attack would begin.

The night sky was paling as the ruins of the once thriving Roman town came into view. Aethelhelm waved forward his force of two hundred-strong Wiltshiremen to head to their planned place of attack on the east. Once there, they would tether their horses in nearby woods and spread out, thirty paces back from the walls and gates to wait for the rising sun, their signal to strike. Paega followed, leading his Berkshire troop of over a hundred to do the same to the north. Alfred waited, giving them time to carry out the plan they'd all gone over last night, before leading his Hampshire army of eighty men to

Seven

take their positions along the western walls.

Alfred's heart pounded as a ribbon of pink spread across the eastern horizon. Soon. Sunrise would be very soon…

Expectation kept him focused on the sight as he silently prayed that Radulf had the Wessex ships in place on the river and Aelfric's troops were guarding the Surrey coast. No route into Wessex for pillaging Danes must be left open.

As the sun emerged, spreading golden light across the land, four hundred Saxon warriors charged into the wakening town, over the crumbling walls or through the Roman gateways, spilling through the streets, with hovels alongside. Shouted orders for the Norsemen to leave the town and never return set men, women and children to flight, down to the river and onto their ships. Those who stood to fight did so for barely moments before Saxon seaxes, swords and battle axes ended their days on Midgard.

Bodies soon littered the streets, lifeblood seeping into the churned-up filth and reeking waste. Gradually all became still, only the groans of the wounded and dying breaking the silence. Alfred picked his way through the carnage, his exhilaration at successfully taking Londinium marred by a sense of revulsion at the need to kill so many. He'd vowed to show no mercy to any who resisted, but now he wavered, knowing his men were waiting for the order to put an end to survivors. If he went back on his vow to kill them all, would they see him as merciful, or weak…?

'Spare none!' he yelled. 'Gather up the corpses into whatever carts you find and toss them into the Thames, then burn these stinking huts they've been living in.'

129

Alfred watched the men set to their grim task, blocking out images of this day's deeds. He wondered whether Aethelred had met with opposition in Lundenwic, and hoped that Radulf and his fleet successfully saw the fleeing Danes sail away across the Northern Sea.

*

Alfred's return to Winchester was a happy and relaxed occasion. After spending almost two months in London to ensure the restructuring and rebuilding works were progressing to his design, as well as attending a ceremony with nobles from across Wessex and West Mercia, his family could hardly wait to see him and bombard him with questions.

Ealhswith was also longing to hear news of her brother, whom Alfred had invited to attend the ceremony. She hadn't set eyes on Aethelwulf for over two years; before Alfred had needed to deal with the Danish attack on Rochester. Unfortunately, that had not been an occasion for celebration or the catching-up of events. The funeral of Lady Eadburh, their overly pious mother, was a solemn affair and Ealhswith had spoken no more than a few words to her beloved brother.

'Papa!' Aethelgifu squealed, breaking off her chat with Asser mid-sentence and charging out of the hall to watch Alfred dismount. She waited patiently while he instructed the men of the Hampshire standing army to pitch camp at Winchester for the night before heading back to their base out in the countryside tomorrow. It was already early evening and too late to be needlessly riding elsewhere. Ealhswith smiled at the look of

Seven

delight on the face of her studious young daughter as Alfred strolled across to greet them. Aethelgifu rarely got excited, but the return of her father was a different matter. Behind her, the other children looked just as happy.

Alfred greeted Ealhswith with a warm embrace before giving each of his beaming children a hug. Even Edward couldn't hide how pleased he was to see his father home, despite griping for weeks about not being permitted to go with him. Ealhswith could see that her husband was weary to the bone, but was refusing to let it spoil his joy at being home.

'Did you get crowned again, Papa?' little Aelfthryth asked once they were seated in a circle in the middle of the hall. 'Mama said you were going to be made a king.'

'Don't be silly,' Aethelgifu chided. 'Papa's already a king!'

At Alfred's side, Ealhswith could not help smiling as Alfred patted his knee, inviting the pouting six-year-old to come and sit on it. 'What Mama meant, Aelfthryth, was that after the ceremony, I'd be accepted as king over a much bigger kingdom. I was just King of Wessex before but now I am called the King of the Anglo Saxons. Which means,' he added as Aelfthryth drew breath to ask the inevitable question, 'that now I don't only rule over the Saxon kingdom of Wessex, but over the Angles of Western Mercia as well.'

'But you've been ruling West Mercia for a few years now, Papa.' It was Aethelgifu's turn to look puzzled. 'What difference did the ceremony make?'

'Nothing, really, except that my title is now official. The nobles of Wessex and Mercia paid me homage and made their vows to accept me as king over both kingdoms.'

'Are you saying that Aethelred is no longer the overlord of Mercia for you, as he was before, Father?' Aethelflaed's face reflected her concern. 'Surely you'll still need him to take care of things there while you're in Wessex?'

'Nothing's changed regarding Aethelred's role or status, daughter, so you have no need to worry on his behalf. I'll be needing him as much as ever, if not more so. But I'll be saying more about Aethelred's future role later on – probably tomorrow, when I feel a little more awake.'

Aelfthryth let out an exasperated sigh and slipped her small hand into Alfred's. 'But what *I* asked, Papa, was whether you'd been *crowned* again. And you still haven't told me.'

The others chuckled and Aelfthryth did her best to scowl.

'No, little one, it wasn't necessary to be crowned a second time. But, between you and me,' he added, whispering in her ear, 'it was quite a pompous ceremony, and I was glad when it was over and I could come back to Winchester.'

Once the evening meal was over and the younger children had gone to their beds, the adults relaxed in the hall, engaged in quiet conversation before retiring to their own bed chambers. Some of Alfred's resident thegns played tabula, and other dicing games, while the scholars discussed their progress in translating the Latin texts with Alfred in their usual corner of the hall. He'd been away for several weeks and they had much to tell him.

Ealhswith sat with Agnes, attempting to continue the embroidery she was doing around the hem of a new tunic for Aethelflaed, while Aethelflaed herself played a game of Hnefatafl with Edward. Ealhswith had never found embroidery an enjoyable pursuit, especially in the evenings when the light was

Seven

poor. Oil lamps and candles were no substitute for good bright daylight but, while Alfred had been away, she had needed to do something at night to stop herself feeling lonely.

It had been so quiet in the hall of an evening for the past few weeks, the silence broken only by the murmurings of the clerics at their work on the scrolls and the muted conversations of the guards that Alfred had left at Winchester. It was easy to sink into a state of total lethargy. Besides, Ealhswith had told herself as she persevered with needle and thread, Aethelflaed needed some new tunics, and embroidery did much to improve the look of any garment. A young woman of seventeen and the daughter of a king was expected to display fine apparel at times, even the odd a piece of jewellery.

But Aethelflaed scorned such things, preferring to be outdoors for most of the day, riding or practising with her bow. Ealhswith smiled at that, knowing that Aethelflaed was so like she was at that age. Ealhswith also knew that Aethelflaed was still determined to challenge Aethelred to another archery contest as soon as she got the chance and wondered how Aethelred would feel about that. Eight years had passed since they were on Athelney.

Earlier, Alfred had said he had things to discuss with them regarding Aethelred's continuing role as Overlord of Mercia, but not before tomorrow, after a good night's sleep. Ealhswith wondered what he'd have to say about Aethelred that was so important, but would not tire him by asking questions tonight. Tomorrow wasn't too far away.

*

Alfred strode through the hall heading for the door, a broad smile on his face as he pointed at Edward and Aethelflaed. 'Come, ride with me, you two. We have plenty of time to enjoy some fresh air before the morning meal. Your mother agrees it would do us all good.'

His two eldest children needed no second telling, readily abandoning the writing tasks their tutor had set them and following Alfred out to the stables. The dozen armed men of their escort were already mounted and the grooms were saddling up Pegasus, along with Edward's sorrel and Aethelflaed's bay mare.

The gallop across the Hampshire countryside in the glorious June sunshine was exhilarating. At Alfred's sides, Aethelflaed and Edward's cheeks glowed pink, their faces revealing their delight in the unexpected outing, so soon after their father's return. Their escort rode six ahead and six behind, alert for any signs of danger. The rolling green downs were swathed in colourful flowers, their scents drifting on the breeze, and on the steeper hillsides, beech, ash and yew seemed to hang over clumps of shrubby hawthorn, dogwoods and juniper. Up high against the blue, skylarks hovered, their distinctive song music to Alfred's ears.

'Are we going anywhere in particular?' Edward asked as they slowed to a trot.

'Does it matter?' Aethelflaed put in. 'Just being out riding is enough for me.' She swept her arm out, indicating the sights before them. 'How could anyone not want to look at this scenery? I think I could spend most of my days out here, inhaling the scents of wild flowers and listening to the tune of the skylark.'

Seven

'Well, daughter, your mother could never get enough of riding out when she was young, either. To be honest, she still loves to do that but it's been hard to find the time for it over the years since I became king. The Danes made sure of that.

'Now,' he said, holding out his arm and pointing at a pond close to a small copse of beech, 'that's where we're heading. As you see, our escort knows exactly which way to go.'

'Is there something you want us to see over there, Father? It's just a pond, isn't it?'

'There's nothing unusual about the spot, Edward, it's just somewhere we can sit out of the sun and talk for a while. I have things to say to both of you and I thought being away from the distractions of the hall would be a good idea.'

Alfred instructed his men to continue their scrutiny of the countryside and sat with his children on a cluster of chalky boulders in the shade of a tall beech, a few yards from the water's edge. For some moments, nothing was said, the light breeze caressing their cheeks as they watched the insects hovering over the shiny surface. Alfred's voice broke the silence.

'You realise that the meeting I called last week was to reaffirm my status as King of the Anglo Saxons now that London is under my control, don't you?'

'Yes, Father, you told us about the oath-taking, and we're all very proud of you.'

Alfred flashed his son a smile. 'Which means that when you become king, Edward, that same status will be passed down to you – and who knows, you could even expand your territory further during your reign. But what I'm saying is that your future is mapped out for you, and only another upheaval like the invasion of the Danes twenty years ago, could stop your kingship from prospering.'

Alfred looked levelly at Edward, seeing a serious and intelligent youth hovering on the threshold of manhood, and silently prayed that his son's kingship would be easier than his own had been. 'Of course, there are still Danes in our lands, in East Anglia and Northumbria for a start,' he continued, and we must remain wary of raids along the Danelaw boundary. Perhaps more of a worry, we have no way of knowing how well the Danes will keep to their treaty once Aethelstan and I have gone. The treaty was between the two of us, and there are bound to be some Danes who will think they aren't bound to keep to any treaty a dead leader made with Saxons.

'I haven't mentioned this to anyone at Winchester yet, not even your mother, but I spent a week of my time away in East Anglia, redefining the boundary of the Danelaw with Aethelstan. It was vital for him to know that London is now under my control and under no account will his people – or any Norseman from elsewhere – be permitted to settle there. Those who come to trade will be carefully watched by men from my standing armies and raids on Mercian villages along the route of the border won't be tolerated. Danes who decline to obey will be severely dealt with.'

He shook his head as his thoughts fixed on the meeting with his old adversary. 'I confess, Aethelstan has aged a good deal since I last saw him. But he is not a well man, and I believe he won't be here for many more years. And, no doubt, my own turn will follow soon after. I pray God that I leave my kingdom at peace when I take my last breath.'

Seven

Edward and Aethelflaed remained silent and Alfred noted the looks of dismay on their faces. But this talk was all about their future, and couldn't be done without the mention of his death. 'I sincerely hope that when you are king, Edward, you will continue to be on good terms with Lord Aethelred. He's a strong and skilful warrior and admired and respected by his men. I like the way he thinks things through and doesn't act on a whim. In a nutshell, he's a man deserving of our trust, just like his father, and I have given him full control of West Mercia, answerable only to me – and you, when your time comes.'

'I like Aethelred, too, Father, and feel certain I could work well with him. He seems very wise and I always appreciate his advice. Will he still be living mostly in Worcester?'

'No, he won't. As soon as the new hall in London is ready, he'll be moving in there and will have complete control of the town's defence and welfare. Naturally, as my court has always done, he'll need to travel to other Mercian estates during the year, but I want him mostly in London for the first year or so. It makes more sense to have him somewhere that relies on trade with foreign peoples for its prosperity than up in Worcester. In Worcester, Aethelred was close enough to hear regular news on Anarawd's antics in Gwynedd, but the Welshman is nowhere near as big a problem to us as the Danes have been. And things seem to have settled down in Gwynedd now, hopefully for some time.'

Both of his children seemed to be mulling over his words, so Alfred went on, 'I've decided to ask Garth if he'd like to act as Aethelred's right-hand man. Aethelred jumped at the idea, but I won't force Garth to leave his home in Somerset.

Although he's not married yet, he'd be a long way from his parents in London, and he'd still be free to return to his own hall once each of his terms of duty is over, as is his right as a thegn. The only difference will be that his duty will be to serve in Aethelred's hall as a resident thegn instead of mine. But I've a feeling he'll be pleased to spend a lot of time with Aethelred.'

'I think Garth will be happy being with Aethelred,' Aethelflaed said, her gaze following the fluttering route of a pretty blue butterfly. 'They're such good friends, and Garth is a good warrior, too – so Aethelred told me.'

'It's Garth's turn to serve at Court next week, so I'll be talking to him about this idea when he gets here. I'm hoping he'll agree, for Aethelred's sake. Now I have just one more thing to say to you, and although it will affect you both, it primarily concerns you, daughter.'

Aethelflaed gaped at him. 'Me? Oh, have the grooms complained that I'm forever in the stables? It's true, I know. Sometimes it's so boring in the hall and I just need to be outside.'

Alfred chuckled. 'Nothing like that. It's something that will come as a surprise, but from what I've seen and heard, one that might not be completely unattractive to you. But I must add, Aethelflaed, that this isn't something in which you have a choice. The decision was made by me, and Ealhswith thinks it's an excellent idea.'

'Papa, just tell me what it is, please. You're making me nervous going on like that.'

'You are to marry Ealdorman Aethelred, and live in Lundenburh with him to start with. You are seventeen now, and

Seven

it's time you were wed – and the marriage will be a perfect union of the two kingdoms.'

Both Aethelflaed and Edward gawked at him, as though they'd misheard, but it was Edward who got the first words out. 'But Aethelred's only an ealdorman, Father. Surely Aethelflaed should marry a king's son. There must be plenty of them in places like the Low Countries and Francia, or even the Welsh kingdoms and…'

'No, Edward,' Aethelflaed cut in. 'Papa's right in choosing Aethelred for me. I probably wouldn't have anything in common with someone from a far-off kingdom, or even speak the same language, and we could end up hating each other. Although marriage was something I had hoped not to think about for a few years, if I must marry, I'd rather marry someone I already know and like.'

'Your answer has made me a happy and proud father,' Alfred said, standing and pulling Aethelflaed to her feet to clasp her in a warm embrace. 'And I forgot to add, Aethelred likes the idea, too, and we've agreed that early September would be the best time for the wedding. That not only gives us time to get invitations out to our many guests – especially those to Aethelred's family in the Danish lands – but it also allows enough time for Aethelred's new hall to be completed and furnished and the ruins of the old Saint Paul's Church to be rebuilt into a place grand enough for the marriage between the daughter of the King of the Anglo Saxons and the Ealdorman of West Mercia.

'So, Edward, in future years, Aethelred will be your brother-by-marriage as well as Ealdorman of the Mercians. There are bound to be times when you'll need to work closely together, and, from what I've seen, I could leave my kingdom in no better hands than yours and Aethelred's.'

*

Ealhswith's delight at the thought of her eldest daughter marrying a man she had liked and admired for several years was written on her face. 'Aethelred is the perfect match for you, and I admit that the thought of you marrying a Mercian made me smile. It's a long time since I lived in the kingdom of my birth, but I still have fond memories of many of the people and places there, especially my brother, whom we've seen so little of these past few years.'

Aethelflaed couldn't help smiling back. 'I know I am fortunate, Mother, and I'll be sure to remind Uncle Aethelwulf to visit you more often. Aethelred is such a nice person. I just hope he doesn't still see me as the annoying child who plagued his life with requests for archery contests.' She stared down at her stitching, reluctant to admit she'd been planning to do just that the next time he came to Winchester.

Ealhswith came around the table at which they were working on Aethelflaed's wedding garments and sat next to her daughter. 'No one could look at you and see a child, dear one. You are a beautiful young woman, with intelligence, confidence and physical strength and stamina to match. No man could find a better wife than you.' She laid her hand over Aethelflaed's, halting the iron needle's continuous motion, in and out of the fabric. 'What he'll make of your fiery and outspoken nature remains to be seen.'

Seven

Aethelflaed stared at her mother, suddenly confronted by a side of her own nature she hadn't considered before. 'You think me *fiery*, Mother? I know I'm outspoken, but that isn't my fault alone. You and Papa reared me to be honest and speak my mind, so that is what I do. But *fiery*...?'

'Dear one, you do have a habit of rising to anger a little too quickly, often saying things you don't mean only to regret having done so later.' Ealhswith's smile belied the spoken criticism. 'Sometimes, perhaps all you need is a deep breath and a moment to consider the thing that angered you before you put voice to words you will later wish had remained unsaid.'

Aethelflaed hugged her mother, no answer coming immediately to mind. Having a fiery nature was something else she hoped Aethelred had overlooked.

Eight

Aros, Danish lands: early July 886

'Good girl,' Freydis cooed, holding out her hands for little Thora to toddle towards her. The happy sixteen-month-old giggled, moving confidently forward on sturdy young legs and throwing herself into her mother's arms for the cuddle she knew would ensue after her efforts.

Yrsa smiled at the sight as she walloped the flatbreads into shape at a nearby trestle. 'Better make sure we leave nothing breakable in her reach – or, of more importance, anything sharp she could hurt herself on… And she'll need constant watching with that firepit.'

Freydis chuckled. 'We've been watching her like hawks since she started crawling.' She tilted her head, gesturing at a barred wooden enclosure. 'And I can't see her being happy in that pen Eadwulf built for her, even though all her wooden toys are in there.'

Yrsa nodded and came across to squat on the floor beside them, wiping floury hands on a clean piece of linen as she did. 'You never know, we could be pleasantly surprised, and she might give us some peace for a while. On the other hand, she could bawl her head off as soon as we take her anywhere near the pen.'

The two women laughed and Freydis suddenly felt blessed by her goddess that Yrsa had been a part of her family for so many years. Although the true daughter of Rorik and Mor-

Eight

wenna, the feisty dark-headed Yrsa had become her adopted daughter since she was no older than Thora was now. And Freydis would be lost without her.

'Thora looks more like Eadwulf every day,' Yrsa said, cutting through Freydis' memories of the fateful death of Eadwulf's mother, the gentle Morwenna, 'especially now she has hair curling round her neck. It's as red as his – and Ameena's of course. I think she'll look a lot like Ameena when she gets older.'

'Probably,' Freydis said, smiling at the thought. She was very fond of Eadwulf's pretty half-sister and valued her help and companionship around the hall and farmlands. Ameena liked nothing better than being outdoors, toiling in the fields, or tending the animals. The weather had to be either extremely cold or wet to keep her indoors.

'Well, Yrsa, let's be brave and see just what Thora thinks of her pen. All her wooden bricks and animals are in there, so let's hope we get some peace while we serve the meal.'

*

Eadwulf stepped through the door and into his hall followed by Hamid and Básim, with Ameena a few steps behind. They were greeted by what Eadwulf could only interpret as Thora's heartfelt disapproval of being in her pen. Freydis and Yrsa seemed to be ignoring her protests as they arranged food on the trestles for the morning meal, scurrying back and forth with trays stacked with flatbreads. The aromas of the pottage simmering in the cauldron over the hearthfire made Eadwulf's stomach grumble, but he headed for the pen to relieve the child of her misery.

'We'd only just put her in there,' Freydis said, stopping in her tracks. 'She hasn't even had time to notice all her toys, which she loves to play with on the floor out here.'

'Well, we won't be able to enjoy the meal while she's bawling, will we?' Eadwulf replied, an impish grin on his face. 'And I'm sure she'll want to eat, the same as the rest of us.' He bent to lift the toddler up and the howling instantly stopped.

Yrsa tutted and summoned one of the serving women over to deal with the food in her place. 'Give her to me,' she said, reaching out her arms to Eadwulf. 'She can sit on my lap and I'll feed her while you eat and catch up on things. Welcome home, you two!' she called out to Hamid and Básim. 'We thought you'd be back either today or tomorrow. You're both looking a little travel weary, but I imagine you enjoyed getting away from farm work for a few days. Did you get the spices I mentioned while you were in Hedeby?'

Hamid grinned, not bothering to conceal his feelings for Eadwulf's half-sister. 'We did enjoy the trip, thank you, *and* we remembered your spices. In fact, we got everything we went for, as well as a few more goats.'

Eadwulf waited until everyone had eaten their pottage before he spoke. 'Hamid and Básim heard some news in Hedeby that may seem unimportant to the rest of us, but it means a lot to them, as it will to Ameena when she hears. I'm not sure there's anything we can do about it, and we may have to accept it simply as news, but I'll leave it to them to explain what I'm talking about.'

'We'd had a good day round the market,' Hamid started,

Eight

his dark-eyed gaze moving between the listeners, 'and headed back to the knarr to load up our goods. Leif had stayed aboard to guard the ship with a few others, and it was he who drew our attention to the Moor berthed further along the quayside. He wondered if we'd like to have a look at it – for old times' sake. We were keen to see where it had come from, and as we got closer, the name *Seville* on a flag fluttering atop the mast answered that question.

'At first the crew seemed surprised when we spoke in the al-Andalusian tongue but after glaring at us for a while, they seemed to accept we were their countrymen and began responding to our questions.'

'Most of the crew were from my home town of Seville but a few came from Cordoba,' Básim continued where Hamid left off, his fluent use of the Danish tongue a credit to his teacher. 'They were in Hedeby to buy slaves and had a big group of men trussed up like chickens on the deck ... and after being captured as a slave myself, I know it's something no one should have to go through.' He glanced at Eadwulf and acknowledged his grim nod. 'A tall, mean-faced Moor noticed us staring and told us the slaves were being taken to the new emir's quarries. He needs a lot more stone so he can build his new palace.'

'The new emir...?' Ameena couldn't hide her surprise. 'What happened to Muhammad? I'm sure he was past his prime, but I would have expected him to live a few more years yet.'

Hamid let out a sigh. This was his natural father they were talking about. 'You're right, sister. Muhammad didn't die of old age; he was assassinated while visiting the quarries. Even his large bodyguard was useless against the scores of riders who swarmed in, some firing arrows, others hacking men down with their scimitars. A well-aimed scimitar strike took my father's head clean off.'

'Doesn't it seem odd,' Eadwulf said, focusing on Ameena, 'that Muhammad eventually met his end in the same place an attempt was made on his life years ago? Our father saved him that day, pushing him out of the path of a boulder hurtling down from the clifftop. The weapons may have been different this time but the intent was the same.'

Ameena could only agree, the mention of her father seeming to momentarily distract her. 'Beorhtwulf was a brave man, and I often think of him and our lives in Cordoba. If not for Salihah's plotting at the time when you and Jorund found him, Eadwulf, I doubt he – or Hamid and I – would ever have left al-Andalus.

'And I can guess who the new emir is,' she added, returning to the present. 'Did they find out who was responsible for Muhammad's death?'

'If you were thinking Rajiv is emir now, you'd be right, sister,' Hamid replied, 'though he's known by his formal name of Al-Mundhir. As for Muhammad's death, no one has valid proof of who organised it, but even if they had, they'd probably be too scared of the consequences to speak out.'

'I wouldn't put it past Rajiv's mother to be behind it,' Ameena spat. 'Salihah was always a treacherous, self-centred witch, and determined her first-born son would succeed Muhammad. No doubt she got impatient waiting for him to die. Why he never suspected her when several of her son's rivals for

Eight

the succession mysteriously died is a mystery.'

Hamid nodded. 'You could be right about Salihah, and even when we were there, most people in al-Andalus were dreading Rajiv becoming emir. According to the Moors in Hedeby, he's a very unpopular emir and needs to watch his back or he'll end up being assassinated, too. But, as Muhammad's firstborn son, he was brought up knowing the title would be his one day.'

'Don't we know it!' Ameena cut in. 'Rajiv was taught to be devious and arrogant by Salihah from the day he was born. Most people in the Alcazar did their best to avoid him and his spiteful ways. His easy, pampered lifestyle meant he never got chance to develop the qualities required of an emir – but he has enough venom to make everyone despise him.'

'Rajiv's been leading assaults on the Muladi, as well as the Asturians far to the north of al-Andalus for some years now,' Hamid added, 'although from what we've been told, the general opinion is that all he does is give the orders for the attacks, leaving his commanders to organise them and carry them out. He's no leader of warriors, that's for certain, and obviously no strategist, either. It's strange that my father didn't realise that…' He scratched his head as he thought. 'Or perhaps he knew exactly what Rajiv's weaknesses were and was threatening to overlook him as his successor.'

'That would certainly have given Salihah a reason to dispose of Muhammad quickly,' Ameena replied, twisting a lock of her red hair round her fingers as she thought. 'She couldn't risk allowing him to live long enough to make his wishes known to his Court, or even write them down.'

'Ameena, we have no proof of that,' Eadwulf cautioned. 'It's a possibility, but until we know more of the facts, we can't be sure what happened.'

Ameena smiled. 'I'd like to find out, though.'

'I'm sure you would, as would Hamid and Básim, no doubt – and me, for that matter. But there's no chance of sailing down to al-Andalus this year with Aethelred's wedding to attend in September. He's marrying King Alfred's daughter, Aethelflaed. They always did get on well, at least once the childish sparring stopped.'

He grinned round as the stunned expressions morphed into delighted smiles. 'I only found out about it myself a short while ago,' he explained, throwing out his hands with a shrug. 'The messengers rode up just as I was about to head back to the hall but I thought I'd let Hamid and Básim get their news out first. We'll leave here at the beginning of September and be in London until early October which, hopefully, will be before the winter gales set in across the Northern Sea. So, you see, if we decide to go to al-Andalus, it will be another year and in the spring or early summer.'

Freydis was the first to remark on the unexpected news about the forthcoming marriage, a huge smile still on her face. 'I'm thrilled for Aethelred and a wedding is something I'm sure we can all look forward to. It's too long since we saw the rest of your family, Eadwulf. But going back to al-Andalus…?' Her smile rapidly dropped. 'You're surely not serious, are you? What do you think you could possibly do there? As far as I can see, you could do nothing that's likely to make a difference. Of course, you could all end up dead, but I hardly think that

Eight

would change anything with this new emir.'

'Freydis, if we did go – and I do mean *if* – it would be for the sole purpose of seeing what's happening for ourselves and allowing Hamid and Ameena to pay their respects at Muhammad's grave.'

'Why would they want to do that?' Yrsa asked, her face reflecting repugnance at the thought. 'After all, the man tried to have you all killed! He's dead, and the way I see it, that should be the end of it.' She stretched across to pat Freydis' hand by way of offering her support.

'You ladies may both be right,' Hamid admitted, 'but it's unsettling news for us. The three of us lived in al-Andalus long enough to call it home, and although my sister and I have no wish to live there now, I'm not sure about Básim, who still has family in Seville.' The young man stared down at his hands, seeming to struggle with his thoughts. But he said nothing, and Hamid went on, 'It's just hard for us to think of the people suffering under this pathetic weasel of an emir. Muhammad may have been strict and his punishments harsh, but his laws made al-Andalus a safe place to live, at least for most of the population.'

Eadwulf rose to his feet, keen to get back to the fields. 'I'd say we get on with our work and let this subject rest, for now. There's no way we can head down to al-Andalus this year, but I promise to give the idea some serious thought once winter's done. But, if we *do* manage to go next year, it will be for two or three weeks, at the most – and that includes the time it takes to sail there and back.'

He smiled at Freydis and she gave a little smile back before turning to relieve Yrsa of the now sleeping Thora.

Nine

Winchester, Wessex: August 886

Aethelflaed's marriage was looming. Most of the replies to invitations sent to nobles and clerics across Wessex and West Mercia had come in, although as yet, Alfred was waiting to hear whether Aethelred's family and friends would manage to get here, especially those from across the sea. He leaned against the outer wall of the Winchester hall, his mind veering between his plans for the future and events of past years. So much had happened since he'd been crowned fifteen years ago, and he'd learned a few good lessons along the way. Not just about ruling a kingdom, but about people and their actions. He could barely suppress a chuckle at the fact that he'd found friendship and trust with a group of people who counted certain Danes as their closest friends and allies. Then again, Eadwulf and his group had also made bitter enemies in the land of the Danes. And now, Alfred's eldest daughter was to become the wife of Eadwulf's son.

'What is London like now?' Aethelflaed asked, suddenly appearing at his side as though his thoughts had conjured her up. 'Not that I've ever been there anyway, but I've heard you all talking about how filthy and unruly the place was before. I know you've cleared the town of the Danes, so is it all clean now with lots of new dwellings?'

Alfred nodded, and ploughed into his description, his enthusiasm for his work in the town carrying him along. 'Our

Nine

new town of Lundenburh is being rebuilt inside the walls of the old Roman city of Londinium. It's already greatly improved, Aethelflaed, though it's by no means finished. When it is, it will be one of our strongest burhs. I'm happy to say that Aethelred is an excellent overseer of ongoing work, and I'm content to leave it in his capable hands while I'm in Winchester.'

A smile spread across Alfred's face as he listed all the work done in the town so far. 'The first thing we did was to rebuild and strengthen the ruined outer walls, gateways and waterfront defences to the standard required for one of our burhs. The town inside has been completely restructured, keeping to the Roman grid pattern of streets. All the hovels built in a random style over the years have been removed, most of them already rendered heaps of ash during our attack. Many of the Mercians and Saxons who lived in Mercian Lundenwic are presently building themselves new, sturdier dwellings in Lundenburh, and once those homes are finished, the hovels of Lundenwic will come down and all trade will focus on the new burh.'

Aethelflaed listened in silence, nodding occasionally at his points. 'But there were two major stone ruins we decided to rebuild,' Alfred continued, 'one being the old Saint Paul's Church, which had belonged to some religious community years ago. Its outer walls and tower were still in good condition so all we needed to do was clear out the weeds growing inside and out, construct a good strong oak door and window shutters, and furnish it with the necessary altar. I also purchased a few statues, cups and chalices and such like for the finishing touches.'

He thought of the elegant stone building with its intricate

carvings and was suddenly reminded of his father, King Aethelwulf, and his opinion that all Saxon churches should be of stone. 'The church is now one to be proud of, daughter, and is a perfect place for your marriage to take place. In the next few weeks I'll be appointing a new bishop, though I have no one specific in mind at present.

'The other structure was once a Mercian royal palace,' Alfred went on, noting his daughter's lack of enthusiasm for his ramblings, 'but it had long since been abandoned. It had originally been built over another Roman ruin, the lower part of which we kept, completing the upper half in solid oak planks and a good, thick reed thatch. I've left the internal layout to Aethelred, since it will be his hall, and a grand one at that. It is where you will both live when you are in the town.'

A small frown creased Aethelflaed's brow, but she remained silent and Alfred went on. 'As I said, work will be ongoing in several areas for a few more years yet. As we speak, the outer defensive ditch is being re-dug and I'm hoping when I return next week to see how things are progressing, the ditch will be filled with water – which hasn't been the case for many years. Then there are the riverside wharfs and buildings to be built, of a design suitable for the incoming and outgoing vessels and goods of a port and trading centre, and buildings to be setup as inns and taverns, for townsfolk and visitors alike. Not to mention a market place and an area of buildings with space enough for craftsmen to live and continue their work. A town does not only consist of houses.'

Aethelflaed could not help a smile, seemingly at his enthusiasm, but the look of anxiety soon returned to crease her face.

Nine

Alfred guessed that after having several weeks to think about her marriage, his eldest daughter was finding it hard to face her future away from her family. But she had asked what London was like, and since she would soon be living there, he added, 'One of my greatest plans for Lundenburh is to build a new bridge where the old Roman one once crossed the Thames. It's a perfect location for connecting most of our Wessex shires with Mercia to the north of the Thames. Aethelred agrees, but I'm afraid it's only a half-formed idea for some distant date at present...

'Lundenburh isn't that far away from Winchester, you know,' he assured, putting his arm round her shoulder when her expression remained downcast, 'and I know you and Aethelred will visit us as often as his commitments allow. We'll also be visiting you whenever we can.'

Aethelflaed gave a wry smile and shook her head. 'You know as well as I do that such intentions have a habit of falling by the wayside. We only need to think of how seldom Mother has seen her parents and brother over the years. I don't want it to be that way with us.'

Alfred took Aethelflaed by the shoulders, twisting her round to face him. 'You are right, we've spent little time in Mercia over the years, but as you well know, since your mother and I married and right up to recent times, our kingdoms have been overrun with Danes. Travelling anywhere was dangerous, and I had no intentions of putting your lives at risk.'

'I do realise that, Father, and didn't mean to imply that you were to blame for the lack of contact with Mother's family. It's just that I cannot bear the thought of living amongst strangers, far away from you all. And yes, I do realise that many noble women face the same situation, your own sister being one of them.'

Alfred looked away as memories of Aethelswith's unhappiness throughout her marriage to the self-centred Mercian king, Burgred, flooded his head. He prayed God that his daughter's marriage would be the love match he believed it destined to be. He drew breath to speak, before realising that Aethelflaed was already speaking.

'I'm sure being with Aethelred will help me to adjust to my new life, and I'll also have Garth to talk to at times. Perhaps Eadwulf and his family will visit us, too. I hope his daughter comes for the wedding with Aethelnoth's family. None of us have met Leofwynn – or Eadwulf's new Danish wife and his two half-sisters. I'm so looking forward to meeting them all.'

Alfred grinned, 'There, you see, you've talked yourself out of feeling down. There are always good people to meet, wherever you live, Aethelflaed. 'I'm looking forward to meeting all those you mentioned, too, and sincerely hope they can find the time to come.'

*

London, Mercia: September 886

Three days before Aethelflaed's marriage was to take place, she arrived in Lundenburh with the rest of her family and a score of her father's retainers, Garth amongst them. This was the first time she and Aethelred had set eyes on each other since

Nine

the decision that they would marry had been made, and it was evident that her future husband felt as awkward as she did when they found themselves face-to-face. Keeping eye contact was difficult for both of them as the visiting party enjoyed the welcomed refreshments, and Aethelred seemed relieved when Alfred asked him to show them all round his new hall.

It was a large, imposing building, her father's use of the word 'grand' seeming inadequate for such a resplendent structure. Aethelflaed admired the bright new tapestries covering the inner, grey stone walls, and marvelled at the fact that the main hall was spacious enough to warrant two firepits. She was duly impressed by the four bedchambers adjoining the hall, and the kitchens and lengthy stables outside. Nor could she deny the value of having so many storage huts, as well as a sizeable garden area that had been dug over ready to be planted with herbs and vegetables for next year's meals.

Aethelflaed found much to like in her future home and convinced herself she would be happy here once the marriage ceremony and feasting were over. But the town itself was a different matter. As her father's cavalcade had entered through the west gate earlier and headed along the overly straight streets towards the hall, Aethelflaed found her dislike of the place mounting. For a start, being inside those tall city walls made her feel cut off from the open countryside she so loved, and everything inside looked so new. Columns of smoke rising from the holes in the roof thatch of some of the newly built dwellings suggested people had already moved in, while others were still being constructed. Despite being thankful that reeking piles of refuse and filth had not yet had time to accumulate, she could only feel that Lundenburh simply didn't look homely and welcoming.

Aethelflaed swallowed hard, thinking of the ongoing building work her father had described that could disturb the peace and quiet for months ahead… As overseer of the work, Aethelred was unlikely to be visiting any other Mercian halls for some time.

Then the restored Church of Saint Paul had come into view, the sight of its lofty tower lifting her spirits and reminding her of places she knew and loved. This church would compare favourably to any Wessex cathedral she had seen, and the day after tomorrow, when she and Aethelred made their vows to each other, she would assess its interior – as well as the newly appointed Bishop Elstanus.

*

The day before the wedding was a hectic one, and Ealhswith and Agnes kept themselves busy helping Aethelred's servants to prepare the abundance of food needed for the wedding feast the following afternoon. Only the hot meats, fish and soups, which needed to be served hot, would be cooked in the morning, along with the breads. In the evening, she spent most of her time with Aethelflaed, now sequestered in her bed chamber, leaving Agnes to care for the three younger children. All the family must be garbed in their finest apparel, and Ealhswith knew that Agnes was more than capable of choosing appropriate garb for the little ones.

But Aethelflaed must look truly stunning.

Nine

Ealhswith fussed over her daughter's bathing and ensured the women rubbed her skin with sweet smelling oils before brushing her gold-brown hair till it gleamed. She smiled as she recalled undergoing the same, age-old rituals before her marriage to Alfred eighteen years ago – although she distinctly remembered her own mother's lack of interest. Eadburh had left all Ealhswith's preparations to the women.

And now, her beautiful, headstrong daughter was to be a bride herself. Aethelflaed's wedding gown lay across the top of a large trunk, just waiting to adorn the young woman for whom it had been made. Ealhswith dismissed the women and sat beside Aethelflaed on the bed. She was exhausted and craved some much-needed sleep, but her daughter's doleful face told her they needed to talk.

'Tomorrow will be a splendid affair,' she started, 'and you will look so lovely that no one will be able to take their eyes off you.'

Aethelflaed smiled, shaking her head at Ealhswith's flattery before fixing her in a searching gaze. 'I know I should feel happy, Mother, and in some ways I do. I'm just a little confused and can't put into words exactly how I feel.'

Ealhswith smiled reassuringly. 'The night before I married your father, I couldn't decide whether to laugh with joy at the thought of spending the rest of my life with him or weep at the thought of leaving behind the only life I'd ever known. It is a hard thing to do, and I imagine few women escape such anxious thoughts on the eve of their wedding. Is that how you are feeling?'

Aethelflaed nodded. 'I suppose it is. I love Aethelred – or

think I do. At very least, I've admired him and thought of him as a friend for a long time, and I know he's an honourable and kindly man who is sure to do his best to make me happy. As, indeed, I will do for him. But I love you all so much that the thought of seeing so little of you in future makes me want to weep. If only I could be with all of you, all of the time.'

Ealhswith took her daughter's hand. 'Dear one, we could say "if only" about many things in this life, but sometimes we must rise above such thoughts and simply move on and do our duty. With Aethelred you have someone to love and care for, and before too long you may have children of your own to –'

'I'm not sure I want any children. I'm frightened of giving birth…' She hesitated, and Ealhswith's stomach flipped, realising what she was about to say. 'I don't think I could cope with losing a babe, the way you lost Winfrith. It would tear me apart.'

Ealhswith wrapped her daughter in her arms. 'Oh, Aethelflaed, I was wrong to allow the babe's death to affect me so badly, and for so long. I wallowed in my grief instead of accepting the loss and resuming the happy life I had with the rest of my family. Just look at the five healthy children I've had! No mother could be prouder than I am, especially when my eldest is to become the wife of a wonderful man we all love. Keep in mind, Aethelflaed, that most babes live.

'And we aren't too far away in Winchester for the greater part of the year, and once most of the building work in Lundenburh is finished you and Aethelred must come and visit. But I've no doubt your father will have been here many times before then.'

Nine

Aethelflaed flashed a bright smile and Ealhswith knew that acceptance of her future had eventually taken hold.

*

The early September day dawned bright and still, the lingering heat of summer hanging on the air, while inside the cool nave of the Church of Saint Paul the many guests engaged in muted conversations whilst awaiting the arrival of the bride. Alfred smiled round, nodding in greeting to any he hadn't yet had chance to speak to. As befitted his title, as well as the occasion, he was garbed in a cloak of deep burgundy with a lining of rich amber silk over a tunic of pale blue linen, and on his wheat-coloured head sat his favourite gold circlet studded with sapphires. His collar-length hair and newly sprouted short beard and moustaches had been neatly trimmed.

On the opposite side of the nave, Aethelred stood calmly with his family and friends who had all arrived in Lundenburh last night. Their reunion had brought a lump to Alfred's throat as he watched the embraces and tears of joy; it had been too long since Aethelred had seen either Eadwulf or Aethelnoth and their families. Alfred gave thanks to God that their respective journeys had been safe and uneventful and hoped that later they'd have time to talk about their lives since they'd last met. Watching them now, he admired the way their apparel equalled that of anyone present, and it was clear that Aethelred had chosen wedding garments in his usual, preferred colour, and had not resorted to any showy display of jewellery or other finery. The mid-green linen tunic and deeper green cloak contrasted well with his shoulder-length red hair, the shades of his attire broken only by a large, ruby-studded brooch that held his cloak at the left shoulder and a belt of finely crafted, interlaced strips of brown leather, with a stunning gold buckle.

At Alfred's side, Ealhswith's smiling face reflected her happiness on their daughter's special day, the agonising grief of the past year seeming, finally, to have lifted. In her overdress of striking deep turquoise, Alfred had rarely seen his wife look so handsomely garbed throughout the eighteen years of their marriage. Nor could Ealhswith disguise her joy at seeing again the brother she adored. At her opposite side, Aethelwulf beamed at everyone, a good-natured man of a muscular and robust appearance, the salting of his dark brown hair at the temples the only indication that he was past his fortieth year. Having lost the wife he'd adored many years ago during a disastrous birthing, he had chosen never to wed again. But today he was here to see his niece married to a fellow Mercian whom he had met on several occasions and his face reflected his joy at being here.

A yard behind them, smartly garbed in rich, deep blue, Edward waited with Alfred's three younger children, firmly holding a wriggling five-year-old Aethelweard by the hand. Edward grinned as he caught his father's eye and Alfred couldn't help smiling at the sight. It suddenly didn't seem so long since his own antics in church had been held in check by his eldest brother as they waited for their sister, Aethelswith's wedding to start.

His memories were rapidly curtailed when murmurings at the lofty arched doorway signalled the arrival of the bride in the porticus. All eyes turned to watch Aethelflaed's four maids of

Nine

honour lead her to her place in the centre of the high-ceilinged nave where Aethelred had now come to stand.

Ealhswith grasped Alfred's arm, giving it a small squeeze as she blinked back the tears of joy. Aethelflaed looked truly stunning. Her long-sleeved underdress of delicate, pale yellow linen reached down to her ankles, its scooped and puckered neckline accentuating her supple throat and neck, around which hung a fine golden chain holding a large crystal of amber. Her calf-length overdress was a rich, deep russet, with sleeves that flared at the elbows to reveal a silken jade lining, matching the colours of the band that held her short head-veil in place over her long, gold-brown hair. A glorious bouquet of late meadow flowers betwixt a variety of gold-tipped, September greenery complemented her attire.

The clear tones of the choirboys reverberating from the chancel signalled the entrance of Bishop Elstanus, whose mitre and richly decorated dalmatic were indicative of a man of his standing in the Church. Alfred watched him with interest, hoping the impression he gave as a friendly and trustworthy man would not turn out to be misleading; too many bishops had played him false over the years. Elstanus smiled at the bridal couple and gestured they should follow him to the traditional place at the doorway, where those gathered inside the church and out could hear them make their vows of commitment to each other.

Alfred heard his beloved daughter pledge love and devotion to the man who had come to mean so much to all his family. He caught Eadwulf's eye and the two fathers exchanged warm smiles of friendship.

*

'Lady Freydis, I haven't yet had the opportunity to thank you for your beautiful gift,' Aethelflaed said, fingering the amber necklace while taking the seat recently vacated by Eadwulf. The wedding feast was well underway. Most people had eaten their fill, for now, and chosen to enjoy their mead whilst circulating the hall and engaging in amicable conversation against a background of soft music from the scop's lyre. Aethelred, Aethelnoth, Hamid and Leofwynn's husband, Oswin, were presently speaking with Alfred, Edward and Aethelflaed's uncle, Aethelwulf, undoubtedly catching up with events in their lives over the past few years. Noticing the empty seat beside Freydis, Aethelflaed had taken the opportunity to get to know her a little better.

Aethelflaed could not help staring at the Danish woman's fair skin and amazingly fair hair, partially covered by a light linen kerchief, and thinking how much she looked like a Snow Queen in her lovely silvery-blue tunic. 'It was so kind of you and the necklace is perfect for today.'

Freydis' smile was warm and genuine, causing her blue eyes to twinkle as she reached out and patted her hand, and Aethelflaed could understand Eadwulf's love for her. 'You are most welcome, Aethelflaed, and it really suits you – just as Eadwulf said it would.'

'I shall treasure it, always, and be reminded of our friends and family from across the sea every time I look at it. Aethelred is so proud to have you all here, and so am I. I've often wondered what you four ladies look like,' she added, glancing along the trestle at Leofwynn, Yrsa and Ameena, who had now been

Nine

joined by Ealhswith. 'And now I've seen you all for myself, I find that Aethelred's descriptions were very accurate – though I haven't yet said more than a couple of words to any but you.'

'I have often wondered about all of you, too,' Freydis admitted. 'Yrsa and I came to know Aethelred's family well during our time at Elston before we returned to Aros, but King Alfred's family remained unknown to us, despite Aethelred's constant chatter about you all on the Isle of Athelney.'

Aethelflaed inwardly squirmed, hoping Aethelred had not embellished her childish habit of challenging him to archery contests. 'Yes,' she replied, 'the men of your group played a big part in our lives when Father was in dire need of friendship. Our time on Athelney was harrowing and uncertain, but the arrival of five strong men offering not only friendship but their battle skills, seemed to give Father the extra determination he needed to succeed.'

Aethelflaed said no more on that, realising that Freydis was a Dane, and would not wish to hear her countrymen demeaned. Instead, she said, 'Losing Jorund was heartbreaking for us all, and Eadwulf and the rest of his group found it hard to cope with. And I know how hard it must have been for you and Yrsa when you heard the news.'

Freydis gave a wan smile. 'It was harder than I care to think about, Lady Aethelflaed. Jorund was such a lovely boy and he and my little brother, Ubbi, were the greatest of friends. It took years for him to put the traumatic events of his early life behind him and I loved him as my own son….' She suddenly flashed a wide smile. 'But we aren't here to speak of difficult times. Your wedding day is for you to enjoy – even though your new husband seems to be penned in by the men of your party! In Elston, Aethelred often spoke of a friend called Garth. I met him today and realise what a fine man he is. Aethelred tells us he'll often be here in London with you.'

'He will, and I'm so pleased about that. When my father asked Garth if he'd be happy to perform his courtly duties with Aethelred instead of him, he was overjoyed. Naturally, he'll need to return to his own estate often in order for it to flourish, but at least we'll have him with us on a regular basis.' Aethelflaed shook her head, a smile on her face as she thought about it. 'The two of them get on so well together.'

Freydis nodded, 'It is good to have close friends near to you,' Lady Aethelflaed. We all need people we trust enough to confide in at times and I know I would be lost without Yrsa, and now I have Ameena, too.' She glanced to where the four women were chatting merrily and turned back to face Aethelflaed. 'Shall we join your mother's little group so I can introduce you properly to the women of Eadwulf's family?'

'I thought you'd never ask,' Aethelflaed replied, laughing as they headed across the hall together.

*

Aethelred woke the following morning as a shaft of sunlight fell across his face. He squinted, trying to focus on various objects around the bedchamber, and grinned when he spotted the heaps of clothing strewn across a wicker chair. Memories of the previous night flooded back and he rolled over to face his lovely young wife.

Nine

'Good morning, lazy bones,' Aethelflaed said in greeting, the smile on her face matching his own. 'I was beginning to think you'd sleep all day! The cockerel crowed ages ago and I was sorely tempted to rise and leave you to your snoring.'

Aethelred was aghast and stared at her, absently admiring the way her hair shone gold as the ray of sunlight reached it. 'I don't snore...do I? No one has told me I do before, and I've slept in halls and barns amongst others on many an occasion.'

Aethelflaed gave his arm a friendly punch. 'And in a few women's beds, I would imagine.'

He stared at her for a moment, then shook his head, unable to prevent the laugh escaping from his throat. 'My dear wife, your brazenness never ceases to amaze me. But this time you have excelled yourself.'

Aethelflaed opened her mouth, making a sound that Aethelred guessed was a squeak of protest. 'Well, I know you'd be lying if you said you *hadn't* slept in many women's beds,' she said, adding an obviously feigned pout.

'Oh, and why is that?'

Aethelflaed threw her arms around him and pulled him close. 'Make love to me again like you did last night and I'll tell you.'

*

The following week passed all too quickly and Aethelred's heart was heavy as his family and friends took their leave. But he realised they'd all left their young ones behind, and could not stay away much longer. Alfred and Ealhswith had left for Winchester at first light this morning and Aethelnoth and the others from Elston had left the previous day. Aethelred knew how much seeing Leofwynn and Aethelnoth leave had upset his father, but Eadwulf was also worried for his own journey home. The weather could be fickle at this time of year; conditions over the Northern Sea even more so. Many a storm had whipped up from nowhere, bringing ships to disaster, their passengers to a watery grave, and Eadwulf had no intention of risking the lives of people he loved for the sake of delaying their crossing by even a few more days.

Aethelred hugged his father as Hamid helped Freydis, Yrsa and Ameena to board the knarr, moored along one of the jetties of the old port of Londinium. It was still early morning and a light mist writhed over the murky, brown waters of the Thames, likely to remain until the day progressed enough for the September sun to gain enough warmth to cause it to dissipate. Fortunately, today the mist was unlikely to cause problems to incoming and outgoing vessels, as Aethelred had seen it do on a few occasions over the past few years. Thick fogs could hang for hours over the slow flowing river. Fears for his father's journey weighed heavily upon him. Although not a praying man, Aethelred intended to make a detour to the Church of Saint Paul on his way back to the hall; his escort would be content to wait outside for a while.

Aethelred admitted to himself that he'd never get over the fact that Eadwulf had chosen to live so far away. He swallowed down his selfish thought; his father must never be told how he felt. He glanced along the length of the quay where rebuilding work continued, and sighed, knowing he could not shirk his duties any longer.

Nine

'We'll try to visit again soon,' Eadwulf said, 'though I'm not sure we could fit it in next year.' He dropped his voice, glancing to make sure Freydis wouldn't hear as she and the other women settled into the ship's hold with the crates of food for the journey. 'I'm determined to get down to al-Andalus with Hamid and Ameena, and Básim, of course. They need to know what happened to Hamid's father and…'

'You don't need to explain again, Father. I agree, they deserve to find out, but I can understand why Freydis and Yrsa aren't happy about it. I won't stop worrying either until I know you got back safely. No,' he said, raising a hand to stop Eadwulf's intended comment, 'don't try to tell me there'll be no danger involved, because I know there will. I was Hamid's apprentice for a long time, remember, and he filled me in on everything you got up to the last time you were down there.'

Eadwulf laughed, glancing again at Freydis. 'I'm glad you didn't mention that after you'd had a few mugs of ale, Aethelred. I know there are risks, and so do Hamid and Ameena, but I don't want Freydis and Yrsa to know that. Now, go back to that lovely new wife of yours and enjoy your life together. We'll see you again as soon as we can.'

Ten

Winchester, Wessex: January 5-6, 887

Alfred rose to his feet and smiled at the faces around the trestles before him. The sumptuous feast had been devoured, unwanted foods and platters now cleared away, and the many guests cradled their mugs of ale or goblets of wine, watching his movements with an air of expectancy. The ceremony they had been anticipating for days was about to begin and Alfred had no intention of keeping them waiting.

'Good people,' he started, 'once again we have reached Twelfth Night, the last night of the Christmastide and the night when it behoves me to show my gratitude to all who have served our kingdom well over the past year.' He held up his silver goblet. 'I salute each and every one of you.'

Knife handles and spoons banged on table tops as the men cheered, and Alfred grinned in acceptance of their approval, then held up his hand for silence. 'Tonight, we celebrate Gift Giving in memory of all the good things that have occurred since the last ceremony, and with thanks to God for granting another year of relative peace in our kingdom. Not only have we successfully ousted the Danes from London, raids around our coasts have been only sporadic, and dealt with by our portreeves or ealdormen– some of whom sit amongst us here.'

Alfred's gaze swept the beaming faces, amongst them his most trusted ealdormen, thegns and clerics, including Aethelred of Mercia, Radulf of Hampshire, Aethelnoth of Som-

Ten

erset and the new Somerset thegn, Garth. Paega of Berkshire, Sigehelm of Kent, Aelfric of Surrey and Unwine of Sussex were also present, as were Alfred's scholars, Plegmund, Werferth, Aethelstan and Werwulf and his newest arrival, Abbot Asser of Dyfed.

'None of us can foresee the future,' Alfred went on, 'and we must pray that in the coming year, our kingdom will be blessed with continuing good fortune.

'And now, before I call each of you to step forward to receive your gift, I have a couple of things to say. Firstly, on a personal note, not only has this year seen us taking control of London, but I have also gained a son-by- marriage, of whom I heartily approve.' More pounding on table-tops demonstrated the men's support of the match.

Alfred held out his arm, fingers aimed at the smiling Aethelred. 'This young man is the grandson of the wise Mercian king, Beorhtwulf, who was admired and respected by many, including my own father. But it is not only Aethelred's bloodline of which I approve; I admire him for himself, his strength of character and his leadership and battle skills, which first came to my notice when we were on Athelney. Though barely into his seventeenth year, Aethelred fought at our sides at Edington and more than proved his worth. And now, he is proving to be a most diligent and well-respected overlord of West Mercia – and my eldest daughter stands at his side. Aethelred, Lord of Mercia, you have my fondest good wishes as well as my sincere thanks.'

Alfred suddenly chuckled. 'And if you should happen to write to that sea-going father of yours in the next month or two, you can tell him that if he does manage to get to al-Andalus this year, I'd like a full account of his adventures down there.'

Laughter filled the room to the accompaniment of more hammering on table tops and Aethelred pushed himself to his feet, a wide grin on his face as he bowed in each direction in response to their cheers of goodwill.

'Secondly,' Alfred went on, in a less jovial tone, for me, tonight is tinged with a degree of sadness at the pending departure of Abbot Asser. He has become a part of our household during his stay, yet now, having been with us since April, he feels it is time to return to his monastery to ensure that all is well in his absence. We can look forward to his return at the end of June.'

Alfred smiled, noticing a definite reddening of Asser's cheeks at being made the centre of attention, but he pushed on. 'Despite my many attempts to persuade the good abbot to stay, at least until the spring, he is determined to return to Saint David's. Understandable, I agree, especially when we recall that it isn't long since the king of Dyfed himself was the monastery's worst enemy! Only the thought that he offered submission to me in return for protection from the sons of Rhodri Mawr is stopping Hyfaidd's unreasonable interference and even raids on Saint David's – for now. But for how long will he keep to his agreement…? Next time I meet with the man, I'll remind him of the consequences if his raids recommence.

'Nevertheless, Asser will be sincerely missed by me and his fellow scholars, with whom he has worked so well. And in all fairness to him, our agreement was that he would stay for only six months at a time, and he has been with us for eight.

Ten

So, my lords, it appears that all my cajoling and pleading did have *some* effect.'

When the chortles abated, Alfred said simply, 'So farewell, my Lord Abbot. Know that you will be in our thoughts as you return to Dyfed, accompanied by our sincere thanks and appreciation. We look forward to your return in June.

'So now we come to the part of the ceremony from which the name of the Gift Giving is derived,' he continued, as Edward came to stand at his side. 'The giving of gifts from king or nobleman to his most deserving subjects is an age-old tradition, bonding leaders to their men. It is a custom I particularly enjoy.'

Alfred handed a scroll to Edward who proceeded to unroll it, reading out the names listed as he did, halting after each to enable the aforenamed to step forward. Alfred duly handed out small scrolls containing the deeds to land or property, or one of the many costly items previously swathed by large blankets on the hall floor: swords, shields, saddles, cloaks, armbands and various other exquisite items of jewellery amongst them.

Lastly, it was Asser's turn. The embarrassed abbot stepped forward, keeping his head bowed. Alfred did not subject him to discomfort overly long, handing him the scroll with the same warm clasping of the arm he'd bestowed on the others. 'We can talk about it tomorrow,' he whispered in Asser's ear before gently urging him back to his seat.

*

Alfred smiled as Asser approached, clutching the gifted scroll in his hand. 'Ah, my Lord Abbot, you wish to speak with me?'

'I do, lord, although now I am here, I find myself at a loss for words.' He held out the scroll he'd received last night, focusing questioning brown eyes on Alfred.

'I fear there has been some mistake,' he continued when Alfred simply tilted his head and returned the quizzical gaze. 'At least, I can find no other reason for what has happened and am obliged to make mention of it before someone in your company feels he's been slighted.'

Noticing Alfred's twitching lips, Asser shuffled a little, but went on with his explanation. 'The gifts referred to in this scroll are generous indeed, and undoubtedly intended for a family member... one of your two nephews, mayhap, or one of the many clerics of your acquaintance for some years, such as the Abbot of Malmesbury, or the Bishop of Winchester, or the –'

Alfred's throaty chuckle halted Asser's deliberations, and encompassed by embarrassment, the abbot averted his eyes. 'Forgive me if my amusement discomfits you, Abbot, and I mean no disrespect to your person. It's merely that a moment ago you declared yourself to be somewhat lost for words, yet now they seem to be tumbling from your lips with ease.'

Asser stared at Alfred, then his face creased into a grin and a hearty laugh erupted. 'I do seem to have suddenly become rather garrulous, don't I? It is simply that my mind is struggling to decide who the scroll could have been intended for – when, of course, you will instantly know when you look at it.' He glanced round the hall, where most of the other guests were assembling for the morning meal. 'Has anyone questioned the scroll they have been given?'

'They have not, Abbot, and nor are they likely to.'

Ten

'Perhaps not in front of others, but would they not seek to speak with you in private?'

'No, they are all perfectly happy with whatever gift they received.'

Asser looked mortified. 'Then you must think me an ungrateful wretch to question your generous gifts. But, believe me, lord, my only concern is for the person to whom these deeds should really have been gifted to.'

'My dear abbot, I will stop playing games with you and put you out of your misery. There *is* no mistake. I gave you the scroll intended for you, as a means of telling you how much your presence and work at my court means to me.'

'But the gift of two Saxon monasteries is far more than I deserve! I do not wish to sound ungrateful, lord, but you have known me for so short a time and tomorrow I must leave again.'

'Yes, you are leaving,' Alfred agreed, nodding, 'but you will be coming back. Besides, the monasteries of Congresbury and Banwell are both in Somerset, so you will need to be in Wessex in order to visit them and ensure their smooth running. During your stay at my court, I will grant you time to do so.'

Asser nodded slowly, his brow creasing a little as he thought, but he did not reply. Alfred smiled to himself, knowing the abbot would be contemplating the benefits of these proposals to both his status and finances. With any luck, owning land and property in Wessex would be a great incentive to Asser to spend longer here in future.

'I've picked a dozen men to escort you to Saint David's, Abbot, and when you are due to return, you need only send word to me and those men will be sent again to guide you to whichever of my royal halls the court is resident in.'

'Thank you, King Alfred. My months here have been most pleasant, and I intend to spend some time today with your wife and delightful children. Aethelgifu never ceases to amaze me with her knowledge and understanding of the way of things, including people. She has a quiet calm about her and wisdom beyond her mere ten years.'

Alfred smiled, knowing his own fondness for his quiet and studious daughter would be evident to anyone who watched them together. 'Aethelgifu has wanted to do nothing but read and learn since she was quite young, Abbot. For some years she avoided meeting people and hid part of her face with a head veil. Ealhswith permitted her to do so in the belief that within a few years the red stain on her forehead would disappear. I confess, it is more vivid now than when she was tiny, and Aethelgifu feels the need to conceal it.'

'I have seen birth stains before and have noted that some of them fade quite quickly while others take their time. Unfortunately, there are also some that never fade. I understand the child's embarrassment; no one likes to be stared at, and people's eyes are invariably drawn to anything unusual.'

Asser reached over and patted Alfred's hand. 'Aethelgifu is a delightful girl and a credit to you, my lord. I shall greatly miss my little chats with her while I'm away and I think she will miss me. We have read so many stories from the Scriptures together and she has asked me to teach her to read and write Latin next year.'

'Well, I'll just have to ensure my daughter has plenty to read in your absence. And unless I am suddenly called to spend

Ten

time away from my court, she and I can share a few stories. But right now, the morning meal is ready, so we should join everyone for that. Then afterwards you can spend as much time as you like with my wife and children. I know Ealhswith wants to say her farewells to you. Oh, and before I forget, there are two more gifts from me that you haven't yet seen.' Alfred inclined his head, indicating a huge wooden crate sitting near the outside door and something wrapped in a blanket on top of it. 'Shall we take a look?'

'My lord, I don't know how to thank you,' Asser said, his eyes suddenly misting. 'Never in my life did I expect to have a garment of silk, and you present me with this exquisite cloak – and after the gift of two monasteries.'

'And inside this,' Alfred said, tapping the crate with the toe of his boot in an attempt to alleviate Asser's raging emotions, 'is enough incense to keep three monastery churches supplied for quite some time...

'As for thanking me, my dear abbot, the best thing you could do whilst you're in Dyfed is to ensure that all is well with your community and that your monks are faithful to their pursuit of God's work. Ensure the doors of Saint David's are open to all, those from the villages and travellers alike. When you return, your mind must be at rest and open to the work ahead.'

Eleven

Aros, Danish lands: April 887

As spring arrived in Aros, work on the land took up most of the day for the men of Eadwulf's homestead. In addition to the ongoing tasks of woodcutting, tool-and-furniture-making, fishing and hunting, the wheat, barley, oats and rye now needed to be sown and cattle and sheep put out to pasture. Over the winter, Hamid had managed to spend more time at his carpentry, aided by his eager apprentice, Básim. As he had done at Elston, Hamid had managed to create many decorative pieces of furniture, which he intended to sell during the next trip to Hedeby or Ribe.

Nor had the women time to dally. Days flew by as the usual rounds of cooking, spinning and making tapestries were fitted in between feeding the pigs, goats and poultry, and searching for eggs hidden around the yard. Work in the dairy was also ongoing, with the cows and goats to milk, and butter, skyr and cheese to be made. And with the arrival of spring, Ameena tended the vegetable and herb gardens, delighted by Freydis' promise of teaching her the techniques of preparing potions for ailments.

As the end of April neared, Eadwulf felt it was time to make a move. If they were to get down to al-Andalus this year, it would have to be sometime soon. He had just begun to plan the journey with Hamid, Ameena and Básim, when Bjorn and his eldest son, Hrolf, arrived at his door.

Eleven

Bjorn grasped Eadwulf's arm in greeting as they entered the small hall out of the blustery wind. 'Your homestead looks as though it's been here for years, my friend. You've achieved much in so short a time.' He shoved his wind-blown hair back from his face, strands of silver glinting amidst the red in the hearthfire's bright glow, and fixed Eadwulf with a questioning look. 'But we've heard you've grown restless to be on the seas again.'

Eadwulf felt a stab of guilt, realising he hadn't yet told Bjorn of his plans. Life on his homestead over the winter months had simply passed by, all thoughts of Muhammad's death and al-Andalus held in abeyance – until recently when he'd made a few enquiries about hiring a crew…

'So, you heard I was asking for crewmen?' Bjorn nodded but said nothing. 'And you did say I could ask around your karls whenever I wanted extra crew for the knarr.'

'I did, and you'll hear no objection from me on that score, Eadwulf. As yet, I've made no plans to go anywhere this year and I know of several of my karls who'll be happy to join you, simply to break the monotony of staying here. I'm just a little bemused as to why you're going back to Cordoba, of all places. I'd have thought you'd never want to see the place again.'

'That's exactly what Yrsa and I have been saying, but will he listen…?' Freydis' face displayed her pique as she plonked the mugs of ale on the trestle and Bjorn laughed out loud.

'In my experience, sister, once Eadwulf's set his mind on doing something, trying to persuade him to do otherwise is pointless. I'm sure he has his reasons for heading back to Cordoba, which I'm hoping he'll be able to share with us.'

Eadwulf explained what Hamid and Básim had learned while they were in Hedeby as briefly as he could, stressing the need for the three from al-Andalus to pay their respects at Muhammad's grave and, hopefully, find out who had ordered the emir's death.

Bjorn scratched his head. 'Come to think of it, I remember Leif saying something about a Moorish ship being at Hedeby last year. He mentioned something about Muhammad being assassinated, too, but I saw no relevance in that news for us. From what you say, this new emir sounds an unsavoury and dangerous character.'

'Will you get to the point of our visit here, Father, or shall I?' Dark-headed Hrolf grinned at the affronted expression on his father's face and continued. 'I don't think it's any secret that Ameena and I have become close over the past couple of years.' He paused, standing and holding out his hand, smiling as Ameena came to take it. 'The thing is, we want to be wed and need everyone's blessings to do so. My parents are delighted with the idea, and I know Freydis is, too. It's just that I'm not sure about you, Eadwulf.'

Eadwulf shook his head, chuckling. 'You don't really think Freydis would have kept your feelings for each other from me, do you, Hrolf? I'm just surprised you've left it this long. Of course you have my blessing – but I get the feeling you've chosen to share your news now for a particular reason.'

'Father and I would like to sail to Cordoba with you. You said you didn't expect to be away for long, so Ameena and I would like to be married soon after we get back,'

'I know this request will seem odd to you, Eadwulf,' Bjorn

Eleven

added, 'but like many of our men, including Leif, me and Hrolf are feeling the need to be out on the sea. Raiding's a thing of the past for me, as you know, but if I recall, there are large markets at both Seville and Cordoba and a trading trip down there would be useful. How would you feel if I suggest we just take one of the knarrs? It would attract less attention than a longship, both when we're sailing and wherever we berth. We could do without another encounter with a load of scimitar-wielding Moors.'

Eadwulf couldn't stop grinning. 'How could I refuse an offer like that? To be all together again is more than I could have asked for, and a wedding to look forward to on our return would round things off perfectly. But I think you're right about not taking the Sea *Eagle*; knarrs would be a safer bet.'

'I've a feeling I could find enough crew to man another two or three knarrs. If so, would that be agreeable to you?'

Eadwulf nodded. 'I don't see why not. A few ships would make it look even more like a trading trip.'

'Good.' Bjorn said, rising. 'And if I tell the men we sail in a week, would that also be agreeable?'

'You must all be mad!' Freydis shook her head, a pained look on her face. 'Don't you *dare* all get yourselves killed! This foolhardy trip could cause Yrsa and me to lose half our family in one go.'

Tears glistened in Freydis' eyes and Eadwulf wrapped her in his arms. 'We came back safely last time, didn't we?' She glanced at Hamid, but made no reply. 'And if I promise we won't do anything foolish, or anything to put our lives at risk, would that ease your fears?'

'If that's all you can say, then I'll do nothing *but* worry while you're away. You must think I have a very short memory, Eadwulf. I well remember the state of Hamid's leg when you got back – and the fact that Muhammad's archers could have killed you all!

'You and my brother have no idea how to keep out of trouble!' she threw over her shoulder as she headed off to rouse Thora from her afternoon nap.

*

In the first week in May, four sturdy knarrs set sail from Aros on the start of a voyage of over two thousand miles. The southerly breeze was in their sails as they headed north for the best part of the day before veering west into the Limfjord. They sailed on through most of the night, leaving the fjord as the sky lightened with the approaching dawn and followed the Danish coast south through the Northern Sea.

Much slower than Bjorn's *Sea Eagle*, the journey to the mouth of the Guadalquivir would take them well over two weeks. Eadwulf and his companions sailed in his own knarr, *Gift of Freya,* with five of Bjorn's men to complete the crew of eight required to man the vessel. Ameena travelled in the ship's deep hold, surrounded by crates of food and casks of fresh water that would last for part of the journey. Finding suitable stopping places along the way to renew supplies, especially of water, was a prime concern.

Thoughts of the long journey ahead did nothing to dampen Eadwulf's joy at being at sea again and to be master of his own

Eleven

vessel, albeit a trading ship. He would never forget Bjorn's generosity in having the knarr made for him. Taking deep breaths of the briny air made him feel so alive and he thanked the gods for giving him such a good life, with people he loved. His only regret was that Aethelred and Leofwynn were so far away – and that Jorund wasn't still with them.

He pushed unhappy thoughts away as they tacked into the rising westerly, increasing their speed and relieving the four oarsmen of their task as they sailed on, south-west past the Low Countries and Northern Francia. For several days, crewmen slept in rotation before they pulled ashore to make camp in Brittany and enjoy their first full night on land in over a week, after sailing over a thousand miles.

'I think we can say we're half way there,' Bjorn said as they ate their cold meal around the camp fire in the fading evening light. 'Leif?'

The old steersman shrugged. 'Aye, must be about that. Tomorrow we set course south-west across the open sea to Northern Iberia. No more hugging the coast until we head south for the mouth of the Guadalquivir. Another nine or ten days to get there, I reckon, depending on how many more nights we spend ashore.'

Bjorn nodded as he prised shreds of cold mutton from between his teeth with his dagger. 'We'll need to fill up with fresh water anyway, so we could probably make landfall for a couple of nights.' He turned to his dark-headed son beside him, whose gaze was locked with Ameena's sitting opposite, flanked by Eadwulf and Hamid. 'I don't know about you, son, but I'm beginning to wish we'd come in the *Eagle*. We'd have been almost there by now.'

Hrolf snapped out of his reverie. 'But, as you said yourself, Father, we'd have been forever expecting the Moors to attack,'

Leif harrumphed 'That's true enough, but who's to say they won't try their luck with our knarrs? And we don't have the speed to escape their fire arrows, or enough crew to stand and fight. We'll just have to hope we pass by unnoticed. Give me a longship any day.'

'Leif, old friend, you've spent most of your life on longships, and have no need to sing their virtues to me. But knarrs serve their purpose and we should show them a little respect.'

'Well now, Bjorn, other than having big cargo holds, I see little about knarrs to crow about.' The old man scratched his near-bald pate. 'For one thing, they're too heavy to be carried on land and as slow as a snail at sea. Yes, they might be wider than most longships, but having more space to move about won't be much use to us if the Moors give chase. I say, we'll be sitting ducks.'

Eadwulf feigned a thoughtful expression and held out his hands. 'So, Leif, I'm guessing you're not too fond of knarrs?'

The rest hooted and the steersman's indignant face cracked as he joined in the laughter.

Ten days later, the small fleet of trading ships was heading north-east along the Guadalquivir, eventually reaching Seville as daylight began to fade. 'Tomorrow, Bjorn and his men will spend time round the market,' Eadwulf told his little group as they made ready to sleep for the night. 'Kata's requested so many goods, he's hoping to find at least some of them here, which will leave him more time to help with our enquiries in

Eleven

Cordoba.' The three of them nodded. 'And you, Básim, need to spend tomorrow seeking out your family.'

Básim's downcast face left little doubt of his feelings. 'I will, Eadwulf, but I have little hope of finding any of them. The raiders took me and my two sisters, and I never saw them again. And I've no idea what happened to my mother and father. I suppose if I head back to our old house, someone in the area might know something.'

'We'll come with you if you like.'

'Thank you, Eadwulf.' The relief in the young man's voice was palpable. 'It's a long time since I was here, and if my parents are… are dead, people will probably have forgotten me and could be unfriendly if I start asking questions.'

'Then that's settled,' Hamid put in, his cheerful voice making the others smile. 'I wasn't looking forward to a day of shuffling round the market and if we ask around after your parents, we could tactfully throw in the odd question about the new emir and the present state of al-Andalus.'

*

The city of Seville was unfamiliar to Eadwulf, the bustling market close to the waterfront being the only area visited when they'd moored here sixteen years ago. He could recall admiring the gleaming white stone and ornate architecture visible over the city walls, and the green hillsides covered in olive trees beyond, but they had not explored the city streets. Nor, it seemed, would they be doing so on this occasion.

Básim led them along the riverfront, avoiding the maze of

narrow alleys and wider thoroughfares of the city itself. He pointed to a couple of partially built stone structures as they passed one of the wide entrances through the city walls. 'As you see, there is much building work going on.' They nodded, and Básim continued. 'A great raid by the Norsemen forty-three years ago left Seville damaged almost beyond repair. The buildings had not been so tall and sturdy then, and the raiders took little time to destroy most of them. But the people did not give in, and the task of rebuilding began.'

'I'd seen some of the work progressing on my visits here with my father and some of my brothers. And half-brothers,' Hamid added with a grin. 'Muhammad told us about the Norse raid, and a couple of failed attempts in later years when the city had learned how to defend itself. It will be a magnificent city one day.' He pointed to a towering building in the city centre. 'That must be for someone of status?'

'It was one of the first structures to be rebuilt for the leader of the city to live in,' Básim confirmed. 'Seville might be under the rule of the emirs of Cordoba, but we still have our own city leaders, and most have been men of honour.'

Hamid grunted. 'I wonder what the present leader thinks of the new emir. Al-Mundhir wouldn't know the meaning of honour.'

The young man's village lay a little over two miles upstream of the city's old Roman walls, a cluster of mere shacks in which many of the poorer citizens lived.

Básim's slumped shoulders displayed his pain as the settlement came into view. 'You can see why the Norsemen were able to attack our village and get away with it. We are a long way

Eleven

from the city, the strike was fast and the raiders were back in their ships before word could reach anyone behind those walls. Besides,' he added, glancing at Hamid, 'most of the people who lived here were not of the Muslim faith. Many were either Jews or Christians, but there were also Muladi families here, like mine. The one thing we had in common was that we were poor, and we managed to get along well with each other. The city soldiers probably wouldn't have been too worried about the loss of outsiders, or poor people in general.'

Hamid nodded. 'I won't deny what you say about people of other faiths, Básim. Even Muhammad was barely tolerant of them. The high taxes he imposed and the harsh punishments inflicted for the least misdemeanour need changing, but Al-Mundhir's more likely to make life even more difficult for them. The sooner he's removed from power the better.'

Ameena's face registered alarm and she reached out to grasp her brother's arm. 'I hope you aren't intending to do something we may all regret.'

'Not yet, but that's only because I haven't had time to think about it. If I can find a way to rid al-Andalus of that scum, I'm willing to try it.'

Eadwulf noted Hamid's words and Ameena's dumbstruck reaction to them. He'd been half expecting Hamid to try something once they reached Cordoba, and had even mentioned his concerns to Bjorn just before they had sailed from Aros. Bjorn had stared at him wide-eyed before laughter erupted. 'Then we'll just have to stand by him, won't we? Just like old times, eh, Eadwulf?'

Eadwulf came back to the present as a group of villagers

emerged from their homes in a movement so fluid that Eadwulf thought it was one well-rehearsed in the event of the appearance of strangers. Village folk stood before them speaking rapidly in the Moorish-Arabic tongue, their confrontational tones and waving arms leaving little doubt of their distrust of uninvited visitors.

Básim stepped forward, responding in words and gestures for some time. Eadwulf could only assume he was explaining who he was and why he was here, but suddenly the group bowed to Hamid before greeting them all as old friends.

An elderly woman pushed her way through the gathered villagers, coming to throw her arms around Básim's neck, her rambling Arabic muffled by sad headshakes and occasional sobs of relief as she clung to the young man.

Básim's eyes clouded with tears as he interpreted her words for Eadwulf's sake, while Ameena wrapped her arms around the distressed old woman.

'This is Bahja, my grandmother. She tells me my parents died in the raid…but, like me, she has not seen my sisters since we were taken. She has lived in hope of seeing at least one of us again before she died and will continue to pray for my sisters. But she can now die in peace.'

'It's an all too familiar story in many lands,' Eadwulf said, almost choking on his shame at being a part of such raids in Francia. He draped his arm across the young man's shoulders as the old woman delivered another tearful monologue.

'Bahja says that now it is not foreign raiders the villagers fear but the new emir's soldiers.' Básim's gaze moved between the three of them, as though willing them to say something to

Eleven

allay his fears. 'Al-Mundhir is cruel and vindictive, and shows no tolerance for anyone outside his Muslim faith. Many people in villages like this feel doomed and know that one day, the emir's soldiers will come and round up the men for the quarries and take the women and children to become slaves in his palaces. News of that happening in other settlements has left them sick with worry.'

Bahja added more to her story, and this time, it was Ameena who interpreted. 'Some non-Muslim families have already left the village to live in the cities, some only as far as Seville, others as far as Rhonda, or even Lisbon – though none would ever move to Cordoba, under Al-Mundhir's nose. They believe they will not be noticed amongst the throngs of a city. But they will need to mingle to work and Bahja fears there will always be Moors in the cities happy to report their presence to the guards.'

'Unfortunately, there is nothing we can do about any of this.' Eadwulf looked directly at Básim. 'But now you a have learned what you needed to know, you must decide if you want to stay here with your grandmother or eventually return to Aros with us.'

Básim needed no time to think. 'It wouldn't matter if I wanted to stay, Bahja won't allow it. She has heard many good things said about Hamid, and is proud to know that I am with you all – and not as your slave.' He suddenly grinned. 'She insists that the kindness in your hearts shines through your eyes – and she will listen for news of Al Mundhir's death.'

Hamid took the old lady's hand and spoke quietly for a few moments. She smiled and embraced him, before moving to embrace Ameena and Eadwulf. Finally, she hugged Básim to her frail frame as though afraid of letting him go, then turned to hobble back to her home.

No one spoke for a while as they headed back to Seville and Eadwulf thought it best that Básim be left to deal with his newly learned sorrows. It came as a surprise when the young man suddenly stopped and looked pointedly at Hamid. 'There's something I should have told you: Bahja is the village seer and her predictions are rarely wrong.'

Twelve

Cordoba, al Andalus: late May 887

The four knarrs pushed away from Seville the following morning, aiming to cover most of the ninety-mile journey to Cordoba before the blazing Andalusian sun made rowing exhausting and uncomfortable. As it turned out, a light southerly picked up mid-morning, driving the ships at a gentle pace along the great Guadalquivir, leaving the men free to enjoy the views along the banks and the variety of vessels heading in both directions.

Evening was drawing in as they berthed along Cordoba's jetties, downstream of the old Roman bridge that Eadwulf remembered so well from sixteen years ago. The men set up camp close to their knarrs, organising a regular watch throughout the day and night while they were there. The stalls and tents of the outer market were barely fifty yards from their camp and Bjorn had no intention of having the goods he purchased in Seville disappear while they were inside the city, or sleeping.

Bjorn gulped down his last mouthful of goat's milk, his loud belch and grimace making his annoyance of having no ale to wash down his evening meal clear to all. He swept his sleeve across his mouth and looked pointedly at Eadwulf. 'So, what now? Have we any solid plans, or are we just heading behind those walls and keeping our eyes and ears open to start with?'

He put down his mug and suddenly grinned. 'But what we could do without this time is having any of us thrown in the dungeons, or having to race off to some distant quarry.'

Eadwulf shrugged, Jorund's reactions coming to mind on the day he was almost knocked to the ground by a group of fleeing tax collectors. 'As far as I know, Hamid and Ameena want to find out more about who was behind Muhammad's death to start with. How we manage that without getting locked up, I don't know. Perhaps we'll just wander around in small groups doing as you suggest and getting into conversations with stallholders and such like. People are often guided by a prompt in the right direction.'

'The rest of you can all do that for a day or so,' Ameena said, her green eyes flashing in irritation, 'but you seem to have forgotten that Hamid and I know this city well. If I can seek out some of the women I used to know, I might be able to discover what most of them suspect. Hamid intends to do the same with some of the stonemasons he knew.'

Eadwulf heaved a sigh, knowing he wouldn't be able to stop either of them doing something they'd set their minds on. 'Promise me you won't take any unnecessary risks and only speak with people you know you can trust – not an easy thing after all these years. People can change, and not always for the better.'

'We'll be careful and try not to draw attention to ourselves,' Hamid assured him. 'Ameena needs to cover her hair, so I'll get her something from this outer market in the morning when I go to buy myself a suitable Arabic robe and headdress.'

'I know who you're expecting to put an end to this the new emir's rule,' Leif remarked, silent until now. He fixed Hamid in his steady grey gaze. 'From what Básim says, the man *will* die, but I'm guessing there must be many folk in this city

Twelve

alone – never mind the rest of al-Andalus – waiting for the right opportunity to bring him down. So, I'd say, you'd best get on with the job, quick as you can.'

Bjorn patted Leif's arm and gave an approving nod. 'Wise words, old friend, and we all need to consider them. But now my tent beckons. Before we traipse around Cordoba tomorrow, I'd like a good night's sleep.

*

Once through the city gates and past the formidable Alcazar with its watchful guards, Eadwulf headed along the narrow, crowded streets, following Hamid and Ameena to wherever they had decided to go first. Beside him was Básim, to whom the greatest city of the emirate was a mystery; poor people rarely travelled far from home. Each of them now wore a headdress, purchased at the outer market earlier, and as the morning progressed and the sun rose higher, Eadwulf was thankful not only for the disguise it afforded, but also its protection from the fierce Andalusian sun.

Passing the Great Mosque, Eadwulf could only gawk at how much it had changed over the past sixteen years. It was now a truly magnificent structure, towering over the city, its white stone bright in the sunlight. Had their intentions in Cordoba been different, Eadwulf would have liked to dally and take a closer look at the remarkable architecture…

Mesmerised by the beauty of the mosque, Eadwulf only just stopped himself from walking straight into Hamid, who had suddenly stopped dead in his tracks.

'I've just spotted an old stonemason I used to know heading down there,' Hamid whispered, grinning at Eadwulf's look of surprise as he pointed to one of the several alleys leading away from the mosque. 'If Básim comes with me, we'll try to catch up with him and have a little chat. As most of the palace workers, Sumayl had no liking for Rajiv, who was always skulking around, trying to find fault with our work. Although, in truth, it was me he wanted to get into trouble. He did it all the time with his half-brothers. I'm hopeful that Sumayl will know something useful, or be able to point us in the direction of others I worked with in the past.'

Hamid and Básim hurried off towards the alley and Ameena turned to Eadwulf. 'It looks as though you must accompany me, brother. As I said last night, I need to find some of the ladies I used to know, although I realise it's unlikely that any will still live in the same place after all this time. Some of the younger ones would have married by now and moved elsewhere, but most of the older women were already married so it's possible at least one or two are in the same houses. Unfortunately, I'm unlikely to find any of those who lived in the Alcazar.'

She smiled, evidently dwelling on a memory. 'Pity, nosy people like my friend Rani, knew more about the private lives of those in power at the palace than anyone I knew at the time. As handmaid to Muhammad's principal wife, Salihah, she had no other choice than to live in the palace and she overheard so much gossip. If not for her, we'd never have known about Salihah's plan to have Hamid assassinated. To run into Rani would be perfect.'

Eadwulf thought it all sounded too hit and miss, but since

Twelve

he had no better plan, he simply agreed. He walked beside Ameena, smiling to himself as he thought of Bjorn and the others in their headdresses, a few even in the flowing robes of the Muslim people. He hoped someone around the market-place would know something that would be useful to them.

Ameena headed purposely towards one of the quieter streets of the city away from the shopping areas. Eadwulf realised they were in one of the wealthy, residential areas of big, fine houses, like the one Beorhtwulf once lived in with his new wife and their daughter Ameena, and her son, Hamid – whose father was no less than the powerful emir, Muhammad.

He shook his head as he thought of the uncertainty of life and the tricks it can play on people when he realised Ameena had stopped walking.

'Do you recognise these gates, brother?'

Eadwulf nodded, remembering his and Jorund's first encounter with Hamid and Ameena in this very gateway. 'How could I forget? But why have we come here? You can't know who lives here now?'

'No, I don't, but I might know a few of the neighbours, unless they've all moved away. Some of their daughters were my greatest friends. We would shop at the market together and spend time in each other's homes.'

Ameena constantly tutted and adjusted her head veil as they walked on. 'It's a long time since I dressed in the Arabic style,' she said, noticing Eadwulf's smirking at her antics. 'I don't miss covering my hair one bit, though I sometimes miss wearing pretty sandals. It's far too hot to wear boots in summer in al-Andalus.' She suddenly laughed. 'But sandals would never do in Aros, especially when I'm mucking out the stables or trudging over the vegetable patch.'

'But you *are* happy in Aros, aren't you?'

'The only thing that could make me happier is being married to Hrolf. But first, we've all got to manage to stay alive to get back to Aros.'

Eadwulf heaved a sigh. 'I can't deny we'll be facing danger here, especially if Hamid attempts what I believe he's planning to do. I won't be happy until we're heading home, and I don't like causing Freydis and Yrsa all this worry either.' He thought of their departure, the tears in his wife's eyes, then brought himself back to the present. 'So, if we do find some of your old friends, perhaps we should keep Hamid's presence in the city to ourselves.'

'I don't want to think about what could happen to my brother if word of his return reached Al-Mundhir.' Ameena shuddered and her face creased with worry. 'But he'll be giving his identity away to any old acquaintances he meets, so we can only hope they'll all be trustworthy and hate the new emir. At least we'll have no need to say anything of Hamid's presence to anyone we speak to. All they need know is that you and I are here with your ship purely to trade. We'll just have to make it sound plausible.'

Eadwulf was again assailed by memories of Jorund as they continued along the street: their first impressions of the high stone walls overhung with colourful foliage and flowers, and the huge, heavy gates concealing the beautiful villas of the wealthy behind. 'How do you suggest we get you into these homes to find out if you know anyone? I imagine all the gates will be barred?'

Twelve

Ameena darted to the nearest gates and took hold of a long, thick cord connected to an iron bell at the top of the gatepost. 'Most are barred on the inside, but many have a bell for traders and suchlike to ring. See, like this one. If we pull this sash... like this... a couple of servants will come to open the gates.'

Sure enough, within moments the gates opened a fraction and a thin, shrewd-eyed, man of middling years appeared in the gap. He snapped out a few harsh-sounding words in Arabic, which meant nothing to Eadwulf other than he was either not happy at being disturbed, or had been ordered not to allow anyone in today.

Ameena flashed a fetching smile and replied politely in Arabic, the only word of which Eadwulf recognised being the name, Jaleel, their father, Beorhtwulf's name when he lived in these lands.

The thin man was shoved aside by an ageing but sturdy individual squeezing through the gap, whose jaw dropped as his eyes fixed on Ameena.

Ameena grasped the old man's hand, the name, Asbat, on her lips. A rapid conversation between them followed and Eadwulf watched and listened as Ameena shook her head when the names Jaleel and Hamid were mentioned, and gestured to Eadwulf when she mentioned his name. Finally, she smiled when Asbat mentioned the name: Galiba.

'It seems that everyone in Cordoba believe Jaleel and Hamid were killed by Muhammad's guards as they'd fled after being discovered plotting to assassinate Al-Mundhir,' Ameena explained. 'They also believe that once I'd heard my father and brother were dead, I left al-Andalus on a trading ship. No one expected to see me again.'

'Then they all think Hamid's a cold-hearted, would-be assassin?'

'I imagine many who didn't know him may think that, Eadwulf, but I doubt that any who knew him would believe such lies! I assured Asbat that the story of the plotting was completely untrue and that the three of us were forced to run when Muhammad's men came to arrest Jaleel and Hamid. All three of us – not just me – sailed away to the northern lands with traders, you being amongst them. I also told him that Jaleel had since died of old age and that Hamid was already happily settled down with a new wife in the Danish lands. I, too, had settled with your people, and would be wed later this year. We had returned here only to trade.

'The good thing is that, as I'd hoped, a woman I used to know well still lives here with her husband and a son who is soon to be married.' She suddenly grinned. 'Apparently, Galiba's been in a dreadful mood since yesterday afternoon. A market trader had promised delivery of several rolls of cloth by then and it still hasn't arrived. We were snapped at because the servants assumed that we were delivering the late cloth – which Galiba has instructed them to refuse to accept. Lateness is a quality she seems to deplore nowadays.'

'So, what now? Did you ask if you could meet Galiba again?'

'I did, and Asbat is happy to take us into the house. He says our visit may well help the mistress snap out of her impossible mood.'

Twelve

*

Galiba was alone in a spacious, sumptuously furnished room at the back of the house, its outer doors flung wide, allowing the fragrance of the flowers and sounds of tinkling fountains from the garden to pervade. She lounged on one of several heaps of silk-covered cushions placed to one side of those doors, her attractive, dark looks marred by the unflattering pout on her face and the constant twisting motion of her finger around a lock of silver-streaked dark hair. Lost in her own bleak mood, she had evidently not heard them enter, and Eadwulf's attention strayed as they waited for Asbat to announce their presence.

He admired the brightly coloured and patterned Turkish rugs on the marble floor and the elegant pieces of dark-wood furniture that stood in the room, the intricately carved legs of a long table reminding him of Hamid's skills in that art...

Asbat's voice cut through his thoughts and brought a little gasp from the room's sole occupant. Galiba jumped to her feet and reeled off what was an obvious reprimand to the ageing servant in Arabic. Her eyes swung between Eadwulf and Ameena, and Eadwulf realised she had not recognised her old friend.

'Hello, Galiba,' Ameena said in the Mercian language. 'It's good to see you again.'

The woman's brow furrowed as she stared at her. 'You speak in the language a dear friend taught me years ago. You even look like her – but that cannot possibly be! She had bright red hair, just like the man you are with.'

Ameena removed her head veil, smiling as Galiba's eyes

opened wide. 'I still have my red hair, and I remember you very well. I sat in this room with you on many an occasion as we played chess, or just chatted about life at the Alcazar, or what we had bought at the market.'

Galiba took Ameena's hands in her own and gazed at her face. 'We all thought you had gone for good. Few women could survive for long on a sailing ship full of ruffians from the northern lands. But before you tell me your story, we shall sit in a shaded nook in the garden and drink some fruit juice, and by the time we come back in here, Asbat will have organised some food for you to enjoy.'

Asbat bowed his head and left the room, but not before Eadwulf had detected his smile of relief at his mistress' improved mood.

They seated themselves on two wooden, high-backed benches with padded red cushions positioned at opposite sides of a square-topped table, Ameena next to Galiba, and Eadwulf on his own. The wide fronds of two tall palm trees provided blissful shade and the tinkling spray from a fish-shaped fountain into an oval pool gave the illusion of coolness. Asbat returned to place a tall pottery jug and three goblets on the table and poured out the lemon-coloured juice before he left.

Galiba twisted in her seat to face Ameena. 'And who is your friend? His hair and eyes are the very same shade as yours, and from looking at his face, I'd say he was a relative – a close one, too – though how that can be I can't even begin to guess.' Galiba stared momentarily at Eadwulf. 'Although, I see now that the square jaw is different to yours...

'Oh, my dear Ameena, do tell me to who he is. Are you

Twelve

related, or are your similar looks merely coincidence?'

Ameena shrugged as she glanced at Eadwulf, her eyes pleading with him to say something that would sound plausible. But on this occasion, Eadwulf decided that only the truth would satisfy Galiba's curiosity.

'Ameena is my half-sister. We have the same father, who passed his colouring on to us. I am much older than Ameena and was born in the northern lands before my father was sold into slavery and brought to work in the quarries at Cordoba.'

Galiba's intake of breath was short and rapid and Eadwulf knew she had realised who he was talking about. 'I remember well the story of the red-headed slave who saved Muhammad's life at the quarries,' she went on. 'Jaleel was a good and honest man, and rapidly rose in favour with the emir. But he would not rest until he'd taken Karima and her young son, Hamid, away from the harem. They were so happy to be married, and a year later, you were born, Ameena. I was privileged to have you all as my neighbours for some years.'

Galiba's eyes clouded with pity as she took a sip of her lemon juice, seeming to search for the right words to say. 'I don't think you know this, but you need to be told by someone, especially if the purpose of your return was to be reunited with them again. Your father and Hamid were killed fleeing from the Alcazar, accused of being in some vile plot to kill Muhammad's firstborn son. Few people believed that either of them would be involved in such a plot, but the fact was, they had disappeared – and so had you, on a ship from the northern lands, it was said.'

'We already know what people think,' Ameena replied,

patting Galiba's hand by way of thanks for her trust in Jaleel and Hamid's innocence. 'Asbat told us – and you were right to believe the story was not true. My father and brother were with me on the ship that took us to the northern lands. None of us were involved in any plot, but someone had evidently wanted people to think we were. We did flee on a trading ship and we settled happily in the northern lands. Hamid is soon to be married and so am I. He decided not to come on this trading trip, but I wanted to see Cordoba just one last time.'

She gestured to Eadwulf. 'Sadly, our father, Beorhtwulf – that was Jaleel's Mercian name – died of old age fourteen years ago, but he had a couple of contented years in his native land and died at peace with himself.'

They sipped their lemon juice in silence for some moments, savouring the scents of the garden. Sounds of tinkling water, and the birdsong high in the foliage of the many trees, drifted to their ears on the gentle breeze. At length, Eadwulf felt compelled to speak. 'More than one market trader has hinted that the city is in a state of unrest at present. Something to do with Muhammad's death and the new emir, who doesn't seem to be very popular. People in Seville were saying the same thing when we were trading there a few days ago.'

Galiba laid her empty goblet on the table and glanced from Ameena to Eadwulf. 'You will have heard that Muhammad was assassinated?' They both nodded. 'It was planned attack at the quarries and they say the poor man was completely decapitated. It shocked everyone, and it seemed as though the entire city went into mourning. He is buried in the cemetery just outside the old Roman walls, and in most peoples' opinion, he was not

Twelve

shown the due respect he was entitled to by his son and heir!

'You are right to sense that Al Mundhir is not popular. In fact, it is true to say that most people hate him – which makes Muhammad's death seem even more tragic. Al-Mundhir's new laws leave little hope for anyone in al-Andalus who is not of the Islamic faith, and so many of them have fled from Cordoba due to his presence here. Indeed, many people in al-Andalus will continue to suffer while he is emir, and I must tell you that there are many of us who believe he and his evil mother, Salihah, were responsible for Muhammad's death.'

'We have heard such rumours, Galiba,' Ameena said, 'but no one could risk doing anything about it. It is all very tragic, and I remember how scheming and vindictive Salihah was, and how spiteful and bullying Rajiv grew up to be. No one liked him even as a boy, and many dreaded the day when he would become emir. It saddens me to see my old city in such a state.'

Asbat reappeared to say that the food had been prepared and Eadwulf deliberately steered conversation away from Al-Mundhir. With what he and Hamid had in mind it would not do to dwell on the subject for too long, even with Galiba. They enjoyed the array of fruits and sweetened cakes, and thanked Galiba for her generous hospitality. Eadwulf headed for the door, while Ameena embraced her old friend. But Galiba's next words made him halt in his tracks. 'I forgot to mention that Rani was married several years ago. You must remember her; you told me several times what a dreadful gossip she was.'

'Oh, I remember Rani very well. She would delight in telling me what she'd overheard from behind some pillar or screen and thought it hilarious that a lowly handmaid should know what the high and mighty in the Alcazar got up to, especially in the bed chamber.'

The two women giggled at that and Galiba added, 'Rani is still one of Salihah's handmaids, but she no longer lives in the Alcazar. In fact, she lives four doors away, and I can tell you, she's as big a gossip as she ever was. If you have time before you sail away, you could always call in and see her. I believe she only works until noon nowadays, so she should be arriving home any time now.'

*

It was easier to gain access to Rani's house than it had been to Galiba's. The lady was already in the garden when they pulled the bell cord, and she hovered behind her two servants to see who could be calling at this time of day.

It had been arranged between them as they left Galiba's that Eadwulf would say nothing on this occasion, mostly because Rani only spoke Arabic. He would pose as a friend who had travelled with Ameena from the northern lands and did not understand the Moorish tongue. He was simply escorting her through the busy city. Once again, Eadwulf watched and listened as servants presumably questioned Ameena's reason for ringing the bell. By standing tall at her side with his muscular arms folded across his chest and a scowl on his face, he made it clear that he was what she was telling them: her bodyguard.

Rani shrieked for joy when she realised who was at her gates and she flung her arms around Ameena before hurling a rapid series of what were obvious questions at her, while throwing the

Twelve

odd, cautious glance in Eadwulf's direction. He was surprised at how short and small-framed the Moorish woman was, the top of her head barely reaching Ameena's chin, and she looked almost as though a puff of wind would blow her away. But her vivacious nature and dark-eyed prettiness would ensure that heads always turned her way.

Ameena readily responded to the embrace, smiling with affection at her old friend, before being pulled through the gates, leaving Eadwulf trailing in their wake.

Heavy scents, vibrant colours and sounds of running water assailed Eadwulf's senses yet again as Rani led them toward the house and, not for the first time, he wondered how many servants were employed to keep these gardens so beautiful. Ameena turned and came to speak to him as Rani waited in the open doorway.

'I'll be in no danger with Rani, so it may be best if you wait out here. I can repeat anything of importance she says later on.' She grinned at his puzzled frown. 'I think Rani finds your fierce demeanour a little off-putting.'

Eadwulf chuckled. 'I'm trying my best to look off-putting, but I'll stay here if it makes your friend feel more comfortable.'

'Find yourself somewhere shaded and I'll ask Rani to send you out a cold drink.'

Eadwulf could do nothing but agree, and found a bench on which to sit close to a fountain, sculpted from shimmering marble in the shape of a sea creature that resembled the whales he'd seen in the far northern seas years ago. He settled down for what began to feel like a long wait. But he was comfortable enough in the shade, and the orange-coloured juice Rani sent out tasted a lot sweeter than the lemon juice they'd had earlier.

He spent the time wondering if Hamid had discovered anything useful from his old colleagues, or Bjorn and the others from people trading around the market. He smiled as he thought of them all in their Moorish dress and hoped they managed to avoid drawing unwanted attention to themselves.

Ameena suddenly appeared beside the bench. 'That was interesting, but I'll wait until we're back in camp before I tell you about it.'

'Probably for the best, especially if it's as "interesting" as you say. Galiba told us little we didn't already know.'

*

Hamid and Básim had taken little time in catching up with Sumayl. The ageing Moor seemed in no hurry and spent some time scrutinising goods on a number of stalls as he passed, his long robes swinging about his ankles. The startled look on his face when Hamid tapped him on the shoulder turned into a huge smile as he recognised the face of his one-time apprentice.

'I knew you weren't dead, despite Muhammad's claims of having you and Jaleel executed!' Sumayl said, enfolding Hamid in a warm embrace. 'He couldn't fool me that easily. So, tell me, where *have* you been these past sixteen years?'

'In the lands far to the north, with the friends who allowed us passage away from here all those years ago. They are good people, Sumayl, and honourable in ways that may seem strange to those of our faith, but I trust them with my life.'

'I wondered if I'd see you again soon, with all that's going

Twelve

on in al-Andalus. I imagined news would reach you sooner or later. Is that why you've returned? Is Jaleel with you... and Ameena? I never did understand how Muhammad could believe those vile stories about you and Jaleel plotting to take his life, but I don't have to think too hard about who started them.' The old man shook his head. 'She's as evil as they come, that one, and I'm certain she's been behind all the supposedly "accidental" deaths in the palace over the years.' He did not need to say the name.

As though suddenly noticing the young man at Hamid's side, the old man's bushy white eyebrows rose. Hamid could barely suppress the smile spreading across his face, partly at his joy in seeing Sumayl again but at the man's way of throwing out seemingly endless questions. 'This is Básim,' he explained, 'who was taken from his home near Seville during a Norse raid three years ago.' He glanced round, ensuring no one was listening. 'If we could go somewhere quiet, I'll explain everything, including why we're here.'

'And, hopefully, you will enlighten me regarding who you mean by "we",' Sumayl said, urging them to move along the alley. 'My home is still where it always was, a few streets away from here.'

*

Sumayl ordered his servants to bring food and drink for his guests and led them into a large, simply but adequately furnished room, its décor predominantly in varying shades of blue, giving the impression of coolness. Its opened windows also faced west, away from the glare of the intense daytime sun. 'I'm sorry to hear of Jaleel's death,' he said, once they had eaten, 'but he was not a young man – several years older than me, as I recall. Muhammad greatly valued his counsel and would have mourned his loss. I came to the conclusion years ago that the emir invented the story of your executions in order to save face with the people; he would not have wanted them to think him a fool who would allow those he trusted to dupe him.'

Hamid nodded. 'That's probably true, old friend, but the threat to mine and Ameena's lives was real. None of us will ever know if Jaleel would have stayed in Cordoba if Salihah's plot to have me killed and Muhammad's desire to have Ameena in his harem had not arisen. The appearance of Jaleel's two sons coming in search of him had thrown him, and he was torn between returning to his homeland of Mercia or staying here with us and the good life he had made for us all. But, in the end, none of us had any other choice than to leave.'

'That has made things a good deal clearer to me, thank you, Hamid. So now we're back to the reason why you have returned.' The ageing stonemason smiled. 'I sincerely hope it's to kill that venomous cur, Al Mundhir. I am convinced it was he and his scheming mother who ordered the assassination of Emir Muhammad and it has been a sad time for al-Andalus ever since. I'm also hoping you will put yourself forward as the next emir of al-Andalus.'

Hamid laughed as Básim's jaw seemed to drop to his chest but he shook his head. 'No, Sumayl, I don't intend to become the next emir, but you have guessed the reason for my return. I do intend to kill Al Mundhir.'

Twelve

The old man nodded, respecting his decision. 'I realise you have your new life to lead and, as you said on our walk here, you have your marriage to look forward to on your return. It's simply that years ago, the Council favoured you to succeed to the emirate, and many of the members of that time will be delighted – and relieved – to know you were not executed for treason.' He held up placatory hands at Hamid's look of alarm. 'But I assure you, they will hear no word of your return through my lips, if that is your wish.'

Sumayl fixed Hamid in his steady, brown gaze. 'Thanks to Salihah's wickedness, there's only one of your brothers left who would be suited to the role of emir.'

'Only one...?' Hamid was shocked. 'There were at least another three or four legitimate sons when I was last here. I was only the son of a concubine, after all.'

'Concubine's son or not, Muhammad held you in high regard, and many people thought he would present you as his successor. But if that is not to be, Abdallah will no doubt take the role. Thankfully, they will also be obliged to expel Salihah from the palace. She will be neither wife nor mother to the new emir and of no use to him – or anyone else – in the Alcazar.

'You may or may not remember Abdallah, Hamid, especially as he would have been a mere child of eight or nine the year you left. He is the son of Muhammad's third wife, an intelligent and thoughtful young man, and when he became the only surviving son other than Al Mundhir, Muhammad had him constantly guarded – the only reason why Salihah's minions did not dispose of him. Yes, he would make a good emir, but not as good as would you.'

'I recall Abdallah as a sparky lad and his mother was not a lady to spoil her children to such a degree as to make them indolent and lacking in any skills. I'm sure he'll serve al-Andalus well and, hopefully, not spend his time persecuting communities of non-Muslims.

'So, Sumayl, is there anything at all you could tell us about the comings and goings in the Alcazar, or any regular outings made by Al Mundhir where I could possibly get close enough to kill him?'

Sumayl thought about that for a moment before standing to head across the room to an elegant ebony chest along the wall. 'There is one thing I can tell you that could be of use to you,' he said, kneeling to lift the lid.

*

The sun was sinking behind the creamy stone buildings of Cordoba as Eadwulf and Ameena headed back to camp and night-time shadows would soon follow. They were both tired and hungry, and the aromas of cooking food as they reached the camp made Eadwulf's stomach growl. He'd had little to eat all day. He was relieved to see Hamid and Básim safely returned, although Bjorn and his men had not yet appeared. But daylight still lingered and he would not succumb to worrying, yet.

Leif came over to sit with them, glad of the company. He'd stayed in the camp, on watch with a few others, and spent some time in the afternoon preparing their evening pottage from meats and a variety of unusual-looking vegetables bought at the market that morning. The cauldron they had brought

Twelve

with them from Aros was suspended from a tripod over the campfire and the aromas of simmering goat stew wafted around the camp.

The old steersman jerked his thumb, indicating the city walls. 'Bjorn and the lads with him will be making a day of it in there and checking out the stalls for goods to take home. And if they've also had a meal, they won't be in any hurry to eat when they get back. Unlike the rest of us.'

Eadwulf nodded. 'Let's hope they've also discovered something useful, although I'm guessing it will be little more than the feeling of general unrest in the country. I doubt if many people would dare to openly voice opinions of the emir, especially to strangers. Al Mundhir could well have his spies about.'

As darkness descended, Bjorn and Hrolf arrived back at camp with their half-dozen men, pulling behind them a couple of handcarts they'd bought, laden with many of the household goods and jars of spices requested by Kata and Yrsa. Seated around the glowing camp fire they enjoyed Leif's meaty pottage whilst sharing what they'd learned around the city.

Eadwulf filled them in on what Galiba had said, stressing the woman's suspicions about Salihah and Al Mundhir being behind Muhammad's assassination and the new emir's disrespect at his funeral. Ameena continued by explaining what Rani had said, her earnest expression making Eadwulf smile.

'Rani swears on her young son's life that she heard Salihah whispering with Al Mundhir the day before Muhammad left to inspect the quarries. Al Mundhir said everything was planned down to the last detail and his men had already set out, taking a circuitous route to the main site of the quarrying. She heard nothing further, so if Rani's story is to be believed, I can only think that Al Mundhir's men would have been waiting for him to arrive, with their plan of attack in place.'

'You're telling us what we'd already guessed, sister, but we can add a little more to that.' Hamid gestured at Básim, nodding at his side and glanced round the listening group. 'As Eadwulf and Ameena already know, I spotted a stonemason near the Great Mosque, a man I had often worked under when I was an apprentice in my father's palace, and fortunately, he recognised me straight away. Sumayl's now well past his sixtieth year and has no need to be inside the Alcazar nowadays, but he has many friends and is keen to keep up with news from around the city. He invited us into his home and we spoke for some time, sharing old memories to begin with, then moving on to the attitudes of citizens to the new emir.'

Hamid nodded, as he thought. 'As we already knew, Al Mundhir - Rajiv as Ameena and I know him – is more than unpopular with the people. According to Sumayl, there are many in Cordoba, and even in the Alcazar itself, who would wish him dead.'

'In the Alcazar itself...' Bjorn repeated, tweaking his short beard. 'Interesting. Would any of those people live in the palace – I mean, sleep there, too, rather than merely work there each day but live elsewhere in the city?'

'There have always been servants who live in the palace,' Ameena supplied. 'Rani lived there for many years before she married. Then there are slaves and concubines who have no other choice than to stay there and are generally strictly guarded in case they attempt to escape. Free citizens like

Twelve

Rani and Sumayl are able to move about, as long as whatever they do doesn't appear suspicious to the patrolling guards. In Rani's case, being Salihah's handmaid entitles her to roam the corridors and private apartments of the emir's many wives unhindered. She even happily stops and chats to the guards, as she knows most of them by appearance if not by name. She said that at least four of them have confided in her of their hatred of Al Mundhir.'

Bjorn nodded. 'What times of the day is Rani inside the palace?'

'Only until noon each day, but she must be in there before sunrise in order to make preparations for Salihah to bathe, and ensure the scented oils to massage into her skin and combs with which to style her hair, are to hand. Then she must lay out the gowns her mistress will wear and set out the foods to break her fast on a tray...'

Ameena smiled at the frowning faces. 'The pampered life of an emir's wife or mother is something most common people find hard to understand.'

Leif scratched his bald head. 'How long after Rani gets there does the rest of the palace start to stir, would you say?'

'Most of the slaves and personal servants rise around dawn,' Ameena replied, 'depending on how much they need to do before the emir's family and palace officials rise. If many of them are as fussy as Salihah over her morning rituals, there could be a number of servants roaming the corridors before sunrise.' She shot a nervous look at Hamid. 'Please tell me you're not thinking of breaking into the palace. You of all people would surely be recognised.'

Hamid gave a sly little smile. 'I have a secret to share, which would make gaining entrance to the Alcazar quite easy.'

'In Odin's name, spit it out, man! If you've a better plan than breaking in and getting Rani to distract guards while we sneak along the corridors to Al Mundhir's rooms – which seems to be the general drift of the rest of us – why didn't you just say so?'

'I wanted to see if anyone had a better plan first,' Hamid said with a shrug. 'Anyway, what do you mean, exactly, by "we"? Dealing with Rajiv is my duty alone and I won't have anyone else put in danger.'

'Well, I'd say that's very honourable of you, my friend,' Bjorn said, shaking his head, 'but I think the more of us involved in this the better. We don't *all* need to enter the palace, but you and Eadwulf need us to keep guard outside and make sure the way is clear for your escape.'

Hamid shot a look at Eadwulf. 'Me and Eadwulf... No! I do this alone and I don't want you risking your life for me.'

'Before you tell us this secret, Hamid, you have to accept that I'll be right with you when you deal with Al Mundhir and Bjorn and his men will do as he just explained. We're in this together, and the ships will be ready to sail the moment we leave the city.'

'So, *does* this secret involve a better plan than relying on Rani to open doors for you?' Ameena asked, breaking the tension between her two half-brothers.

After a moment, Hamid opened the leather pouch attached to his belt and drew out a large iron key. The rest of them gaped at it.

Twelve

Leif tutted. 'Don't just sit there waving the thing at us, lad. We can see it's a key but unless you decide to tell us, we'll never know where it's for, will we?'

'The key is from Sumayl and I think it will solve a lot of our problems.'

'But where's it *for*?'

Eadwulf smiled to himself; Leif was becoming impatient in his old age.

Hamid grinned like a child tasting his first honey cake. 'It opens a door at the end of a tunnel that starts in what looks like a pile of unused boulders along the western side of the city wall. Sumayl came across it by accident years ago when he was overseeing the rebuilding of a section of the old wall. He followed along the tunnel once and says it's quite long, and dark too, so we'll probably need a lamp with us. It drops beneath the city wall, then under the thick, outer wall of the palace.'

He held up the key and it shone in the glow of the firelight. 'As to where Sumayl found this, he claims to have trodden on it on the earth outside the door, which was, naturally, locked. He didn't go through at the time, but he worked out which room the door opened into from plans of the Alcazar, and eventually tried the key from there when no one was around. I don't suppose we'll ever know who dug out the tunnel or why. It could have been there since the Romans were here.'

He paused, glancing round at the rapt faces and Eadwulf began to feel as impatient as Leif.

'There's just one snag,' Hamid eventually continued. 'After Sumayl left the tunnel he had some of the slaves close the gap that leads to the passage, so we'll need to drag away the biggest rock on the northern side of the pile to find it again – which will probably take two or three men. And while we're in there, the rock needs to be pushed back into place until we've done the job.'

'No problem there as far as I can see. A group of us intended to hover near the gates, anyway, so we'll stay near this rock pile instead.'

'Thanks, Bjorn. And there's something even more interesting…'

Leif rolled his eyes. 'At this rate, I'll be on my funeral pyre before you get this story out! Whatever else you're good at, Hamid, you'll never make a skald.'

The chuckle that rippled round was a nervous one as everyone waited to hear what else Hamid would reveal.

'The tunnel ends in a small room in which the walls appear to have been covered in alternating sections of wooden planks and marble tiles. One of the wooden sections is actually a door – a door with a keyhole that fits this key.'

Eadwulf was sceptical. 'Why have none of the servants ever seen it, then?'

Hamid smiled. 'All the wood-planked sections are decorated in keyholes etched into the wood, each one with an actual hole bored into the middle of it. Of course, all but one of the holes is imitation. There is no furniture in this room other than a table in the middle laden with drying cloths and sweet-smelling oils used only by the emir when he bathes, so the doorway won't be blocked as we enter.'

'Are you're saying this secret passage ends somewhere in the emir's private apartments?'

Twelve

'The room I'm describing is a mere fifteen yards or so from the emir's sleeping chamber, Eadwulf. So, all we need to do is get from that room into Rajiv's without patrolling guards seeing us, deal with him and get back through the hidden door before any servants arrive to prepare things for his morning routine.'

'Not a lot, then,' Leif said, shaking his head.

Thirteen

A thin sliver of moon cast enough light for Eadwulf, Hamid, Bjorn and half a dozen of his crew to find their way round the edge of the outer market to the western side of the city wall. Eadwulf didn't dwell too much on the task that lay ahead. It was simply something that needed to be done before they could sail home. He'd killed before, and recognised in himself the same steely resolve that always set in at such times. The only difference now lay in the fact that it wouldn't be him doing the killing – unless something went wrong with the plan he and Hamid had devised.

In a sheath at his belt, the dagger given to him years ago by Leif was the only weapon he carried, and Hamid had a similar weapon with him. Without doubt, Eadwulf knew that everything hinged on timing: they needed to be out of the palace and rowing like the Furies down the Guadalquivir before any stall-holders arrived to set out their wares at the market, or servants arrived at the palace to make preparations for the day – and entered the emir's bed chamber. The knarrs were ready to push away, their belongings loaded, and men waited at the oars. Dawn was still a few hours away, but any unexpected hold-ups could throw their well laid plans awry.

The rock pile was easy enough to locate, and Eadwulf could only wonder why it had sat there for so long. Perhaps the simple fact that it was on the outside of the city negated the need to move it.

It took three men to drag the biggest of the rocks a little

Thirteen

under two feet, creating a gap just wide enough for Eadwulf and Hamid to squeeze through. Before the rock was pushed back and darkness engulfed them, Eadwulf lit a small oil lamp and led the way into the narrow tunnel.

'Watch your head, and duck when I do,' Eadwulf threw over his shoulder as the tunnel descended steeply for some yards before levelling out. 'There are some jagged rocks hanging from the roof in places.'

The tunnel continued in a straight line for a while before rising again, the incline less steep this time. Eadwulf suddenly stopped. 'I think we've just come under the outer wall of the palace,' he whispered, 'so we should now be below some area of the building. How far beneath the palace floor we are is anyone's guess, so we should only speak if we have to.'

Hamid nodded and they moved on, the glow from the oil lamp casting dancing shadows along the earthen walls. The passage became a little wider and less oppressive at this point and started to curve and gradually rise. At length they came to what at first appeared to be a dead end, but on nearing, a wooden door came into view with a clearly visible keyhole halfway up, on the right.

Eadwulf held his breath, his ear to the door. All seemed silent, though he knew that meant little. There could be guards on the other side playing board games, or dozing while waiting for their shifts to end. He swallowed hard, placing the lamp on the earth, praying it would still be burning when they made their escape, and pushed the key into the keyhole.

Hamid's rapid intake of breath displayed his unease as metal grated on metal and Eadwulf attempted to turn the key. But the old key repeatedly refused to turn, as though it did not fit the hole. Eadwulf's hopes of gaining entry plummeted and he glanced up and down the door to convince himself there was only one keyhole. Then he saw it, just above his head at the left-hand side of the door: a second keyhole, positioned where few would think of looking.

The key turned first time and Eadwulf pushed the door ajar. Still no sound. They waited a few moments and stepped into the room, which was dimly lit by light shining through the part-opened doorway opposite. The outline of a long table heaped with folded cloths and various baskets and jars stood in the middle, just as Sumayl had described to Hamid.

Hamid crept across the room and poked his head round the door. 'There's a marble-floored corridor through here that I remember being outside the emir's apartments. If I'm right, the door into Rajiv's bed-chamber is less than ten yards to our left. No guards about now… but it won't be long before they're back.'

The first thing they noticed on closing the heavy door behind them was that the spacious bed-chamber was not swathed in darkness. Flickering light shone through the flimsy drapes of three floor-to-ceiling windows to their left, providing just enough light for them to move around without walking into the pieces of ornate furniture – or the wide, canopied bed against the facing wall, with silken sheets that draped the form of the sleeping emir.

Eadwulf sidled over to the closest window to locate the source of the light, observing the wide balcony immediately outside and a courtyard below with a flaming torch in the

Thirteen

centre of each of the walls. Then, as planned, he headed back to the door to listen for sounds of movement along the corridor outside. But the only noise to disturb the silence was the soft, regular snoring of the sleeping Al-Mundhir.

Willing Hamid to work quickly, Eadwulf watched as he lifted a velvet cushion from one of the couches and crept silently towards the emir's bedside. For some moments he stood, motionless, as though transfixed by the rise and fall of his half-brother's chest, the cushion in his hands hovering over the detested face. Then, snapping out of his trance, Hamid plunged the pillow down and pressed hard.

But Al Mundhir did not succumb without a struggle, tugging on Hamid's arms and writhing about so much that Eadwulf feared he'd succeed in wrenching Hamid's hands away, or squeal so loudly that someone would hear. He darted over and leapt on the bed, straddling the emir to stop his legs from thrashing while grasping his arms and pinning them at his sides. As the life force of the hated ruler of al-Andalus deserted him, the death throes gradually ceased until he lay still, vacantly staring up at the canopy of his ostentatious bed.

Working fast, Eadwulf closed the emir's eyes and helped Hamid to roll him onto his side, straightening the pillows and lifting one of his arms to curve in languid pose around the top of his head before pulling the silken covers up to his shoulders. To anyone looking from the doorway it would appear he still slept and, with any luck, they'd be glad to leave him that way for at least a while longer.

They listened behind the door for some moments before opening it a little, heaving silent sighs of relief to see the corridor still empty, and hurried back to the small preparations room. But this time it seemed that their luck had run out.

The servant was no weakling of a man, with thick, bared arms and a barrel of a chest. He tossed down the drying cloth he'd been in the process of folding, his heavily bearded face thunderous as he hurled himself at Hamid, the first to enter. Hamid dodged to one side, so that the Moor was now between him and Eadwulf – and unsheathing a long, curved knife that hung from his belt. Waving the knife menacingly before him, his eyes darted from one to the other.

Hamid was the first to move, shifting his stance a little, as though about to attack. The big man's attention focused on him a moment too long… and Eadwulf took his cue. Unsheathing his own dagger, he dived at the Moor, thrusting the blade up beneath his ribs. A wave of sympathy engulfed him at the look of surprise on the servant's dark face as his knees gave way and he crumpled to the floor. But Eadwulf had no time for regret, and pulled him onto his back before twisting the piercing blade a couple of times to ensure he was dead.

'Get that door open,' he whispered, retrieving his weapon, 'then help me clean up the blood in here.'

Eadwulf dragged the body into the hidden passage, where it would stay and rot. They mopped the blood from the clay-tiled floor with some of the drying cloths and water from a pail, tossing the bloodied cloths into the passage with the body, then straightened up the items on the table so they looked untouched.

Voices of the guards sounded from along the corridor as they darted into the passage and relocked the door behind them. The deed was done.

Thirteen

Dawn was breaking over al-Andalus as the four knarrs pushed away from Cordoba, rays of golden light dancing on the waters of the great Guadalquivir. Eadwulf watched the city grow smaller and smaller, then disappear from view as they rounded a bend. Relief washed over him that it was over and that no palace guards had fired at them, though his thoughts were far from easy. Innocent people would suffer once the search for the emir's murderer was underway. Guards and palace officials and servants would be ruthlessly questioned; some would no doubt confess to being involved in the plot under the agony of torture and mutilation. Others would give the names of innocent people to deflect the blame from themselves...

Eadwulf forced away such thoughts, replacing them with images of al-Andalus under the leadership of a far more honourable and just emir than the unscrupulous Al Mundhir. He pulled the large key from the pouch at his waist and tossed it into the Guadalquivir, then relieved Básim at his oar port as images of his family and home filled his head.

Fourteen

Wilton, Wiltshire: June-December 887

Abbot Asser returned to Alfred's court in the last week of June, just as it settled in for its two-month long stay at the royal manor of Wilton. His wagon trundled in, flanked by the mounted men that Alfred had sent out to Saint David's as escort, and fond greetings were made all round.

Alfred was delighted to see Asser back, and keen for him to recommence his work on the texts with the other scholars. Since January, Alfred had spent much of his time travelling back and forth to Lundenburh, checking on the building works in the new city, very aware that for any town and port to function fully, a variety of buildings were needed besides family homes: areas for trade and commerce – including homes with yards attached for a variety of craftsmen to operate – inns, hostels and stables for travellers were all drawn into Alfred's plan, and he needed to be sure it was being followed.

He need not have worried. Aethelred was following it precisely, and the city was beginning to take the shape of the one in Alfred's mind, even down to the new quayside with its large, riverfront storage structures. And now, having spent more time with his daughter and son-by-marriage than the rest of his family, they had come to Wilton to enable Alfred to relax for a while before he began travelling around his kingdom to inspect some of the newly fortified burhs.

But Alfred's mind was rarely at rest, and he wandered out of

Fourteen

the hall to be alone while he considered his plans for the future.

So much had already been achieved in improving the defences of his kingdom, and he was pleased with the speed with which his new mounted armies could muster and travel. But work was still ongoing and, although Wessex was now enjoying a period of peace, deep down he could not believe it would last forever. His success at Edington and the treaty he had made with Guthrum had bought him a few years of peace – but, at best, it was an uneasy calm. The Danes had left his kingdom and, with a few exceptions, those not content to stay in the lands of the Danelaw had since been focusing their attacks on the Low Countries and Francia. But for how long would that continue? How long before the Franks defeated them, or simply paid the Norsemen enough geld to leave their kingdom? If either of those possibilities occurred, Alfred was certain the invaders would, once more, set their sights on his kingdom. And when that happened, he was determined they would not find it as easy to infiltrate and defeat as they had done in Halfdan and Guthrum's time.

He inhaled deeply, allowing the beauty of the Wilton estate to calm his mind. How peaceful it was, standing by the clear waters of the River Wylye, with the breeze playing through the wispy leaves of the drooping willows. Wilton held so many memories for Alfred: of his father's love of the place, and the battle that took place close by, during which his beloved elder brother, Aethelred, sustained the wound that ultimately killed him. Yet despite the sharp poignancy of his memories, like his father, Alfred always felt at peace here, if not feeling the deep-seated love he had for his manor at Wantage.

He glanced at the hall, a straw-thatched structure pleasing to the eye, the lower half of stone to honour his father's desire to see more Saxon buildings created from that material. It had been built sixteen years ago to replace the old one that had been burnt to the ground by Halfdan's Danes before the Battle of Meretun.

'What are you thinking?' Ealhswith asked, coming to stand beside him.

Alfred smiled at his wife. 'Oh, just memories, again. There's something about this place, new hall or not. Whenever we come here the air seems thick with images of past times just waiting to take seat in my head. We came here so often when I was young and I have to be careful not to allow the couple of bad memories to override the many happy ones.'

'We must enjoy it while we can, Alfred. I know you have no intention of being idle, but here, you can at least take each day as it comes, and you have no need to leave home for any length of time. The abbot told me earlier he is eager to get back to working on translating the texts with the other scholars, as well as working with you and Aethelgifu on your Latin.' Ealhswith smiled at the thought. 'It will be good for our daughter to be learning alongside her father, and she greatly admires the abbot.'

'I'll be happy to work with Aethelgifu and it will give us something extra to talk about. She's such a clever young thing and will undoubtedly understand it much better than I do, but I'm determined to keep trying.'

Ealhswith turned to head back to the hall. 'Are you coming back in? I thought you had things you wanted to discuss with Asser.'

Fourteen

'I do. I'm just giving him a day or two to rest after his journey and settle in, but I'll speak to him soon.'

But, the following day, Alfred's illness struck again, the gruelling pains and sudden diarrhoea sending him to his bed for the next three days. When he eventually rose, he felt so weak, he could do little more than sit in his high-backed chair, either in the hall or outside in the early July sunshine, and watch as life went on around him.

'Papa, you will be well soon… won't you?'

Alfred gazed at Aethelgifu who had silently appeared beside him as he watched his youngest son and daughter playing chase between the sheds and storage huts. The worried look on her face made him smile and he squeezed her small hand. 'I will, daughter. I'll get a little stronger every day, until I'm bouncing around like… like Aethelweard.'

Aethelgifu's giggle was a delight to his ears. 'Are you enjoying being here as much as they seem to be?' he asked.

'I enjoy being anywhere, as long as I'm with my family, you know that, Papa. Strangers make me feel a little uncomfortable, and shy.' Inadvertently, her hand moved up to touch her red-stained brow, despite the mark being mostly covered by the head veil. 'I feel badly enough about this when Aelfthryth teases me about it, and –'

'Aelfthryth is old enough at eight to know better than to tease you about that,' Alfred cut in. 'She needs to be made aware that hurting people's feelings is unkind, and no one likes anyone unkind. I'll speak to her about it later. Don't worry,' he added, noting her look of alarm. 'Your sister will not know you told me about it. After all, it could have been anyone in the hall, which is what I'll lead her to believe – that she was simply overheard.

'Other than that, you say you like it here? You have plenty to do to keep you occupied?'

'I love to sit with Abbot Asser and read the Scriptures, Papa. Those stories fill me with a kind of joy. I thought about some of Christ's teachings a moment ago, when you said that no one should be unkind. He teaches of doing good deeds and helping others less fortunate than ourselves – like all the poor people out there.' She swept out her arm in a dramatic gesture that made Alfred laugh.

'Do you know, Aethelgifu? After talking to you, even for so short a time, I'm feeling a lot better already.'

'Good. Then I shall be sure to come and sit with you for a while every day until you are properly well. That will be one of my daily good deeds.'

'I will look forward to that very much,' Alfred replied, and meant it.

After another two days of resting and being fussed over by everyone, Alfred decided it was time to get back to work. Aelfthryth had soon got over her pique at being chastised for cruelly teasing her quiet older sister – nothing could keep such a boisterous child down for long – and things in general were running smoothly at Wilton. Alfred was now keen to have the talk with Asser he'd planned for several days ago, so after the morning meal he led the abbot out of the hall to sit beside him on a wide bench, carefully placed out of the sun's glare beneath the willows lining the Wylye.

Asser turned to face Alfred once his request had been

Fourteen

voiced. 'So, you are asking me to look into the possibility of you acquiring Frankish scholars to join your court?'

'I am, Abbot. I seem to have temporarily come to the end of my list of suitable scholars from our own kingdoms and, although I realise that Francia is plagued by Norse raiders at present, I still feel the Franks owe us a favour in this respect.'

Asser looked puzzled. 'They do, lord?'

'They do, indeed. Ever since Charlemagne's time, a number of our scholars have been requested – or perhaps lured by promises of numerous gifts – to work in Francia's court school which, to my way of thinking, means it's high time the favour was returned. Do you, perhaps, know of any Frankish scholars who would be suitable?'

'One certainly comes to mind. Grimbald of Saint Bertin is both a learned scholar and devout monk and is, I am told, of a pleasant and amiable disposition. He is highly favoured by Fulco, the archbishop of Rheims, who intends to appoint him to a bishopric. So it may well transpire that the archbishop will not wish to part with him.'

Alfred stroked his short brown beard as he thought. 'It's possible, though I won't know until I try. I'll write to Fulco, stating my desire for the services of Grimbald at my Court, and out of courtesy, he'll be compelled to reply. Obviously, what I do next will depend what he says. If his answer is yes, I will be delighted, but if it's an outright refusal, I shall respond by expressing my deep disappointment, considering how many Saxon and Mercian scholars are working in Francia. I'll stress the need to continue the mutual goodwill and co-operation that exists between our kingdoms which, hopefully, will play on his guilt at refusing. If it does not,' he added, grinning at the abbot, 'then I'll resort to the age-old trick of bribery. Highly-prized gifts can work wonders.'

'Ah, at last I understand why I now own two monasteries and a beautiful silk cloak.'

Alfred momentarily stared at Asser, wondering if the remark was intended as rebuke, but the abbot's twitching lips and ensuing hearty laugh allayed his fears.

'Yes, I was indeed fooled by your gifts, King Alfred, but I know I can do much good owning and running those monasteries. I hear the abbots of both are lax and the communities suffer because of it. I had it in mind to appoint new abbots at both.'

'Then while my court is still here, closer to Somerset than is Winchester, I suggest you call on both monasteries. If you intend to appoint new abbots, you will need to spend time at each, which I will happily grant you. A score of my men will accompany you so the monks realise you have my support in this.'

A slight frown appeared on Asser's brow and Alfred smiled, sensing the cause. 'Be assured, my lord abbot, it will be to *your* authority the monks bow down. They will already know you keep the monks of Saint David's on a tight rein and show no lenience to those who fail in their duties to God and pursuing the work necessary for the community to flourish. My authority in religious houses is only called upon in the face of total failure in these things and the abbot or bishop is either complicit in the misdeeds, or simply powerless to control the errant monks or priests.'

Fourteen

'I am most grateful, lord. To run a monastery so poorly is a sin against God, and I will do all in my power to rectify the situations at each.'

'Leave here in two days, Asser, which will also give your escort time to make ready, and I'll give you until late August to assess the situations and perhaps hold elections at each monastery to ascertain who the monks themselves deem suitable as abbot before you have the final say in the matter.'

Asser nodded. 'You are certain my work here can wait all that time?'

'I think dealing with your monasteries is more important at the moment than translating texts or teaching me Latin, and your absence will give me time to work through some of the tasks that must be done this year. I'll start by making my request to Archbishop Fulco. I'm hoping he'll see the sense of the monk joining me, but if not, I'll begin working through the strategy I outlined – a tedious mix of letter-writing, reminders of mutual goodwill, bribery and gift-giving.' He grinned. 'Let us hope Fulco is a reasonable man.

'Oh, and when you return to us, I'd like to discuss with you the fact that in the next year or so I intend to start work on the construction of the first of two new monasteries.'

Asser nodded his tonsured head in approval. 'Have you decided where they will be located?'

'I have,' Alfred said, standing and pacing back and forth to stretch his legs. 'The first to be built will be on Athelney. The isle is dear to me and was very much a part of my success in ridding our lands of Guthrum and his Danes. Building a monastery there is my way of showing my thanks to God, as well as my deep gratitude to the fen folk for the help they gave us, especially when we first arrived. I am hopeful that much of the produce grown and livestock kept by the monks will greatly benefit the island people, especially in mid-winter or times of hardship.'

'And the second?'

'Shaftesbury, most likely, and I intend it to be an abbey for nuns. We have few places for the most devout women amongst us, so I wish to rectify that. Of course, building work at Shaftesbury will not begin for at least a year after Athelney is finished and I am satisfied it is being well run.'

Alfred stopped pacing and seated himself next to the abbot again. 'I also want to begin designing a new bridge across the Thames from Lundenburh to Surrey… in the same place as the remnants of the old Roman bridge, so we'll need to remove the rotting timbers of that one first.' Asser nodded. 'Ealdorman Aelfric tells me there's a settlement developing along the river's south bank and a bridge would be more than useful. It's a few hundred years since the old bridge was usable.'

'King Alfred, I know little about building work itself, but I'd be glad to assist with the design of the bridge as well as the monasteries.'

'I hoped you'd say that, and of course I'll also need your help in the selection of an abbot for Athelney.'

'And an abbess for Shaftesbury, I imagine.'

Alfred shook his head. 'No, Abbot, I already know a young woman who will make the perfect abbess there. Not that she will be told about it for another few years.'

Asser gave a knowing smile. 'In the meantime, we must

ensure that the young woman in question becomes proficient in the reading and writing of Latin.'

*

Once the Wessex court returned to Winchester, the weeks flew by for Alfred in a constant round of visiting Lundenburh and other towns that were undergoing fortification at that time. On the relatively few occasions he was in Winchester, he was largely occupied with learning his Latin beside Aethelgifu and designing a bridge and monasteries with Abbot Asser. But there was no rush for the plans, since building would not be starting on any of them until late next year, so they were able to take their time and enjoy the process, frequently seeking the opinions of the scholars working their way through the ever-growing mound of scrolls. On a couple of occasions, he managed to get out with Edward and his thegns to fly their falcons and hawks. Edward loved the sport, and the peregrine Alfred presented him with gave him immense pleasure. Alfred felt so at peace during those times, and prayed they would continue.

His initial letter to Archbishop Fulco met with little success, and the reply did not arrive until mid-October. As Asser had guessed, the archbishop was not too keen on parting with Grimbald. He made it clear that the monk was destined for great things in Francia and questioned whether Alfred would find similar opportunities for him in Wessex.

'The man is obviously wanting to play the game,' Alfred said to his scholars as they sorted through a newly arrived batch of scrolls together. 'He writes an eloquent letter, I admit, littered with praises of me and the good relations between our kingdoms, but it's evident he won't be letting me have Grimbald too easily.' He grinned at Asser. 'Time for gift-giving, I think, and an equally eloquent and flattering missive from me in return. Three good hunting dogs will be my first gift, to help protect him from the many wolves that roam around Francia. Edward can pick them out from our pack tomorrow and they can be sent straight to Francia before the seas become too rough for travel. But I imagine I won't get a reply from Fulco until well after the Christmastide.'

December came around all too quickly and the Advent was upon them. As always, invitations to spend Christ's Mass at the king's hall were sent to several of Alfred's closest nobles and their families, including Aethelred and Aethelflaed and Garth. To Alfred's and Ealhswith's disappointment, it seemed that none of the three would be able to come.

'Garth's been called back to Somerset to visit his mother who is quite ill at present,' Alfred said as he read through the letter. 'As soon as she's feeling a little better, he intends to take all his fenland family back to his Glastonbury manor for the Holy Season. Aethelred has given Garth full permission to do so and does not expect him back in Lundenburh until his next term of service in March.'

'I was looking forward to seeing Garth again,' Edward put in.' He's good company, especially when he's with Aethelred. Perhaps all three of them will visit here before Eastertide?'

Alfred shook his head. 'I doubt it. The reason Aethelflaed and Aethelred aren't coming here for Christmastide is because Aethelflaed is also feeling unwell.'

Fourteen

Ealhswith jumped to her feet and crossed the hall towards Alfred. 'Pray God it's nothing serious,' she said, her face creased with worry. 'Our daughter was well when you saw her in October, wasn't she?'

'I'm not sure, now I come to think about it. She spent much of her time in the women's bower, even taking her meals in there, leaving Aethelred to discuss important issues with me – which I assumed was because he was more familiar with the building progress than she was. She didn't look ill, although she wasn't her usual robust self, either...

'And now that I've read this letter, I understand why.'

'Well...? Is her illness serious, or not?'

'I'd say it is very serious, Ealhswith.' Alfred glanced round the hall, noticing that everyone had stopped what they were doing to listen to this conversation. Aethelflaed was dear to them all.

'Aethelflaed isn't going to die, is she, Papa?' Aelfthryth looked close to tears and Alfred realised he'd kept them in suspense for too long.

'No, your sister probably feels as though she is, but ask your mama how she felt when she was in the early months of carrying a child.'

Ealhswith let out a little squeal of delight and the rest of the hall cheered. 'Our daughter is with child! Oh, Alfred, it was cruel of you to make us think she had some awful illness. Does Aethelflaed say when the child will be born?'

'In late May, so at least it should be warm and sunny for the new babe. And since Aethelflaed is feeling too sickly to travel here, I'll arrange for us to travel to Lundenburh for a week as soon as the winter weather is a little less severe – the beginning of March, perhaps? Garth will probably be back there by then, too.'

'Thank you, Papa!' Aethelgifu said. 'That would be lovely. But I do hope Aethelflaed is feeling a little better by then.'

Ealhswith laughed. 'If your sister is anything like I was, I doubt she'll be feeling really well until after the child is born.'

Fifteen

Winchester and Southampton, Wessex: February 888

As the new year started, Alfred was kept busy dealing with correspondence with a number of clerics from abroad as well as travelling to Southampton in early February to discuss with Eadgar, the portreeve, the construction of another three ships of a design that Alfred had spent several snow-blocked days perfecting in mid-January. He was obsessed with the thought that the Norsemen held sway over the seas for one reason only: their ships were still superior in so many ways to his own. They were lighter, with wide but shallow draught hulls which made them faster and so much easier to manoeuvre than any in his Wessex fleet. Having scrutinised several of the ships he'd captured in the past, he had designed a similar vessel of his own.

'It doesn't take long to see where you got the idea of this one from,' the rotund portreeve said, surveying the parchment laid on the trestle in the shipbuilders' warehouse near Southampton's quayside. 'Of course, these low hulls make them easier to board during attack than our own ships, but you're right, they should be much faster, both when in sail and being rowed, so will make for a faster escape, when necessary.'

'Then I'll leave things with you, Eadgar. If you have problems in finding materials or with any part of the design, let me know and I'll try to get down to see you.'

The portreeve nodded. 'Hopefully, we won't need to do that, lord, but I'll let you know when we've made progress on the first ship anyway, and if you can manage it, you can come and see what you think. If it's satisfactory and you don't want to alter anything, we'll push on with the other two vessels as well.'

Alfred handed the portreeve a substantial bag of silver coin. 'Then I'll look forward to seeing what you create for me. My court will be in Winchester until the end of July when we head to Wantage for all of August, although we also intend a short stay in Lundenburh during the first week of March.'

'We've all heard your family's good news, lord, and I'd be grateful if you'd pass our congratulations on to Lady Aethelflaed and her husband.' Eadgar suddenly chortled. 'And when the child is born, I'd appreciate your views on what it feels like to be a grandfather. I'll be one myself in August.'

*

As Alfred had anticipated, Archbishop Fulco's response to his gift did not arrive until late February, and was one of overwhelming and superfluous gratitude for the three handsome hunting dogs. His wording was dramatic and obviously intended to soften the stipulations he laid down in his missive regarding the necessary elevation of Grimbald within the Saxon Church, should he be permitted to serve at Alfred's court. The haughty Archbishop of Reims went to great lengths to stress the high esteem in which he held this monk, and that he would expect him to succeed to the position of Archbishop of Canterbury very soon after.

'Fulco has evidently heard of the passing of Archbishop

Fifteen

Ethelred in January,' he said to Asser as they sat in the hall to discuss whether or not the archbishop would send Grimbald to Wessex, as he had totally evaded agreeing to Alfred's request in his letter. 'If he thinks having a Frankish monk as the archbishop of Canterbury will give him a say in Saxon affairs, he can think again!'

Alfred took a few deep breaths. 'I want someone in that position I can trust, this time, Abbot, unlike Ethelred who spent most of his days wishing me dead. There isn't one of my ealdormen who thinks I was right in forgiving him for his betrayal of me to Guthrum all those years ago. I imagine he didn't regret what he'd done, either, though he kept his word and did not betray me again.'

'I daresay he would fear the consequences if he did, my lord.'

'Oh yes, Asser, I made very clear to him that one step out of line would see him executed. But now he has simply died of old age and, this time, I want someone I can trust and rely on in such a high position in our Church. I'm afraid some unknown priest simply would not do. I don't intend to appoint anyone until I've had time to think it through and assessed the worth of possible successors. So, I'll reply to Fulco – with another gift, of course – telling him that I'll give every consideration to Grimbald's appointment as archbishop. Hopefully, by the time I do appoint someone, Grimbald will have been in Wessex for some time and the esteemed archbishop of Reims will have forgotten all about him.'

*

Lundenburh: late May-June 888

Aethelred paced the rushes of the hall's expansive floor, unable to sit or even stand still as he waited for word from the bedchamber. For the past few hours he'd been expecting one of the nurses to rush in with the news he longed to hear: that Aethelflaed had been delivered of a healthy child and was wanting to see him. His mind was awash with possibilities, and not all of them pleasant. If anything went wrong and he should lose Aethelflaed, he'd be a broken man. It had been hard enough watching her suffer from the wretched sickness throughout her term, and he longed for her to feel well again. And now, this birthing was taking far too long. Outside the long May day was beginning to fade and his wife's birthing pains had become strong enough to arouse the midwives well before dawn. Mildrithe had anticipated a birthing by late afternoon, but that time had long since passed

Garth had done his best to help him remain calm, although Garth knew as little about the birthing process as he did. All he could do was put his trust in the two midwives sent by Lady Ealhswith following their visit in March. After all, they were both highly experienced and had delivered Aethelflaed herself, as well as her four siblings.

The door from the bedchambers creaked open and Hild stepped into the room. 'You have a beautiful daughter, my lord. Both Lady Aethelflaed and the babe are well, but your wife is extremely tired and needs to sleep, so I would ask that on this occasion, your visit be a short one.'

Hild left the hall amidst a babble of congratulations and

Fifteen

Aethelred grinned from ear to ear as he followed the midwife back to the bed chamber. He was greeted by the lusty voice of his daughter as she objected to being wiped clean with a damp cloth, but his heart went out to Aethelflaed who looked totally exhausted, despite having been washed and dressed in a clean nightgown. Her need for sleep was obvious, but she held out her hand as he came to her and he could see she was also still in a good deal of pain. But he did not remark on it, deciding to ask Mildrithe about her condition later.

Aethelred bent to kiss her pale cheek and perched on the edge of the bed. 'Well done, my love, and thank you for giving me a daughter to cherish. We'll have to decide what to call her.'

Aethelflaed gave a small smile. 'I've always liked the name Aelfwynn. Would that be agreeable to you?'

'Aelfwynn…' he repeated. 'Yes, I like it. It's a pretty name.'

Mildrithe brought the now sleeping babe, wrapped in a warm blanket, and placed her in Aethelred's arms. He stared down at her perfect little face, the tightly balled fists and the light covering of brown hair across her tiny head. 'I wonder if she'll have the same hair colour as you and your mother when she gets a little bigger. It's hard to tell until it grows a little.'

'And even then, hair often changes colour as a child grows,' Mildrithe explained as she gently lifted the babe from Aethelred's arms. 'I've known some children with flaxen hair to become quite dark-headed once they're fully grown.

'Now, my lady,' she continued, laying Aelfwynn in her crib, 'we'll leave the little one to gather her strength after the rigors of birthing. It's no use trying to get her to suckle if all she wants to do is sleep.' She gave a little chortle. 'Believe me, we'll know about it when she *is* feeling hungry!

'I must ask you to leave, for now, my lord and I need to speak with the servants about serving Lady Aethelflaed's meals in here for the next few days so I'll accompany you to the hall. Hild will keep an eye on things here until I get back.'

Aethelred kissed his wife's brow. 'Try to get some rest yourself while Aelfwynn's asleep,' he ordered, bringing another little smile to her lips as he turned to follow Mildrithe out of the room. 'I'll be back to see you a little later.'

Once in the hall, Mildrithe drew him to one side. 'I need to tell you that Lady Aethelflaed did not have an easy birthing, my lord, as you have probably guessed from the length of time it took.' He nodded. 'That means she will take longer to recover than is usual. Thankfully, the babe was birthed the right way round but her entry into the world stretched my lady's flesh too far and it tore quite badly in a couple of places.'

Aethelred gestured they should sit at a trestle away from the occupants of the hall and Mildrithe twisted to face him, her confident brown gaze on his as his thoughts darted in all directions. 'The ragged tears will need to be drawn together with a few stitches as soon as your wife has rested, which will greatly help the flesh to knit together. Needless to say, she will be in some pain for a while and continue to feel sore for a few weeks after that.'

Aethelred's concern for Aethelflaed welled. 'Is there anything you can give her to ease the pain…?'

'There are pain-easing medicines we could use under normal circumstances, my lord, like belladonna or willow bark.' Mildrithe's brow creased in thought. 'Unfortunately, even a few

Fifteen

drops of belladonna would be far too strong and keep Lady Aethelflaed asleep for long periods – not something we want with a new babe to care for. But willow bark is a possibility… though again, not whilst my lady is suckling the babe. Either potion would, doubtless, get into the milk, and who could say what it would do to such a tiny infant?'

'Then perhaps we need a wet nurse – though I'm not sure what Aethelflaed would think of that. She has mentioned many times how Lady Ealhswith would have no one but herself feed her babes.'

The midwife nodded. 'That is true. Lady Ealhswith was determined on this issue, but all women have their own views on the matter and I have yet to discuss things with your wife. If she chooses to feed the infant herself, we would need to rely on salves and ointments, which will, at least, bring some relief from the pain. As I said, for the first week after the stitching, she will be in much discomfort, even when merely sitting.'

She paused, glancing down at her hands, and Aethelred could see she was struggling to put her thoughts into words. At length, Mildrithe said, 'I must stress, my lord, that although the pain will gradually ease, the tears will need some time to fully heal and must not be exposed to… to anything that could cause them to reopen.'

Aethelred patted her clasped hands. 'Don't worry, I won't be demanding Aethelflaed joins me in my bed for quite some time. As you say, she needs time to heal, and all I want is for her to be free of pain.'

'Thank you, Lord Aethelred. I'll get back to the birthing room now and if my lady is awake, I'll discuss her intentions regarding feeding the child and the possible use of ointments and salves. I'm sure she will tell you of her decision next time you see her.'

By the end of the first week in June, Aethelflaed had been on her feet for over a week and between sessions of caring for Aelfwynn, had recommenced some of her duties around the hall. Though still undeniably sore and moving more slowly than was her norm, the willow bark she was now able to take afforded her a good deal more relief than the ointments she had used during the first two weeks following the birthing, when she had suckled the babe herself. But now, she was more than content to hand her daughter to Alys at feeding times, a pretty and motherly young wet nurse with a small boy of two of her own who was happy to play with his wooden shapes whilst his mother fed the new babe. After all, Aelfwynn was the second babe Alys had suckled since she had stopped nursing him, and he was used to it. And though Aethelflaed's love for her daughter was wholesome and strong, the act of feeding her and constantly feeling wet and sticky was something she would rather do without.

Aethelred seemed content with his role as overlord of Mercia. The ongoing building works around Lundenburh were coming along well and he'd organised several of his thegns to oversee their progress on a daily basis. But recently, he'd admitted to feeling the need to be further afield in the kingdom he loved so much, and Aethelflaed sensed he was considering doing just that.

'You know your father gave me free rein to make improvements in Mercia wherever I see fit,' he said one evening as

Fifteen

they sat in the hall, Alys having retired to her chamber to feed Aelfwynn and settle young Stepan in his bed for the night. Aethelflaed nodded, guessing her senses were about to be proven correct. 'Well I think it's about time we started fortifying some of our Mercian towns to the standard of your father's burhs in Wessex – and Lundenburh, of course.'

Seated beside him, Garth nodded, and Aethelflaed realised she was about to hear something the two of them had already discussed while she had been occupied with their new daughter. She swallowed down her rising indignation, knowing she had been in no state to take part in any discussions recently. 'Which did you have in mind to start on?' she asked. 'We have several towns along both the Welsh and the Danelaw borders in much need of improved defences.'

'That's true,' Aethelred admitted, 'but I had a conversation with Bishop Werferth when we were last in Winchester and he mentioned the neglected state of Worcester – which I know only too well after living there for a few years. He feels that the people in the city would be powerless to defend themselves should the Welsh attack; after all, Worcester is very close to the Welsh border. But it's also near enough to the Southern Sea to become a target for raiding Norsemen. They've raided settlements along both the northern coast of Devon and the southernmost Welsh kingdoms many times in the past, and if they continue up the River Severn, it will take them straight to Worcester.'

'Has Werferth discussed this with my father?'

Aethelred nodded. 'He has, and Alfred's response was as I said to you. He simply told Werferth to suggest that we undertake the fortifying of the city, since it is our concern anyway.'

'This talk with Werferth must have been some time ago. We haven't been to Worcester since before I became with child.'

'The very reason why I haven't mentioned my thoughts on it until now,' Aethelred said, reaching out to take Aethelflaed's hand. 'You were so unwell during those months, and I still had work in Lundenburh to occupy me then. But now that the quayside is more or less finished, I feel I could be of more service to Mercia by making improvements elsewhere.'

Aethelflaed nodded, knowing what her husband said was true, though she hated the thought of him leaving her behind, especially in a city she still found hard to like. 'Will you leave for Worcester soon?'

'Hopefully, within the next three or four weeks, once you're feeling able to cope with things. Garth and half a dozen thegns will be with us and I'll leave the other half dozen here with the servants to ensure the safety of the hall.' Aethelflaed nodded, seeing the sense in that. 'It's over a hundred and thirty miles to Worcester from here,' Aethelred went on, 'and with wagons to consider, we need to allow at least five days for the journey. I'll send a few men out to arrange meals and beds for the night in the halls of some of our thegns along our route and, of course, once we get there, we'll stay in my hall in Worcester.'

Aethelflaed's heart seemed to leap for joy. She wasn't to be left in Lundenburh after all. To be able to travel again meant so much to her. 'That all sounds perfect. Worcester is a lovely city and, I agree, its location alone demands its defences should be the best we can make them.'

Aethelred smiled at her enthusiasm. 'We'll only be away

Fifteen

for a few weeks for our first visit, Aethelflaed, just long enough to draw up plans for the outer wall, order the stone from the local quarry and hire some reliable men to do the work. I'm hoping we'll be ready to start the actual building work by mid-September, so it will be finished before the worst of the winter weather can hold us up.'

'I hope Alys will be happy to leave her hometown for a while,' Aethelflaed said, suddenly concerned that she might not be. 'She's never been away from Lundenburh in her life, so she might not like the idea at all and refuse to come with us.'

'Or she might be glad of a chance to see new places. I know I was, the first time King Alfred invited me to Winchester.'

Aethelflaed flashed Garth a smile. 'Then I must hope Alys will feel the same. After all, she has no family to consider other than Stepan and, as you know, her husband died of a fever soon after the child was born – which is why Alys has needed to earn coin as a wet nurse,'

'Then I don't see how she could refuse,' Aethelred said, 'especially if I offer her an extra piece of silver or two for her trouble. Alys is a sensible young woman who seems to love her position as wet nurse with us. Plus, she will also realise that if she refuses to come with us, Aethelflaed, it would mean that you would also be unable to come.'

Aethelflaed knew only too well what it would mean, and silently prayed Alys would be happy to see the city of Worcester. 'Alys is such a kind and cheerful person, and I don't ever want to lose her, even when Aelfwynn is weaned. I'm considering asking her to become our daughter's regular nurse… providing you have no objections to that. If she accepts, it will also mean

245

she won't have to be a wet nurse for the next twenty years!'

Aethelred shook his head. 'I think it's a splendid idea and I'm sure Alys will be more than happy to stay with you.'

'Unless she should marry again,' Garth put in, his eyes averted. 'I can think of many a man who would be happy to have a wife as kind and pretty as Alys, myself included.'

Aethelflaed laughed as Garth's cheeks took on a crimson glow. 'Indeed they would, and I suspect you may have a few rivals for her affections before too long; I've noticed several heads turning her way as she passes, both around the city and in this hall,'

Aethelred slapped his friend on the back, a smirk on his face. 'Don't worry, Garth, we won't reveal your feelings to anyone. We know how to keep a secret, don't we, Aethelflaed?'

'We most certainly do,' she agreed. 'Things will work out, one way or the other, in their own good time. Besides, I imagine Garth would never speak to either of us again if we so much as breathed a word of what he just said.'

*

Winchester, Wessex: late July 888

As the Wessex court prepared to travel to Wantage for the month of August, a messenger arrived from an aide of Pope Stephen in Rome. Although not entirely unexpected, given her age, news of the death of Alfred's beloved sister, Aethelswith, filled him with an aching sadness that alternated with periods of seething rage, aimed at her long-dead, selfish and cowardly

Fifteen

husband. If not for Burgred, Aethelswith would have spent her final years close to her family, who loved her dearly. Instead, she had spent the last fifteen years far away, first in Rome and then in Pavia, where she had recently been buried.

For two days, Ealhswith watched Alfred sink into a state of deep melancholy, in which memories dominated his thoughts. Aethelswith had been so dear to him as a child and her love for him could not be doubted. But once married to Burgred and living in Mercia, the odious man had rarely permitted his wife to visit the family she adored, nor was Alfred's family made welcome at his court.

Ealhswith felt his pain as he expressed his feelings to her and, for the most part, she could only agree. She had greatly admired and loved her beautiful and gentle sister-by-marriage.

'Come to bed, Alfred,' she said, finding him in a corner of the hall, long after the household had retired on the night before they were due to leave for Wantage. 'You'll be in no state to travel tomorrow if you do not. Your sister will be in our thoughts for some time, but you must take comfort in knowing that she is now at rest and with God. And we know from her letters that she had found solace in Rome for several years after Burgred died. I also believe that she and her daughter found happiness with the new friends they made from Pavia, which is probably why they moved to that town.'

'You're right, but news of my sister's death has caused my loathing of Burgred to resurface. I know it's wrong of me, especially since the man's been dead for almost twenty-five years, and I need to pray for forgiveness for succumbing to such unchristian thoughts before I try to sleep. I also need to write a note of condolence to Mildrede; she is, after all, my sister's only child, and the two of them were very close.

'I won't be long, I promise. As you implied, I don't want to be falling asleep on Pegasus. Good natured as he is, he might become a little anxious if I should suddenly slump in the saddle – or, worse still, slide right off.'

Ealhswith smiled at the thought, pleased that the dark clouds of mourning hanging over her husband were beginning to fade. 'Good, then think about Wantage and riding Pegasus across the Vale when it's swathed in its glorious summer foliage. A more pleasing image would be hard to find. Let us look forward to it together.'

*

August in Wantage passed far too quickly for Ealhswith, and tomorrow, the last day of the month, the court would begin its journey back to Winchester. As the sun sank to the western horizon, she sat in the hall, watching Alfred chatting to the scholars while the servants cleared away the remnants of the meal, and contemplated what a peaceful and carefree time they had all had. Now, summer was over and they had the glorious colours of autumn to look forward to… But they would see those colours in Winchester, not here in this lovely place.

Ealhswith and her children had spent many happy hours out in the sunshine, often riding across the Vale of White Horse, sometimes as far as the top of the Ridgeway to investigate the strangely shaped white horse, or the mysterious burial mound their people believed to have once been the home of

Fifteen

Wayland, the god of metal-working. Or to simply admire the views. At twelve and ten, Aethelgifu and Aelfthryth were already competent riders, but at only seven, Aethelweard rode in the same saddle as one of the bodyguards, or that of his father or elder brother when they were able to join them.

On days when Alfred and Edward stayed in the hall to work on affairs of state, they would walk alongside the winding chalk stream known as Letcombe Brook that flowed past the hall, or through the nearby woods, identifying the different trees or listening to birdsong in the canopy above. As long as their bodyguard was with them, Alfred was content to see his family enjoying themselves.

Ealhswith was so proud of her children. The three younger ones were growing fast, their individual talents and foibles becoming more evident with the passing months. Like Aethelgifu at seven, Aethelweard already showed signs of a studious nature and a deep love of learning. He would sit for hours, delving into work set by his tutor, or reading through texts written in their Saxon tongue. And Alfred had recently suggested to Asser that the boy should join him and Aethelgifu in their Latin lessons once they returned to Winchester.

In contrast, Aelfthryth showed little interest in studying, though she could read and write well enough and happily listened to stories being read to her. She was a pretty child, and like many children her age, she could be noisy and mischievous. But she had a loving nature and generally liked to please people. Ealhswith was certain that, one day, Aelfthryth would make someone a perfect wife.

Her thoughts turned to her middle daughter, Aethelgifu,

and she sighed. Now on the cusp of womanhood, the burden of living with the vivid birth stain on her brow had caused the girl to withdraw inside herself for many years. At an early age, she had begged to be allowed to wear a head veil that covered her brow to avoid the humiliation of anyone outside the family staring at her. Yet over the past year or so, Aethelgifu had learned to overcome her embarrassment, and for that, Ealhswith knew she had Asser to thank. The abbot had done all in his power to boost the girl's self-confidence and spent many hours helping to increase her knowledge and understanding of the scholarly pursuits she loved. So it came as no surprise to Ealhswith to hear Aethelgifu professing her love of God and her wish to enter a nunnery. Only time would tell if that desire would last.

As for Ealhswith's two elder children, no mother could be prouder of the adults they had become. News of the birth of Aethelflaed's daughter had filled her with joy and she could hardly wait to visit the family and meet her new grandchild. Aethelflaed's role as wife to the overlord of Mercia suited her well, and no one could doubt how happy she was to be with Aethelred. And Edward, her eldest son and heir to the throne, was fast becoming skilled in the many-faceted art of kingship. At seventeen he was tall and broad with dark good looks that were likely to melt the heart of many a young woman. It would not be too many years before he could be wed: after all, Alfred was only seventeen when he was married…

'That look on your face tells me your thoughts are not in this hall right now,' Edward said, bending to kiss his mother's cheek before sitting down beside her. 'We are all sorry to be

Fifteen

leaving, even Father, although he has so many things he wants to do now that summer's over, and he needs to be in Winchester to do them.'

'I know he has, and I'm happy to have had such a lovely time here. But I realise that Winchester is where we need to be. It's just that thinking about leaving tomorrow has filled my head with thoughts of you all and how fortunate I am to have such a wonderful family.'

She smiled at her son's intent gaze. 'Your father tells me the first thing he'll do when we get back to Winchester is instigate the building of the monastery on Athelney.'

Edward nodded. 'That's what he told me, too. A letter from Ealdorman Aethelnoth of Somerset arrived a few days ago, saying that all is ready. The plans Father drew up with Asser are with the men chosen to do the work and the timber Aethelnoth ordered is already on the isle. They're all just waiting for Father's signal to start. Let's hope they get most of the outer buildings up before the midwinter weather puts a stop to it.

'And while we've been here,' Edward continued, 'Asser has written to a monk in eastern Francia with the odd name of John the Old Saxon, requesting his presence at the Winchester court. Father is considering him for the role of the Athelney abbot. But as far as I know, there has been no reply from him yet – which is annoying Father quite a lot.'

Ealhswith laughed, glancing over to where Alfred was still sitting, now perusing more texts. 'You should know by now, Edward, that nothing makes your father more irritable than being kept waiting.'

'I learnt that years ago, Mother, and now I realise it's because he always does tasks promptly himself so he can't abide tardiness in others.'

Ealhswith could only agree, and looked steadily at her son. 'I'm wondering what else September will bring. We've seen so many changes in Wessex over the past few years, as well as enjoying a wonderful peace. Do you think peace will last?'

'We can only hope it will,' Edward replied with a shrug. 'But I must be honest and say that the many communications Father has had with Frankish scholars have led him to believe that our peace may soon be over.'

Ealhswith felt stricken, black clouds of battle suddenly obscuring the blue skies of her thoughts. Alfred had said nothing of this to her. 'But why? What is happening in Francia that could affect our kingdom?'

'Nothing is certain yet, Mother,' Edward said, giving her hand a squeeze, 'so please don't upset yourself. You know how Father is, and as the king, he has to be alert to the possibility of threats to our lands.'

'I realise that, Edward. Alfred has said so many times that it was his failure to consider likely future moves by the enemy in his younger years that lost him many battles against Halfdan and Guthrum. So, what is happening in Francia?'

'You knew that the Danes were raiding Paris again?'

'Yes, I had heard that much.'

'Well, after many assaults on the city, they failed to break through its formidable defences. Eventually, they laid siege to the place, a siege that dragged on and on until the Danes ran out of food – exactly what they'd hoped would happen to the Parisians. In the end the Danes were forced to accept

Fifteen

the terms offered by the emperor, Charles the Fat. According to Archbishop Fulco, he offered them seven hundred pounds of silver on the understanding that they would sail on, up the Seine to eastern Francia and Burgundy to continue their raiding if they so wished.'

Edward paused, and Ealhswith knew her feelings about such an act would be showing on her face. 'It sounds unbelievable, I know,' he continued, 'but Charles actually assured them he'd turn a blind eye to their raids in those regions if they agreed to leave Paris alone.'

'And he calls himself a Christian emperor!' Ealhswith shook her head. 'How could any god-fearing ruler do that? He actually gave free rein to bands of callous, thieving pagans to raid any part of his empire on the understanding they leave his own little domain alone?'

Edward nodded. 'That's what Archbishop Fulco said, so Father thinks it won't be long before the Danes bleed those regions dry and set their sights elsewhere. And he's convinced that the "elsewhere" will be our lands.

'But on a positive note, Mother, if the Danes do come back, they won't find Wessex the same place it was the last time they invaded. Our network of burhs and the prompt responses of our standing armies – both in the fortified towns and the mounted armies in the field – make easy travel though our kingdom a thing of the past.'

Ealhswith's heart swelled at the pride she saw in her son's eyes. 'I pray to God that by the time you are king, Edward, the Danes will have left our lands for good.'

Sixteen

Aros, Danish lands: early September 888

As noon approached, Bjorn appeared in the doorway of Eadwulf's longhouse, a smile on his face as he glanced around. Freydis and Yrsa were busy at their looms while three-year-old Thora played with her toys on a blanket on the rushes under the watchful eye of a young serving girl.

'Good morning, brother,' Freydis said warmly, staying her hand guiding the shuttle between the threads. 'If you're looking for Eadwulf, he's in the stables with Hamid and Básim.'

'Ah… The foaling?'

Freydis nodded. 'It's the mare's second season, and though it's a little late in the year for foaling, we aren't expecting problems, so feel free to go and have a word with him.'

'I was hoping to speak with all of you, so I'll go and see if they'll be back soon.'

'I wonder what that's all about,' Yrsa said once Bjorn had gone. 'It can't be anything bad with that smile on his face.'

'Exactly what I thought, but Bjorn has always liked to keep people guessing, even when he's had little of interest to say. We'll find out what's on his mind soon enough.' Freydis suddenly stopped and scrutinised the bleary-eyed face of her adopted daughter. 'Go and rest for a while, Yrsa. You've done nothing but yawn all morning and you won't get much weaving done if you're feeling unwell. Your husband will say the same when he gets back.'

Sixteen

'I'm fine, Freydis, and I've told Hamid that many times. Though I never thought carrying a child could make anyone feel so wretched – and I've still got six months to go. Sometimes I feel so tired I could nod off where I sit – or even stand. Ameena mentioned the same last year when she was carrying Einarr, but to my shame I thought she was exaggerating. Now I understand the reality of it all.'

Freydis reached out and stroked Yrsa's pale cheek. 'I've known some women to truly blossom during their term, dear one, but generally not in the early months when the sickness affects so many of us. Ameena positively glowed during her later months, and I'm sure you will be the same.'

Before the conversation could continue, the men arrived back, Bjorn with them. 'If we all gather round, I'll explain why I'm here,' Bjorn said, striding across the room and sitting on a bench alongside a trestle. The others followed and waited for him to start and eventually he said, 'Dainn arrived in my hall last night saying he's done with raiding.'

Freydis gasped. 'Dainn's here... with you? Why hasn't he been to see me?'

'That's easy to answer, sister. He had no idea where Eadwulf's homestead was until he'd seen me. And,' he added, holding up a hand to halt Freydis' next question, 'it was far too late when he got here last night for us to traipse over fields to see you. He–'

'Did he tell you where he's been for the past three years?'

Bjorn heaved a sigh, his annoyance belied by the grin on his face. 'He did, and I'll tell you if you give me the chance.'

Freydis reached across the trestle and patted her brother's

hand, returning his grin with a guilty smile. 'Sorry, I won't interrupt again. I'm just so impatient to know how he is.'

'Hmm,' Bjorn huffed. 'Now, where was I? Oh yes… Dainn arrived in Ribe in mid-August and after a short stay with Aguti, he decided to come and see you. He'd been–'

'Is he waiting in your hall?'

'No, Mother, I'm here,' Dainn said, stepping through the partially open doorway.

Freydis flew across the hall, leaving Bjorn in mid-sentence, and flung her arms around the son she hadn't seen for seven years before pushing him to arm's length to look him up and down. Satisfied he hadn't been maimed in any way she led him to sit beside her at the table, relief coursing through her. She had feared she would never see him again. 'So, you decided to leave Hastein and come home. What made you change your mind?'

'I suppose I just realised a little later than Aguti that I didn't want to spend the rest of my life raiding. I want to settle down and raise a family, though I've yet to decide where I want to do that. I would not impose upon Aguti to take me in, especially now he has a new wife of his own.'

Freydis understood her son's reasoning. 'You've met Kristen then?' Dainn nodded. 'Then you will know that she and Aguti look forward to the birth of their first child just before the Yule?'

'I do, and I can say that Kristen's a good wife to my brother, and a lot more agreeable than Frida. I was relieved to find he'd divorced that one. She had a spiteful nature and a vicious tongue, but Kristen is just the opposite. She is kind and cheerful, and makes Aguti happy, and he's overjoyed that

Sixteen

he's soon to be a father. Seeing them together made me even more determined to have the same in my life.'

'We all agree about Frida… and about Kristen,' Yrsa put in. 'The two are as different as night and day.'

Freydis took her son's hands in her own. 'I can't tell you how happy I am to hear you want to settle down. I've been so worried while you've been out there, raiding. The dread of hearing you'd been killed rarely left me and –'

'Now we need to find you somewhere to live,' Bjorn finished for her. Freydis glared at him, then nodded, realising that now wasn't the time to put voice to her fears.

Dainn shook his head. 'Thank you, Uncle, but this isn't your problem and I would not impose on you, either. I'll travel for a while and, hopefully, find somewhere I can build a homestead.'

'As you wish, of course, but if you change your mind, I have plenty of available land here, either further along the coast or a short way upstream, close enough to the River Aros for your water supply.'

'Think about what Bjorn is offering, Dainn,' Freydis pleaded, searching her son's eyes. 'To have you nearby would mean so much to all of us.'

'You'd be welcome to stay with us until your own home is built,' Eadwulf added. 'And if you choose a site close enough, we can also help with the building work.' He gestured to Hamid and Básim who nodded in agreement. 'If we start soon, it should be ready well before the Yule.'

Dainn glanced round the grinning faces. 'How could I refuse an offer like that? It's far more than I deserve after deserting you all for so many years, and I–'

'Hush,' Freydis urged, placing a finger on her son's lips. 'You are here now, and that is all that matters.'

'Tell us, Dainn, where was Hastein's band when you left? Three years ago, he told us he was planning to strike Paris the following year and news of the city being assaulted has reached us from several sources. We supposed it was my cousin's doing. Was it?'

Dainn's face became sombre as he glanced at his family and friends waiting for his answer. 'It was, and I was with his band when the attack was made, Bjorn, starting in the spring, two years ago. But, as large as Father's army was, our every attempt to gain entry to the city was prevented by its strong outer defences – not to mention the Frankish soldiers lining the walls. They blasted us with arrows whenever we got near, as well as hurling burning hot oil, wax, and pitch over the walls. After several weeks and the loss of many of our men, Hastein ordered us to lay siege to the place in the hope of starving them into submission.'

He shook his head, a mirthless laugh escaping his throat. 'As we later learned, Paris was well stocked with food and there are a couple of wells behind its walls, beside which the Franks had ways of getting in and out of the city unseen by us. The siege lasted throughout the rest of that year and until the following spring. The long, icy winter months were the worst and by March we were running out of food and ready to give up the siege. Only later did we discover that the Parisians were smitten by disease and desperate to bury the mounds of reeking bodies, and would have been unable to hold out for much longer.'

Sixteen

'Are you saying the siege was abandoned and you moved elsewhere to raid?'

'Not exactly, Eadwulf. We did leave but, in the end, we were not totally empty-handed. As I said, the Franks had places where they could get in and out of the city despite our siege lines, and once the snows cleared in March, the city leader, Count Odo, must have sent out for help. The next thing we knew, we were surrounded by a vast army of the Frankish emperor, Charles the Fat. We all thought we'd be slaughtered where we stood, but no attack came. Instead, Charles offered Hastein seven hundred pounds of silver to leave Paris alone and continue his raids in Burgundy, further east.

'Needless to say, Father accepted, and to give him his due, he shared the silver out between all of us. But by that time, a couple of shiploads of men had decided they'd had enough and wanted to sail home. I confess, Hastein wasn't too surprised when I told him I wanted to go with them – he'd always known my love of raiding was not as strong as his, and that I wanted the chance to settle down. And the silver he gave me ensured I didn't rely on my shipmates to pay for my food during the passage home. As far as I know, Hastein is still raiding out in Burgundy and I have no idea where he intends to raid after that.'

Bjorn absently scratched his head, a wistful look in his eyes. 'I often think about him and wonder if he'll ever come home. We had some good times when we were young, and Eadwulf was with us for some of them.' Eadwulf nodded, though Freydis knew that her husband's memories of that particular venture into Francia were not altogether happy ones.

'Raids on Paris were not so difficult then,' Bjorn continued, 'and many bands of our countrymen tried their luck with the city, which doubtless resulted in the building of those defences you spoke of, Dainn.

'But now I'll leave you in peace, and tomorrow morning well take a look at a few possible sites for this homestead of yours.' He clasped Dainn's arm across the trestle. 'It's good to have you in Aros, Dainn, and you've made your mother a very happy woman.' He glanced at his sister and grinned. 'And you know what…? You'll make her even happier when you find yourself a wife.'

*

Winchester, Wessex: November 888 - March 889

The autumn weather held dry and mild and many of the buildings of what would become a fine monastery on the Isle of Athelney were well underway. The outer, wood-planked walls and thick, reed-thatched roof of the church filled Alfred with pride, and the dormitory, kitchen, refectory, library and scriptorium had also begun to take shape. By the time he returned to Winchester in early November after a two-week stay on the isle, a cubiculum had also been started. It was essential for the abbot, prior and senior members of the community to have their own private place from which to conduct the business of running the monastery, including keeping a careful record of its financial incomings and outgoings.

As yet, the stables, byre, workshops and storage huts and

Sixteen

other features necessary to the working life of the community were little more than markings on the ground, but Alfred had every confidence in his workmen, most of whom were Fenmen, to complete the outer walls of all structures before the snows or heavy rainfall of winter made further outdoor work difficult, if not impossible. Throughout those cold, bleak months they would make pieces of indoor furniture, and women in the area had agreed to weave woollen blankets for the beds, and stuff large sacks with straw for use as mattresses. As long as Alfred sent the materials, they were more than happy to earn a little coin for their efforts.

There seemed so much to be done, and all must be ready by spring when Alfred planned to officially appoint John the Old Saxon as abbot before any hopeful monks made an appearance. He had great hopes for this man, considering he'd been a monk for some years in a monastery in the far eastern Frankish lands. He would know exactly how one should be organised and run.

John arrived in Winchester two weeks prior to Archbishop Fulco's favourite, Grimbald of Saint Bertin. Alfred was immediately impressed by John, whose ready conversation and sharp mind became evident as they spoke, and his years of experience in military encounters impressed him even more so. Alfred smiled to himself, realising that John reminded him of a number of warrior bishops he'd known in the past: men like Bishops Ealhstan and Heahmund, and a man he'd truly respected, Ceolnoth, Archbishop of Canterbury who had crowned Alfred's beloved brother, Aethelred. Like those men, John was tall, muscular and broad shouldered, and despite the restrictive dark robes of his Benedictine order, his agility could not be disguised.

Yes, Alfred decided, John would make the perfect abbot for his Athelney monastery, and until next spring, his experience in teaching would be a great asset in his hall.

Compared to John, Grimbald was a quiet and reserved man, evidently used to spending time on his own, and in no way suitable for the very public role of Archbishop of Canterbury desired for him by the archbishop of Rheims. Alfred had no intention of elevating an unknown priest – especially a Frankish one – to such a position in the Saxon Church and was relieved to hear Grimbald's thoughts on the matter.

'I have never sought to hold such an exalted position, my lord,' Grimbald said, once introductions to Alfred's court had been made and Alfred outlined possible roles for him in Wessex, stressing that Fulco's request for him was not one of them. 'I can only wonder why the archbishop should believe me capable of holding a position of such responsibility. The role of archbishop demands a leader of influence and authority, and I confess, I am neither of those things.' He shook his head at the thought. 'I am a humble mass priest, and would be more than happy to serve you in that manner. I am also a scholar; learning means much to me, and to work with you and your companions on Latin translations and teach others of your countrymen to read and write would give me great pleasure.'

'Then you will be my own personal mass priest, and hear my weekly confessions,' Alfred replied, taking a liking to this self-effacing man. 'And there will be plenty of work for you in my hall, including teaching some of my thegns to read and write. I agree, the position of Archbishop of Canterbury is a distinguished one that does require a certain exuberance and would be better suited to someone with more experience in dealing with people.'

Alfred reached out and clasped the priest's arm. 'Welcome to Wessex, Grimbald. I hope you enjoy your work with us and that some of your enthusiasm for learning rubs off on my thegns.'

*

In mid-March the following year, John the Old Saxon was appointed Abbot of Athelney and Alfred stayed on the isle, anticipating a goodly number of both potential and experienced monks to arrive over the next few weeks. Yet by the end of April, no more than four had made an appearance, which worried Alfred. He was anxious to see the monastery at work, perhaps even a few crops sown ready for this year's harvest, before he returned to Winchester.

John, too, was puzzled by the lack of interest from the Saxons. 'It is, indeed, unusual,' he murmured to Alfred, as they wandered round the monastery site, discussing the situation. 'In my experience, the opening of a new monastery attracts potential monks like bees to the honey pot, and often many are turned away, disappointed. Athelney could not be better placed for monks seeking peace and solitude away from the noise of everyday life, so I am struggling to see where the problem lies.'

'True,' Alfred agreed, 'but you know, the more I think about this, the more I'm convinced the lack of interest is because Saxons are fearful. Many of our monasteries and abbeys have been raided and even burnt down by the Danes over the years, their monks killed or grievously wounded.'

'We have lost many beautiful monasteries in Francia, too, lord, but our priests and monks have been united in refusing to be denied their calling.' John nodded as he thought about that. 'And your kingdom is not presently invaded, so surely men who feel the need to serve God would be willing to turn again to the Church and other religious houses to work for the good of the community.'

'Perhaps, but people have long memories. We've believed Wessex to be safe from their cursed raids before, but then they've come back. We might have had over ten years of relative peace this time, but as long as the Danes are active across the Narrow Sea, we all fear that peace could soon be over.'

John stroked his tonsured head. 'Are you saying we must put aside all hopes of establishing the monastery on Athelney, King Alfred?'

'No, I'm saying we must look elsewhere for monks to fill it. If, as you say, there are men in Francia seeking monasteries in which to serve, it seems to me that Francia is where we must look. It may well be too late for growing corn this year by the time we get any of them here, but with the four monks you have got, a vegetable garden could be created, and I can send men out to purchase livestock for you and ferry them over to the isle, or across the causeway if it's showing. We'll buy a bull and few milch cows, as well as a few young females to start with, as well as some older stock to keep you supplied in beef. A few goats and hens would also be useful. All you need to do while you wait, is to ensure the byre and outside enclosures

Sixteen

are ready to put them in.

'It's not in my nature to give up, John, so once I'm back in Winchester, I'll write to Archbishop Fulco and some Saxon scholars known to be working in Francia, and request a list of any monks and priests who would be happy to serve God in a new monastery, and any families of the old Gallic race in need of a home.'

John's eyes opened wide. 'Gallic families, lord?'

Alfred held out his hands, his shoulders hunched. 'What better way to ensure monks for the future of this monastery than to have the children of families left homeless by Danish raids educated here? I'm hoping that in future years, some of those children will feel able to join your monastic order. But only time will tell how it will all work out.'

*

Once back in Winchester, Alfred was true to his word. Letters were duly written and sent to various parts of Francia, and although he knew it could take months, he eagerly awaited the replies, particularly regarding the Gallic families. It seemed to him that homeless people would jump at the chance of having permanent roofs over their heads, of being regularly fed, and clothed in garments that were not filthy rags. But Alfred curbed his impatience by turning his thoughts to planning his new abbey at Shaftesbury.

'I was pleased with the way the Athelney monastery turned out,' he said yet again as he and Asser set out a blank parchment on a trestle at the side of the Winchester hall with the plan of the Athelney monastery beside it. 'And I remain hopeful that by next year it's filled with Francian monks and Gallic families.'

He said no more on that subject. Asser had heard it all before and the poor man didn't deserve to be constantly bombarded with Alfred's hopes. 'So,' he said, refocusing on his proposed new abbey, 'as far as I can see, the nuns will need the same types of buildings as the monks at Athelney – in which case, Shaftesbury Abbey could probably be built to the same design.'

Asser laughed. 'In that case, my lord, surely we don't need the new parchment? I would think the builders can work from this plan.'

'That's true regarding the positioning of the buildings,' Alfred said, his brow creasing in thought, 'but Shaftesbury will be an abbey rather than a small monastery, so the buildings need to be on a grander scale. For a start, I intend the church to be built of stone. There's no shortage of beautiful limestone in Dorset, after all. I was content to have the church at Athelney built of wood simply because of the difficulty we would have had in transporting heavy stone across to the isle.'

Alfred took the abbot's nod as agreement and pushed on, 'A stone church will need skilled men to build it, so perhaps some of our scholars will know of reputable builders and stonemasons in their home regions.' He paused, knowing his next statement would get Asser's attention. 'I also want at least one stained-glass window fitted into the church and a number of sculpted statues of some of the saints and such like to adorn the inside.'

The abbot's eyebrows rose considerably, though he kept his thoughts to himself. Alfred knew he'd be thinking that although

Sixteen

stained-glass windows were not unknown, the cost made them unattainable by many. 'And since Shaftesbury Abbey is to be a nunnery,' he continued, 'I am very aware of the need to make it as safe for the women as possible. The encircling wall will also be of stone, high and thick, with perhaps only a single sturdy oak gate barred by metal strips. If the Danes come back, a nunnery would be a prime target and they've invaded Dorset before. Yes, Abbot, I truly fear for the women's safety, despite the fact that it will be on the edge of the town. And once the nunnery is running, I will ensure a section of the Dorset standing army is stationed close by.

'As for the work around the site, the nuns will have no choice other than to tend the gardens, workshops and farm themselves, although there's bound to be plenty of local cottars willing to earn a few coins for undertaking some of the heavier tasks.'

'Are you still planning to appoint Aethelgifu as abbess?'

'I am, Abbot, but I have no intention of telling her until the abbey is built and ready for use, which is not likely to be for a couple of years. By that time, my daughter will be fifteen, an age when many young women are married. I've no doubt Aethelgifu could handle the financial and administrative sides of abbey life even now, but another two years will give her greater confidence in herself in dealing with people and, hopefully, an air of strict authority, especially as some of the new nuns will probably be much older than her.'

Asser smiled and nodded, and Alfred knew how fond the abbot was of Aethelgifu, as well as being extremely proud of her achievements. His daughter had taken to Latin with ease and in so short a time was happily reading and translating prayers and hymns alongside his resident scribes and clerics. Alfred's middle daughter was a true scholar, and had no interest in becoming a wife. Aethelgifu already felt the Church to be her calling and Alfred was determined to enable her to embrace it.

'Speaking of appointments, Lord Abbot... You know that Bishop Wulfsige of Sherborne has been very ill since Christmastide?'

Asser nodded. 'He was confined to his bed the last time I visited him in late February, and I have to agree, even then I feared he might not last another week.'

'His physicians now fear the same, and though I will mourn the loss of a good and wise bishop, I will soon need to appoint a suitable replacement for him.'

'And you would like my thoughts on the matter? Leave it with me, lord. I just need a little time to consider who is available for the post before we can discuss it.'

'No need to do that, Abbot, I've already selected an eminently able and reliable cleric for the position. I just need to approach him with the offer and see how he responds.'

'May I ask who you have in mind, lord?'

'You can, Lord Asser. It's you.'

*

Chippenham, Wessex: April 890

At the beginning of April, the Wessex court arrived at Chippenham, where it would spend the Eastertide before moving on to Wedmore for May and moving back to Winchester for

Sixteen

the summer. Ealhswith loved spending time at Alfred's various manors and being with people she hadn't seen for months. She was also looking forward to the arrival of Aethelflaed and Aethelred with their young daughter, Aelfwynn, in June. It seemed so long since they'd been together in Lundenburh at Christmastide. There was so little time for family visits, with everyone busy with affairs of state and building schemes. Whilst Alfred had been concentrating on his new monastery and abbey, Aethelred and Aethelflaed had been spending weeks at a time in Gloucester, setting up a new priory dedicated to Saint Oswald. Ealhswith looked forward to hearing their progress in that.

How fast the years seemed to pass. Ealhswith could hardly believe that by June, little Aelfwynn would have passed her second birthday, and her own youngest child, Aethelweard, would be nine later this year. And had Winfrith not died, he would have been six…

She put all sad thoughts from her head, determined to embrace the joys of spring and peace in their lands.

A week following the Eastertide, three of Aethelred's men arrived from Lundenburh with news for Alfred. The messengers bowed before him in the Chippenham hall and their spokesman withdrew a folded parchment from a leather bag attached to his belt.

'Our ealdorman wasn't sure that the news from East Anglia would have reached you in Chippenham yet, lord, and instructed us to see you got his missive with all possible speed. He also said to assure you that he'd be keeping his ears open regarding future developments.'

Ealhswith watched her husband reading Aethelred's message, hardly daring to breathe and dreading to hear that the East Angles were invading Wessex again – or Lundenburh, so close to the Anglian lands. Guthrum was old now, and not the powerful, feared ruler he used to be, and if his subjects had lost faith in his leadership and returned to their old ways of raiding and looting, Alfred would have no other choice that to confront them.

'By the time you receive this notice, my lord,' Alfred read Aethelred's words out loud, 'Aethelstan will have been dead for a little over two weeks and given Christian burial in a churchyard in Thetford. As yet, no one has been chosen to rule in his place and we've had no reports regarding who the contenders might be. Nor have we heard rumours of unrest in the Anglian kingdom, but my spies in Thetford will keep me informed if that should change.'

'So, Guthrum is dead,' Ealhswith said, feeling no sorrow on hearing that news. The Dane would happily have seen her husband dead, had he been the victor at Edington. 'And the East Anglian Danes are without a leader.' She acknowledged Alfred's thoughtful nod. 'Does that bode ill for Wessex? Could those leaderless men return to their pagan ways and again invade our lands?'

Alfred shook his head. 'Until they have an overall leader, I think that unlikely. And even then, it would depend on whether Aethelstan's successor is Christian or pagan, honourable or otherwise. As my godson – and to honour his baptism – I would imagine Aethelstan would have appointed at least *some* Christians to his Council. All we know for sure is that he kept his vows to me regarding not invading Wessex again, but no successor will feel bound by those vows.'

Alfred's amber gaze swept the listeners in his hall: his family, his resident thegns, scholars, servants and messengers. 'My biggest fear is that if the East Anglian Danes remain free to make their own decisions regarding who they show allegiance to, some of them will be tempted to join the Norse bands now raiding in Francia and the Low Countries. From what we hear, there are hundreds of them beleaguering those lands.'

Alfred threw back his head as though beseeching the heavens for assistance. 'When the day dawns that those bands tire of Francia and set their sights on Wessex, that, my friends, will definitely become our problem. But until then, we continue to improve our defences and keep our armies strong. I fear it won't be long before they are put to the test.'

Seventeen

Boulogne, Francia: August - September 892

The once Roman port of Boulogne on the coast of northern Francia heaved with disgruntled and increasingly worried Norsemen. In June, the bands of Danes who had wreaked havoc plundering the country for the last ten years had broken camp, fleeing to their ships and horses, intent on reaching the coast and sailing elsewhere. Behind them, devastation reigned – and for once, the marauders were not responsible. In early May, a wicked blight had swept the land, destroying all crops in its path, and with no food sources left, the Franks and their livestock were soon dropping like flies. The Danes were determined not to join them.

August was nearing an end and they'd been skulking around Boulogne for two whole months. Provisions in the town were almost exhausted and, like their comrades in other bands, Hastein's men had resorted to fishing. He squinted into the lowering sun as he watched the ships bobbing about a short distance from the quay and hoped their nets would be better filled than they had been yesterday. He thanked the gods that although their meals were flavourless and dull, at least they were keeping them alive.

All bands were desperate to get away, to sail across the Narrow Sea to a land where food was plentiful. Yet, with the many women and children who had joined them, and the dozens of horses acquired, there were too few ships to carry them.

Seventeen

Hastein's band alone needed another three or four vessels and other groups were far bigger than his. Who else could supply those ships than the citizens of Boulogne? Surely, they'd see the wisdom of providing the Danes' only means of leaving? If they did not, both Franks and Danes would soon succumb to starvation.

But as the days passed and no ships appeared, a change of tactics became necessary, and a hastily arranged meeting between Norse leaders and town councillors proved most rewarding. The good citizens fervently agreed that finding ships for their oppressors was infinitely preferable to watching a dozen of their number put daily to the sword.

Over the next two weeks, ships began to appear in the harbour, seemingly from nowhere. By the first week in September there were more than enough to provide comfortable passage for the entire company of Danes. Hastein's fleet now numbered eighty ships and the larger force, collectively, an impressive two hundred and fifty.

By the end of the second week of September, the ships were loaded and ready to leave the beleaguered port and its disease-wracked hinterland. Hastein smiled to himself, imagining what lay ahead. On the other side of the Narrow Sea was Wessex, a wealthy kingdom, as yet unconquered and ripe for the taking. The Saxons wouldn't stand a chance against the combined force of thousands of men.

He gripped the hilt of his sword, its comforting feel stirring long-forgotten memories of conflict. It was too long since he'd seen action and he looked forward to pitching his wits against the great King Alfred that Eadwulf seemed so fond of. And, much as Hastein had come to admire and love the Mercian, Eadwulf had stolen the heart of the woman he adored – and above all else, he was not a Dane. Besides, Eadwulf was in Aros, whereas Alfred was straight ahead.

Hastein mulled over their carefully laid plans, feeling confident they would work. The great fleet of three hundred and thirty ships would sail for Kent, all but Hastein's eighty aiming for the south coast where they would establish a base from which to strike at churches and settlements to their hearts' content. Hastein's ships would head further north, sail into the mouth of the Thames to make landfall on the north coast of Kent and raid settlements there. The two-pronged attack to his kingdom was intended to cause the Saxon king such confusion he would not know which way to turn.

Hastein approved of the plan, but in choosing the north coast of Kent he also had another idea in mind. News of discontented Danes in East Anglia had been reaching his ears for some time – as had news of Guthrum's death two years ago. As King Alfred's Christian godson, Guthrum had stifled the way of life of many red-blooded Danes. To be unable to raid and plunder made men resentful and bitter, like caged birds, desperate to break free and just fly; to live their lives in the way that generations of Danes before them had done.

Yes, Hastein mused, many East Anglians would jump at the chance to bring doom to the king who had brought them so low. The mighty King Alfred would soon be on his knees, grovelling for mercy.

*

Seventeen

Winchester and Maidstone, Wessex: mid-September 892

Aethelred chuckled to himself as he watched his young daughter following Aelfthryth around the busy Winchester hall. At twelve, Aelfthryth had a caring and motherly way with younger children and had taken it upon herself to keep her little niece amused during their two-week stay at Winchester. Aethelred knew Alys was pleased, as it gave her a little more time to keep on top of her many chores, as well as freeing a little of her time to be with her new husband, Garth.

'My sister has got a way of dealing with little ones,' Aethelflaed said, as though reading Aethelred's mind as she sat down next to him. 'She'll make a wonderful mother one day, just like our own mother. Ealhswith was at her happiest when we were all young.'

'My mother was the same. Leoflaed would probably have had at least another three children if she hadn't died in childbed.' Aethelred looked levelly at the wife he adored, and lowered his voice 'I can understand you not wanting any more children, but that you rarely want me in your bed is a torment I don't deserve.'

Aethelflaed turned away, staring silently at Aelfthryth amusing Aelfwynn with her puppets. Aethelred bristled. This wasn't the first time his wife had refused to be drawn into this conversation. He reached out and laid his hand on her arm, resting it there until she turned back 'You must trust me to be careful – as I have been on the few occasions we've been in the same bed since Aelfwynn was born. My seed does not have to be spilled inside you, as we have proved.'

'More than anything I want us to be close, Aethelred, and yes, you have managed to spill your seed outside my body so far,' Aethelflaed admitted, eventually facing him, the struggle she fought with herself reflected in her eyes. 'I'm just terrified of being with child again and going through all the pain of the birthing. Next time could even be worse and the babe, or I, could die. No Aethelred, I won't go through months of worry to be rewarded by weeks of pain, or agonising loss.'

Aethelflaed stood and headed over to join Ealhswith, as always, their failing relationship and the problem of sharing their bed unresolved. His wife seemed intent on forcing him to take a concubine.

Aethelred heaved a sigh, putting such thoughts from his mind. As so often in the late afternoon, women were busy either at their looms or tapestries, or preparing foods for the evening meal, and Alfred was still working with the scholars. Edward and Garth had headed outside for some air and Aethelred suddenly felt the need to join them, perhaps even suggest a ride out.

'We're over here, by the barn,' Edward yelled, waving at Aethelred as he wandered around the outbuildings looking for them. 'We wondered how long it would be before you'd had enough of the noisy hall.'

'It's a perfect autumn day,' Garth added, shading his eyes from the sunlight as Aethelred sat beside them on the mound of straw. 'We've been watching some of the servants threshing the wheat and others loading sacks with vegetables and forest fruits for the winter. It looked a good crop of apples.'

'Hmmm,' Aethelred murmured, shaking his head and

Seventeen

tutting at his two friends. 'In other words, you're just sitting here doing nothing.'

'That just about sums it up,' Edward admitted. 'But now you're out here as well, I have a problem I'd like to talk to you both about.'

Garth shrugged, indicating he had no idea what this 'problem' was either, and Aethelred said, 'We're all ears, but that doesn't mean that either of us can offer suitable advice.'

'But you're both married men so you might understand.'

Aethelred and Garth shared a look, both determined not to laugh at the worried look on Edward's handsome face.

'As you know, I had my twenty-first birthday in January,' Edward started. They both nodded. 'Father thinks I should wed – but I haven't met anyone I like enough to marry… Well,' he amended, 'that isn't strictly true. There is one woman, but she's the youngest daughter of the portreeve in Swanage and I'm not sure Father would think her grand enough for me.'

Aethelred reached out and patted Edward's arm. 'You do your father an injustice in thinking that. I'm sure he'd be pleased to know you like a woman enough to want to marry her. If she'd have been a ceorl's daughter, it might have been different, but a portreeve's a respected position.'

'So, you both think I should mention her name to my father and, of course, tell him how happy I'd be to wed her?'

Garth nodded, 'I agree with Aethelred. Your father would prefer you to be happy than to marry someone you either don't like or don't even know. So, what's her name and is she beautiful?'

Edward threw back his dark head and laughed. 'She is very

beautiful, with glossy dark hair and bright blue eyes, and a body a man could die for. Her name is Ecgwynn.'

'Then what's holding you back?'

Edward looked momentarily speechless before a smile creased his face. 'Nothing at all, Garth. I'll tell my father as soon as I get him alone.'

*

The following morning, three messengers arrived at the Winchester hall, begging audience with the king and falling to their knees as Alfred approached, flanked by Edward, Aethelred and Garth.

'You have news for me?' he asked, indicating they should rise.

'Ealdorman Aethelbold sent us, lord. The Danes are in Kent!'

Alfred's heart seemed to skip a beat and he prayed he would hear it was only a small band, raiding randomly along the coast. 'Go on,' he ordered the spokesman.

'Two groups of them, a huge fleet making landfall in the south and a smaller one on the north coast.' Alfred stared at the man, causing him to momentarily falter before he added, 'Reports say there are two hundred and fifty ships in the south and around eighty in the north.'

A deep groan escaped from Alfred's throat. 'These two groups arrived at the same time?'

'Within a day of each other is the most accurate we can say, lord. Those in the south were the first to arrive.'

Seventeen

'Where were they both when you left?'

'The southern fleet rowed about four miles up the River Rother until they reached the edge of the great forest, Andredesweald. The first thing they did was raid a half-finished burh at Castle Toll and kill all the workmen there. But that was almost three days ago and they've probably moved elsewhere by now. The smaller fleet sailed into the Thames and set up base on the Swale Marshes on the north coast of Kent across from the Isle of Sheppey. But they could also have moved on by now.'

Alfred nodded. 'Have the shire's field armies been called?

'Aethelbold was doing that as we left, lord, and they'll muster at Maidstone, close to the middle of Kent.'

'Exactly what I would have done,' Alfred said, his mind working fast. 'Whatever else we do we need to make sure these two bands don't link up, or even contact each other. If, as you say, there are around three hundred and thirty ships in total, we could be facing many thousands of Danes and I'd rather face them as two separate bands than one enormous force. As things stand, we'll need as many men from our shires as possible.'

No one moved, the stillness in the room reflecting Alfred's tension.

'Messengers will ride to the ealdormen of Berkshire and Sussex with orders to lead their armies to Maidstone as soon as possible and you will do o the same in Surrey on your way back to Aethelbold. I'll leave here once the Hampshire armies are mustered, and if we start alerting them immediately, that could be the day after tomorrow.'

Alfred paused, considering the task ahead, determined not to let it daunt him. He'd faced huge armies before, and prayed that these bands would not be joined by more of their countrymen. 'I'll also send men to the ruling Danes in East Anglia, whoever they might be since Aethelstan's death. They need a reminder of the oaths their former king made to me to keep the peace between us. I also want further oaths from them that they will resist joining these new bands of their countrymen in Kent.

'Edward, you will take charge here. You'll have several contingents of the Hampshire armies to raise should any of these Danes attempt to take Winchester, or any other part of the shire. I intend to leave you with between two and three hundred men, and all will be ready, should you call. And of course, Radulf will be in Southampton should you need his advice. His physicians won't allow him to travel here, of course.'

A wave of deep sadness spread through Alfred at the thought that this would be the first time since his crowning that Radulf was not riding beside him. Well past his sixtieth year, old age and illness had suddenly caught him up and he was barely able to ride, let alone fight. But he remained his usual cheerful and clear-thinking self and Alfred saw no reason for relieving him of his position as Ealdorman of Hampshire just yet. Radulf had two strong sons, both capable of seeing his orders were carried through.

'I'll notify Aethelhelm in Wiltshire to ensure his armies will be ready to join yours if the need arises,' he added and Edward nodded. 'I'll also send the same request to the ealdormen of Dorset and Somerset.'

He turned to his son-by-marriage. 'You and Garth need to get back to Lundenburh, the sooner the better. Summon as

Seventeen

many of your Mercian troops as possible and ensure the town is as impregnable and as well defended as it can be. You would also be wise to have an army ready in the event of attacks in Mercia itself. The Danes camped on the north coast of Kent could well sail up the Thames and attack the city, or they could just as easily spread into Mercian countryside. Pray God they haven't done either already.'

'We left the city in good hands and well defended,' Aethelred replied, 'and the new walls are unlikely to be breached. I'm confident the city won't fall, but you're right, lord, we do need to get back and call up more forces.' He glanced at Garth. 'We'll leave within the hour.'

Aethelred gestured to his men who'd been playing tabula in the hall. 'You six… round up the rest of our escort. We leave for Lundenburh as soon as they strike camp.'

*

The next two days sped by as Alfred's Hampshire armies were summoned and gathered at Winchester. By mid-morning of the third day, an army of over a thousand men was heading for Maidstone, a ride of almost a hundred miles. The route took them north for half a day before they turned east across Surrey, joining several contingents of the shires standing army on the way. By the time they reached Maidstone, after a gruelling three-day ride, they were an army nearing two thousand strong.

Ealdorman Aethelbold's Kentish army had been camped at Maidstone for the past two days, and added another two thousand men to those arriving with Alfred, making an impressive force of almost four thousand fighting men.

'We couldn't have asked for a better response,' Aethelbold said as they ate a hastily cooked meal that evening. 'The southern horde is a big one and would likely be unstoppable against a smaller army than their own.'

Alfred's brow creased in thought. 'Our numbers are encouraging, although three hundred and thirty ships could mean we'll be facing many thousands of warriors. In which case, we need an army of at least six thousand. I don't intend to confront both bands of Norsemen at the same time, but we could find ourselves having no other choice at some point. I also have a feeling that Danish numbers will swell with an influx of East Anglians – and even Northumbrians – before too long.' He heaved a sigh. 'But it isn't time to get downhearted just yet. We still have the rest of the Surrey forces to arrive, not to mention the Berkshire and Sussex armies. I'm praying they won't fall short of expectations.'

'And we still have men in the burhs, so we also need to take those numbers into account. Along with the strengthened defences, our men have proved effective in repelling attack, no matter how large the enemy army.'

Alfred shoved his last piece of bread in his mouth and pushed himself to his feet. 'You're right, and I have every confidence in my warriors' skills and the training they've had. But right now, we're wedged between two armies and need to plan our first move. Your scouts will be here by late morning tomorrow, you say?'

'That's what we arranged. I sent men both north and south, and once they get back, I'm hoping we'll know more about en-

Seventeen

emy numbers and any moves they've made in the last two days.'

Both groups of Aethelbold's scouts rode into the camp at Maidstone before noon the following day and Alfred was not surprised to hear that their reports were similar.

'The name of the leader is Hastein,' a wiry blond named Drew reported of the northern band once they were all seated around a campfire. 'We didn't see him – at least, if we did, we didn't know who he was – but from what we heard, he's a seasoned warrior and well respected by his men. He's been raiding in Francia for several years now.'

Alfred nodded thoughtfully, the name sounding familiar, though it was a common enough Norse name. 'They have eighty ships?' Drew confirmed that as true. 'How many men, would you say?'

'Not as many as you'd expect from eighty ships, lord. Less than a thousand, we reckoned, probably not many more than eight hundred.' He gestured to his two comrades, who nodded in agreement. 'Most ships were manned by as few as ten or a dozen men, but they were crammed full with women and children, as well as horses and what looked like looted goods.'

Alfred grunted. 'If they've come here intending to settle, they can think again! But the number of warriors is encouraging. I was expecting at least fifteen hundred from eighty ships. Pray God that number remains unchanged and no East Anglians or Northumbrians decide to throw in their lot with this Hastein. Where was this fleet when you left?'

'Still on the northern coast close to Milton, opposite the Isle of Sheppey. We heard no plans from them about a mass move elsewhere, although smaller raiding parties ride out every few days, attacking nearby villages for food. Most are small settlements, but all have the harvest in the barns and storage sheds by now, which the Danes empty at will, leaving the village folk in a sorry plight for the coming months. They even take some of their livestock, which they slaughter once back in camp.'

Alfred rubbed his forehead, determined to curb his mounting temper. 'Our people suffer yet again at the hands of these cursed pagans. But as God is my witness, they will not do so for much longer!' He fixed Drew in his intense gaze. 'You say you heard no plans from them for a mass move out?'

'No, lord, but some of the things they talked about amongst themselves made us think they were waiting for news of something.'

Alfred grimaced. 'They'll be waiting for reinforcements from the Danish kingdom across the estuary, I'm certain of it. It's been my biggest worry all along. My thanks to the three of you. I hope to know more on this once the men I sent to East Anglia get here.'

He turned his attention to the four men who had been sent to spy on the large fleet menacing the south coast. The four confirmed the number of ships, and that they had, indeed attacked an unfinished burh.

'Have they used Castle Toll as their camp?'

'No, lord,' a youthful warrior with a cheerful manner replied. 'They moved on to Appledore on the edge of Romney Marsh. We reckoned it was a good defensive site, between the marsh and the dense forest of Andredesweald.'

'You're right, Ryce.' Aethelbold nodded. 'We'll need them to move out of there or we can give up any hope of confronting

Seventeen

them in all-out battle.'

'They'll move out soon enough,' Alfred said, confident in his assertion. 'They may stay at Appledore for a while, but they haven't come to Wessex to hide away in our marshes and forests forever. They'll need to find sources of food for a start.' He turned to young Ryce. 'Did you catch the name of their leader?'

'No, lord. Many names were used in conversations, but there was nothing to suggest that any of the men named were in command. But as far as we could make out, there are several bands working together, so we guessed there was no one overall leader, as in the northern group.'

Alfred nodded slowly as he digested that fact, deciding it made little difference to his army whether there was one leader or several, especially if it came to a full-scale battle. All warriors would be drawn up in the shield wall. He returned his attention to Ryce. 'What's your closest estimate of fighting men?'

The young scout gestured to the men sitting on the opposite side of the campfire. 'Like Drew's group we expected to see many more warriors than we did. Two hundred and fifty longships could carry six thousand or more men, but like the northern fleet, the ships at Appledore were full of women and children and a good supply of horses. Fighting men could number between three and a half to four thousand.'

'Your scouts have served us well, Aethelbold,' Alfred said. 'I'm relieved that neither group has yet moved further into Wessex, and our task is to make sure that's how things stay. It's too early in the year for them to dig in for the winter, so the only way we can stop them moving on is to counter every move they make.'

He paused, contemplating possible strategies and problems that could arise. 'The size of this southern horde alone gives cause for alarm,' he admitted, 'but once our armies from Sussex and Berkshire get here, our own force will be far larger – large enough to confront both groups, I hope. And, as you said yesterday, Aethelbold, we still have our warriors in the burhs.'

Alfred slammed his fist into his open hand, his face contorted with rage and determination. 'The pagans will *not* be given free rein to plunder and kill in Wessex!' He inhaled deeply in an effort to control his seething emotions. 'But, unlike years ago when Halfdan and Guthrum invaded, I am confident that Wessex can now not only withstand attack, but repel and defeat the enemy as well.'

*

Throughout the winter months, Alfred's system of rotating his warriors in the field, along with his well-established network of moving supplies back and forth, ensured that he kept a fresh and powerful mounted army firmly lodged between the two forces of Danes. Occasional forays were also made by warriors from the few fortified Kentish burhs: those from Rochester thwarting northern raiding bands, and men from Eorpeburnan and Canterbury attacking bands in the south. Alfred exulted in the success of his reorganised system. Thanks to the better training and efficiency of his Wessex fyrd, the improved transport system and fortified burhs, neither group of Norsemen was able to gain a hold over the shire nor constantly plunder Kentish villages.

Seventeen

Yet Alfred was only too aware that the invaders were still in his kingdom and with the onset of spring, they would renew their efforts to move further afield – and along with that was the likelihood that their numbers would swell still more with incoming raiding bands from the continent or the Danelaw. Stopping such vast numbers from taking his kingdom was a far cry from confronting relatively small raiding parties seeking food.

By the beginning of March, Alfred's decision was made. He had no other choice than to make his move now, before the situation became impossible to control. The size of the southern force remained his biggest worry, and he could not afford to split his army in the event of facing attacks from both armies at the same time. But if he could successfully rid his kingdom of the smaller, northern band before then, his own armies could focus on the southern horde.

'And just how do you intend to go about this feat of getting rid of Hastein's band, lord?'

'Tried and tested methods are always the best, Aethelbold.'

'You're thinking of paying him off?'

'Something like that. I'll visit him personally and put my terms to him.'

'Then I hope the treaty lasts longer than the ones we made with Halfdan… or Guthrum.'

'I'd say our dealings with Guthrum ended satisfactorily, wouldn't you?'

'Perhaps, but it took enough years to reach that state. And right now, we have no idea what kind of man we're dealing with in Hastein.'

Eighteen

Milton, Kent: early-late March 893

'Thor's balls, if we don't see some action soon, I'll go crazy!' Hastein yelled, stomping around the Milton camp, kicking at stones and stray objects in his way.

Few of his men cast him more than a passing glance; they were used to him venting his frustration now and then. Not that Hastein was seeking an audience. Bound up in his own impatience, he let out a sound, midway between a groan and a growl, and sat on a log to massage his temples, as though the act would stimulate his mind into productive thought… which it did not. But it did help him to focus more clearly on their present predicament.

After hanging around in Boulogne all last summer doing nothing other than fishing, they'd done little more for the entire winter in Kent. It was now early March; time to be heading out on some good, healthy raids. They'd already taken all the food nearby villages had to offer and needed to move further afield. But it wasn't food alone that Hastein craved. There were Christian churches, monasteries and noblemen's estates out there just waiting to be relieved of their trinkets, and plenty of land on which his people could settle.

The main obstacle to his plans was the prolonged wait for Danes from across the estuary to join his band. His messengers to the East Anglian kingdom had returned at the beginning of November with positive intentions from disgruntled Norse-

Eighteen

men over there, many as keen to get back to their old ways as Hastein himself. But, as yet, none had made an appearance in Kent. Hastein could only hope they were simply sitting out the winter before making a move. Their added numbers would be a great boost to his own, and, hopefully, give his men a good fighting chance against the Wessex king. They would still need to be watchful, of course. Getting too close to the cursed Saxon army that had cut his men off from their comrades in the south could prove disastrous. This king seemed to know what he was doing, all right, and the speed with which he'd raised and moved so large a force last autumn was worrying.

In mid-March, Hastein again sent men across to East Anglia, but before they returned, he found his camp surrounded by sword-wielding Saxons. Too late to muster in defence, his men could only watch as the Saxon warriors closed in, the occasional snort of horses breaking the deathly hush that had fallen. Then a voice rang out.

'Hastein. Show yourself!'

Curiosity overrode Hastein's sense of danger as he took in the Saxon lines, estimating around thirteen hundred mounted men, before stepping forward and focusing in the direction from which the voice had sounded.

'I am Hastein, leader of this band,' he replied, finding little need to raise his voice against the silence. 'I imagine you aren't here to welcome us into your lands.'

A warrior astride a powerful white stallion dismounted, the two men at his sides doing the same. Hastein watched as the three stepped towards him, judging the central figure to be the one who had spoken and unable to help himself comparing his fine quality sword, mail-suit and helm to his own unarmoured state. The man appeared to be slim but muscular and of similar height to himself, though some years his junior. His proud stance displayed confidence in his role as a leader of men and his stony expression gave nothing away of his intentions. Hastein suddenly wondered if this was the Saxon king himself – and whether he'd come to do battle, as the armoured state suggested, or merely to talk.

But the warrior remained silent, his owl-like eyes breaking contact with Hastein's stare to sweep across the camp, seeming to take in every small detail.

'So, my lord king,' Hastein started, breaking the discomfiting hush, 'welcome to our temporary home… It is King Alfred I address, is it not?'

The warrior's attention swung back to Hastein, his amber gaze boring into him, assessing him from head to toe, as he had done to Alfred only moments ago. 'I am indeed King Alfred, and you, Lord Hastein, are in my kingdom uninvited.'

For some moments, neither man spoke, amber and hazel eyes locked together in silent appraisal. Then Alfred said, 'You look much as Eadwulf described you, although I believe he hasn't set eyes on you for some years.'

'It wasn't too long ago, as a matter of fact.' Hastein shrugged. 'Must have been eight years since, in Francia. But I'm sure you don't want to hear about that – at least, not until we're better acquainted.'

Alfred gestured to the camp. 'What I have to say shouldn't take too long, but I'd feel more comfortable if we could sit. Most of my men will be happy to dismount and stay with the

Eighteen

horses.' He beckoned a further two dozen of his warriors to join him. 'Your presence with me in camp would be appreciated,' he told them, grinning at Hastein. 'Just until the Danish lord and I become better acquainted, shall we say?'

Once seated on some sawn-off tree trunks, with his selected men clustered around him and several Danes at Hastein's back, Alfred put forth his proposition.

'If you're intending to settle somewhere in our lands, Hastein, I'd like to think there is peace between our peoples.'

Guessing where this conversation was heading, Hastein nodded. 'You mean like the peace that existed between you and Guthrum?'

'Ah, I see you know something of our recent history.'

'I do. I also know that Guthrum is now dead but my countrymen still dwell in the kingdom known as East Anglia, as well as Northumbria and parts of eastern Mercia.'

It was Alfred's turn to nod. 'The people of those areas are mixed – Danes, Angles and Northumbrians, but they are ruled largely by Danes and the entire region is known as the Danelaw.'

Hastein remained silent, appearing to mull things over.

'As far as I can see, you have two choices,' Alfred went on. 'Either we do battle here and now, or we make peace and you can take your people to settle in the Danelaw or sail back across the Northern Sea. You will sign a treaty to this effect and swear oaths never to raid Wessex again.'

'And if I choose not to make peace, what then?'

Alfred swung out his arm, indicating his men. 'Look around at my army and compare it to the size of yours. I have over fifteen hundred men and you have eight hundred, at most. At a given signal from me, my warriors would move in on your camp right now and, as you can probably imagine, there would be few of you left when we'd finished. Or, we could do the honourable thing and meet in a shield wall tomorrow. That way, your women and children would remain unharmed. But, either way, there would be few of your men left to limp off at the end.'

Hastein didn't need to think twice about his reply; he'd been expecting such ultimatums and knew exactly what he would say. 'Making peace is the only sensible option, as you well know, Alfred, and I imagine you've already had a treaty drawn up?' Alfred confirmed that. 'Then if you are agreeable, we can sign it and make our oaths now. We'll strike camp at first light tomorrow, load up our ships and sail up to East Anglia. You won't see or hear of us again.'

'It's not that simple, Hastein. I have another condition I want your agreement upon before you leave Wessex. Guthrum readily agreed to it fifteen years ago, and I'm hoping you will do the same.'

Hastein feigned ignorance of what Alfred had demanded of Guthrum, smiling to himself at how predictable this Saxon king was. No truly hot-blooded Dane would be bound by Christian principles and beliefs. 'Then you'll need to explain this condition which, I hope, is something we can accept.'

'You and a dozen of the more influential warriors amongst you will be baptised into the Christian faith and be absolved of all sins during the ceremony. Then you will swear on our holy bible never to raid and plunder in Wessex again.'

Eighteen

Hastein glanced round at his men behind him, sharing an inconspicuous wink with a few of them. They'd been through this a few times before in Francia and the Low Countries. It seemed the foolish Christians never learned that being baptised into their faith was no more binding to Danes than swearing oaths never to raid again. Besides, few Norse warriors would risk being on the receiving end of Thor's wrath.

'I'm sure there are at least a dozen of my men who would be glad to receive Christian baptism,' he said. 'But, in my case, I have no need of it.'

'Then, Lord Hastein, we have no more to say to each other. Tomorrow morning, we will meet in the shield wall on the wide stretch of beach west of this camp. And I wouldn't suggest attempting to set sail tonight. My army will be staying right where it is.'

'King Alfred, I fear I explained myself badly. I have no need of Christian baptism simply because I am already of that faith, and have been for the past fifteen years. I was baptised in the holy city of Rome. But if you insist, I will undergo the ceremony again.'

Alfred stared at him. 'You are a Christian, yet you continue to raid other Christian kingdoms!'

'The faith of a kingdom has little to do with where my people raid, Alfred, be it Christian, Muslim or even a land in which the people are followers of the Norse gods. Nor does being a Christian prevent us raiding if our people are starving. I simply pray for Christ's forgiveness, and I believe he has bestowed it upon me on various occasions.'

'Then, as a Christian, will you swear on the Christian bible to leave Wessex and never come back?'

'I will, although I can't speak for all of my men,' Hastein replied, assuming a thoughtful expression as he brushed imaginary dust from his breeches. 'Those faithful to my leadership will stay with me, wherever I go.' He gestured to the men behind him.' Several of these men are leaders of smaller bands that have joined together to create the army under my overall command. If these leaders agree to baptism, it's likely their men will follow.'

Alfred looked sceptical, but Hastein saw no need to push the matter further. 'What I can suggest, King Alfred, is that to show good faith, I will undergo the ceremony again and my twelve-year-old twins, Raud and Davyn, could be baptised with the dozen leaders you mentioned. I would be honoured to have my twins embracing the teachings of the Christ-god.'

'Then that is what we shall do. I'll organise the baptism to take place in the city of Lundenburh in five days, so you can have tomorrow to make preparations to leave and ensure the smooth running of your camp in your absence. The following day those to be involved in the ceremony will ride along the coast of northern Kent, accompanied by me and thirty of my warriors. The journey is a little over fifty miles, so we should cover that in a couple of days, giving us a day or two to find passage on vessels crossing to the north side of the river and rest in Lundenburh before the ceremony.'

Alfred raised his hand, halting Hastein's imminent remark. 'And, in case you were wondering, the rest of my army will stay at your camp until your return – just a precaution, you understand, in the event of the rest of your warriors attempting

Eighteen

to sail away elsewhere.

'In Lundenburh, you will be greeted by my son-by-marriage, Ealdorman Aethelred who, effectively, rules Mercia. He has been based at the city for the last few years, overseeing its improvements.'

'Ah… Aethelred I already know, and no doubt he will remember me. I last saw him years ago, when he was a lad of nine, and Eadwulf talked about his role as Lord of Mercia when he and my cousin, Bjorn, came out to Francia eight years ago.' He grinned at Alfred's raised eyebrows. 'No, they didn't come to raid – even Bjorn lives a quiet life nowadays. They were searching for my older sons, Dainn and Aguti, as my former wife, Freydis was worried about them. She is now married to Eadwulf.'

'I had the pleasure of meeting Lady Freydis when my daughter, Aethelflaed, was married to Aethelred seven years ago. She is a delightful lady and made quite an impression on my daughter. Perhaps you already know that she and Eadwulf have a daughter? She must be eight by now.'

Hastein looked away, his mind awash with distant memories. 'The child was born just before Bjorn and Eadwulf set out for Francia. Thora, they called her, after Freydis' kindly mother who lived with us in Ribe until she died. It all seems so long ago now… Growing old has little to offer, Alfred. I know that for certain.'

Evidently having no suitable reply to that, Alfred just nodded and steered the conversation back to the baptismal ceremony. 'So, Hastein, tomorrow I'll send some of my men out with instructions to all who will be involved in preparations for the baptism and, as I said, we'll leave for Lundenburh the day after that.'

He glanced at the faces staring at them from the clusters of rough, hide tents and rose to his feet. 'Evening is drawing in and your women hover around the cooking pots, eager to begin your meal. Your camp will remain encircled by my army and naturally, we never sleep without our vigilant guards keeping an eye on things, including your ships. No one will leave here, by river or road until I say so.'

Hastein found nothing to contest in Alfred's statements. He had every intention of undergoing another baptism. From past experience in Francia and the Low Countries, he knew the ceremony would involve much feasting and gift-giving on Alfred's behalf. Just what he needed before heading into the Danelaw to recruit fellow Danes to his band. Then, with a large enough group to be proud of, he would head back to Western Mercia and Wessex to continue his raids.

The voice of the Wessex king as he strode from the camp cut though his thoughts.

'I bid you goodnight, Hastein.'

*

Aethelflaed sat by the window of the Lundenburh hall, constantly scanning the bustling, workday town for the familiar figure of her husband. Though anxious for Aethelred to return from the baptism of those seedy Danes, she dreaded their presence in her hall for another two whole weeks, knowing her father would constantly shower them with gifts and they

Eighteen

would be treated as comrades and friends... equals in the Christian faith.

Having arrived in Lundenburh the previous afternoon, the thieving pagans had already spent a night in the hall, which had required Aethelflaed to provide an evening meal as well as early morning oatmeal and breads to break their fast. And once the initial baptism service was over, they would return to enjoy the baptismal feasting and festivities. The mere thought of it turned her stomach and she could only applaud Ealhswith's decision not to attend. But, as wife of the Lord of Mercia in whose hall the festivities would take place, Aethelflaed felt it her duty to be at his side to oversee the serving of the many meals and personally pour the mead cups...

Yet Aethelflaed had not envisaged taking such a dislike to the Danish leader himself, with all his insincere charm and too-ready smiles. No, she wasn't taken in by Hastein for one moment but, as yet, she'd had little chance to express her feelings to Aethelred. She'd fallen asleep before he reached their bed last night and this morning had been a rush to serve the food before they headed to the church. But thoughts of Hastein caused a shiver of dread down her back: he was not a person she could ever trust.

Tired of sitting and restless to do something useful, she moved about the hall, chatting for a while with servants putting their final touches to the foods for the lavish feast that would follow the baptism. Then she stopped for a game of I-Spy with Aelfwynn and Stepan, allowing Alys time to feed her three-week-old daughter.

It was hard for Aethelflaed to stop smiling when she

thought how happy Alys and Garth had been since their wedding four years ago. Aethelflaed knew she was being selfish, but she always dreaded Garth's term of service at Lundenburh coming to an end and the little family returning to Somerset.

At the opening of the hall door and Aethelred's appearance, Aethelflaed jumped to her feet and headed towards him, eager to catch him on his own. 'You need to watch your back with this Hastein around,' she said, the moment he stepped over the threshold. 'From what I've heard, he's about as slippery as an eel and as trustworthy as a wolf. I know he was your father's friend, but that was a long time ago and –'

From behind her husband, Hastein stepped out, garbed in his white, baptismal robes. He had that usual, derisive grin on his face, marring his otherwise handsome features. Only the scattering of grey threads in his braided, pale ginger hair, and the few lines etched around his mouth and twinkling hazel eyes suggesting he was well past his prime. His gown did little to mask his lithe physique and well-muscled chest and shoulders and his infuriatingly relaxed bearing indicated confidence in himself.

'I am happy to see you again, too, Lady Aethelflaed,' Hastein murmured, moving through the doorway to allow Garth to enter before bowing in an elaborate fashion that made her smile. 'Though I am saddened to know of my slippery reputation in these lands. Most of my friends find me quite easy to keep hold of and perfectly trustworthy. But I have heard the odd comparison to a cunning old fox.'

'I've heard reference to foxes including the word, "sly", Lord Hastein, and truly hope that description does not apply

Eighteen

to you.' Aethelflaed smiled sweetly, curtsying in response to his bow, determined not to let his glib mockery goad her into a temper. He was not a welcomed guest in Mercia, after all, and she decided to avoid conversation with him as much as possible. 'Excuse me,' she added, noting Aethelred's glower at her attitude, 'but I need to instruct the servants to bring refreshments for you all.'

She turned to stride away, throwing over her shoulder, 'When it comes to being cunning, Lord Hastein, I doubt there's a man alive who could match my father.'

His amused chuckle rang in her ears, and she prayed that the next two weeks would be quickly over.

*

'It is a strange ceremony, the Christian baptism, is it not, Aethelred?' Aethelred nodded, having nothing to say that would counter Hastein's opinion. 'Raud and Davyn were quite bemused by the meaning of it all, and the need for godfathers and wearing white robes. Although they found being daubed with holy oils, eating salt and having their heads plunged into the font to be somewhat funny, whereas I always found it a messy affair, especially when that disgusting spittle is smeared on our faces.'

Hastein grimaced in accord with his words as they ate, his eyes dancing with merriment. Around them, the hall buzzed with conversation and flurries of activity as servants scurried around trying to keep food bowls and wine cups filled. 'That you are now Davyn's godfather and King Alfred is Raud's, is also interesting,' he went on, 'though I do wonder what part either of you will play in my sons' future lives. Perhaps time alone will answer that question.'

He shook his head, as though finding it all too confusing. 'I imagine each part of the ceremony is of some importance to the Christ-god, but I can't see what relevance it holds for young babes, who would remember none of the event in later life. But I must confess, I found today's ceremony interesting, and I congratulate King Alfred on creating such a beautifully ornate church. The Christ-god obviously enjoys a little ostentation.'

Aethelred nodded. 'Alfred was determined to reconstruct the Church of Saint Paul, and indeed, to ensure it matched some of the most renowned cathedrals in our lands in its grandeur. The beauty and splendour of our churches and cathedrals is a symbol of our love and respect for God.' He hesitated, struggling to find more to add in response to the Dane's odd questions. 'Our Lord gives us life and cares for us, and if we love and believe in Him in return, live good, humble lives and are kind to others, when we die, we will spend the rest of eternity with Him in Heaven.'

'Not so different to my warrior's desire to spend eternity in Valhalla with Odin, then – except of course, that to earn a place in Valhalla, we must die killing enemies in battle. And all you Christians need to do is behave yourselves and be kind to others. As for being humble…' He rolled his eyes heavenward. 'I don't believe that to be a quality much admired by Odin, and it's one that I shall personally find extremely difficult to achieve.'

Aethelred shrugged, wishing that Hastein would direct his questions and observations about religion at Alfred, rather than

Eighteen

him. He had hardly been raised a devout Christian, considering Eadwulf and Aethelnoth's beliefs, but nor could he profess to be a pagan. Religion was just too confusing and he'd prefer not to think about it at all.

'I shall also be interested to see how you celebrate your Eastertide Services next week,' Hastein continued, 'and be pleased to enter the beautiful Church of Saint Paul again. Just standing beneath that splendid ceiling amidst magnificent treasures and relics fills a man with a sense of peace and calm and –'

'Mead, Lord Hastein?' Aethelflaed thrust the brimming earthenware jug to within a finger-length of Hastein's nose, effectively cutting off his rambling words. He blinked, startled, and despite being relieved that the monologue had stopped, Aethelred gaped at his wife's audacity.

'It is our finest brew,' she added, 'and I will continue to serve it while my father speaks to us all in celebration of your glorious baptism. I hope you are comfortable wearing such flattering attire.'

Hastein threw back his head and roared. 'My dear Lady Aethelflaed, I've been baptised many times, and can say that I found none of them to be glorious occasions, nor any of the gowns to be comfortable. But King Alfred and Lord Aethelred are proving to be generous and engaging hosts, and although your husband does not seem to admire your wit right now, I can tell you that I am thoroughly enjoying it.'

Aethelflaed's lips turned up at the edges and a smile spread across her face before rapidly falling again as she filled his mead cup. 'I shall take that as a compliment, although that doesn't mean I approve of your presence in our kingdom for one moment. And I tell you this: if you break your oaths to King Alfred, he, my husband and my brother will never stop until they break you. Enjoy that thought while you drink your mead and have Alfred's gifts thrown at you.'

She stalked off, leaving Hastein grinning and Aethelred squirming in embarrassment. He excused himself from Hastein's company and followed Aethelflaed across the hall to their bedchamber. 'What on earth's got into you?' he hurled at her. 'Alfred won't be pleased to hear you've been rude to his guests... and just remember, they'll be here for almost another two weeks!'

Aethelflaed looked crestfallen. 'I know, Aethelred, but something just snaps when I look at that man with his mocking grin. I feel such forebodings about his presence in our lands, no matter that my father believes he'll abide by his vows and head off to the Danelaw as Guthrum did. Hastein's a hardened and determined leader and raider, despite all his charm. He wants our lands and he'll leave no stone unturned until he gets them.

'I fear for your life, Aethelred, as well as the lives of my father and brother. Hastein is slyer than a fox and lies pour from his mouth as easily as mead from a jug. Don't let yourself be taken in by him.'

Aethelred held his wife and kissed the top of her head. 'I'm not sure how you can know that much about the man when you've only just met him, but I promise to stay wary of him, whatever he says. But, for Alfred's sake, we have to be civil and get through the next two weeks without harsh words from anyone. Now, we'd best get back into the hall. Your father will expect us to be there while he showers the visitors with gifts.'

Eighteen

*

Hastein twisted in his saddle, glancing at his men riding behind, his two sons on their ponies at his sides. Four substantial carts trundled along in the midst of his convoy, in which the fabulous gifts bestowed by the foolishly generous Saxon king were being transported to their Milton camp. He sucked in great breaths of fresh, spring air as the oppressively walled-in Saxon town disappeared from view. Confined in such a place was no life for free-spirited Danes, and he was elated to be in the open again.

Yet being cooped-up behind stone walls for the last two weeks had been worth it, and Hastein could barely suppress a chuckle as he thought of the way things had played out. The ease with which this 'danegeld' in the carts had been acquired, with the days of lavish feasting thrown in, seemed too good to be true. And Alfred really believed that the lives of the six hostages Hastein had given him would ensure he kept his pledges. How little the man knew of the nature of the Dane. Anyone as trusting as Alfred deserved to be duped. Perhaps the pious king should have listened to the doubts of that headstrong daughter of his.

Now Aethelflaed *had* impressed him, and she'd been so right regarding his true nature and intentions in this well-endowed kingdom. Hastein had learnt how to be sly over the years, and cunning, and no red-blooded Dane alive felt the need for honesty with Christ-lovers, whether they be Saxon, Francian, Frisian or Roman. And Aethelflaed seemed to have seen right through him. Hastein could not help admiring the woman's outspokenness and knew, deep down, it was because she reminded him so much of Freydis, the love of his life. If Freydis had loved *him* and not Eadwulf, perhaps he would not have become the embittered man he was now.

Still, Greta had been a good and loving wife for over thirteen years and had given him two more fine sons, as well as a pretty daughter. His life with Freydis was in the past and he rarely thought of it nowadays. It was just seeing Aethelred again, now a grown man, and looking so much like Eadwulf, that brought it all back. In truth Hastein felt no animosity towards Eadwulf, and had taken a liking to his son. But if he ever faced Aethelred in battle, the young man would simply become another enemy to be dealt with.

Now he must focus on the weeks ahead. His days of idling in Milton were over, and from now on he would raid to his heart's content. It was unfortunate that teaming up with their countrymen from Boulogne was not an option. Getting his army through Alfred's forces had never been a possibility, so there was only one thing he could do. He would sail his fleet across the Thames to Benfleet and raid mercilessly in West Mercia. With any luck, doing so would tempt a goodly number of East Anglian Danes to join them.

Nineteen

Winchester, Wessex: April 893

Whilst Alfred was with his armies in Kent, Edward was given his first taste of leadership. Left in control of the more westerly Wessex shires, he kept his scouts in the field, ensuring he was regularly updated of events, particularly those occurring further east. If, at some stage, his father should call for reinforcements, or the kingdom was attacked elsewhere, Edward intended to be ready. Failing his father was not an option.

Since last September, Edward had amassed a sizable army at Winchester. In addition to a substantial Hampshire force left by Alfred, he had gathered armies from Wiltshire, Dorset, Devon and Somerset – though he'd been careful not to leave those shires without fighting men in the event of unexpected attack. Nonetheless, with close to a thousand men, Edward felt his numbers were impressive, and all were camped within a hundred yards of the Winchester hall.

The second week of April brought heartening news. Alfred had achieved his first real success in ridding the kingdom of this new Danish scourge, albeit a peaceful one. Hearing that the seasoned Norse leader, Hastein, had readily agreed to baptism and thereafter would leave the kingdom, boosted Edward's hopes that the rest of the pagans would soon be ousted. As yet, he knew nothing of his father's intentions regarding the enemy camped at Appledore, but he trusted Alfred's judgement and knew he would send for more men if the need arose.

Informed that the Danes to be baptised were now in Lundenburh, with two weeks of baptismal festivities ahead of them, Edward's thoughts turned to Aethelflaed. He couldn't help wondering how his intolerant and sometimes judgemental sister felt at having her hall bursting with enemy Danes. And Aethelred, how would he be coping with the notorious Hastein under his roof – a man who had once been his father's friend?

The Eastertide in the second week of April was a quiet affair at Winchester, the situation in Wessex negating the possibility of inviting many guests. Edward joined his mother and two youngest siblings for the services at the cathedral, although the absence of Alfred, as well as Aethelflaed and Aethelgifu, was felt by all. They'd seen little of Aethelgifu over the past two years, but the family was content to know how happy she was in her role of Abbess of Shaftesbury. The last time they'd visited her, no one could doubt that Aethelgifu had found her true calling in life.

As the late-April evening drew in, just a week after Eastertide, three of Edward's scouts rode in, their fatigue evident, their horses well lathered. That they'd had need to ride like the wind sent a bolt of dread through Edward's chest. 'Tell me, quickly, Chad,' he ordered as they followed him into the hall and sat round a central trestle. 'The king isn't –'

Chad held up his palm, halting Edward's words. 'No, lord, King Alfred is well and still in Lundenburh, although he plans to return to Maidstone soon. It's the Danes who were camped at Appledore. They've –'

'*Were camped*...? You're saying they've moved further into Kent?'

Nineteen

The ageing scout nodded, his brow wrinkling further as he spoke. 'They'd been kept in check until the Eastertide by frequent attacks from the king's armies at Maidstone, but they must have guessed our men wouldn't strike during our holy days and moved deep into Andredesweald. They'd raided several forest villages in the first two days, but by the time our armies arrived the thieving bastards had disappeared into the forest again.'

Edward cursed, his thoughts on the great, black Forest of Andred, so deep and thick, and stretching as far west as Hampshire, and as far north as Surrey, it was said that a man could be lost within moments of entering. 'We'll have no chance of finding them while they're in there. Are they moving in any particular direction?'

'From the villages they'd plundered by the time we'd left they seemed to be heading north-west.'

'Likely aiming for the heart of Wessex?'

Chad nodded. 'They moved fast across Sussex, raiding as they went. I'd say you've little time to lose if you intend to meet them as they leave the forest and move further into Surrey – possibly even northern Hampshire. There are a couple of fair-sized settlements in that area, the most obvious one probably being Farnham on the borders of northwest Surrey.'

'There's always the possibility they could attack Guildford, a little further northeast, of course,' Edward said, 'although if it's Wessex heartlands they're after, they're probably more likely to try their luck at towns like Farnham and head into Hampshire or perhaps Berkshire, from there. Or they could just be intending to cross the Thames into the Danelaw.'

He gestured to several of his men. 'Get out to the camp and have the thegns ready their troops to ride at dawn. We'll head in the general direction of Farnham. It's little over thirty miles and if we leave early enough and ride at a brisk pace we could be there by mid-afternoon.'

Edward's men left the hall and he turned back to the scouts. 'You've done well to find this much out, and I know you'd have my father's thanks as well as mine.' He stopped, a further thought entering his head. 'What about their ships… are they still at Appledore?'

'No, lord. Around half their men – somewhere between fifteen hundred and two thousand – sailed them back down the Rother to the south coast. Last we heard they'd sailed past Dover and were heading north. But where they were aiming for is anyone's guess.'

'Well, my guess is that it won't be too far north, not while the rest of their army is still south of the Thames. Which means that once the villages along their route have been drained of food and loot, the raiders will continue to head north, probably needing to ford the Thames at some stage.'

'Seems that way, lord.'

'Then we arm ourselves for battle and do our damnedest to stop them.'

*

By the time Edward's army reached the torched Surrey village of Wrecclesham, just two miles south of the town of Farnham, the raiding Danes had plundered settlements across the shire

Nineteen

as far west as Hampshire and as far north as Berkshire. The lives of many of the villagers at Wrecclesham had been saved by the arrival of forces from local burhs who had come to their aid. Although they'd been unable to defeat so great a number, they'd at least made the Danes think, and move on.

Edward removed his helm in order not to distress the distraught and bereft, and his men did the same. 'Do you know where these troops are now?'

The old man to whom Edward had directed his question continued to rock the bloodied body of a young boy, his grief-filled gaze flicking briefly up at him before refocusing on the child. When he eventually spoke, his voice rasped in his throat.

'The scum'd started firing our homes and would've killed us all if our warriors hadn't come. My grandson ran for the woods, like his mother had told him, but he was seen and, young as he was, they cut him down! Savages, that's what they are!'

'I'm sorry,' Edward said, knowing how trite that sounded and that no words of sympathy could lessen grief such as this. His own eyes prickled at the sight before him, smoke from torched homes lingering on the still afternoon air.

'It was King Alfred's men that stopped them, from those new towns with the high walls. Brave lads, all of 'em! Charged right in, outnumbered more'n three to one they were. But it did the trick. The heathens were quick enough to leave when they arrived.'

'Where are the king's men now?' Edward persisted, 'or which way were the raiders headed?' He glanced round at the distraught faces and devastated village; the bodies not yet buried. The swelling lump in his throat threatened to waylay all speech. 'We have to stop them, though I'm sorry we didn't get here before… before *this*.'

'The Danes went that way.' The old man swept out his arm, indicating the greening woodlands beyond. 'Along the path that follows the edge of the woods before it curves round to join a track heading to the Wey valley. The Wey flows through Guildford and continues north until it joins the Thames a few miles west of Londinium - or Lundenburh as the king renamed it. They won't have got too far, mind, with the cartloads of loot. Moving like snails, they were. Chances are, they'll be only a few miles from here now.'

Edward knelt down beside him. 'Did the king's troops go after them?'

The old man shook his head. 'Stayed here for a while, helping to put out the fires and tend the wounded before they left. Edric was alive when they carried him back to us, but he died in my arms soon after. His mother's dead, too, and his father won't last the day. The king's men rode off back to Farnham, to join with more of their men. I'm guessing once they've done that, they'll be on their trail.'

'Mount up!' Edward's commanding voice carried across the village. 'We'll get the bastards who did this!'

*

Little more than a mile north of Farnham, thuds of hammering on shields and the taunting howls of pending battle were the first indications Edward had that his army had caught up with the marauding Danes. The resounding clash of shields

Nineteen

and accompanying roars soon after told him the two shield walls had met.

On rounding a bend along the woodland path, the situation became evident. In an open stretch of meadow, a large army of Danes was already ramming into a far smaller company of Saxons. It was also apparent that without his army's aid none of these brave Saxons would still be alive by sunset.

No time to stop and dismount, Edward led his men in a mounted charge that came crashing down on the Danes in a cacophony of thundering hooves and slashing swords. Assailed from all sides, the Danish attack wavered, yet bloodied and battered they fought on as men continued to drop to the churned-up, blood-soaked earth. Then, cries of 'Torsten is fallen' rang out, at which the surviving raiders turned and fled, their cartloads of plunder abandoned.

Radulf's elder son, Raulf, drew rein at Edward's side, his expression alternating between exhilaration at their victory and concern at the enemy's flight. 'They're heading for the Wey valley, as the old man guessed they would. Taken their wounded jarl with them, too – although the word is, he won't last long. Do we give chase?'

Edward steadied his horse as it snorted and sidled at the acrid stench of blood and excrement. 'We do, but the men from Farnham and the burhs will stay here and get the wounded back to the town before nightfall. Tomorrow they can retrieve the dead. Oh, and Raulf, get some of the local men to take the loot back to Farnham. We'll think about how to return it to the various villages it came from later.'

He swept the back of his hand across his clammy brow,

feeling in great need of water. 'Give our men time to take a drink then instruct the thegns to have them ready to ride after the rest of those swine. They'll be moving fast and probably keep going all night, desperate to reach the Danelaw. If their jarl's badly wounded, he's unlikely to live for long astride a galloping horse, so we may well find his body along our route.'

*

For the first few hours of a gruelling chase, no body of an affluent Norse leader lay across their path, suggesting the jarl was either clinging on to life, or his body was being carried along by his men to be honoured with a funeral pyre later on. Edward gave no further thought to the jarl and focused on the route ahead. Daylight was rapidly fading, and a waxing gibbous moon was already on the rise.

'Keep going,' he yelled, his order repeated along the column behind. 'As long as the moon's out the Danes are unlikely to stop, and I don't want them crossing the Thames.'

Throughout the darkest hours, the moon continued to light their way, its face only fading as the sky lightened with the approaching dawn. Already drained by the exertions of a long ride and battle the previous day, the Saxon force kept moving, Edward allowing only a few stops to rest the horses. Their efforts paid off. As the rising sun pinked the eastern horizon, the distant, shadowy shape of the raiders came into view. But reaching them before they crossed the Thames was a different matter.

Edward heeled his mount to the gallop, his men following

Nineteen

his lead, and the gap between pursued and pursuer gradually closed. Yet the fleeing Danes were still two hundred yards ahead when Edward watched them splashing into the shallow but flowing waters of the Thames. Inwardly groaning, he had no other choice than to follow after them.

Horses half-waded, half-swam across the river, their riders emerging soaked to the chest. No time to stop and empty their boots, the chase continued north along the valley of the River Colne as it wound its way south-west to join the great River Thames. By mid-morning they were close to the village of Iver, at a point in the river where its course parted to flow around a small island in the middle of its channel. Without hesitation, the Danes splashed through the flowing waters and seized the uninhabited isle, a good thirty yards from either bank.

Edward very soon realised the futility of following; doing so could result in the loss of at least half his men. The Danes had already assumed a defensive position, arrows nocked and ready for loosing at anyone who attempted to do so. Although the Colne was shallow here – shallower than the point in the Thames where they had crossed earlier – wading through it would still be slow and they would seem like sitting ducks to those bowmen. He deeply regretted having so few archers in his own army.

Raulf's voice suddenly cut through his thoughts. 'I don't think they'll last for long out there. Thorney Island's naught but a build-up of mud with a covering of grass and low, shrubby trees. There are probably birds of various types in the shrubs but I doubt anything with fur and four legs lives there.'

'I hope you're right,' Edward said, scanning the isle. 'As

far as I can see they brought no food with them, other than, perhaps, a few scraps in their saddle pouches. Though I suppose they could resort to slaughtering their horses if they become desperate enough. But they can't stand there, aiming their arrows at us forever. Something will give very soon, but until then, the only thing we can do is to lay siege and hope for an early surrender.'

Edward pulled his cloak close as a chill gust of wind caught him and glanced up at the gathering clouds. 'The first thing we need to do is build some makeshift shelters. Looks like we're in for rain.'

'Edward, there's something you need to know.'

Edward, stared at him. 'Something I won't like, by the look on your face. Well…?'

'Our men are grumbling about their terms of service being almost up, most saying they can't stay for more than another week or two.' He shrugged. 'As you know, the agreement they have with the king is that they serve for a set time then go back to their villages while another group takes their place. Right now, they're worried about the safety of their families while they're out here, not to mention the spring ploughing and sowing that needs doing.'

'They have every reason to be worried, Raulf, especially with raiders in our lands. And I admit, I hadn't thought to ask how close to the end of their terms any of the men were before we set out. How many are wanting to leave?'

'More than half of them.'

Edward groaned. 'Which would leave our army far smaller than the Danes' and if they decided to break out, we'd be unable

Nineteen

to stop them. We'll just have to hope they surrender before our army falls apart. If they don't, we'll all have to retreat.

'But for now, we deal with the situation we have and get some of our men across to the far bank.' He thought for a moment as Raulf nodded. 'You and your brother, take half our men and ride far enough downstream to be out of range of the archers. Cross the river then circle back to the opposite bank. We can't leave any escape routes open to them, and I know I can trust you and Uhtric to keep a watch going. The Danes are unlikely to wade further upstream, especially with their injured jarl, and they won't be heading back to the Thames. But we'll still need to keep a lookout, in case I'm proved wrong on that one. There's woodland over there so you can build a few shelters, and take half our food supplies with you.'

For the next few days, the Danes kept a line of defensive archers along both sides of the island, partly concealed behind a low earthen wall they'd built, topped with branches from shrubs and spindly trees. The grumblings of Edward's men and their need to get home grew louder, and to make matters worse, Edward knew that their own food supplies were becoming dangerously low. Having no other choice, he sent three of his thegns to his father with a plea for food and reinforcements for the siege.

At the start of the second week the messengers returned. 'If you have news for me, spit it out,' Edward said, praying the news wasn't bad. 'You spoke with King Alfred?'

'We did, lord,' a red-headed young thegn said, slipping down from his saddle. 'He wants you to know that by the time we got back, he'd be on his way with reinforcements. They should be here in a couple of days.'

A cheer went up from the men and relief washed over Edward. 'Thank the heavens for that!' He lowered his voice as he spoke to Raulf and Uhtric. 'Now that the men know help is on the way, it wouldn't surprise me if many of them decide to slip away over the next day or two. Pray God the king gets here soon.'

Twenty

Late April - early May 893

A week after Hastein's departure, Alfred made his farewells to his daughter and son-by-marriage in Lundenburh. News that the Appledore Danes had managed to leave their base completely unseen and disappear into the depths of Andredesweald and raid Saxon settlements filled him with rage. Were the men he'd left at Maidstone all blind – and where were the spies while they were making this move? Incompetent fools, all of them! All his plans to deal with this group as he'd done with Hastein's would now be impossible.

With the army of fifteen hundred men that had been with him since he'd confronted Hastein in Milton, Alfred set out on the four-day ride back to Maidstone, crossing the Thames at the Reading ford. During the ride, the tension and anxiety holding him captive gradually released its grip and he was able to think things through. The conniving pagans could have tricked anyone, including him, and they would have made their move in the darkness of night. Then his spies would have taken time to return to Maidstone with their report. He knew his army would have pursued the Danes as soon as they could, but by that time, the marauders would have been well and truly concealed in the vast, dark depths of Andredesweald.

On arrival at the Maidstone camp, Alfred was greeted with the news that the Appledore Danes had plundered villages across western Surrey as well as Sussex and were now attempting to reach their ships in East Anglia.

'Come and sit, lord, and I'll bring you up to date with the rest of the details while the meal finishes cooking.' Intrigued, Alfred followed the Kentish ealdorman to sit on a hefty beech log close to the campfire. The April evening was drawing in and a chill hung on the air. He drew his cloak around him, his stomach growling as aromas of meaty pottage reached him.

'After a few days, we could track the Danes' route from the locations of ravaged villages.' Aethelbold shook his head as they were handed cups of watered ale. 'The poorest of the forest folk had little to start with and many now have nothing at all. The thieving Danes took everything they owned, and more than a few villages were torched.'

Alfred nodded, having nothing to add to Aethelbold's summary, tragic though it was. The ealdorman had described the Danes' usual pattern when they rampaged through an area. 'Are they still in Surrey?'

The ealdorman's reply was a complete surprise. 'No, they are not, thanks to young Edward. He mustered his troops and headed to Surrey to stop them, caught up with them at Farnham and beat them in battle. The surviving Danes fled up the Wey valley with Edward's army after them, obviously aiming to cross the Thames and head east to the Danelaw and their ships.'

Aethelbold scratched his head as he thought. 'I'm guessing they'd hoped to reach the ford at Reading, but with Edward's army on their tails, they probably had a quick change of plan.'

'They crossed the Thames there and then?'

'They did, and Edward followed right after them. The river's

Twenty

fairly shallow at that point, but I think their horses would've still had a bit of a swim in places.'

Alfred smiled at the description and a feeling of pride welled in his chest. 'And Edward continued to follow them into West Mercia?'

'He did that, so you've every right to feel proud, King Alfred. The Danes headed up the Colne valley. Last thing we heard, they'd seized a small island in the river at Thorney, near Iver, about six miles north of where the Colne meets the Thames. There are archers in their band and Edward can't get across to them, so he's laid siege in the hope that their food will run out and he can force them to surrender.'

Little more was said that night and Alfred silently planned his move to send reinforcements to his son. But on the arrival of Edward's messengers the following morning with the worrying news of the men's demands to go home and requests not only for reinforcements but for food, Alfred's plans promptly became actions.

*

Alfred's army of three thousand well-armed men rode west across the ancient track that ran across the Downs north of Andredesweald. Their aim was to reach the ford at Reading late the following day, a distance of almost eighty miles from Maidstone. It would then take them another half a day to cover the thirty miles to Thorney. They were barely fifteen miles from the Maidstone camp when four riders caught up with them. Their horses skidded to a halt and the breathless men swung from their saddles and fell to their knees before him.

Alfred's heart pounded as he feared the worst. Pray God his son wasn't dead. 'Speak. Your news is evidently urgent.'

'Lord, we've ridden from Exeter, hoping to find you at Maidstone. Ealdorman Aethelbold sent us this way.' The messenger's panted words wavered and he glanced at Alfred, who nodded for him to continue. 'The Danes have attacked our city and we haven't enough men to hold them off for long. There are a hundred shiploads of them; over two thousand men. Even the city's new fortifications will be strained under a prolonged attack by so many.'

'Exeter is one of our strongest burhs and should withstand assaults for some time,' Alfred replied, his brow crinkling as he thought. 'Although, I confess it hasn't yet been put to the test, and wooden gates are a weakness on all our fortresses.

'A hundred shiploads… with women and children aboard?' Alfred's mind reeled as he struggled to see why the Danes from Appledore would have sailed to Exeter while half their crew was still besieged by Edward – unless, of course, the attack on Exeter, a long way from Thorney Island, was intended as a distraction and means of splitting Alfred's forces still further. 'Do you know where these ships came from?'

'Not exactly, lord. Lookouts in Hampshire sent word that a large fleet of a hundred and forty ships had been spotted heading west along the south coast, but where they'd sailed from, we don't know. Only a hundred of them turned into the Exe, so we thought the rest must have carried on towards Cornwall. As far as we could see, there were no women and children with them. They spent some time eyeing up our de-

Twenty

fences, then they attacked. Our portreeve sent us to find you and beg for help.'

His decision made, Alfred swung Pegasus round and singled out three of his Hampshire thegns. He could not deny Exeter the help it needed, so Edward would just have to cope – though not entirely alone.

'Alwin, Ormod, Edgar, take two hundred of our men and head for Reading. Cross the Thames, then head back east to Thorney Island. It's sixty-odd miles to the ford from here, then another thirty to the isle, so the journey will take you over two days. I trust you to ride as fast as possible without causing exhaustion to yourselves, or breaking the horses.

'Curse the lack of bridges over the Thames!' Alfred suddenly raged, thumping his fist into his palm and causing Pegasus to sidle. 'What madness when so many of the old fords have been unusable for years and the earliest one now isn't until Reading! Why is it that only the Romans saw the need for bridges? I swear, once we've rid our lands of these Danes my first task will be to rebuild the Roman bridge at Lundenburh!'

The men remained silent while Alfred calmed and refocused on the Exeter messengers. 'I must ask you to take a request to Ealdorman Aethelred in Lundenburh, so you will also need to cross the Thames. Fortunately, for just four of you it will be much simpler. Head north to the Surrey riverbank where a settlement is developing opposite to Lundenburh. Seek passage on the first ship you see that is heading straight to the city.' Alfred paused, opening the drawstring of the pouch at his belt and retrieving three coins, one gold and two silver, plus one of his own, frequently worn rings that all Saxons would recognise.

'The ring will ensure those you approach believe you were sent by me. One of the silver coins is for a skipper who can only take you across, in which case you will need to use the second silver coin to pay a different ship's master to return you to Surrey. If, by chance, you find one prepared to wait and ferry you back once your request is delivered, pay him the silver coin for the journey across and show him the gold coin. Tell him it will also be his as soon as you berth back in Surrey to collect your horses.

'Once you're in the city, ask to see Ealdorman Aethelred. Show him the ring and tell him to rally his army and head to Edward's aid at Thorney Island, near Iver. It should be little more than a twenty-mile ride for him. The warriors riding with my thegns may, or may not, have arrived by the time Aethelred gets there, depending on how soon he moves out from Lundenburh. But I'm hoping that with his help, the siege will be brought to an end; the Danes will accept our terms and give their oaths to leave our lands.

'Convey my hopes to the ealdorman.'

*

Aethelred listened to Alfred's orders with Garth and Aethelflaed beside him. It was already dusk, so rounding up troops and leaving that night was out of the question. But he was determined to head out tomorrow. For tonight, all he could do was send men out to the camps outside the city walls, instructing them to be ready to ride at dawn and remind them to pack enough food to last at least a week.

Twenty

'It's fortunate our armies have been at Lundenburh since the Danes arrived at Milton,' Aethelflaed said, inviting the four messengers to sit as she filled their ale cups, 'although now that Hastein's baptism is over and he's across the Thames in Benfleet, my father assured us we would be safe.'

'The Danes being besieged by Edward aren't Hastein's men,' Garth reminded her, joining the men at the table. 'They're part of the horde that had been camped at Appledore.'

'I know that, but they arrived at the same time as Hastein's and I can't seem to separate the two. Raiding Danes are all the same… thieving pagans! I just hope the other leaders aren't as sly as Hastein with his condescending smirk. I didn't trust him when he was here and I don't trust him now. If other Danes are raiding in our kingdom, the devious cur won't be able to stop himself from doing the same. Christian or not!'

The messengers glanced at each other and then at Garth, who was unable to conceal his grin as Aethelflaed flounced off.

'My wife is Alfred's daughter, as you will know,' Aethelred said, coming to join them, 'and has strong views on a lot of things. You also need to be aware that she is rarely wrong in her assessment of people, or situations. Her reasoning has convinced me that Hastein hasn't finished raiding in our lands. And another thing, where have the Danes attacking Exeter come from?'

The messengers shook their heads and the oldest in the group said, 'None of us in Exeter know that, but with so many Danes in these lands, it could have been from anywhere.'

Aethelred sighed. 'I agree with you, and if all these groups start working together and co-ordinate attacks in different parts of our kingdoms, the task of countering them will be very difficult – although with Alfred's burhs and standing armies, I'm reluctant to say it would be impossible.'

'My father would skin you alive if he thought you believed the Danes would beat us,' Aethelflaed declared on her return. 'After the years he's spent improving the defences of these lands, he has no intention of letting any pagans take them from him.' She grinned at Aethelred's affronted expression and patted his hand. 'So I'm glad to hear you think we can still beat these Danes, husband.'

Aromas of meats sizzling around the hearthfire filled the room and servants busied themselves carrying in the breads, cheeses and desserts from the small kitchens beside the hall. Aethelflaed smiled as the stomach of one of the men growled. 'The meal is ready and you are most welcome to share it with us. We also have spare beds in here if you'd like to stay until morning – unless, of course, you need to get back across the river tonight.'

'We'd be honoured to share your meal and have a bed for the night, my lady,' the older man replied. 'The skipper sails back at dawn, so we'll head down to the quayside at the same time as your armies set out for Thorney Island.'

Aethelflaed gestured to the servants as they stacked steaks of various meats on the platters. 'Good, so let's all enjoy the meal, then the serving women and I will gather as much food together as we can to send to my brother. It's a good thing we have plenty of smoked meats and cheeses in store, and we can always slaughter a couple of sheep,' she added, as she wandered off to oversee the servants. 'But I think we'll also need to spend some time after the meal baking a lot more flatbreads.'

Twenty

*

Alfred's army reached Exeter just after noon in the middle of the second week of May, ending a gruelling two-hundred-mile ride that had taken them five long days beneath an unseasonably hot May sun. Having been pushed to near-exhaustion to cover over forty miles a day, horses were hobbled and left to graze in a lush meadow beyond the city walls while their battle-trained riders silently circled the town.

It soon became evident that the Danes had not yet abandoned their efforts to take the city. Roars and howls and the clashes of an ongoing assault carried through the still, May air. It also became clear that despite trying for a week and a half, the assailants had made little progress in breaking down the city's defences. Rams had done little more than splinter the solid, heavy oak gates, and Alfred's reinforcements of the already thick, stone Roman walls had made the city well-nigh impregnable to attacking forces. Relief and pride flooded his senses, along with the desire to cut these murdering Danes down here and now.

Sudden panicked shouts of 'Saxons!' rang out and Alfred waved his men forward. A dense wall of glinting metal and unsheathed swords closed in on the Danes; a tidal wave sealing off all escape save for the longships waiting along the waterfront. The panicked Danes needed no telling they were no match for Alfred's army in size or focus and rapidly fled to their ships.

But Saxon blood lust was up, and Alfred's men were trained to show no lenience to marauders who intended harm to Saxon people or seize their kingdom. Danes who were injured or too slow to reach the quayside were hacked down as they ran, their bodies tossed into the Exe to be carried out to sea on the outgoing tide.

Alfred's praise for the men of Exeter was as genuine as his praise of the burh itself and he enjoyed the feeling of confidence and pride that gave him. 'Your quick thinking deserves every credit, Nerlan,' he said as he and his thegns enjoyed a meal in the portreeve's hall that evening. 'You were right to send to me for help. It was just unfortunate that I was more than two hundred miles away at the time. If the burh had not withstood the assaults so well, we might have been telling a different tale tonight.'

'We also had two of the nearby standing armies rally to our aid, lord, so we must praise those men, too. They held up assaults on our gates a few times, although we could have done with another few hundred of them to make a lasting difference.'

Nerlan's steel-grey hair fell across his eyes as he nodded and, instinctively, he raised a wrinkled hand to shove it back. 'The joint response of men stationed in the burhs and in the field is proving a great success and I can only thank you for devising such a system, King Alfred. And the fortifications have proved invaluable. We've lost many of our people to Norse raiders during the twenty years I've been portreeve at Exeter and I thank God that things are different now. This new fortress is a match for any raiding Danes.'

'I'm more than relived myself that the system is proving so effective,' Alfred admitted. 'This is the first time it's been fully put to the test. Until this year, only Rochester had been raided since Guthrum's invasion and –'

Twenty

He suddenly broke off, the mention of Guthrum throwing a thought into his head. 'Have you any idea where this fleet of raiders came from, Nerlan? Perhaps a shouted instruction or name heard during an attack…? Could they have been East Anglians?'

'As far as I know, none of my men heard anything, lord, but some of them captured two of the fleeing Danes today, thought we might want to question them. Quick thinking on their behalf, that was, and I've praised them for it. One of the captives is a puny little man but the other has the look of a leader about him – arrogant as hell and his sword is not one a poor man would have. It's on that trestle in the corner over there.'

Alfred wandered over to take a look, marvelling at the quality of the weapon with its emerald-studded hilt. 'Fine workmanship,' he said, testing the feel and weight of the sword in his hand. 'It looks Frankish, so it was probably taken in a raid.

'Where are these two men now?' he asked as he sat with the portreeve again.

'Under lock and key in an empty, rat-infested storage hut, guarded by the men who captured them.'

'Have them brought to me. I have one or two questions to put to them.'

*

Alfred glowered at the two Norsemen, taking in every detail of their appearance and agreeing that Nerlan was right in his descriptions of them. One was of little note. In his middling years and of a grey and jaded appearance, his lack of height and girth were in sharp contrast to the figure of his striking companion. This man stood tall and broad and, despite being bound at the wrist, his stance was arrogant and derisive. His tunic and breeches were not the usual poor man's garb and his black hair was held back from his face in a number of tight braids.

The big Dane's dark, contemptuous eyes fixed on Alfred. 'Sigeferth made it back to his ship; I saw him sail away myself. You'll never catch a man like him, for all your kingly title and big armies. My cousin will plague your shores till his dying day. Compared to his, our lives are of little worth, so just kill us now and be done with it. It's what you're planning, so the sooner the better.'

Alfred gave him a long, mirthless smile. 'Tomorrow will be soon enough for that; tonight, you are in this hall to talk. Don't worry, it won't take long. I don't wish to deprive you of the company of your long-toothed friends. As for this cousin of yours, whoever he might or might not be is irrelevant to me. He's just another pagan who will get his full due in the end. Our Lord God will see to that.'

The puny Dane shuddered. 'Perhaps if you tell them what he wants to know, Harald, this king might see fit to let us live.'

Alfred was silent for a moment, nodding a little as though in thought. 'That could be a possibility, although it would very much depend on exactly what you have to say. If you tell me nothing of use, then it's back to the hut to spend your last night of life with your furry friends.'

'Ask me some questions, lord. I know as much as he does about why we're here.'

Twenty

Harald made a menacing move towards the shorter man, raising his bound hands to strike but two of Nerlan's guards stepped between them and shoved him back. 'You scrawny little toad!' he yelled. 'Don't tell these pigs a thing. If they want to know anything, let them find out somewhere else!'

Emboldened by the Saxons' firm hold on Harald, the little man's words poured forth, his pleading eyes searching Alfred's. 'I've a wife and children back in Northumbria, lord, and I'm desperate to get back to them. I only came here because I was too scared to refuse the call from Harald. Everyone knows he's cruel and vicious and he would have made us all sorry if we'd said no.'

Alfred nodded, inclined to believe him. Harald looked a brute and probably treated his countrymen as badly as he did his enemies. 'What's your name and what position in your village does Harald hold?'

'I am Gils, lord, from Northumbria, and Harald's been our jarl for the last six years. Things were different when his father was alive. He treated his villagers fairly.'

'So, Gils, are you saying that all the men who came to attack Exeter are Northumbrians?'

'Not all of them, lord. Of the hundred and forty ships, thirty of them were Sigeferth's and Harald's, and another sixty were from across Northumbria. The other fifty came from East Anglia, some of them carrying men who had only arrived at Mersea Island a few weeks ago. It was their jarls who sent word to Danes across Northumbria and East Anglia to join them in raids on Saxon lands. The promise of booty was too much to resist.'

Alfred inwardly fumed. Despite his repeated demands that the Norsemen in the Danelaw respect their treaties with Wessex, at the first temptation they had broken their oaths and returned to their old ways.

'What about the forty ships that didn't turn into the Exe with you?' Nerlan asked. 'We know they sailed on towards Cornwall, so where, exactly, were they heading?'

'Wouldn't you like to know!'

It took every bit of Alfred's self-control to stop himself from striking a hefty blow at Harald's sneering face and watch blood trickling through that well-trimmed beard. Instead, he forced a smile. 'So be it. At sunrise you both die and your bodies will be tossed back into the hut for the hungry rats to feast on.'

Harald merely shrugged, but Gils fell to his knees. 'Lord, If I answer your question, will you let me live?'

'Possibly... but how will I know if you are lying?'

Gils' face reflected his panic. 'Why would I lie? I am telling you the truth so I can go home to my family.'

'Then spit it out, and I promise that if we find you have been truthful, you'll be released. Unfortunately, that might not be for some time. Meanwhile, you will stay here under guard, although Nerlan will find you better accommodation than the rat house, and you will be regularly fed. Does that sound a fair bargain to you?'

'It does, lord.'

'So where were those forty ships heading?' Nerlan repeated.

'Around Cornwall to raid along the North Devon coast. I heard say there's a fortress there they want to try their luck at, though the name escapes me right now. Could have been

Twenty

something like Courtsburn… or Countsberg.'

Nerlan grinned. 'Could it have been Countisbury?'

'That's it – but I've no idea where it is, so no use in asking me that.'

'Thor strike you dead, you traitorous scum!' Harald hurled at Gils, struggling to break from the hold of the two guards. 'If you're in that hut with me tonight, I swear I'll break your neck!'

Alfred shook his head. 'There's no possibility of that happening, Gils. Tonight, Harald will be playing with his ratty friends all by himself and tomorrow the rats will feast.' He nodded at the two guards. 'Get him out of my sight.'

Alone with his thoughts, Alfred made his plans. Tomorrow he'd send word to Eadgar, the Southampton portreeve. His orders would be simple: sail a dozen of their fastest ships round the south-west coast of Wessex and ensure the Norse fleet led by Sigeferth is unable to raid anywhere along the shores of their kingdom. Alfred had no idea how many ships had managed to flee from Exeter with this supposedly notorious raider. Gils had mentioned only the one, so Sigeferth could well be sailing alone. But Alfred was taking no chances.

A wave of sadness took him as he thought of Radulf, ill and possibly dying in Southampton. The role of leading the Wessex fleet had always been his in the past, and Alfred had relied on his wise counsel over the years. But now was not the time for sad thoughts and Alfred focused on planning his army's ride across country to the North Devon coast. Those forty shiploads of Northmen would not find raiding in Devon an easy task at all.

Twenty One

Aethelred's army of six hundred and fifty Mercians reached Thorney Island to find the two hundred men promised by Alfred had already arrived. The three thegns were speaking with Edward and Radulf's two sons while their men spread out and settled in the camp. It didn't take long for Aethelred to notice that none of Alfred's men had, as yet, been sent to boost the sparse number of Saxons keeping lookout on the opposite bank of the river and he promptly sent Garth with half of his army to join them.

Edward hurried over to embrace his brother-by-marriage, the relief on his face evident. 'Thank God you're all here. I doubt I'd have had an army in another couple of days without reinforcements. By the time the next groups of the standing army got here the Danes would have been miles away. And I thank you for sending those men across to the far bank. Our numbers were badly depleted on both sides of the island.'

'You will know that Alfred sent us,' Aethelred said, squinting into the May sunlight as he tried to focus on movements on the isle. The Danes were surveying the new arrivals and probably reconsidering their options. 'He was on his way here when a call for help came from Exeter. The city was being attacked by a huge force of Danes and would not have been able to hold them off for much longer without the king's help.'

'So we've been told. I realise my father must go to wherever the need is greatest but I'm thankful he had you to send in his stead. Without reinforcements we wouldn't have been able to

Twenty One

stop the Danes from fleeing into the Danelaw.'

'Happy to oblige, my friend. With Alfred's two hundred, we have brought you another six hundred and fifty men.' Aethelred gave Edward's arm a friendly punch. 'Besides, if I'd refused, your sister would have skinned me alive!' He pointed to the packhorses being unladen by his men. 'The message said you needed food as well as men so Aethelflaed and the women put together as much as they could at short notice. Garth's already taken a share of it for the men across the river. I swear, if we hadn't needed to get to you in a hurry, your sister would have had us herding half a dozen sheep here for you as well.'

'Yes, that sounds like Aethelflaed,' Edward said, laughing at the image. 'But we're all more than grateful you're here and for whatever food you've brought. We've been relying mostly on foraging since we arrived. None of us had much food in our saddle packs when we set out, and we weren't expecting to lay siege.'

Aethelred nodded as they wandered round the camp, well able to understand their predicament. 'So, what's been happening on the island?'

'For one thing, the Danes out there will be desperate for food by now. At least my army's been able to hunt for hares and such like; we even speared an odd deer. But as far as we can tell there's little to forage on the island and the Danes would have been on the verge of surrendering if not for my dwindling army!'

Edward rubbed his brow in frustration. 'One thing's for sure, I'll never make the mistake of not checking the men's terms of service again, and I can't force them to stay.'

'Don't be too hard on yourself. Your quick thinking in sending for help has prevented the Danes from breaking from the island.'

Edward shook his head. 'My oversight with the men's terms of service is inexcusable but the fact that you and my father got these men to me so quickly will, hopefully, stop an imminent breakout. The Danes have been watching my army gradually shrinking for the last week and we reckoned they were just waiting to see how low our numbers dropped before they tried. In another day or two we'd have had no chance of stopping them. Now your forces are here, they'll be thinking twice about any conflict. And for all we know they may still have their leader to consider.'

Aethelred's raised eyebrows and cocked head were enough to encourage Edward to explain. 'Their leader, a jarl called Torsten, was wounded at Farnham and we didn't expect him to last long. But if he's dead, his men haven't bothered with a funeral pyre or we'd have seen it. If he's still alive and suffering, getting him off the island during a breakout would not be easy for them.'

'If you put that together with their weakened state due to near starvation, I'd say breaking out won't be their preferred move, especially since our arrival.' Aethelred looked intently at Edward. 'Tell me, what would your father do in this situation?'

Edward grinned. 'We both know that Alfred would do what he usually does and offer them terms. He'd allow them to leave the island and head to the Danelaw on the condition they swear oaths never to raid his lands again. He'd also demand at least six hostages, who would be killed if oaths were broken. And

Twenty One

you know what, Aethelred? He'll expect me to do the same.'

All was quiet in the camp following the meal that night, but in the grey light of the predawn, another group of the Wessex standing army silently drifted away. Aethelred watched the figures meld into the gloom, his main thought being that these men had, at least, set off for home with their bellies full.

The rest of that day was uneventful, but at mid-morning the following day, the Danes had stirred and were massed along the edge of the island. Saxon and Mercian troops stood ready for the breakout that Edward had been expecting for days, though far enough back from the bank in the event of archers suddenly emerging through the lines, aiming to kill as many of their men before the battle began.

Then a mounted figure pushed through the Danish lines and hoisted a tree branch with a scrap of white cloth attached to it. Aethelred watched as he held out an arm, waving it about, seemingly to stress whatever he was saying. But the Dane's words were drowned in the wide gap and the continuous gushing of the river's flow.

At Aethelred's side, Edward gestured for the flag-bearer to advance and the Dane urged his horse into the water.

'I am Gunnarr,' the Dane said, dismounting soaked to the waist. 'I've come to speak to your leader.'

Edward needed no prompting. 'Well, Gunnarr, I am Edward, son of King Alfred of Wessex.' He gestured to Aethelred standing next to him. 'And this is Aethelred, Lord of West Mercia. We are joint leaders here, so you can say your piece to both of us.' He indicated some thick logs that had served as seats. 'Come and sit. Your horse will be taken care of until you return to the island.'

Aethelred took in the gaunt face and lank brown hair of this man of middling years as they sat on the logs. Lack of food had done him no favours. 'We respect your courage in coming to us alone and swear no harm will befall you since you hold the flag of truce.'

Gunnarr grunted, as though the assurance meant nothing, his sunken brown eyes flicking between Edward and Aethelred seeming to assess the authority and experience of the two young leaders. 'My father is dying and we need to be with our people to honour his body on a funeral pyre. So, we surrender, in the hope that you will let us to go on our way. Our comrades and families wait for us on the Anglian coast, ready to sail home.'

'In your present situation it's easy to say what you intend. But it would be even easier to forget those intentions once you've left here and built up your strength again.'

Aethelred's words earned him a scathing look from Gunnarr. 'Not all Danes are liars! My father will not live for more than another few days. He's been a respected jarl for years and our people at Mersea will want to honour him at his funeral ceremony.' He heaved a sigh. 'We are in no state to do battle with you. As you said, we need to find food to regain our strength. I am offering you our surrender, and hope you can find mercy enough to let us leave.'

Aethelred glanced at Edward, who took his cue. 'We accept your surrender, Gunnarr, but your leaving here will be on our terms.'

Gunnarr's eyes narrowed, suggesting an outburst was imminent, but he held his temper in check. 'Go on.'

Twenty One

'First, we want your oaths that you will leave the Anglo-Saxon kingdoms and never return to raid and plunder. You will swear that on whatever amulets you have with you to your gods.'

'That can be arranged. Many of our men wear necklaces of Thor.'

'Good. Then you will select six of your men to be our hostages. If you should happen to forget your vows and raid our people again, each of those six will forfeit their lives.'

Edward waited for the reply as Gunnarr seemed to think the demand over. 'If you refuse there will be no surrender and you can return to the island to starve with what's left of your large army from Appledore.'

'Then I have no other choice than to agree.'

'No, Gunnarr, you don't.'

Aethelred stood, breaking the glowering eye contact between Edward and the Dane. 'I suggest you get back to the island and choose three others who will take the oaths with you. They must, of course, have some standing with the men. Then you will pick six hostages. As long as you keep your vows they will be fairly treated.'

Edward headed back to where the Dane's horse was being held, leaving Gunnarr no alternative than to do likewise. 'We'll expect the ten of you by mid-afternoon,' he said as Gunnarr remounted. 'If you don't arrive, we'll assume the siege is still on and you will all likely die of starvation.'

The oath taking was a straightforward affair. The hostages were led away by Radulf's two sons while Gunnarr and three others made the necessary vows on their small amulets of

Thor's hammer. Aethelred listened, knowing from his father and Aethelnoth how little oaths of any kind meant to Danes. Nor would they have any concern for the lives of the hostages. Unless they were men of status, specifically picked by leaders of the opposing army, hostages were usually the runts of the pack, the weakest or the cowardly, and as such they were expendable.

Tomorrow, Edward would head back to Winchester with those six hostages and the remaining men of his standing army. But Aethelred was in no great rush to return to London just yet… at least, not before he knew what the angry-eyed Gunnarr intended to do once he reached the Danelaw.

*

Alert in their battle lines, the joint armies of Saxons and Mercians watched the Danes make their exodus from Thorney Island. Aethelred scanned the mass of riders, wondering how the dying jarl was being transported. No one so close to death could ride unsupported, yet a makeshift pallet dragged behind a horse would slow the company down too much. Whereas, if Torsten was dead, his body could simply be tied across his saddle. But, hidden in the midst of moving horseflesh, both the jarl's state of health and manner of travel remained a mystery.

Aethelred watched until the Danes disappeared from view, seemingly heading north-east to cross the shallow, upper reaches of the River Lea before turning south-east towards Mersea Island on the Anglian coast, as Gunnarr had said. Yet, somehow, Aethelred still couldn't accept that Gunnarr had been honest. After all, honesty wasn't a prized trait amongst

Twenty One

Norsemen, particularly when they were intent upon raiding and plundering. But if the Dane *had* been lying about their destination, where else could they be heading?

A possible answer suddenly flashed into Aethelred's head: Hastein was in Benfleet. News of his move across the Thames from Milton had reached Lundenburh within days of the baptised Danes leaving the city. At the time, neither Alfred nor Aethelred had thought anything of it, considering that Hastein was simply on his way to East Anglia in search of somewhere to settle. But now, Aethelflaed's voice rang in his ears:

Hastein is slyer than a fox and lies pour from his mouth as easily as mead from a jug. Don't let yourself be taken in by him.

Perhaps Hastein has no intention of settling in the Danelaw.

Wanting to share his suspicions, Aethelred sought out Edward, who was busy striking camp with his men. 'Gunnarr might be heading north-east right now, but once he's crossed the Lea, I'd lay odds he'll veer in a more south-easterly direction than he led us to believe.'

'Why would he do that?' Edward looked puzzled. 'The rest of his people are at Mersea and he sounded pretty keen to get back with them again.'

'I'm not certain that particular group of Danes will still be at Mersea or, at least, not all of them. Many of the men are likely to have sailed south to join Hastein at Benfleet – probably on Hastein's invitation. Perhaps you hadn't heard that Hastein went straight to Benfleet after the baptism?'

Edward shook his head. 'There was no news of it while I was in Winchester, although messengers could have arrived when we were on our way to Surrey. I imagine news got to

Lundenburh quickly enough.'

'It did, but like your father, I believed Hastein had simply stopped there on his way to settle in Anglia. Now I'm not so sure. The thing is, Edward, as far as we know, he's still in Benfleet and I've started wondering *why* he's still there… I don't suppose you know that Aethelflaed took an instant dislike to Hastein at the baptism ceremony?'

A grin crept across Edward's face. 'What did she say about him?'

'Lots of things, including describing him as being "as slippery as an eel and as trustworthy as a wolf".'

Edward's grin grew wider. 'Yes, that sounds like Aethelflaed's kind of phrase.'

'What I can't get out of my head right now is her worried face when she spoke about Hastein. She has such forebodings about the Dane's presence in our lands, baptised Christian or not. No matter that your father trusts him to keep his vows and settle in the Danelaw, Aethelflaed truly believes Hastein craves our lands and won't be satisfied until he gets them. And, you know what, Edward, having had time to think about it, I'm inclined to agree with her.'

'Having not met this Dane, I can't agree or disagree with my sister's estimation of the man, other than to say that we shouldn't discount her feelings about him. Aethelflaed has a way of seeing through people's boasts and lies that less observant people miss.'

Despite feeling Edward's comment to be partly aimed at him, Aethelred could not disagree with his brotherly praise of Aethelflaed. 'The embarrassing part was when she challenged

Twenty One

the Dane's slyness to his face, only to stomp away, livid, when he laughed at her. I can tell you, your sister wasn't easy to live with for those two weeks.'

Edward laughed out loud. 'You'll never change her, you know. Aethelflaed has always charged right in and told people she disliked what she thought of them. She's embarrassed all of us many times, even Father. Nevertheless, we'd be wise to keep her opinion of Hastein in mind should future dealings with him arise.

'So, is this little story about my sister leading up to you telling me something?'

Aethelred nodded. 'I know you need to get your men back to Winchester but I have no reason to return to Lundenburh just yet. I've almost six hundred and fifty men here with me and I intend to follow Gunnarr. Our scouts will keep us informed of the direction they're heading, although I'm almost certain it won't be to Mersea.'

'What will you do if he does reach Benfleet?' Edward looked sceptical of the plan. 'If Hastein's band from Milton has already been joined by the Danes from Mersea Island, as you believe, once Gunnarr's band of seven hundred gets there, you'll be vastly outnumbered. And have you considered that other Danes may also have joined Hastein?'

'I have, but I don't think Hastein is ready for all-out battle yet. He'll still be building up his army and will probably keep to small-scale raids until he commands a force as big as Halfdan and Guthrum's. So, to answer your question, Edward, I'll wait and watch. If I can catch Hastein out raiding at least I'll have proven that Aethelflaed was right about him. As to what

I'll do about it, events will dictate that. Confronting smaller raiding parties is a possibility.

'We'll set off as soon as our horses are saddled and we've got food in our packs. I can't see us being able to forage, especially once we get further into the Danelaw.'

*

The ride across the south-eastern corner of Aethelred's kingdom of West Mercia revealed that several villages had been attacked and their occupants mercilessly hacked down. Torched homes blackened the landscape, bodies of the slain already ravaged by rapacious crows, buzzing insects and night-time predators. The state of decay indicated that most of the raids had taken place over a week ago, which meant that Gunnarr's men could not be held responsible. It didn't take Aethelred long to point the finger at Hastein.

'By all that is holy, Garth, I swear Hastein will pay for this!' he snarled at as they rode past the fourth desecrated village that day. 'And I'll never question my wife's feelings about anyone again!'

Gagging on the stench of rotting, insect-infested flesh, Garth could do no more than nod.

Early the following morning, two of Aethelred's scouts returned to his overnight camp on the edge of the Danelaw. One piece of news was as Aethelred had expected: Gunnarr's band was now back in the saddle and heading in the direction of Benfleet. The other news, although not expected, did not really surprise him.

Twenty One

'They camped at the edge of some woods last night and some of them headed out to hunt. A few of them came back with hares, or ducks and geese from a nearby stream, but one little group had taken an old stag; another group, a small pig.'

'Then they ate better than we did… but, I suppose, those freshly roasted meats would have been shared by over seven hundred men so perhaps they each had very little. And now, Eafa, if you two have nothing more to report, get some food in your bellies then head back on watch. Stay on Gunnarr's tail until he gets to Benfleet. I want to know for certain whether he joins up with Hastein.'

'The Danes' meal wasn't my point, lord,' Eafa said with a grin, 'but there is something you might like to know.'

'Go on.'

'A group of them spent some time digging while their food was cooking. We'd moved pretty close to their camp by then, and even from behind the trees we could see they were digging a grave, and someone was definitely buried.' He gestured at his companion. 'We guessed it was the old jarl, Torsten.'

'Gunnarr's wish to honour Torsten with a funeral pyre didn't last long then,' Garth said, shaking his head. 'Though I don't suppose we should be too surprised at that. The jarl either died on the journey or was dead before they left Thorney, and Gunnarr couldn't be arsed to take his body into Hastein's camp.' He thought about that for a moment. 'I wonder why they didn't build a funeral pyre where they camped? They don't know we're following, so they couldn't have been worried about being seen. And they had enough campfires going to cook their food.'

'A burial's just quicker,' Aethelred replied. 'After a pyre, they'd still have Torsten's ashes to collect the next day and Gunnarr's probably keen to reach Benfleet.

'And I'm keen to see what they all get up to when they do.'

*

Three days after they had left Thorney Island, the two scouts returned to report that Gunnarr's army was now in Benfleet.

'The town's changed a lot since the last time we were there and it became part of the Danelaw.' Eafa scratched his dark head as he thought. 'It's much bigger for a start, and there are now heavy earthworks around it with a palisade of sturdy sharpened stakes along the top. Breaching those could take some doing. The three gateways through the defences look solid, too, and would likely take some time to break down, even with a ram. If they have a walkway behind the top of the palisade, we could well be facing archers, which would make it almost impossible to approach, let alone break down the gates.'

Aethelred harrumphed. 'All Hastein's doing, no doubt. My father always said he was a quick thinker. Did you see signs of any archers?'

'There was no movement at all behind the palisade and, if we hadn't known better, we could have wondered at Benfleet's need for such defences. Two of the gates were wide open and both men and women were casually wandering in and out.'

Aethelred took in that information and considered what to make of it. 'It could be that Hastein and his people feel safe at Benfleet, far away from the clutches of Wessex or West

Twenty One

Mercian troops. If that's the case, they may well not be on the lookout for danger – which would be in our favour. But it could as likely be that they've concocted a display to fool any attackers into thinking that besieging Benfleet would be easy.'

'Either way, we'll find out when we attack the place.' Garth shrugged. 'There could be hundreds of armed men inside and archers behind that palisade. Gates can soon be shut, or deliberately left open, depending on where the Danes plan to meet any attack. But I think we can be certain of one thing: Benfleet is now Hastein's, so it isn't simply some peaceful settlement. His people are here to take our lands.'

'Truly spoken, my friend. So, we give ourselves time to watch before we make our move.'

'Oh, and something else, lord,' Eafa said. 'One side of the stronghold opens up to the jetties along the little river that leads down to the mouth of the Thames. There are dozens of longships moored there.'

Aethelred nodded. 'I thought there might be. Some of them will be Hastein's, but I'm guessing the rest belong to the Danes from Appledore with, perhaps, some East Anglian and Northumbrian ships.'

'Hastein must be gathering a fair-sized army,' Garth said, reinforcing Aethelred's feelings. 'He seems to be planning to do more than raid small villages.'

'Eventually, maybe, but before he challenges Alfred, I think he'll want to see just how large a force he can gather. He'll allow time for more Northumbrian and East Anglian Danes to join him, and perhaps any who've been raiding in Francia and the Low countries this spring. But until then he'll continue to raid homesteads and churches across eastern Mercia.' Aethelred heaved a sigh. 'We'll have to try to stop them, but with our small army pitched against Hastein's ever-growing force, right now, Garth, I don't know how we're going to do it.'

*

The joint army of Saxons and Mercians closed in on the Benfleet fortress at mid-morning three days later and tethered their mounts in nearby woods. For some time, they hung back, silently observing people moving in and out of the open gates, seemingly in pursuit of their daily tasks. None appeared to be wary of pending danger. A party of some two dozen men set out on foot with their spears and bows, heading for the dense forest a mile to the north, their pack horses and carts suggesting they intended to hunt. Aethelred sent fifty of his men to ensure none of them returned to help defend the fortress.

Women and children scoured the edges of the woodland, gathering twigs and small branches which Aethelred guessed to be kindling for their hearthfires. Daytime Benfleet was at work, just like any other village. But he knew that at night, when those gates were closed and bolted, Hastein's stronghold would be almost impregnable.

By noon, most of the women and children had retreated inside and Aethelred realised it was time to move; before long, those gates would close. Warriors stormed the fortress from all sides, surging through the open gates into the large settlement inside. Aethelred estimated no more than fifty Danish warriors stood to meet them in combat and, vastly outnumbered, they

Twenty One

were soon cut down. Panicked, screaming women and children fled, some succeeding in making it through the still-open gates, others raced for shelter into their reed-thatched homes.

'Forget those who got away, just round up the rest,' Aethelred yelled. 'I want them out here, where I can see them.'

A handful of aged or wounded men and well-nigh two hundred terrified women and children were wrenched from their homes to huddle together in the centre of the fortress, surrounded by Aethelred's men.

'You... explain where the rest of your warriors are,' Aethelred demanded, jabbing a finger towards a man of middling years hobbling on one leg with the aid of two stout crutches. His right leg was missing from the knee down, the binding cloths stained with dried blood suggesting the grievous wound was not too recent. 'And I don't mean the few we saw going out to hunt.'

The Dane opened his mouth as though to reply, then shut it again and glanced round at the rest of the captives.'

'Speak, man, or you may well lose the other leg.' Aethelred silently cursed his own rash words, knowing he could never order the taking of a helpless man's leg and praying he would speak.

'Let him be,' a woman called out as she pushed through the huddle. 'He has suffered enough. If you want answers, I will give them.'

'And you are...?'

'Greta, lord.'

'Then tell me, Greta, where are all Hastein's warriors?'

Greta momentarily stared down at the earth, absently

tucking a strand of fair hair back beneath her short head veil, then looked up and glared at him. 'They went out to raid. We need food if we are to survive here.' Her voice held more than a hint of defiance.

Aethelred felt his rage mounting, and waited for his mind and body to calm before he spoke. 'Are you saying that the gathering of food involves the slaughter of innocent people and the destruction of their villages?'

Greta's blue gaze remained locked with Aethelred's green. He knew she'd be weighing up her chances of staying alive if she said the wrong thing. 'No, it does not. But… but there is too little food to be foraged to feed all of us, so our men must take it from the villagers. It is only because they resist that they are killed.'

Aethelred scowled, knowing that to be untrue. 'What about the Christian churches? It is not only food they take from them, is it?'

Greta continued to hold his stare, though she seemed at a loss for an answer.

'Is it?' Aethelred snapped, forcing her to reply.

'No, it is not. Our warriors raid churches to provide us with plunder, which we sell or trade for other things we need.'

'Where do they raid from here?'

'Mostly villages close by, in Essex, but also in East Mercia and sometimes into the west of that kingdom, as they have done this time.' Her eyes flicked to Aethelred's outraged face and she quickly added, 'It is only until we leave Benfleet and settle in East Anglia.'

Aethelred breathed deeply, keeping himself calm. If he

Twenty One

continued this line of questioning, he would not be able to control his temper. 'We've been informed of the arrival of a new band on Danes in Benfleet. Is this true?' Aethelred half expected the woman to lie, and was surprised when she did not.

'Yes, a new band arrived three days ago but I didn't ask where they had come from.' She shrugged. 'New groups often join us.'

'Which of the bands are you with Greta?' he said instead. 'Have you come to our lands with one of the fleets that sailed from Francia, or are you from Northumbria, or perhaps East Anglia?'

The panicked look that flashed in the woman's eyes did not escape Aethelred, though her sudden loss of composure came as a surprise.

'I came here from Francia with Jarl Hastein's band,' she said, throwing herself to her knees, her pleading eyes fixed on Aethelred's. 'I beg mercy for us all, lord. Most of the women here have children to care for. I have three of my own.' She gestured to the mass of Danes behind her and two boys and a young girl pushed through the crowd.

Aethelred stared at Greta's two sons and recognition hit. 'Raud and Davyn... you are Greta's sons?' The twins nodded and Aethelred focused on the young girl, who looked no more than seven or eight. 'And what is your name, and how old are you?'

'I am Inga, lord, and I am almost seven.'

'Well, Inga, I have never met you before today but I have met your brothers. Perhaps Davyn didn't tell you, but I am his godfather and King Alfred is Raud's.' He refocused on Hastein's wife, the children's mother. 'I see now why you are fearful for your safety, Greta. Hastein's family will be worth a lot to us – or rather, to King Alfred. Now, on the lives of your children, tell us truthfully, when do you expect this raiding band back?'

'Not for some time yet. They left two days ago and are often away for more than a week.'

'I take it the new arrivals rode with them?'

'Most of them, lord, but a few were too weak to ride. Hastein told us to make sure they were well fed and rested.'

Aethelred singled out a few dozen of his men. 'Take Greta and her children as our hostages, along with another dozen women and children and a dozen of the more able-bodied of the men. Then search every building for plunder. There's bound to be some, especially from the churches raided. Find enough carts to carry both loot and hostages and enough horses to pull them. They'll either be stabled somewhere in here, or out in a paddock. Remember to bind the men's wrists – and those of any women who show signs of defiance. Then get them all outside these walls until we're ready to leave.'

He took a deep breath, his gaze sweeping his men. 'The rest of us will deal with their ships. We'll row any that look seaworthy a hundred yards downstream where they'll be berthed until we've finished at the quayside. The vessels left here will be either smashed to pieces or torched. Make sure none are left repairable. Is that clear?' The men nodded. 'Then Garth will pick some of you to sail the seaworthy craft across the estuary to Rochester, where they'll stay until King Alfred decides where he wants them. You men will need your horses aboard or you'll be walking back to Lundenburh from there.'

Twenty One

Aethelred turned to face Hastein's people. 'Those of you not taken as hostages will be left here. You can wait for your men to return, or not, whatever you choose. But be aware that if you do stay here, there will be no houses for you to live in. Once Benfleet is empty, we'll be burning it to the ground.'

He strode off to the quayside, followed by the rest of his men, and yelled over his shoulder, 'I don't need to tell any of you that all this must be done quickly. 'Greta could well be lying through her teeth, and having Hastein's band returning before we leave is something we can do without.'

Twenty-Two

Winchester, Wessex: mid-May, 893

Ealhswith's green linen skirts swept the rushes of the Winchester hall as she paced, the newly delivered missive crumpled in her hand. After opening it in the hope of reading that Alfred was on his way home, its contents returned her to the state of misery that had consumed her for months. News of her husband's success at Exeter was heartening, but the fact that he was now heading into Devon to confront the fleet of forty longships that had sailed past the mouth of the Exe, filled her with dread. Having not set eyes on her husband since he left for Maidenhead eight months ago, she longed to have him safely home. Any encounter with the Danes was laden with possible consequences of disaster.

Ealhswith now faced the truth that Alfred would not be home for some time. He'd already sent word to the Southampton portreeve to sail their ships round the Cornish coast and up to North Devon. With Eadgar's men following them at sea and his own army along the coasts, Alfred was hopeful the Danes would find raiding settlements difficult, if not impossible.

Around her the constant chatter of the clerics working on Alfred's behalf mingled with the clatter of servants about their chores and children at play. The hall was rarely silent these days, for which Ealhswith was thankful. It helped to stop her from fretting over the safety of those she loved. It wasn't only Alfred she worried about now, but also Edward, and even Aethelflaed's

Twenty-Two

husband, Aethelred. At least Edward was safe, for now. Her eldest son had arrived back after his siege at Thorney Island a couple of weeks ago and the success he'd had at Farnham had done much to bolster his confidence in himself and his ability to lead. Ealhswith was so proud of him, but she knew how much he, too, longed for this Danish invasion to be over. His marriage to Ecgwynn would not take place until it was.

As for Aethelred, Ealhswith's son-by-marriage was proving to be a great leader, justifying Alfred's faith in him. Not only had he rallied to Edward's aid at Thorney, but had taken it upon himself to destroy the Danish hornets' nest at Benfleet. Aethelflaed had previously written of her forebodings regarding the Dane called Hastein, and Ealhswith knew she'd be pleased to have been proven right. But being right would not stop Aethelflaed from worrying as much as Ealhswith over the safety of her family.

Ealhswith cursed Hastein and his savages to everlasting hell and prayed their journey there would be soon.

'Are you feeling ill, my lady?' The gentle voice and the fleeting touch of her elbow jerked Ealhswith from her seething thoughts and she smiled at the look of concern on Asser's face.

'I am well enough, thank you, Bishop,' she replied, laying a hand on his arm. 'I will worry until Alfred is home and the Danes have left our kingdom, so take no notice of me and my moods.'

'I have one piece of news that may hearten you, Lady Ealhswith. My monthly letter from Aethelgifu arrived some moments ago.' Ealhswith nodded, happy to know that the friendship between her abbess daughter and the now Bishop of Sherborne still flourished. 'Aethelgifu asked me to pass on the news that she will be paying you a visit next week.'

'Oh, that is good news. Thank you for letting me know, Lord Asser. It's almost a year since we saw Aethelgifu and we now have something nice to think about and preparations to make. Did she say how many others will be with her?'

'I believe it will be simply Aethelgifu and a couple of her nuns, with a bodyguard of a dozen.' The bishop smiled. 'The abbess is not coming on business for Shrewsbury Abbey, merely as a chance to see the family she greatly misses.

'I wonder if I might put an idea to you, my lady,' he continued, his face becoming serious. 'It concerns my work here for King Alfred, although I confess, it is not something he requested. Yet I think he would be pleased to have it done. After all, it's about his life and the way in which future generations will see him, and perhaps come to understand all that he did.'

Ealhswith laughed. 'Lord Bishop, I'm afraid I can't begin to guess what you are talking about unless you make it a little clearer.'

'No, of course you can't, so perhaps if we sit down, I will try to do that.'

Glad of the distraction, Ealhswith sat with Asser at a bench as he explained. 'I'd like to start writing the story of King Alfred's life and work. Despite his absence, the king has spoken with me about his early life on many an occasion and I feel I know enough to make a start. Finer details can always be filled in once Alfred returns, if need be.'

Ealhswith considered Asser's tired face and the way his simple, grey robe hung on his slight frame, and inwardly sighed.

Twenty-Two

This dear man was not one to care about either his looks or his health, and she already feared he was spending too many hours a day working. Since becoming Bishop of Sherborne two and a half years ago, he spent much of his time travelling between the places where his duties lay. 'I'm sure Alfred will think that a splendid idea, as do I,' she said, reaching out to take his hand. 'But, my dear Bishop, do make sure you don't overtax yourself with this work. You need your sleep just as much as the rest of us. I know you are often still working long after most of us have retired for the night, oftentimes on nights when you are due to travel the following morning.' She smiled at Asser's look of surprise. 'There isn't much that escapes the notice of the servants, and even they are worried for your health.'

Asser's broad smile masked the fatigue that Ealhswith knew he must feel, though his reply did not convince her for one moment. 'I shall make every effort to be in my bed at the same time as everyone else in future, my lady.'

'Good,' she replied, 'then all I'll need to do is make sure you eat a little more. You can't spend all those hours working on an empty stomach, you know.'

*

'Thor strike the Saxons dead while they sleep!' Hastein raged, circling the remnants of his destroyed fortress. Most of those who had escaped Aethelred's onslaught had remained, for want of somewhere else to go. Even many of those who had managed to flee had returned, keen to stay with the rest of the band.

'In Odin's name, you're saying they took the loot and destroyed our ships as well! So, what have we left…?

'Nothing!' he ranted on, as much at himself as anyone else, and inwardly admitting he should never have left the fortress with so few fighting men. But how was he to know the women would be foolish enough to leave the gates open? He'd built them a strong, defensible base, yet they roamed outside as though they were still in their homeland! And yet… deep down, Hastein knew the fault lay with him. So keen had he been on raiding, he'd given no order to stay locked inside the stronghold in his absence.

But to be so humiliated by Aethelred… Eadwulf's son of all people! Worse still, he'd even *liked* the young ealdorman. At this moment, it seemed to Hastein that everyone he'd ever trusted or loved had eventually turned their backs on him. All except Bjorn.

By now the cursed Alfred would have a few dozen of Hastein's people in his grasp, including his own wife and children. But he would not let that defeat him. Women and children were expendable, and the men taken were weak and useless. Their loss would cause him no sleepless nights. He would find another base, and once he'd had time to think things through, he'd make these Saxons and Mercians realise that, no matter what they did, Hastein was here to stay.

Within a few days, he had moved the remainder of his men and their families to Shoebury, ten miles east of Benfleet along the Essex coast. But he had no intention of spending time fortifying this town. It would be nothing more than a temporary place to store the booty taken in raids in western

Twenty-Two

Mercia and to keep his army together until he could think of somewhere better.

Their plundering of local settlements continued, and with the passing days, groups of Northumbrian and East Anglian Danes began to arrive. Soon, fleets of them were sailing up to the Shoebury quay. But many of these new arrivals were men who'd had long-standing dealings with Alfred of Wessex.

'Staying here isn't a good idea,' Soren said as the band of fifty rode back after three days of raiding churches and settlements in the area surrounding Shoebury. The seasoned warrior shook his balding head and jerked his thumb at the packhorses carrying the few bags of loot. 'If this is all Essex has to offer, we'd best be moving on. But with all those fortresses the Saxon king has had built in Wessex and the southern parts of West Mercia, and the camps of his new standing army that criss-cross the open country, raiding in those places would be too risky. What I'm saying is, we need to find somewhere well away from Alfred's eye.'

He suddenly caught Hastein's cold stare. 'Course, it's up to you, but most of my men are looking for richer and easier gained pickings and I can think of a few places where we could do that.'

Hastein held Soren's gaze, knowing him to be amongst those who had come to these lands with Guthrum and would have had a bellyful of the Wessex king. He would also, no doubt, have kept up to date with the improvements made by Alfred to his armies and towns.

'I'd already made the decision to move on, long before you got here, Soren, and for the same reasons you've just given.

I've also chosen somewhere I believe will be suitable.' Hastein's tone was sharper than he'd intended, but no newcomer was going to ride in and tell him what he should or shouldn't do. He let out a loud sigh and said more affably, 'Which is why we haven't even begun to fortify Shoebury. Believe me, before the end of this week we'll be on the move.'

*

Leaving over a hundred warriors to stay with the women and children and guard the Northumbrian and East Anglian ships at Shoebury, Hastein's army of almost a thousand rode west across the open country of the Thames Valley. After six days of hard riding and covering over a hundred and seventy miles, stopping only to raid settlements for food and snatch a few hours' sleep each night, they turned north along the valley of the River Coln. Eventually they reached the Severn Valley and followed it north.

After another four days they reached the village of Buttington, weary after riding so far and sweating beneath the hot June sun. The village nestled close to the banks of the Severn in the Welsh kingdom of Powys. It was also beside Offa's Dyke, the long earthwork constructed by the Mercian king of that name to separate his kingdom from the Welsh a hundred years ago. Relieved to have reached here unchallenged, Hastein looked forward to many weeks of raiding poorly defended West Mercian settlements, churches and abbeys, before returning to Essex with all the plunder. He was also sure that the sons of Rhodri Mawr would welcome him to their kingdom. After

Twenty-Two

all, weren't they just as much Alfred's adversaries as the Danes?

Hastein smiled, priding himself on his choice of location in which to pillage. He was elated to think that Alfred, still chasing Hastein's countrymen around Devon, could do absolutely nothing about it. Buttington was also far away from the clutches of the Wessex king's cursed ealdormen with their standing armies. All his men had to do now was build themselves a suitable base – and Hastein had spotted the perfect place. Surrounded by hills in a gap in Offa's Dyke, where the Severn had cut its way through, the site would provide a secure and defensible camp for months. From there, they'd be able to ride out and raid to their hearts' content.

After two days of constant work, the fortress was complete though, as yet, his men had not had much time to raid, and replenishing dwindling food supplies was now a priority. Hastein slept well that night, his mind filled with visions of future raids. But as the rays of newly risen sun streamed across the land, a huge mounted army swept in from the south, its numbers equalling those of Hastein's company. They lined the eastern side of the dyke, a menacing presence that would effectively block his army from raiding anywhere in Mercia. Then, at mid-morning, another large force rode in from the east, further strengthening their comrades' stand.

Cursing to all the gods that Alfred's armies were so well-trained and disciplined to be able to act without him, Hastein realised he was left with only one course of action. His army would flee into the Welsh mountains and hope to find allies among the sons of Rhodri Mawr.

No sooner had they saddled up to ride west than another

large army drew up along the banks of the Severn. Hastein swallowed a sickening dread. Leading this army were Anarawd, Cadell and Merfyn, the three sons of Rhodri Mawr. Even the Welsh had turned their backs on old comrades, preferring instead to honour their treaties with Alfred of Wessex.

A million curses on them all! Like fish in a net with nowhere left to swim, Hastein knew his army was well and truly trapped.

*

Later that June evening, Aethelred met with ealdormen, thegns and Welsh princes to discuss the best way to handle the situation. He gazed at the many familiar faces, his friend, Garth amongst them, focusing first on the ageing Aethelhelm.

Aethelred had only the highest praise for the Wiltshire ealdorman's swift actions. No sooner had his scouts reported the Danes to be riding north-west along river valleys to the Welsh borderlands, than he had rallied his armies and tracked the Danes' route, sending word to Aethelred and Aethelnoth of Somerset to do the same. Aethelhelm had also called on the oaths of allegiance made to King Alfred by the Welsh princes, demanding their help should this army reach their lands.

Despite having only recently returned to Lundenburh with the captives from Benfleet, Aethelred did not hesitate to do as requested. The loyalty and efficiency with which these seasoned leaders had served their king over the years truly impressed him. Alfred could trust men like them to think on their own and do their utmost in the defence of Wessex. It suddenly made Aethelred very proud to be numbered amongst them and he'd

Twenty-Two

do all in his power to repay Alfred for that trust.

For some time, a number of suggestions to storm the fortress were considered, but the idea did not win total approval – the strength of the Danish defences being a major concern. Eventually, tweaking his grey-streaked beard, Aethelhelm stood to sum things up.

'Taking into account that the Danes are already behind these defences, laying siege sounds the best option,' he started, glancing round the earnest faces. 'For one thing, they've only been here for a couple of days and spent most of that time building their stronghold – which means they won't have had much time to hunt or forage. Given a few weeks, I reckon they'll be starving and begging for terms of surrender. Whereas we could last here for months with King Alfred's standing armies supplying us with food.'

Anarawd pulled himself to his feet and focused deep, dark eyes on Aethelhelm before gesturing to his brothers, Cadell and Merfyn. 'We came to that conclusion the moment we got here. By laying siege, we can best the Danes without our own blood being spilt... whereas, a good number of these marauders will likely die. Our kingdoms have had enough of them and their thieving ways in the past and we don't want them here again!'

He glanced at Aethelred, a mocking grin on his face. 'Besides, we've made treaties with King Alfred in return for his protection of our lands and we intend to honour them.'

Aethelred grinned back, wondering at Anarawd's double-edged words. The Mercian people living close to the Welsh border could say the same thing about the thieving Welsh constantly raiding their lands. But he admitted to himself, the Mercians had done much the same thing in the kingdoms of Wales.

'Very honourable of you, Anarawd,' he said. 'I'll reassure the king of your ongoing support next time I see him.'

'Well then,' Aethelnoth put in quickly before this exchange developed into something undesirable, 'it seems we're all of one mind, and we make preparations for a siege. I suggest we start by building a few shelters. Summer it may be, but summer storms aren't something we want to face out in the open.'

*

The siege continued through the rest of May until early September, by which time Hastein knew his men could survive no longer without food. Desperation had forced them to slaughter their emaciated horses, and now there was nothing left. Dozens of his men had already died, the nauseating stench and swarms of buzzing insects compelling the rest to bury them before their fortress became even more unbearable.

Yet it galled Hastein to think he'd have to plead for their lives. He'd already grovelled enough before the Wessex king and his pride wouldn't take any more. No, if they were to leave here at all, it would be with a fight. When he put his views to the rest of his men, he was pleased to hear that most agreed with him.

'Then we strike out tomorrow, before the sun is up and most of the Saxon dogs will still be asleep. Taking them by surprise is the only way we'll stand a chance.' He rubbed his throbbing head, knowing that the rest of the men would feel

Twenty-Two

just as weak and exhausted as he did. 'What other choice do we have?' he ranted, as much to himself as the rest. 'If we risk breaking out, one way or another we'll get our just reward. We'll either get away – as I believe is possible for some of us – or we'll die killing our enemies and earning our places in Valhalla. Surely, either of those is preferable to staying here until we meet an ignoble and ugly death?'

His arm swept out to indicate the mass graves: the men who had already succumbed to starvation's cruel grip. 'There will be no one left to bury those of us who linger to the end.'

Silence hung over the camp, until Soren spoke up. 'I'm with you, Hastein, and I want to know who else will be joining us.'

As one, the men rose to their feet, swallowing down their cheers before the breeze carried them to the besiegers beyond the ramparts. Hastein acknowledged their support with a raised hand. 'Our best chances lie in breaking out on our eastern side, despite the numbers of Alfred's men out there. To risk heading west into the Welsh kingdoms would mean facing not only Anarawd and his brothers' armies but also crossing the Severn. Finding a ford or shallow enough crossing place could take days and result in our downfall.

'To those of you who survive, I pray that Mighty Thor will watch over you as you flee across Mercia and back to Essex.'

*

In the shadowy, grey light of the pre-dawn, seven hundred starving Danes unbolted the gates and burst from the fortress that had become their prison for the past ten weeks. But in thinking they'd take their besiegers by surprise they had been greatly mistaken. Hastein's shrieked curses were drowned as the army of Saxons and Mercians rammed into them. He should have known that a constant watch would be kept throughout the night, and that trained warriors would sleep with weapons and armour to hand. As his men unbolted the gates, the shouted alarm rang out and by the time they had surged through, Saxon and Mercian troops had drawn up into a shield wall and were moving in to attack.

Hastein knew his men could not withstand such force. In their weakened state, their only hope had rested on taking the enemy by surprise. Yet, in desperation, they fought hard, striking out with battleaxe, seax and sword at the fit and well-fed warriors they faced. Many a Wessex warrior fell back, wounded and unable to continue the fight, but outnumbered and too close to starvation to maintain the struggle, more and more Danes began to fall.

The lightening sky with the approaching dawn revealed the horror of the Norsemen's fate. Mutilated bodies littered the earth, their life blood seeping into the churned-up soil. Followed by fewer than a hundred of his men, Hastein fled across West Mercia, clutching at his throbbing arm in an effort to staunch the bleeding, Though not deep, the gash was wide and bled profusely, despite the strips of tunic that Soren wrapped round it once they were well away from Buttington.

The trek across country was slow and gruelling, the desperate need for food slowing them down in a number of attempts to hunt or pillage the odd village. By the time they reached Shoebury it was nearing the end of September.

Twenty-Two

'If we stay here in Essex, we'll be sitting ducks for the Saxon and Mercian forces who'd hoped to finish us off at Buttington,' Hastein said, his hazel gaze sweeping the remnants of his once huge community gathered in Shoebury's market place. Among them were the men and women he'd left in the town as well as the survivors from Buttington. 'As far as the Christ-loving Wessex king is concerned, we've broken our treaty with him and he'll be after our blood. He might be still in Devon, but he's got plenty of ealdormen to see his wishes carried out. And I've no intention of fortifying this town. It isn't worth the effort.'

One of Hastein's original crewmen from Francia spoke up. 'Lord Hastein, if we're leaving here, what will you do about the hostages taken by that ealdorman from Lundenburh? Remember, your wife and children are amongst them.'

Hastein glowered at the man, not wishing to be reminded of the destruction of Benfleet or the taking of his family. 'In Thor's name, Erik, there isn't a single thing we can do about it! We can't just ask to have them all back. The hostages are the forfeits of our defeat, and I imagine once Alfred returns from Devon, he'll decide whether they live or die. If they live, they'll be handed out to any of his noblemen in need of thralls on their estates.'

Erik hung his head and Hastein knew he was thinking of his own wife and young daughter who were among the hostages.

'One thing I do think, Erik, is that the Wessex king's Christian beliefs won't let him order the execution of women and children. Men are a different matter – I know Alfred's executed hostages before when oaths were broken.'

He let out a deep sigh, the gesture intended to impress the

listeners with the concern he felt for his people. 'Many of us may never see our families again, but I think we can be sure that at least the women and children will remain alive.'

'If we aren't staying here, where are we going? I can think of one place we'd be safe from Saxon clutches.'

'If you're thinking Mersea Island, Soren, you'd be right – at least, partly. Tomorrow we sail up the coast to Mersea, where we know the women and children will be safe. We'll wait there for a couple of weeks in the hope of recruiting more Northumbrians and East Angles. After our losses at Buttington, I'm hoping for a good response. Then we make another attempt to get ourselves some plunder. I won't let the pious, god-fearing Alfred beat us!' He inhaled deeply, determined to staunch his rising temper. 'I know of an ideal place, a long way from him or any of his ealdormen, and close to our countrymen in Northumbria in case we need a quick escape route.'

Soren shrugged and held out his hands. 'Do you intend telling the rest of us where this ideal place is…?'

Hasten nodded. 'I do. It's the old Roman fortress of Chester.'

Twenty Three

Aros, Danish lands: mid-October 893

The mellowing October sun touched the western horizon, framed by a sky splashed with multiple shades of crimsons, ambers and violets. It was time for the people of Aros to say their last farewells to a man who had been their friend and comrade for as long as most could remember.

Barely able to swallow with the lump in his throat, Eadwulf stared at the lofty funeral stack. Resting on top of the mounds of stout logs and thick branches infilled with kindling was the body of Bjorn's much-loved old steersman, Leif. Eadwulf could recall so many happy times with this man, whose kindness had meant the world to him as a lad. Soon, Leif's flesh would be devoured by raging tongues of flame, rendering his spirit free to fly along the Bifröst to Asgard, the realm of the gods. There, Leif would spend eternity in Valhalla, the hall of mighty Odin…

At least, Bjorn and many of the villagers had prayed it would be so, and that Odin would welcome Leif in through his great doors of polished oak. It worried them all that the old man had not died while killing an enemy in combat. Despite having survived many battles and killed many enemies in the past. Leif had lost his life while killing a wolf that had been menacing the village for days.

'Surely,' Bjorn had said, 'a wolf is just as much our enemy as a man when it threatens our lives?'

Leif had taken it upon himself to end the beast's prowling hunt. No human child would become its next meal. If only the old man had declared his intentions and taken others along to help him, he might have remained on Midgard a few more years.

Bjorn lifted one of the flaming torches circling the gathering and thrust it into the stacked timber pile, while the people of Aros looked on in mournful silence. The sparking and crackling of dried kindling rapidly became the roaring flames of the funeral pyre,

They watched, transfixed, until the burning pile collapsed and all that remained was a glowing heap on the ground that would eventually fizzle away to leave only smouldering ash. Eadwulf knew it would stay there until it had cooled enough for them to sift out Leif's remains to bury in a funeral urn with the respect the old man deserved.

'Good people of Aros,' Bjorn yelled to gain their attention before gesturing to his wife, Kata, and the rest of his family. 'Return with us to my hall, where we will feast and drink and retell our tales of Leif. That we all mourn his loss cannot be denied, but tonight we will celebrate a life well lived for almost seventy years. Our love and praises will help to carry him on his journey to Valhalla.'

Two days later, Leif's ashes were returned to his family to be buried in the little cemetery at the foot of the rise behind Bjorn's hall. It was a quiet, early morning ceremony, attended by Leif's immediate family and close friends. Memories swam in Eadwulf's head as he watched the urn containing his old friend's ashes laid in a shallow, boat-shaped grave with some

Twenty Three

of his belongings. Bjorn placed a steering oar from one of his knarrs beside the urn to represent Leif's role in his crew, while his aged wife brought bowls of his favourite foods, a mug of ale and two of his best tunics. Others added Leif's shield and battleaxe, still others his little scramseax and a dagger similar to the one he'd given Eadwulf all those years ago.

Eadwulf fingered the dagger in its leather sheath at his belt, thinking of all the times it had come in useful over the past thirty-four years and knowing he could never part with it, even more so now.

Eventually the soil was replaced and built up into a low mound before large stones were positioned around its edges, marking out the shape of a ship: a fitting resting place for the remains of a committed man of the sea.

No feasting followed today's ceremony and everyone went their own way. Eadwulf returned to his home with Freydis and their eight-year-old daughter, Thora, hoping his old friend had felt the waves of love flowing to him from all who had been touched by his kindness.

'He'll be so missed,' Freydis said as they closed the door on the chilly October day and Thora squatted on the rushes to play with her new puppy. 'He's been part of our lives for so long, and I don't know what Bjorn would have done without him at times. I suppose he'll have to find a new steersman now. Not that he goes too far nowadays; the *Sea Eagle* hasn't been out at all this year.'

'Perhaps he'll give it to Hrolf before too long.' Eadwulf had been wondering that for some time. Now into his sixtieth year, Bjorn felt his days of long sea voyages were over. The furthest he'd been for some time was to Hedeby in one of his knarrs.

'Speaking of Hrolf,' Freydis said, her back to Eadwulf as she arranged items on a trestle for making flatbreads later on, 'he and Ameena asked if they could call in sometime today with their children. We haven't had time to chat to any of our family for a while so I asked Hamid and Yrsa and their son to come too, and Básim of course. So, I thought I'd invite Dainn and Una round as well. We can have our evening meal together and catch up on everyone's news. Leif's funeral wasn't the place to do that and we didn't get the chance at Bjorn's the other night.'

'Why do I get the feeling there's something you're not telling me?' Eadwulf said, coming up behind her and wrapping his arms around her as she worked. 'I've a sneaking suspicion the rest of you are up to something.'

Freydis turned to face him, and smiled at his exaggerated frown. 'I don't know what it's about so I can't tell you anything, but I doubt if anyone's "up to something". I just know that Hamid and Yrsa have news to share with us. Whether or not the others know what it's about, I don't know, either, but I'm hoping the news will be good and not something we don't want to hear.'

'Well, I'm happy they're all coming to see us,' Thora squealed, her red curls bouncing about her face as she chased after the puppy with her shoe in its mouth. 'It's *ages* since I had my cousins to play with. I haven't even got Básim since he went to live with Hamid and Yrsa.'

Typical of the women in their family, Yrsa, Ameena and Dainn's wife, Una, arrived in the afternoon, insistent on helping Freydis prepare the meal. The four men made their

Twenty Three

appearance in the early evening, enjoying a mug of ale with Eadwulf while the women fussed over the cooking. From their cheerful banter, Eadwulf decided the young men were relaxed and carefree, and didn't ask Hamid what news he had to share. No doubt it would be revealed at the meal table when they were all together.

Freydis swallowed the last mouthful of her dessert, savouring the sweetness of the honeyed pears against the tang of the creamy white skyr as she placed her spoon on the dish. She waited until everyone else had finished before suggesting the children went off to play for a while. 'Now,' she said, looking intently at Hamid and Yrsa opposite to her, 'Eadwulf and I are eager to know just what it is you have to tell us. Am I right in thinking that we are the only ones here who don't know?'

Yrsa shook her dark head and glanced at her husband who was staring down at the tabletop. 'No one in the village knows about this except for Hamid and I, and Básim. We haven't even told our son. I know he's only four, but he's a sensitive child and might not take well to change.'

'Oh Yrsa,' Ameena said, 'you're expecting another child! How wonderful. I'm sure Aron will adapt very well and accept the new babe from the start. Our two boys are the best of friends.'

Yrsa laughed at the clever guess. 'Well, that wasn't going to be our news – at least, not the main piece of it. Our second child will be born in mid-May, but before you all get carried away with your congratulations, there's something of more immediate importance to tell you all. I'll leave Hamid to explain.'

'A few days ago, messengers from al-Andalus came here

looking for me,' Hamid started, ignoring the intakes of breath at the mention of his homeland. 'As most travellers, they went straight to Bjorn's hall asking for directions to wherever I lived. Of course, Bjorn sent them to me.'

He paused, glancing at the confused faces. 'I imagine you're all thinking that Bjorn must know what they wanted, but he doesn't. He didn't ask them because he'd just received news of Leif's death and was pretty distraught. He did ask me after the burial this morning and I said we'd explain once we'd told the family. So here we are.'

'And we're all ears, Hamid,' Dainn said. 'I'm the only man at this table who hasn't been to al-Andalus, although I've heard a lot about it from Hrolf here. Sounds like a dangerous place to me.'

'You're right, it is dangerous, though like most places, it has its periods of peace, when it's a wonderful area in which to live. The cities are beautiful, with towering buildings that glow in the sunlight in a way you could never imagine. Ameena will agree with me about that.'

'I will, brother. I had a happy childhood there, except for the death of my mother. But the sunshine isn't everyone's idea of perfection, and I'm more than happy here with Hrolf and our sons.'

Hamid nodded. 'As am I, although sometimes I feel guilty knowing I've evaded my duty. I may not be a legitimate son of an emir, but Muhammad treated me well, and I know he had hopes for me in either his government or his army.'

'I think it's time you came straight out with it, Hamid.' Eadwulf's heart pounded, hoping he'd misread Hamid's evasive

Twenty Three

words. 'You're about to tell us you're going back, aren't you?'

'No!' Freydis shrieked, jumping to her feet. 'We can't lose you now, Hamid. We love you too much for that. And what about Yrsa and your son, and Básim…? Will you just abandon them?'

'No, Freydis, he won't.' Yrsa's voice was soft as she took Hamid's hand. 'We're all going, but not until after the babe is born. And Básim has become so much a part of our little family now, he asked if he could go with us, too. That is, of course, if you don't object, Eadwulf?'

Eadwulf shook his head. 'I have no objection, other than the fact that we'll miss him, just as we'll miss the rest of you. Básim's a free man, and you're right, he's been part of your family since you moved into your own home.'

Tears rolled down Freydis' cheeks and Eadwulf held her close as he spoke. 'I know the three of you would have not have made the decision to leave lightly, so if you explain the reasons behind it, we might understand a little better. Perhaps you should start by telling us what the message was about.'

'The letter was from Sumayl, the stonemason I once knew. He was a wise man, and loved his country. If not for him, our journey to Cordoba six years ago may well have failed.' Hamid's dark eyes flicked from Eadwulf to Ameena, Hrolf and Básim, his companions on the venture. Eadwulf didn't expect him to elaborate on events during that visit. They all knew. 'Sumayl was old and frail the last time I saw him, and in his letter, he says he's dying. But before he left this world, he wanted to let me know about the situation in al-Andalus.'

'Not another assassination!' Ameena looked aghast. 'I

thought Abdallah would be popular.'

'He is, very much so – and no one's been assassinated. According to Sumayl, Abdallah has proven to be a wise and well-respected ruler, and for most of the six years he's been emir, the country has prospered and largely been at peace. Taxes have lowered for most of the poorer people and the persecution of groups like the Muladi and Jews have stopped. Unfortunately, the Asturians are still causing havoc in the north, constantly pushing south and spreading their Christian beliefs. The area around the River Duero, which has been a mix of Muslims and Christians for many years, is being pounded by both sides. But more and more of it is being taken over by the Christians.'

Ameena's expression reflected her confusion. 'If that's your reason for going back, Hamid, I can't see what you can do about the Asturians. I'm sure Abdallah has plenty of good men to lead his armies up there.'

'No, that isn't my reason; I was simply summing up the state of the emirate nowadays. Further south in al-Andalus there has been little unrest, other than the odd coastal raid by Northmen or pirates from across the Middle Sea. Sumayl had something different in mind for me. It seems that Abdallah's chief advisor died recently and he can't find anyone he can trust well enough to take his place.'

'You'll take on the same role that Beorhtwulf used to have?'

'I hope to, Eadwulf.'

'I imagine Abdallah remembered Sumayl from the days when he worked in the Alcazar?' Hamid nodded. 'And it was Sumayl who suggested you for the role?'

'It was, and he explained to Abdallah where I'd been these

Twenty Three

past twenty-two years. It seems he was very glad to know I was safe and well, and that he already knew I wasn't dead. Muhammad had confided in him years ago, once he'd named Abdallah as his successor.

'There's another role for me, too. Like your father, I will become High Counsellor and preside over matters of the Law. There are crimes in al-Andalus, the same as anywhere else. And Básim will have the dual role of my scribe and chief bodyguard.'

'It sounds perfect for you, both,' Ameena said, her green eyes moist with tears. 'Though I don't know how I'll cope with you so far away. You've been there for me since I was born, brother.' She brushed a tear from her cheek and attempted a cheerful smile. 'I wonder where you'll all live. It will probably be somewhere close to the Alcazar.'

'Abdallah will give us Beorhtwulf's old house – where we both lived, sister. He intends to have it redecorated and refurnished ready for our arrival. So, if any of you manage to get down to Cordoba, you know we'll have plenty of rooms in which to accommodate you.'

Chatter continued for some time, though no more was said about the intended move. The evening ended on a happy note when Dainn's dark-headed young wife, Una, spoke up, her face red with embarrassment. She took her husband's hand and flashed a wide smile. 'We have news to share, too. We expect our first child at the end of March.'

Congratulations erupted and Freydis suddenly said, 'With Dainn and Una's little one, Aguti and Kristen's two, and Yrsa and Hamid's two, I'll be a grandmother of five! Now that makes me feel *very* old.'

Twenty Four

Chester, Mercia: late October 893

By the time Hastein had been back in Shoebury for four weeks, almost two hundred East Anglian and Northumbrian Danes had arrived to join his band. Confident that his plans to overwinter in Chester would succeed, he was impatient to move out and create a suitably strong fortress before the snows and driving rains of winter made that difficult.

Their journey of over two hundred and fifty miles took them to the north of Mercia, before they circled across country, so avoiding Alfred's permanently manned burhs and well-trained standing armies further south. More and more Northumbrians arrived to join his band as they edged the border between the two kingdoms, swelling his numbers to over five hundred strong.

After a gruelling ten-day ride, with a bitter northerly to contend with for much of the way, they reached their destination in the far north-west of Mercia. Bounded on one side by the River Dee, the long abandoned Roman city looked grim. Miles away from any settlements, it stood desolate, its lofty walls crumbling in places, though Hastein was certain they'd keep out the worst of the winter gales as well as providing substantial defence. There were also enough partly roofed, stone buildings inside to keep rain and snow at bay.

Hastein smiled to himself as he mulled over his plans.

Much of the surrounding land was pasture, perfect for their

Twenty Four

horses to graze, and the extensive, dense woodlands could well harbour game birds, perhaps even a few deer and wild boar. The river, too, was home to ducks and geese and, undoubtedly, fish swam in its depths. But, Hastein mused, should the area fail to provide for their needs, they would ride into the Welsh kingdoms and raid, a few months earlier than spring, as he had planned.

For the next three days, Hastein's band swept across the surrounding land, gathering fruits, berries, nuts and other remnants of autumn's bounty from meadow and wood. Hunters returned with hares and other small mammals as well as several deer and a few wild boar. Archers took ducks, geese and swans from the river banks and fishermen netted a few salmon, trout and eel. Still others felled trees and cut logs for their cooking fires and to keep them warm. All were stored away in shelters and Hastein was certain that despite the lack of wheat for bread, what foods they had would last until the end of December. And in another couple of weeks, weather permitting, his men would hunt and fish again.

As daylight seeped into Hastein's shelter with the arrival of the following day's dawn, pandemonium erupted outside. Panicked yells and pounding footsteps made his heart thud. He shot through the rickety doorway to join his men lining the walls, and gasped at the sight. Saxons surrounded the city down to the river, leaving them no way out. Engulfed by rising panic at the prospects of a long winter siege, Hastein clutched at possibilities of fighting his way out. But the Saxon army looked huge, far larger than his own five hundred. Thank Odin they'd spent the last few days gathering in food supplies. At least their survival for a few weeks was assured.

Pulling at his right ear lobe, Hastein retreated to his shelter to think.

*

'Spending the winter here isn't something any of us want.' Ealdorman Aethelnoth scowled at the prospect as he assessed the situation at Chester with Aethelred and Aethelhelm. Around them, their joint forces waited, several lines deep, grim determination on their faces. 'But there's no way we can afford to let these bastards out to rampage across our lands again. It's obvious they've already taken whatever foods they could find around here, so they aren't likely to starve just yet. But winter lasts for a long time, and they won't see their horses again.' The Somerset ealdorman's throaty laugh made Aethelred and Aethelhelm smile. 'What fools to leave the beasts outside! Did Hastein really think he'd be out of our clutches right on the very edge of Alfred's kingdoms?'

'God alone knows what these pagans think,' Aethelhelm replied, his focus swinging from his appraisal of the Danish fortress to fix on Aethelnoth. 'We'd have little chance of getting through Chester's defences, so laying siege seems to be our only option. As you say, they'll probably already have enough food for a few weeks but without their horses to eat when it runs out as they did at Buttington, after that they'll be struggling to feed themselves and eventually surrender. We'll just have to sit here and wait for that to happen.'

Aethelred shook his head, certain he had a better plan. 'Yet,

Twenty Four

starving and without mounts as the Danes were at Buttington, many of them still managed to break out of their stronghold. And although only one of our men was killed, many were badly wounded – something we should try to avoid this time.'

'What alternative do we have?'

'First we send our men out to collect any remaining berries and nuts in the area and capture any wildlife suitable for our own use.' Aethelnoth and Aethelhelm nodded. 'Then we fire all the surrounding land – woodland and meadow alike – to be certain nothing edible is left. We'll stay here until the winter snows arrive which, if this northerly is anything to go by, aren't too far away. Then we'll leave the Danes to either starve throughout the winter months or die trekking on foot to distant places to raid. As I see it, by then our presence will not be needed.'

No one disagreed with Aethelred's words. They all remembered how King Alfred had laid bare the lands surrounding Chippenham fifteen years ago, resulting in the surrender of Guthrum and the remnants of his army after the battle of Edington. On this occasion, Alfred's faithful ealdormen had the coming winter in their favour. The biting winds and snow-covered land would keep the Danes penned in until the spring, by which time they would be facing starvation.

*

Devon. Wessex: mid-February 894

Over nine months had passed since Alfred's arrival in Devon and it galled him that the Danes who had sailed from East

Anglia with the Exeter raiders were still at large in the shire. Together with Ealdorman Odda's standing armies, his forces had succeeded in curbing most of the Northmen's looting, but they were evidently doing enough to keep themselves fed, even during the deep snows of winter. There was wildlife aplenty in the Devonshire forests, something Alfred knew the Danes had made full use of. A few of their archers and spearmen had been spotted by scouts, but catching them had been a different matter.

All in all, it had been a worrying and frustrating time for Alfred. To make matters worse, during these nine months, he had succumbed to the ravages of his old illness on three occasions. The same griping stomach pains and diarrhoea kept him confined in Odda's hall for several days each time, leaving him no other choice than to entrust the leadership of his armies to his loyal Devonshire ealdorman.

On the fourth day of Alfred's most recent bout of illness, he crawled from his bed to attempt a few spoons of pottage while Odda reported on his last encounter with Danish bands.

'Looks like they've finally realised they aren't going to get mounds of loot in Devon. Soon as they spotted us heading their way, they turned tail and fled. We'd have been outnumbered if they'd stood to fight, but they didn't seem interested in conflict. I've a feeling these Danes might be thinking of sailing off pretty soon, especially now the snows are thawing and spring isn't too far away.'

Alfred gave a weary sigh. 'I hope you're right. After nine months I feel we've achieved nothing, although most of their raids over the winter have been for food rather than loot. One

Twenty Four

thing's for sure: we may not have booted them from the shire, but at least we've managed to contain them within it. They probably expected to move into Somerset and Wiltshire once they'd drained Devon dry.'

'It's a pity we couldn't get rid of them as fast as Eadgar chased off Sigeferth. I wonder how that treacherous scum is enjoying raiding his countrymen in Dublin. I hope they're giving him a good walloping over there, too.'

Alfred smiled at the thought, the treachery of Danes never failing to amaze him. But his portreeve's success had given him one less thing to worry about. 'I know how relieved you'll be to have the raiders out of Devon, Odda. I'll be more than relieved when they've left our shores for good and we can all go home. Right now, knowing that the rest of my kingdom is being attacked from all sides is my biggest worry, and until these bands are out of Devon, I can do nothing about it. Thank God my ealdormen are capable of dealing with them. Hastein has outdone Guthrum in his duplicity and I feel ashamed when I think how well he played me for a fool. Christian baptism is no more than a game to him, and he even drew his two sons into his lies and deceit. May God watch over their souls.'

Odda did not dispute Alfred's words. 'Hastein will take some time to recover from his latest encounter with our ealdormen at Chester, especially so soon after his defeat at Buttington. This is the second time he's been left with no horses. Serves the pillaging swine damned well right – if you'll excuse the language, lord. But it might make him realise that wherever he raids in our lands, he can't win, so he might as well go home.'

Alfred harrumphed. 'You mark my words, Odda, he'll

find a way of raiding somewhere, with or without horses. If he can't raid in Wessex or Mercia, he could well try his luck in the Welsh kingdoms. His band could steal dozens of horses and collect a nice stash of booty before Anarawd realises they're even there. Hastein won't want to go home empty-handed. His pride is at stake here, and that is something he prizes more than anything else in life.'

*

Chester: early March 894

Throughout the long winter months, Hastein despaired of ever leaving Chester. The land was shrouded in deep snow and ice, constant fresh snowfalls creating great drifts against Chester's outer walls, making it impossible for anyone to even get out to the river to supplement depleted food supplies with fish and water birds. At first their fires had provided them comfort when the bitter winds whistled or the punishing cold turned water solid. But since January, stacks of firewood had become dangerously low and for most of the time, fires were fuelled by little more than spindly sticks. By late February, Hastein's band was not only in a state of near-starvation but shivering in the perishing cold with no way of keeping warm. And there was nothing anyone could do about it.

The first week of March saw an end to the snowfalls and the beginning of the thaw. Hastein was as weak from lack of food as his men and needed no telling that if they didn't eat soon, death would claim the weakest amongst them, just as it

Twenty Four

had done at Buttington.

His men trudged west, their most prized possessions strapped to their backs or hanging from their shoulders, and battleaxes and seaxes ready at their belts. Some carried bows and quivers across their backs. All had high hopes of raiding before the day was out, the desperate need to find food uppermost on their minds.

In the early afternoon they crossed the border into Anarawd's kingdom of Gwynedd. The early March air was still piercingly cold, the rays of the watery sun as yet too feeble to challenge it. Shivering, weak and starving as they were, food and shelter for the night were becoming more desperate as they walked, and men constantly scanned the land for signs of rising columns of smoke that signified human settlement.

Hastein silently prayed to mighty Thor, the god of warriors, thunder and storms, to keep his men alive. They would repay him by raiding every church to the feeble Christ-god they came across, taking the silver crosses and chalices before slaughtering the pathetic priests and burning their places of worship to the ground.

By mid-afternoon, Hastein felt his prayers had been answered. A substantial settlement stretched out before them, with at least a dozen round-houses, several outhouses and two good-sized barns, from which the sounds of softly lowing cattle reached their ears. He divided his men into groups, each to take a house or barn.

'No mercy to any inside,' he yelled. 'Anyone you see, you kill, whether man, woman or child. This place will be ours alone for the next few days and I don't want word of our arrival to spread. We eat our fill and build up our strength before setting out to gather as much loot as we can to take back to Mersea.'

No one questioned Hastein's orders and his men were already unstrapping battleaxes and seaxes as they crept forward, silently observing and seeking out possible dangers once they charged.

The screams of the villagers broke the silence of the Welsh afternoon.

Bodies were tossed into empty huts, where they would stay until some passer-by, friend or relative came calling. By which time Hastein would be miles away, raiding in Gwynedd and Powys before heading back to Mersea through the kingdom of their Northumbrian comrades, laden with plunder. Alfred's cursed ealdormen would not be following them there.

*

Lundenburh: April 894

The arrival of spring in Lundenburh did little to lift Aethelflaed's spirits. The harsh winter had taken its toll on her temper and she despaired of ever having the hall free of her Danish 'guests'. Not that she could say they had caused her too much trouble, it was simply that they'd been here for so long. By next month they would have been in Lundenburh for a year and their continuous presence, combined with Aethelred's all too frequent absences, had become hard to bear.

Hastein's wife, Greta, had done little more than mope about the place, constantly bemoaning her fate and the injustice of

Twenty Four

keeping her and her children confined here. Sharing the meal table with this woman with her constant whines and demands to be set free had so annoyed Aethelflaed that on more than one occasion, she had threatened to sell them off as slaves – the fate that had already befallen the rest of the hostages taken from Benfleet by Aethelred.

Thankfully, once Aethelred had returned from Chester in November, his absences had been curbed by the snowfalls. But with the thaw at the end of February, he had declared he had responsibilities in the rest of Western Mercia to tend to and left for Worcester. Once again, Aethelflaed was left alone with no idea of when her husband would return.

'Play nicely, or not at all!' she yelled at Aelfwynn, who was chasing round the hall after the young son of one of the serving women, shrieking like a banshee. Inga took it upon herself to walk over and calm the younger girl down, then led her to a corner to play I-Spy.

Admitting to herself that Inga was a sweet child and the two boys, Raud and Davyn, were well-mannered and polite, Aethelflaed chided herself for being so intolerant with their mother, simply because she loathed her devious husband. She imagined herself in Greta's shoes, contemplating how she'd feel if snatched away from Aethelred and left wondering whether she and Aelfwynn would live or die. Deep down, Aethelflaed knew she'd probably whine just as much as Greta.

Her father's sudden appearance in the doorway caught Aethelflaed deep in thought and off her guard. 'What a nice surprise,' she called, putting down the embroidery she was doing half-heartedly and rushing over to give him a hug. 'We'd heard you'd driven the Danes out of Devon, though we'll want to know how that came about. We also heard they'd tried to attack Chichester on their way back to Mersea Island. It seems they hadn't reckoned on another fortified and well-defended burh and were swiftly chased back to their ships by our standing army stationed there. Is that true? How is everyone in Winchester, by the way? It's ages since I saw any of them.'

Alfred laughed. 'What would you like me to talk about first?'

'Sorry, Father,' she replied, laughing with him as she led him to sit near the hearthfire, signalling to a serving girl to bring refreshments. 'It's just so long since I saw you.'

The glow from the flickering flames seemed to deepen the lines around Alfred's sunken eyes and enhance the grey that had finally consumed the rest of his wheaten hair. He looked dog-tired and Aethelflaed's concern for his health soared. The year in Devon had done him no favours. 'But I'm sure you'll explain everything once you've had a mug of ale and something to eat. You look in dire need of refreshment after your ride. I'm afraid Aethelred isn't here, though. He went to Worcester a few weeks ago and I've no idea when he'll be back.'

'Aethelred's here with me and will be in as soon as he's had a word with his men. He finished his business in Worcester in a matter of days and, as soon as he heard I'd left Devon he decided to head down to Winchester to bring me up to date with recent events elsewhere in the kingdom. I'd heard some of it but it was interesting to hear the details. He also wanted to ask about another matter, which we'll speak of later on. And no, before you ask,' he added, holding up his hand to halt the

Twenty Four

intended question, 'it has nothing to do with the Danes.'

Elated to know that both her husband and father were here, Aethelflaed did not question this other matter. She would hear about it soon enough. 'You know, of course, that Hastein's wife and children have been here for almost a year,' she said, sitting beside him at the trestle. Alfred nodded and Aethelflaed glowered at the Danish woman who was blatantly listening to their conversation. She lowered her voice. 'I hope you're here to tell us what you intend to do with them. The sooner they've gone from here, the better, as far as I'm concerned.'

'I'll be telling the woman of my decision as soon as Aethelred comes in. He already knows, of course, and isn't particularly happy with it. I know he expected me to inflict a life of slavery upon them. But my decision is final and not open to discussion.'

Aethelflaed swallowed hard. There were only two decisions her father could have made and it seems he'd chosen the one that even Aethelred would not have considered. Putting the family into slavery would have been well justified in the face of Hastein's betrayal of her father's trust and goodwill. Aethelflaed could have come to terms with that. But not this...

She glanced at Inga's three children, determined to plead with Alfred on their behalf. Although she had not enjoyed having the woman around, she would not wish to see any of them dead.

The serving woman placed a mug of ale and warm flatbread on the table just as Aethelred entered the hall. 'I'll fetch the same for you, lord,' the serving girl called to him, heading back to the kitchens.

'Make that two more, if you would.' Alfred's order coincided with his gesture to the Danish woman to join them at the table. 'Now that Lord Aethelred is here, I won't keep you wondering what your fate will be any longer, Greta,' he said as she seated herself. 'You've been in Lundenburh long enough and I think my daughter would like her hall back to herself.'

Greta visibly paled, though she glared at Aethelred, her captor. But after barely tolerating the woman's presence for so long, Aethelflaed's pity for her welled.

'You realise that your husband's deplorable actions in breaking our treaty and openly raiding in my kingdom are enough to warrant I inflict the harshest penalty upon you, don't you, Greta?'

'Lord, do what you will with me, but I beg you to have mercy on my children. They are innocent of any crime.'

'As are you, Greta, as far as I can see. But any punishment on Hastein's family would be, indirectly, my punishment of him. As I'm sure you know, the fate of all hostages taken in battle rests with the oath-taker keeping his vows. Unfortunately for you, Hastein did not, and is still out there raiding, seemingly without a care as to what will happen to you.'

Greta took a panicked glance at her children, then hung her head. She was close to tears and Aethelflaed could not help herself reaching out to take her hand. The woman looked up and gave Aethelflaed a wan smile. 'I realise all that, lord, but I still beg you to spare the children. Kill me, if you must, but send the children back to Mersea. Hastein will go back there sooner or later.'

'Last I heard he was raiding in northern Powys,' Aethelred

Twenty Four

told her. 'The people of Worcester were praying his band wouldn't head further south and cross the border into West Mercia. So it doesn't look like he's planning to head back to Mersea just yet.'

'But he will go back, eventually.' Alfred nodded as he thought. 'And when he does, I'm hoping he'll be leaving our lands for good. His raids in Wessex and Mercia have come to nothing and he's lost hundreds of men and endured two long sieges. The fact that he's still at large in the Welsh kingdoms tells me he's having more success there, but if he's taken a lot of plunder, he'll want to get it back to Mersea in the end. Which suits my plans.'

Alfred looked levelly at the Danish woman. 'The fact that Hastein hasn't even tried to negotiate with me over the release of his family, or ask what I had in mind for your future, is sad for you, Greta. To have such an uncaring husband must cause you pain.'

Greta bristled, though her voice was calm and controlled. 'Hastein is not an uncaring man, King Alfred. You don't know him well enough to make that judgement. It is the Danish way for a jarl to ensure the men in his company are not disappointed in their expectations of gaining plunder. Women and children must take second place in this. I know Hastein loves us and will return to Mersea when he and his men have loot enough to pay for our food and clothes in the coming months.'

'As someone baptised a Christian, Hastein should not be raiding anywhere!' It was Alfred's turn to bristle. He put down his ale mug and glared at Greta. 'He kills too readily, which no good Christian would do. Killing in battle, defending one's home and people, is a different matter. Raiding, killing and raping for sheer enjoyment is not acceptable. If Hastein is so worried about keeping his family and people fed and clothed he should be at home in his hall, overseeing his farmlands and livestock. That's what good Christians do.'

Aethelflaed laid her hand on Alfred's arm and his composure returned. 'Father, will you tell us what you've decided to do with Greta and the children. We need to know.'

Alfred nodded. 'They will be escorted by a company of my men to Mersea. If Hastein is back by the time they get there, all well and good. If not, at least they'll be with their own people while they wait for his return.'

'You are not going to kill us… or send us somewhere as thralls?' Surprise and relief mingled in Greta's voice. 'You are just sending us back… back to Hastein?'

'I am.'

'Lord, I am humbled by your compassion and my sincere thanks don't seem enough. To know that my children will not be harmed means everything to me.'

'It is the only Christian thing to do, Greta. After all, I am Raud's godfather and Aethelred is Davyn's, and Christian baptism is binding. The boys are our spiritual kinsmen and we must care for them as we would our own families. So, it is our responsibility to see them safely reunited with their father. Of course, you and Inga will be shown the same lenience.

'I confess, it took me some time to convince Lord Aethelred that this was the only thing we could do,' Alfred continued, flashing a wry smile at Aethelred. 'He is almost as unfamiliar with Christian baptismal duties as you are, Greta, but he didn't

Twenty Four

wish you all to be slain, or put into slavery, so I convinced him that this was the only option left.'

'We can never repay such kindness, lord.' Greta was overcome with emotion. 'And I'm certain that Hastein will feel deeply indebted to you.'

'Perhaps, but if he does feel that way, he can show his gratitude by taking you home across the Northern Sea. Now,' he said, turning the conversation to the pending travel. 'Tomorrow we will feast, then in two days' time your escort will be ready with a wagon big enough for the four of you to travel in and sleep in at night. If Raud and Davyn prefer to ride, a couple of horses will also be provided.

'We now have other matters to discuss, Greta, so you may go back to your children. I'm sure they'll be pleased to know they are going back to Mersea.'

The smile on Greta's face reflected her relief and Aethelflaed shared it with her. Soon, the Lundenburh hall would be back to normal. Her father's voice snapped her out of her thoughts.

'In the second week of May, the marriage between Edward and Ecgwynn will take place in Winchester Minster. It's almost a year later than Edward would have liked, but with Danes overrunning our lands, the opportunity simply hasn't arisen. It gives us barely three weeks to get the ceremony organised but I'm convinced we can do it, even if there are fewer guests than we would have hoped for. We can't risk leaving it until later in the year. Right now, we have a rare period of peace, but who knows what the later months will bring?'

'I hope Ecgwynn's family has enough time to prepare her wedding apparel,' Aethelflaed remarked, remembering how long she and Ealhswith had taken with her gown alone. 'But I suppose that if the marriage is at Winchester, the wedding feast will be in your hall, Father?'

'It will, and your mother is more than happy to organise it. She tells me that Edward's been driving her mad with his moans about having to wait so long to be married. And I've asked Archbishop Plegmund to officiate. The man is dear to us all, and he's done more in the four years he's been Archbishop of Canterbury than his predecessor, the traitorous Ethelred, did throughout his nineteen years of office.'

'Will Garth be invited to the wedding?' Aethelred asked. 'It's just that he'll be doing his term of service here at that time and his wife and children always accompany him. Like me, he was rarely at home last year, being part of Ealdorman Aethelnoth's Somerset army. It will be good to have them all here again, and I know he and Edward are good friends.'

'Edward has made his own list regarding who he wants to invite, and I can tell you, Garth's right at the top of it with the rest of the family. We're hoping Aethelgifu will be able to join us, too. Most of the invitations have been sent and we're hoping they'll all come.

'Now, where's that little granddaughter of mine? I haven't had time to greet her since I got here but I am glad we've got the two most important issues sorted out – and we'll have a great feast to look forward to tomorrow.'

'Before I fetch Aelfwynn, you did say you'd tell us about Devon. But if you'd rather not until you're better rested, I'm sure we can wait.'

Alfred rolled his eyes. 'I'm not on my deathbed yet, Ae-

Twenty Four

thelflaed, and explaining events in Devon won't take long.'

'Then we'll be pleased to hear about them, Father. And while you chat with Aelfwynn, I'll check on tonight's meal and sort out some of the foods we'll be cooking for this feast you're insisting on having for our houseguests tomorrow.' She heaved a sigh of relief and lowered her voice. 'You have no idea how much I'll enjoy bidding them farewell.'

Twenty Five

Mersea Island, northern Essex: late May 894

May was drawing to a close by the time Hastein and his band arrived back in Mersea. The men trudged between the extensive array of variously shaped hide tents, sweating in the warmth of the sun, their faces etched with pride. Cheering camp followers flocked to welcome them back, some tearfully shuffling away again knowing their comrades or loved ones would not see Midgard again. People gawked at the little Welsh ponies laden with sacks of plunder that would serve them all well.

Hastein glanced around, hoping that Greta and the children had, somehow, escaped or had been released from wherever they'd been held. But they were nowhere amongst the crowds and, yet again, he wondered whether they were even still alive. Or had they been condemned to a life of thraldom on the estates of Alfred's noblemen, the four sent to places miles apart, destined never to see each other again? Trying to find them across the expansive Anglo-Saxon lands would be a task that could only end in bitter disappointment.

Not for the first time, Hastein swallowed down the pangs of shame and guilt he felt at his own callousness in refusing to negotiate their release. Yet if he had done so, these profitable raids in the Welsh kingdoms would not have occurred, and he'd have been scorned as a leader who failed to deliver his promises to his men. He thought of Greta's selfless care of him in Antwerp all those years ago. Without her love and devotion,

Twenty Five

he would have long since been dead.

For the rest of the afternoon, Hastein sat in the camp speaking with the men who had been through so much with him. Several, like Erik, whose family had also been taken, had been with him since he'd sailed along the Somme in Francia. Others, like Soren, were later arrivals from East Anglia or Northumbria. All had given him their loyalty and trust. Younger warriors amongst them were still boastful of their achievements in Gwynedd and Powys and keen to continue trying their luck in these bountiful lands. Older men, like Hastein himself, were weary to the bone. Their raiding days were over and many longed to end their days in a place of harmony and peace.

'I'm considering sailing back to the Danish lands as soon as I have a ship built,' he told them. 'I just need to find a group of shipwrights who can get the job done in the next month or so. There's nothing left for me here, and there are plenty of leaders with their own bands who may well choose to continue raiding.'

'None of us is getting any younger,' Soren admitted, raking his fingers through wiry grey hair as though to stress the point. 'I left the settled life I'd had in East Anglia in Guthrum's time for the thrill of raiding again, but now I know what a mistake that was. The bags of booty don't make up for the family I lost and the peaceful life I once had. So, if you're heading back to our homeland, Hastein, you can count me in.'

'Me, too,' Erik said. 'My raiding days are over. Losing my family told me that. To be honest, I didn't expect to survive when we were in Chester, and d'you know what…? I didn't want to. My wife and daughter are probably thralls somewhere out there, but looking for them would be hopeless.'

Hastein nodded slowly, knowing exactly how he felt. Though barely into his middle years, Erik had the look of a man broken beyond repair, his cloudy blue eyes devoid of hope. Yet, Erik had been loyal to Hastein for too long to deny him the chance of going home. 'If you sail with us, Erik, you must be prepared to row with the rest of the crew. I don't need anyone who wants to simply sit and mope.'

'I understand, lord. Thoughts of returning to my homeland are enough to keep me from that. Like the rest of us, I have plunder to trade or sell, which will be useful in helping me to settle in a place I can call my own.'

Before long, Hastein had enough men to crew a new longship, and tomorrow he would seek out a shipwright. But for tonight, he needed to put up his tent and find himself something to eat. If he offered a few silver coins, perhaps he'd find a family prepared to let him share their meal. While he did that, he would consider exactly where in his homelands he would head to.

*

The old woman shook her head in response to Hastein's question and handed him a platter of steaming pottage, the meaty aroma making his stomach gurgle. He had eaten nothing all day. 'You've been away a long time, lord. The hostages were taken from Benfleet over a year ago, and you ask me if I know what became of them. How could any of us here know that?

Twenty Five

We'd heard that the Saxon king held your family.'

Hastein swallowed down the first few spoonfuls of pottage, his tongue flicking out to halt the gravy threatening to mingle with his whiskers as he noted the downcast eyes of the rest of the group. Rekindled despair and grief surged as the hopelessness of his situation sank in.

'I just thought… or hoped… someone might have heard what became of at least some of them. And you're right about my family. They were taken into King Alfred's clutches, but I imagine he would have sent them into thraldom with the rest by now.'

'Or he could've had them killed.' The shrewd-eyed old woman momentarily stared at Hastein before glancing round at her own family, two of whom had been with him in Chester.

'We've heard of your good fortune in the Welsh kingdoms, lord, and know that the loot you took was needful, but the cost of your raids in the lives of our men is high indeed. We wondered where you planned to pillage next.'

Hastein nodded to suggest he was thinking about her words while he finished his pottage and returned the platter, deciding to ignore the overt criticism. The woman had lived amongst warriors for long enough to know that to all Norsemen, the possibility of heaps of plunder was worth the risk of injury or death during raids.

'My raiding days are over, Mette, but there are several jarls here at Mersea who may well continue with them. I'm going back to the Danish lands to–'

'So, you're just going to sail away and leave us. Again!' The woman's voice was contemptuous and emotional but Hastein recognised it. He jumped to his feet, twisting to face her, too ashamed to rush to her side. He was thankful to see how well his wife looked after a year as a hostage. Even her clothing was of a good quality.

'It didn't take you long to decide not to bother looking for us. I should have known not to expect anything else.'

'Greta… that's not how it is.' He looked away, the guilt he felt escalating beneath her scathing scrutiny. 'Alfred let you go?'

'Unlike you, Hastein, King Alfred is a man of honour… and feeling! He knows that families are to be cherished. I watched him with his own and it filled me with envy. To know that my own husband cared nothing for me – or our children – is a hard truth to accept. Do you know, that noble king even said how sorry he was that I had such an uncaring husband! Shame on you!'

Stung by Greta's words, Hastein could find nothing to say in response and the suffocating silence closed in on him. 'Are the children here?' he asked at length.' Greta nodded. 'Are they well?'

'As well as they could be after learning they have a father who doesn't love them. They know you're here and have heard you are returning to your homeland. You are abandoning them yet again, so how do you expect them to feel about *that*?'

Hastein knew she didn't expect an answer as she turned away, the slump of her shoulders revealing her battle with her emotions.

'I never intended to leave without you or our children, Greta. I didn't think Alfred would have had you killed… As you say, he's an honourable man and his Christian beliefs would not permit the revenge-killing of women and children. But I thought his counsellors would insist he inflicted thraldom on you.' He stared vacantly across the camp. 'I just didn't know where to look for you across these kingdoms.'

Greta did not move or speak and Hastein suddenly realised he was not going to win her back. 'Look at me!' he suddenly raged.

Startled out of her misery, Greta turned and stared at him, the contemptuous glare returned. 'I am getting *old*,' he said, tugging at his grey-streaked ginger beard. 'I never intended to still be raiding in my sixty-first year. You and the children could have been taken anywhere in these kingdoms, perhaps to estates far away from each other. I would likely have reached my deathbed and still not found any of you.'

Greta's hysterical laughter had everyone in the gathering staring at her, then at each other, their puzzlement evident.

The laughter abruptly stopped. 'You could have been killed a hundred times or more during your reckless raids over the years, Hastein. Thoughts of that didn't stop you, though, did it? You were almost dead when I met you more than fifteen years ago in Antwerp, but you are completely dead to me now. I want nothing more to do with you. Go back to your homeland to be with Dainn and Aguti, but don't expect *this* family to join you. I've made arrangements for us to return to Ghent in a few days' time.'

Greta strode away and Hastein stared after her as she disappeared amongst the hundreds of tents.

'If you want my advice,' Mette said as he slumped to the ground, 'you'll go after her and tell her how much she and the children mean to you. I happen to know how much they all love you, although *why* is anyone's guess after the way you've treated them. Greta may or may not come around, but if she does, I suggest you take them somewhere in the Danish lands far away from the "other" family she mentioned. You mark my words, she won't be prepared to share you with them.'

'You knew they were here when I asked about them, didn't you?' Hastein's hazel gaze swept all those seated, the accusation tempered by a tolerant smile. 'Did Greta ask you to keep quiet about their presence?'

Despite the warmth of the evening, Mette pulled her shawl close around her shoulders then nodded slowly. 'They've been with us for a couple of weeks, escorted here by King Alfred's men. Greta told us of her kind treatment by the Saxon king and how his daughter, Lady Aethelflaed, struggled to cope with their long stay at Lundenburh at times. But they were all well fed and clothed and it seems that Inga enjoyed looking after the Lady's young daughter.'

'So, they were held in Lundenburh with Aethelred's feisty wife… Aethelflaed would have loved that, considering her opinion of me.' Mette didn't question his words and Hastein thought that Greta had probably told her of his clashes with Alfred's daughter. They had amused him, at the time. But now he was grateful for her care of his family: the family who didn't want him any more.

Mette pulled herself to her feet, her old knees creaking. 'Well don't just sit there looking sorry for yourself, Lord Hastein. If you want to make amends with your family, the only way is to tell them how sorry you are and beg their forgiveness – the sooner the better, I'd say. Now would probably be a good time. They all love you, so the rest is up to you.'

The grinning old woman pointed out a route between the tents. 'Keep going through there and you'll find their tent beside the stream. But don't expect Greta to take you back with open arms immediately. She claims that all the gifts she received from the Saxon king have made her wealthy enough to provide a good home for herself and the children in Ghent –without your help.'

Hastein's hopes plummeted, yet again, and Mette laid a crinkled hand on his arm. 'Between you and me, your wife's harsh words are because she is deeply hurt. I'd lay silver on the fact that she'll be hoping you seek her out and beg forgiveness.

'In case you hadn't noticed in all the years you've been together, Greta has a very forgiving nature.'

*

Winchester: early June 894

Alfred heaved a sigh as he dismissed his witan. Having spent the last two days outlining his plans for further improvements in his kingdom, he was tired, and his temper more than a little frayed. The last few days had been difficult, the main cause of dispute amongst the councillors revolving round the costs and acquisition of materials required. But with fervent words of support from Aethelred of Mercia, Alfred's proposals were eventually accepted.

'Surely they can see the need for new burhs!' Alfred ranted, sinking into his high-backed chair after the council members had left and signalling to Edward, Aethelred and Asser to sit with him. 'They have short memories if they've forgotten how the new defences have saved several of our towns from Danish raids…

'And I'll have the old Roman bridge at Lundenburh rebuilt if it's the last thing I do! Haven't I been saying for years how valuable a bridge across to the new settlement in Surrey would be?' The three men murmured agreement. 'The plans you drew up for me seven years ago went a long way in persuading them, Lord Asser. Realising we'd be building on the existing Roman foundations was a help.'

'A bridge at that point will not only be useful to the people of Lundenburh and Surrey, but to travellers from all south-eastern Wessex shires heading to West Mercia,' Aethelred said for the second time that morning, 'and I'm glad the council eventually saw that. Unfortunately, building the bridge is likely to take some years.'

Edward nodded. 'All the more reason to get started as soon as possible. At least they found nothing to object to in your decision to move the bulk of our fleet from Southampton to Rochester, Father. No one could deny it's a logical step, considering the occupation of East Anglia and Mersea Island by restless Danes, and the ease with which raiders can still sail up the Thames to Lundenburh and beyond.'

'So, you're leaving for Lambourn in the morning,' Alfred said, feeling the need to change the subject. 'I hope you and Ecgwynn are enjoying life out there. As you know, your mother and I spent some time there after our marriage and the manor

Twenty Five

is dear to us. I'll need you back in court sooner or later, but I think I can cope without you until at least the end of July.'

'Thank you, Father. The Lambourn Downs are so peaceful, and we could both happily stay there forever. We've spent so much time out riding and simply relaxing.'

The loud guffaws from both Alfred and Aethelred said exactly what they thought 'relaxing' entailed.

'Enjoy it while you can, Edward,' Alfred said, still grinning. 'I don't trust any of the Danes on Mersea Island or in East Anglia, or those in Northumbria come to that. Who knows what Hastein will do once he gets back over there? There are plenty of regions in our kingdom he could raid next, although I'm hoping the fact that I sent his family back to him will make him think twice about raiding anywhere under my control.'

Determined not to let thoughts of Hastein's betrayal get him down, Alfred turned again to Edward. 'In your absence I'll continue working on my life story with Bishop Asser as well as updating a number of our laws and, naturally, my ongoing translations of the prayers and psalms from Latin. I plan to involve your young brother in some of this work. Aethelweard has become quite learned, largely thanks to our many hard-working scholars. If I'm honest, at thirteen, his knowledge of Latin already surpasses my own.'

'The boy has a rare aptitude for learning,' Asser agreed, a fond smile on his lips as he glanced across the hall to where Aethelweard sat reading amidst the scholars. 'Though that doesn't mean your own efforts are in any way lacking, King Alfred. Your ability in reading and writing Latin is not to be sneered at. Aethelweard's enthusiasm is praiseworthy and he very much reminds me of Aethelgifu in that, although he is more interested in secular matters than spiritual ones. Interpreting aspects of the Law should suit him well.'

'I'm certain it will. Aethelweard's learning has already prospered under your guidance, Bishop, and can't fail to continue doing so. And now that our meetings are over, I see no reason why the work on the Law shouldn't begin in a couple of days. Before then, I'll send word to Eadgar in Southampton to organise the movement of our fleet to Rochester. I also want to have new fortifications at Reading started soon, then hopefully they'll be finished before winter sets in. Fortunately, once I've talked over my building plans and designs with Reeve Unwin, I can trust him to order materials and oversee the work.

'As for the Lundenburh bridge,' he added, glancing at Aethelred, 'work on that will wait until next spring. That way, the witan can't complain I've drained our coffers all at once.'

Aethelred nodded. 'Then we'll all have to hope this period of peace lasts at least until next spring.'

*

Ribe, Danish lands: mid-June 894

'Seems we're about to have visitors, Aguti.' Kristen hovered in the doorway of the Ribean hall and peered across the water meadows down to the river, her right hand shielding her eyes from the glare of the midday sun. 'One of them looks like a woman and three of them are youngsters. I can't say I recognise any of them, so they can't be from around here.'

Twenty Five

Kristen came into the hall, placing her basket of herbs on a trestle and checking that eleven-month-old Gytha was still sleeping in her crib before sitting beside her husband.

Aguti shrugged. 'I suppose we'll find out when they get here – which should be any moment now…'

The rap on the door was not overly loud. Had the couple's young son, five-year-old Steinolf, been in battle mode with the rest of the hall's children just then, it might not even have been heard. But Aguti had been listening for the approaching footsteps and headed to the door at the first tap.

'Father! By Odin, I'm pleased to see you. Come in and we'll greet each other properly.' Once through the door, Aguti flung his arms around the man he hadn't seen for the past eight years, tears of joy in his eyes.

'I can't tell you how good it is to see you, too,' Hastein replied, returning the hug. 'It's a long time since I set foot in our homelands.'

'And Greta,' Aguti gushed on, turning to embrace Hastein's second wife. 'It seems too good to be true that you're all here. And just look at you two lads! Last time I set eyes on you both, you were *this* high.' He held out his hand, waist high, and laughed. 'You were only four, as I recall, with gingery hair just like your father's, which hasn't changed one bit. So now you must be… what… thirteen?'

The two lads nodded, each holding out their hands for a handshake, only to be pulled in for a hug from Aguti before he turned and smiled at the fair-headed girl standing close to her mother.

'So, Greta, this must be the babe you were carrying when

I left you in Francia almost nine years ago.'

'It is, Aguti,' Greta confirmed, smiling down at the girl. 'Introduce yourself to your step-brother, daughter. I can tell you, he's a very nice person.'

'I am Inga, and I am eight. We've come all the way across the Northern Sea from Mersea Island to see you – and I'm glad we did. You all look very nice, and I'm very happy to know you.'

Aguti laughed. 'We are happy to meet you, too, Inga. And as soon as I get over my shock of seeing you all, my wife, Kristen – the lady with the dark hair peeping out of her head veil coming over to greet you– will order food and drink and you can meet our two children.'

As though on cue, little Gytha started to chunter and Greta and Kristen shared a smile. 'Well then,' Kristen declared, 'it seems Gytha wants to share our refreshments with us, so I'll call Steinolf and we'll get to know each other while we eat.'

'So, you've decided it's time to settle down, at last.' Aguti put down his empty ale mug and looked steadily at Hastein. 'I'm a little surprised, since the last thing we heard, you were enjoying yourself in giving the Wessex king a hard time.'

Hastein's smile did not reach his eyes and Aguti could see how weary he looked. But there was more to it than that: his father had the look of a man defeated.

'Giving King Alfred a hard time and getting the better of him are two different things, Aguti. Alfred has created such a well-defended kingdom that even travelling through it is barely possible without having his armies on our tails. Believe me when I say that all our manoeuvres ended in disaster.' Hastein's eyes squeezed shut as he spoke, seeming to Aguti to

Twenty Five

recall the number of times his army was brought to its knees. 'Only by staying within the Danelaw boundary did we ever feel safe from their clutches.'

'I take it you didn't want to settle in this area called the Danelaw?'

'I am getting too old for raiding, and many of our countrymen in that region still crave the taking of Alfred's lands. No, son, it was time to come home, not only for my benefit, but for Greta's and our children's. I was hoping you might find a patch of land on your estate where we can build our homestead.'

Aguti inwardly breathed a sigh of relief, having wondered whether his father would want to take his hall back. He and Kristen had been happy raising their family here.

'Father, you are more than welcome to stay in this hall until your new home is ready to move into. I can think of a few suitable spots, which you will know well, so we can ride out tomorrow and have a look. They're all close to the Ribea, so there's plenty of mooring for any ships –'

Aguti stopped abruptly. 'Speaking of ships, did you cross the Northern Sea in a ship of your own, or find passage in one sailing this way?'

'I've had several ships since I last saw you, but the last one was burnt to a crisp with many others in Benfleet. I've just had a new one built and guess what I called it.' Aguti shrugged and held out his hands. 'It's the *Jormungand 2*', Hastein supplied, a grin on his face. 'We berthed right behind the *Jormungand* on the Ribea out there and I was amazed to see my old ship still afloat.'

'I've looked after her Father, although I confess, she's seen better days. I rarely sail very far nowadays. We visit the family in Aros a couple of times a year, and sometimes carry on down to the market at Hedeby, but mostly the *Jormungand* just sits out there…'

'You won't know this, but Yrsa is now married to Hamid.'

Hastein smiled at that. 'I can see how that would be a good match. Yrsa was smitten with Hamid when she tended his leg wound on our return from al-Andalus more than twenty years ago.'

'They already have one child, a boy called Aron, and are going back to live in Cordoba after their second is born next May.'

'Understanding their motives for *that* will take some doing,' Hastein said, pulling a face. 'I hope they've thought it all through. I can imagine how your mother feels about Yrsa living in distant Cordoba!'

'Mother's not at all happy about it, but Hamid and Yrsa have thought about it carefully, and to them, it's the right thing to do. The decision stems from a visit they all made to Cordoba seven years ago, which I'll tell you about later on. You also need to know that Dainn is married to a nice young woman called Una, and has had a homestead built on Bjorn's land – as have Hrolf and Ameena.'

Hastein shook his head as the deluge of news hit him. 'It seems I have a lot of catching up to do. It's many years since I saw any of them.'

'And, although I once thought I wouldn't, I'd love to meet the rest of Hastein's family and friends,' Greta said, squeezing her husband's hand. 'I'm hoping we can visit them before winter gets here.'

Aguti nodded approvingly. 'That would be a good trip for

Twenty Five

all of us to make and can easily be arranged. But for now, there are more pressing things to talk about, such as whether your crewmen are still on the ship.'

'They are,' Hastein confirmed. 'They're waiting to hear if they should wait for us or sail on to Ribe. I wasn't sure how you'd feel about us living here, so I kept the men on hold, just in case. If you're sure you're happy to have us on your lands, I'll head over and let them know there's no need to wait.'

'What about your ship?' Kristen asked. 'Will your crew sail it back here for you in a few days?'

Hastein shook his head and gestured to his wife and children. 'If we are to settle here, I have no need of a ship. I decided if that were the case, I'd give the *Jormungand 2* to Erik, who's been one of my regular crew for some years. His family was taken from him at Benfleet and although a longship won't fill that gap, it might help to ease the pain of his loss. He's young enough to benefit from owning a good, seagoing vessel, though he may have to hire more crewmen in Ribe, depending on where the rest of the present crew decide to head off to. I'll give him enough coin to buy food for a voyage to wherever he chooses to raid, or settle, but the rest will be up to him.'

'All I can say is that having you here in Ribe will be a blessing to us.' Aguti reached across the trestle to take his father's hand. 'Our children will come to know their famous grandfather, whose deeds so many people can only talk about.' Hastein laughed at that remark. 'Oh, it's true, Father, your reputation as a great warrior has equalled that of the notorious Ragnar Lothbrok, so you'll have to get used to the stares and questions thrown your way whenever you venture further than this estate.'

Twenty Six

Lundenburh: mid-November 894

The rapid knocking on the door of the Lundenburh hall interrupted an intense game of *hnefatafl* between Aethelred and Garth. It was mid-morning on a grey and blustery day and the two friends had snatched a rare moment's relaxation following the meal before heading out to make their rounds of the city.

Aethelred bounded for the door, leaving Garth to clear away the wooden warriors, bemoaning the fact that his *hnefi* would have reached a corner of the board, had they continued.

'Raiders, Lord Aethelred,' the portreeve gasped, panting after his run up from the riverbank. 'Must have been over forty longships heading upriver. With a good few horses aboard.'

'Not again,' Aethelred groaned, all thoughts of a peaceful winter shattered by Oswin's words, and he wondered if the leader was again Hastein, with the Danes from Mersea Island. Would the damned man never give up!

'You and you, with me,' he yelled, jabbing a finger towards two of his thegns. 'You, too, Garth. We might be in time to catch a glimpse of this fleet.'

Donning their thick winter cloaks, they sped down to the river, arriving just in time to see the tail end of the Norse fleet disappearing round a bend. Thinking quickly, Aethelred spat out his orders. 'You two, send a dozen of our men to raise our closest standing armies. I want them ready to ride with me soon after daybreak tomorrow.

Twenty Six

'Garth, you and three others, take word of the present direction of this fleet to Alfred. I'll be following them along the banks with my army and won't move against them without authority from him, unless they attack us. I hope only to discover their intentions at this stage, and, of course, I'll inform him of whatever we find out.'

Aethelred grinned at his friend's frown. 'Don't worry, I'll write all that on parchment, so there's no need to commit it to memory.'

'As good as done,' Garth replied, hurrying back to select three warriors to accompany him.

By early afternoon, the strong easterly had subsided. Aethelred stood on the quayside with Edric and the men who would ride with him to Winchester, watching the river's murky water flowing on its journey to the Northern Sea and trying to ignore the stench of raw fish that drifted their way from a fishing boat unloading its catch barely twenty yards downstream. His thoughts momentarily strayed to the last time he'd seen his father: the day Eadwulf sailed away back to Aros following Aethelred's marriage to Aethelflaed. That was more than eight years ago now, though sometimes it seemed just like just yesterday…

Not for the first time, Aethelred wondered whether he'd ever see his father again.

The scraping sounds of a barge berthing close by brought him back to the present and he noticed that several other craft had now resumed their business, ferrying a variety of goods and passengers across the Thames to Surrey and back.

Aethelred handed Garth the parchment for Alfred as the

four men prepared to lead their mounts onto the barge. 'Ride with care, my friend. It was lucky we found a skipper to take you across the river. Seventy miles is a long enough ride without adding an extra dozen with a detour to the Reading ford. The skipper's been generously paid to take you across, and this,' he added, handing Garth a leather pouch containing several silver coins, 'is to pay for a ferry-ride back on your return.'

'Thanks for that,' Garth replied, adjusting the leather baldric across his chest, holding his prized, jewel-hilted sword from King Alfred. 'We'll head straight back with the king's reply, so expect to see us in five or six days – unless, of course, he detains us for any reason.'

Aethelred watched the barge push away from the quay and headed back to the hall to wait for confirmation that his army would be ready to ride by morning.

*

A low mist hung over the Thames as Aethelred's army of two hundred rode west from Lundenburh along the northern edges of the great river. The reed beds, so needful for the thatching of homes, stood tall and dense along its banks, strangely obscured in patches by the writhing haze. Guided by the word of local villagers and their sightings of menacing longships, at little under two miles from the new burh, where the River Lea added its waters to the Thames, the riders turned north to follow the course of the narrower river.

They continued at a steady pace for a further twenty miles until, in the mid-afternoon, a vast, semi-circular Norse

Twenty Six

encampment came into view, its sides reaching down to the river where their ships were moored.

'An interesting site for a camp – or fortress, more like,' Edric remarked, drawing rein beside Aethelred as the army halted a hundred paces from the Danes. The sturdy Mercian thegn gestured to the partly constructed earthen embankment which would eventually shield the array of variously shaped hide tents. 'They must have worked non-stop to get that much done in a single day. The soil will be from a ditch they're digging out behind it, probably a deep one, too. And as far as I can see, there'll be three gateways – no doubt with sturdy gates, if those tree trunks lying around are anything to go by.'

Aethelred nodded, any hopes he'd harboured for storming the camp rapidly fading. 'They've also made good use of the river as part of their defences, especially as it means they can keep an eye on their ships. They've evidently no intentions of leaving just yet. Curses on them!' he suddenly raged. 'The last thing we need is pillaging Danes overwintering so close to Lundenburh!'

He inhaled deeply, saying nothing for some moments while his temper cooled. 'You're right, Edric, it is an interesting spot. The town of Hertford isn't too far away and three smaller rivers flow into the Lea at this point, after which, the Lea flows south to join the Thames, as we've seen. The interesting thing about *that* being that the Lea forms part of the Danelaw boundary from Lundenburh as far as the town of Luton, flowing through Hertford on the way. I'm sure you can see how useful that would be to these Danes.'

'A clever choice as well as an interesting one, then.' Edric nodded as he thought. 'They have their ships if they decide to sail back down the Lea to raid close to London or even further south, and they're on the edge of the Danelaw should they need to get away in a hurry. It looks like they learned something from events at Chester, too, because they've taken their horses inside. The idea of raiding on foot again obviously didn't appeal to them. The question now is, what do we do about all this?'

Aethelred pushed his fingers beneath his helm to scratch his head. 'Nothing, except report what we've seen to King Alfred. It's hard to know exactly what these Danes intend to do, other than overwinter here. Which means that local villages will be plundered for food, at the very least. I told Alfred we wouldn't attack unless we had to, and looking at that fortress, I'm guessing we wouldn't stand a chance if we did, especially as we've no idea how many men they have. There could be over a thousand of them in there, although having so many horses aboard their ships could mean that number is a couple of hundred lower.

'But right now, we're attracting more than a little attention, so I'd say it was time to leave.'

*

Winchester, Hampshire: Christmastide 894

Ealhswith gazed round the festively decorated hall, happy to see all the people she loved most in all the world looking carefree and relaxed. Sitting around the trestles or standing in small groups, their guests were catching up with each other's

Twenty Six

news while enjoying the seasonal foods. Even Aethelgifu had put the problems of running Shrewsbury Abbey behind her for the past few days. Deep in conversation with her father, Abbot Asser and Aethelweard, she looked so dignified in her dark over-gown and headdress. Ealhswith's heart swelled with pride every time she thought of her wise and intelligent daughter. Devoted to her work, there was no place in Aethelgifu's life for a husband... unlike Aelfthryth, who was now approaching a marriageable age.

Soon to reach her sixteenth year, Aelfthryth seemed content with the knowledge that she must soon marry and move away from her family home. 'I long to have a husband and children of my own to love, Mother,' Aelfthryth had said on several occasions recently. 'Caring for them all will bring me the greatest of pleasure.' Ealhswith knew that was true; her youngest daughter had a loving nature and a desire to bring children into the world. Only recently, Alfred had expressed the need to search for a suitable husband for Aelfthryth during the coming year. He already had a couple of possibilities in mind, though as yet, had not shared them with anyone, even Ealhswith.

Aelfthryth was unlike either of her older sisters, a thought that brought a smile to Ealhswith's lips. For Aethelgifu, God and the Church were her life; her nuns were her children, whom she cared for with utmost devotion. And her pursuit of knowledge remained as passionate as ever. As for Aethelflaed... Ealhswith's eyes fixed on her eldest child, at ease beside her husband, Aethelred, and in deep conversation with Archbishop Plegmund and Bishop Werferth of Worcester. Aethelflaed had always been strong-minded, proud and wilful, and had developed an ability to aid in the running of Mercia since her marriage to Aethelred eight and a half years ago. She had the unusual gift of being able to judge a person's character, to see right into their hearts and minds and discern whether they were being honest and truthful, or scheming and deceitful, as she had declared Hastein to be. That she adored her husband and child could not be denied, but Aethelflaed had made clear to all that Aelfwynn, now a delightful girl of six, was the only child she ever wanted.

'I've been watching you for the past few moments, Ealhswith, and I always know when happy thoughts are filling your head.' Alfred sat next to his wife on a high-backed bench, putting his arm around her shoulders. 'We've come a long way and been through so much since we first met twenty-six years ago and our children have been a blessing to us. It's a rare and wonderful thing to have them all together under one roof these days, so it's good to enjoy this time while it lasts.'

'Am I so easy to read?' Ealhswith asked, a question to which she already knew the answer. 'You're right, as always, I've been contemplating each of them as they are today and feeling very proud. Even Aethelweard is no longer a child to be fussed over. Indeed, he has the head of a scholar, and I feel that is where his destiny lies – though not in the Church.'

'That's true,' Alfred agreed. 'There's still much work for him to do here with Asser, but if he becomes restless to visit other lands once he's old enough, I see no reason to stand in his way. Nor does Edward.'

Ealhswith focused on her eldest son, chatting quietly to the

Twenty Six

vivacious, dark-headed Ecgwynn, his wife of seven months. Their first child would be born in May and Ealhswith was delighted at the prospect of a second grandchild.

'Edward will make a good king, Ealhswith, I've no doubt of it. He probably won't have an easy reign, but he's wise and strong enough to shoulder it, especially with Aethelred's help. The two have become as close as brothers, and when Garth's with them, it's like having triplets around the place. They're almost inseparable.'

Ealhswith laid her head on his shoulder. 'We all need friends, Alfred, as you and I both know.'

She would not speak of the Danes who could destroy their peace and happiness during the coming year, though she knew that, despite his silence on the matter over the Christmastide, the Danes presently overwintering on the River Lea were constantly on her husband's mind. His restless nights and daytime pacing were enough to tell her that. Perhaps the raiders' intentions would become clear with the onset of spring, but until that time, Ealhswith was determined to make Alfred's life as easy as she possibly could and remind him every day that even after twenty-six years, he still meant the world to her.

*

Lundenburh: late-June, 895

'Edward's little son is a delight,' Aethelflaed gushed on their arrival back in Lundenburh after a brief visit to Winchester to greet her new nephew. She turned to speak to the servants regarding the evening meal and settled Aelfwynn at a trestle with a mug of buttermilk. 'The babe looks so like Edward,' she continued,' although Ecgwynn's hair is dark, too, so Aethelstan's black curls are to be expected, I suppose.'

Aethelred only half-listened to Aethelflaed's words as he focused on the more pressing matter of the Danes still camped along the Lea. Now that early vegetables were bearing fruit and the hay was golden in the fields, their raids on local villages had escalated. They'd also seized many spring lambs and cattle, now out at pasture, and Aethelred was finding it hard to stand by and let it happen. He'd made Alfred aware of events on more than one occasion, but, as yet, his father-by marriage had given no order to move against them. Although Aethelred agreed that breaking through such a well-fortified stronghold could result in the loss of many men's lives, he was becoming increasingly impatient with the inaction. He was also determined not to let the bastards get their thieving hands on the coming harvest, leaving the villagers to starve next winter.

'If these pagans think they're getting silver from me to leave our lands, they can think again!' he raged, suddenly overcome with the hopelessness of the situation. 'None of our people within miles of Hertford – even Lundenburh itself – will be safe this summer if we don't act now.'

'Aethelred, if you act without my father's authority and you don't succeed in driving these Danes out, you will have to live with the knowledge that he will never forgive you. If I know him, he'll already be planning some kind of action, so we just have to be patient.'

'Tell that to the villagers when they bury their dead and

Twenty Six

rebuild their torched homes.' Aethelflaed turned and headed into the kitchen and Aethelred rubbed his aching brow. He hadn't intended to vent his frustrations on his wife and deep down, he knew she was right. He would send messengers to Winchester and ask Alfred's permission to attack the Danes. If he refused, then so be it. He'd just have to be patient, as Aethelflaed said.

'Are you going to say you're sorry to Mama now, Papa?' Aelfwynn's worried voice at his side startled him out of his thoughts. 'She looked very angry when she went into the kitchen.'

Aethelred gave his young daughter a hug. 'I was just about to do that, little one. I admit, I was the one at fault, not Mama.'

'Well,' she said, her small hands now firmly planted on her hips, 'you'd better do it soon or she might stay in the kitchen for the rest of the day – and she promised to play tabula with me later.'

*

In the obscurity of pre-dawn shadow, Aethelred's army of well-armed and well-armoured men silently crept forward to surround the strategically placed Danish fortress, their aim to oust the marauders who had blighted their land for the past seven months. June was nearing an end, and left here unchallenged for much longer, the Danes would claim the harvest and the entire region would starve.

The night sky was paling fast and Aethelred prayed they'd manage to cross the earthworks and strike before either daybreak or observant guards roused the camp. His army of seven hundred was, undoubtedly, outnumbered, its success resting upon a neatly executed surprise attack – which entailed killing as many of the enemy as possible before they were fully awake and arming themselves.

Aethelred raised his arm, its downward strike the signal to attack. The forward surge was soundless but by the time they attempted to scale the earthen wall, Norse warriors reared into view along its top, hefting swords and battleaxes, ready to defend their lair.

The three gates were suddenly flung open and Danes streamed out, weapons swinging at the Mercians, who instantly fell back and attempted to form a shield wall. But too late… Danes crashed into them, fragmenting their would-be wall and ensuring the battle became a full-scale clash of individuals.

Aethelred and Garth kept each other's backs, slashing and thrusting with their swords and blocking attacks with their shields as fighting raged on around them. Between them they took several Norsemen down, and Aethelred prayed the rest of his men were doing the same. But reality soon revealed itself in the mounting number of Mercian dead. His army had been crushed by the far greater number of opposing Danes. Aethelred had no other option than to signal retreat.

They fled back to their horses, knowing the enemy would be on their heels – until the racket of hammering on shields and jeering laugher reached them. Aethelred did not need to look back to know that the Norsemen were mocking their pitiful attempt to storm their stronghold.

'Ride for Lundenburh!' he yelled, choked for words as

Twenty Six

humiliation at their rout overwhelmed him. He could well imagine what Aethelflaed would say, and daren't even think how her battle-wise father would react. Disappointing Alfred was not how Aethelred had imagined this manoeuvre would end. The Danes were still here, and he'd lost several good men. Holding his head high would not be easy for quite some time.

*

In the first week of July, Aethelred arrived in Winchester to report his failed attempt to oust the Danes from their stronghold on the River Lea to Alfred. Having listened to Aethelflaed's criticisms, he expected even worse from the king.

But Alfred did not scold or deride, nor did he demean Aethelred's efforts to strike the fortress. He simply invited his son-by-marriage to walk with him alongside the River Itchen where they could be alone to talk.

'I can't deny I would have celebrated had you been successful,' Alfred started, as they strolled, the bright July day seeming at odds with the misery Aethelred felt. 'In truth, when I gave my consent for you to deal with those Danes, it hadn't crossed my mind you might attempt to take on an entire fortress. My spies reported almost nine hundred men in there, and you had, what… fewer than seven hundred?'

'Yes, lord,' Aethelred replied, averting his gaze in shame.

'In which case, a better strategy would have been to have remained in the area for some time, repeatedly striking and harassing smaller groups of Danes when they came out to raid. To have worn them down and lessened their numbers gradually would have been to our advantage.'

Alfred was silent for some time and Aethelred could see he was deep in thought.

'At this moment, my main concern is the loss of our men during your attack,' Alfred eventually continued, 'and the fact that we now need to replace four of your thegns. I'll leave that in your capable hands, of course: you know your men better than I do, and the areas of Mercia they come from.'

Aethelred nodded, already realising that was something he'd have to do. Taking news of the men's deaths had been a gruelling task. Knowing their deaths were due to his own bad decisions was hard to bear.

As though reading his mind, Alfred said, 'All leaders make mistakes, Aethelred, especially in the early days of their commands. I should know, I made enough of them in my younger days: misjudgements and misinterpretations of people and situations, as well as failing to take note of advice, even when I knew it to be wise. The only thing I could do was to learn from those mistakes and make sure I didn't make them again.'

Alfred halted to grasp Aethelred's arm as though in greeting. 'Be assured, Aethelred, I value your judgement and your ability to rule Mercia, and I don't want this one incident to make you think otherwise. Now, while you're here in Winchester I want you to hear how I plan to deal with the cursed Danes on the River Lea once and for all.'

Twenty Seven

In the last week of August, Alfred led his army of twelve hundred men to camp close to the Danish fortress on the Lea. The harvest was ripening fast and he was determined it would be the villagers doing the reaping and not the pillaging Danes. Even his new city of Lundenburh was partly reliant upon the produce of the Hertford region and deprived of it, the citizens would suffer great hardships.

Over the next couple of weeks, Alfred's men positioned themselves to stand guard each day while the people gathered in their crops and herded their livestock into the byres. The wheat and barley, so vital for their daily baking of flatbreads and brewing of ale, were carted into nearby burhs, safe from further plundering.

'At least we've overcome the immediate problem of keeping our people fed through the winter,' Alfred said to Aethelred as the reaping came to a close, the golden, sun-kissed beauty of the season a momentary balm to his frustrations. 'The Danes would have expected to have the harvest all to themselves but now it is they who face a winter of starvation.'

Aethelred twisted in his saddle to face Alfred as they returned to camp. 'What now, lord? Once we ride away from here, the Danes may well sail back to the Thames and we could still be facing raids on Lundenburh and the coastal areas to the south.'

'The very reason why we make certain that doesn't happen.'

'How do we do that, other than by laying siege to their

fortress all winter, or by following them along the riverbanks as they sail?'

Alfred shook his head. 'I have no intention of inflicting the discomforts of laying siege on my men, Aethelred, or of following the Danes around like sheep. But I do intend to make sure they can't reach the Thames, and by a much simpler method. It's one that has worked in West Francia for some time now and if Edward has followed my orders correctly, he'll be instigating the start of important building work as we speak. And tomorrow, we move our camp to join him a short way downriver.'

*

Aethelred was happy to be with Edward again, whom he hadn't seen since he'd visited Winchester to welcome his newborn son in June. The younger man looked extremely well and Aethelred decided that marriage and fatherhood obviously suited his brother-by-marriage. His dark hair curled about his collar and his newly sprouted dark beard accentuated his handsome face, now pinked from hours in the early September sun. After brotherly hugs and back-slaps, and enquiries after the health of family members, Edward led him to survey the building works in progress on both sides of the River Lea.

Edward did not seem surprised that Aethelred hadn't been told what to expect to see here, despite the fact that he'd arrived with Alfred. 'It's typical of my father to keep you guessing,' Edward said, matter-of-factly, 'so don't take it as a snub. He does the same thing with me all the time, so I'm used to it. If you ask me, I think he just enjoys springing surprises on people. I know how highly he thinks of you, and that he plans to ask your opinion on what he's doing here once you've had time to consider it. So, what are your first impressions?'

Aethelred shrugged, seeing no mystery regarding Alfred's intentions at this spot. 'It's obvious you're building defensive settlements on either side of the Lea – burhs, if I'm not mistaken by the ditches being dug and the ramparts already up. They aren't too different in that to the Danes' fortress further upstream.'

Edward nodded at his estimation so far and Aethelred went on, pointing to the activity inside the outer ditches. 'With the timber and thatch you've brought here, some of your men are building structures needed for the settlements to function: houses, stables, a forge and workshops, and such like. And, as they are to be burhs, on completion both will be manned by regular forces of the standing army, ready to halt the passage of enemy longships.' He pointed along the riverbank. 'I see you've also brought a dozen of Alfred's ships here, and I imagine you'll be bringing more – at least enough to successfully block the river and give battle, if need be.

'Alfred's decision to build these burhs is a clever one,' Aethelred mused, rounding off his thoughts, 'and the siting of them here, where the river narrows, is ideal. The Danes will think twice about trying to pass this way, and sailing upstream from their present camp would be pointless. The Lea becomes little more than a shallow brook a short distance upstream, dwindling further as it nears its source in the Chilterns, just twenty miles from their present camp. They'd soon be forced to abandon their ships anyway. All in all, I'd say, the Danes will be well and truly hemmed into their fortress with nowhere to sail…'

He nodded slowly as a thought came into his head. 'Unless they decide to abandon their ships and flee elsewhere overland. That is, of course, if they make that move before they're forced to eat their horses as Hastein's army did at Buttington.'

He laughed at Edward's nods of approval. 'You forget, Edward, I was involved in the development of Lundenburh, and I picture both of these settlements as smaller versions of that.'

'Not a bad summary at all, my friend, considering this is the first time you've seen the building work. You're also right about the ships. We expect another dozen to arrive from Rochester in a day or two. But there is one thing you haven't mentioned. Have *you* forgotten that Father has always griped about there being something missing at Lundenburh?'

Aethelred thought for a moment and grinned. 'I haven't forgotten, it just slipped my mind for a moment. A bridge linking these twin burhs would be a perfect deterrent to raiders. Archers and spearmen along a bridge could decimate a ship's crew, as well as being an invaluable means of communication between the two burhs. I know your father is still hoping to start work on the Lundenburh bridge once we rid the kingdom of these Danes and, in my opinion, we need to build bridges across many of our rivers.'

'Given time, I'm sure they'll be built,' Alfred said, coming to stand between them. 'It won't be in my lifetime, but I'm certain that future generations will continue where I left off.' He looked pointedly at Edward, his eyebrows raised and a silly

Twenty Seven

grin on his face that made the two men laugh.

'As for asking your opinion of these burhs and their usefulness, Aethelred, there's no need for me to do that now. I've been perched on that rock over there, shamelessly eavesdropping on your conversation. I'm glad you approve.

'Oh, and Edward… it isn't in my nature to "gripe".'

*

The Danes remained at their camp for another three weeks before abandoning their ships and fleeing across country on horseback. Three days later, Aethelred had mustered a thousand-strong army and was following behind them, heading north-west along the Danelaw boundary before veering due west once they were twenty miles south-west of Leicester. As daylight faded on the second day of their pursuit, Aethelred's scouts rode into their overnight camp.

'They reached Bridgnorth on the River Severn just after noon two days since, lord, and it looks like they're planning to stay.' The fresh-faced young man nodded in agreement with his words. 'A group of them spent some time looking round the site, pointing at different places as they walked. We guessed they were deciding where to build their earthworks, though we weren't close enough to hear what they said.'

Aethelred's spirits plummeted as thoughts of the long, cold months ahead filled his mind. By the time his army reached Bridgnorth, the Danes would have their ramparts built and attacking the stronghold would be pointless – as he he'd proved to himself on the River Lea. Prospects of laying siege during the winter months loomed, despite Alfred's reluctance to inflict siege conditions on his men. But in this, Aethelred knew he had no other choice. The Danes were in West Mercia, and as the Lord of Mercia, it was his role to deal with them.

'What are the advantages of this particular site to them, Eafa?'

'For a start there's a stream that flows into the Severn right next to them, with woodland within half a mile where they could hunt and gather firewood. There are also numerous settlements they could harry within a day's ride… You're thinking of laying siege, lord?'

'Much as I'd like to say no, at this stage I can't see any other way of dealing with this.' Aethelred's smile at the young scout was grim. 'As you say, they've already started digging themselves in so they're evidently planning to overwinter at Bridgnorth. We can't just ride away and let them ravage our villages.'

'Aethelred, as your friend, I have to remind you of what happened to Edward at Thorney Island.' Garth's face reflected his concern. 'His siege almost failed because of the terms of service of many of the men of the standing army coming to an end.'

Aethelred nodded, needing no reminder of that. 'I'll organise some of our thegns to do a check around the men, but whatever the outcome, I can't stop any of them leaving once their terms are up. Let's hope the Danes' food supplies don't last long and they surrender. We've no way of knowing how much hunting and foraging they'll have done by the time we get there. It's a big enough army to have some of their men out raiding and gathering food while the rest are digging out

Twenty Seven

the earthworks. So, it looks like we're facing a repeat of events at Chester and on the Lea.'

*

The siege of the Bridgnorth camp had been ongoing for over two months, and the early December weather was growing colder by the day. White-rimed mornings had become the norm, while writhing mists embraced their knees. Aethelred stamped his feet and shook his hands in a vain effort to stop them from tingling with the cold. Cursing the Danes to everlasting damnation, he prayed they would soon surrender and they could all go home. Surely, they must be nearing starvation by now.

'You realise that many of our men are complaining of wanting to be home with their families for the Christmastide, don't you, Aethelred, even though no terms of service are up before February? They know that going home before then is unlikely, so I suppose they're just bored.'

Garth paused, grinning as he watched his friend performing his strange warm-up dance, his exhaled breath clouding as it mingled with the freezing air. 'When the men aren't on duty, they're idling in their tents playing dicing games,' he went on. 'To my way of thinking they'd be better out here, keeping themselves fit in case the Danes decide to try a breakout. The exercise would warm them up a lot more than sitting around on their arses brooding about Christmastide.'

'You're probably right, but I can understand them wanting to take shelter. If you tell me your balls aren't frozen out here,

I won't believe you. I daren't even piss in case it freezes before it reaches the ground.'

Garth's laughter was enough to jolt Aethelred from his self-pity and he joined his friend in a hearty laugh.

Two days later, without forewarning, Alfred rode into the Bridgnorth camp with a small contingent of his men. Aethelred led his father-by marriage into the large tent he shared with Garth and two other thegns in order to talk, leaving the rest of the new arrivals to pitch their tents. Although pleased to see Alfred, and the distraction from the monotony of the siege his visit brought, Aethelred knew that the king would not have ridden all this way without good reason, especially as it seemed he was planning to stay.

For some moments Alfred stood before the glowing brazier in the centre of the tent, the blissful warmth he enjoyed reflected in the look on his face 'Not the weather for riding almost a hundred and fifty miles,' he said at length, turning to face the two younger men while rubbing his hands together to contain the heat a little longer. 'Nor is it weather for sitting out a siege.' He held up a hand to halt Aethelred's inevitable questions. 'So, before you bombard me with whys, wherefores and what-ifs, let's sit and I'll explain the purpose of my visit.

'First, let me say that you seem to have everything in hand here, with plenty of guards around keeping watch. None of us would wish for the Danes to break out, but it has happened in the past – at Buttington, for instance. The loss of life in battle is not something we want, or need, to accept as an appropriate end to a siege. But we all know it's a possibility, one which you have obviously thought much about.'

Twenty Seven

Aethelred and Garth stayed mute, knowing Alfred well enough to realise he hadn't yet reached his main point.

'I imagine you've had dismal thoughts of staying here for the rest of the winter, but I've come to relieve you of the necessity of doing that… Your faces tell me you're confused and probably think I've lost my senses: an army of only thirty men could not lay siege on so large a Danish force. Well, I can assure you, that is not my intention.'

'Then what *are* you going to do' Aethelred asked, unable to stay quiet now. 'You say you're relieving our army, so whose army will you put in our place?'

'There'll be no need for any army once I've paid the Danes to leave our lands for good. I've brought enough silver with me to persuade them to head back to Mersea Island. What they do then is up to them. Many of them will have had enough of trying and failing to take our lands, and settling in Northumbria or East Anglia may sound like a good idea. But if they hope to find allies to ride against us amongst the Northumbrian Danes, they'll be sadly disappointed. You may have heard that I sent Ealdorman Aethelnoth up to York last year to negotiate a peace treaty with the Danish king, Gunfrith?'

Both men nodded and Garth said, 'Aethelnoth mentioned it to me when he got back to Somerset. He was surprised at how readily Gunfrith agreed to sign the treaty.'

'That's because the old king's years of warring with neighbouring Norsemen over the rulership of Rutland had just ended,' Alfred explained. 'He wanted nothing more than to enjoy some years of peace, so signing a treaty with me was to his advantage.' He gave a wistful smile. 'I can only say that he and I share that sentiment…

'So, any of these Danes from the Lea who want to continue raiding will not be welcome in Northumbria. They may find a few allies amongst the East Anglians but I doubt there'd be many, especially after Hastein's experiences in trying to get the better of us. I'm guessing that any would-be raiders will be heading back to Francia.'

'What about the ships they left on the river?'

Alfred shook his head. 'Oh no, they don't get those back, Garth. The seaworthy vessels are now part of my fleet at Rochester and the rest we burnt. I'll allow them to keep their horses; it's how they came to Bridgnorth, so that's all they get.'

'Are you saying that once these Danes have ridden off, we can all go home in time for Christmastide?'

'That's exactly what I'm saying. We've had four years of these Danes in our lands and I think we can now say, this move will see us finally rid of them. And if I ever see your father again, Aethelred, I'll tell him exactly what I think of his good friend, Hastein!'

Twenty Eight

Aros, Danish Lands: early-July 896

Aros was abuzz with activity as Hamid and Yrsa prepared to leave for Cordoba with their two small children and faithful friend, Basím. Bjorn had offered to take them in the *Sea Eagle,* with Eadwulf, Hrolf and Dainn along for company, and tomorrow they would sail with the dawn. Now the men were busy loading wooden crates full of family clothes and cherished possessions onto the ship.

Freydis was not happy about any of it, and had fought back her tears for days, determined not to let anyone see her distress. Already upset about losing her adopted daughter and grandchildren – the youngest a tiny girl of only six weeks whom they had named Alith – her husband, brother and one of her sons would also be gone for some time. Freydis dreaded the empty weeks until at least, some of them returned. But the gap in her life made by Yrsa leaving would never be filled.

As the sun rose on the eastern horizon, she stood on the bank of the River Aros with Kata, Ameena and Una, waving as the *Sea Eagle* grew smaller and smaller until it eventually disappeared from view. She would fill the next few weeks as she always did when the men were away, caring for Thora and overseeing the servants to ensure the smooth running of her household and farmland. At times, she and Thora would enjoy the company of the other women whose men-folk had sailed off on the *Sea Eagle* to al-Andalus, whiling away the hours in shared domestic activity and idle chat.

Eadwulf had promised to be home by late August, in time for a visit to Mercia. A recent letter from Aethelred had informed them that Wessex and Mercia were enjoying a period of peace and he intended to visit his sister Leofwynn and old friend Aethelnoth in early September. He would be overjoyed to see his father and his family there at the same time.

It was almost ten years since Eadwulf had seen his older children and he was determined not to miss the opportunity on this occasion.

'Come on, Thora,' Freydis urged, taking her daughter's hand. 'Let's go back to the hall and make some honey-cakes. Your papa will only be gone for a few weeks, then we'll sail across the Northern Sea to meet another of your half-brothers, and a half-sister as well. They are both grown up of course, but they have children of their own, so I'm sure you'll make some new friends.'

'I'd like that a lot,' Thora said, her face lighting up. 'Do Papa's children have red hair like mine?'

'Aethelred does, but his young daughter, Aelfwynn, who must be eight or nine by now, has the same gold-brown colouring as her mother, Lady Aethelflaed. Aethelred's sister, Leofwynn, has auburn hair, a deeper red than her father and brother's – or yours. She has the same hair colour her mother, Leoflaed, had.

'Now, let's go and make those honey-cakes. Then we'll take a batch to Una and see how much little Hals has grown since we saw him last week. It's hard to believe he's already five months old. Time passes so quickly, and I'm hoping it will sprout wings and fly between now and the end of August.'

Twenty Eight

*

Winchester, Hampshire: early August 896

Ealhswith paced the hall floor, trying to avoid the servants as they set up the trestles for the morning meal and wringing her hands as her anxiety rose. Alfred was in his usual place in the corner of the hall amidst his scholars, poring over a large sheet of parchment spread out before him, his drawn face and sunken eyes testament to the fact that he'd missed yet another night's sleep. Surely, he'd exhausted his list of ship designs by now…?

Alfred had been so unwell recently, stricken, yet again, by his old illness. As was typical of her husband, when he was well, he declared there to be nothing to worry about; he was simply growing old and his body could not fend off the attacks as easily as it had in his younger days.

Although Ealhswith could not deny that Alfred was ageing, as indeed, was she, she could not accept that age was the sole culprit here. To her way of thinking, the cause of his worsening illness was the fact that he had worked himself raw, constantly denying his body the rest it craved. Few of the twenty-five years of his reign had been free of Danish attacks, and rest had become a luxury that Alfred had never managed to capture for long. Even now, with no major invasions to contend with, Alfred had rarely been at home…

Ealhswith thought of how the year had started on such a positive note. The siege at Bridgnorth had ended and the Danes had fled from Mercia. Alfred had been pleased to know that some had settled peaceably in Northumbria and East Anglia and others had done as he'd predicted and sailed back across the sea to Francia. For a blessed few weeks, Alfred's kingdom had been free of Norse invaders. But with the onset of spring, coastal raids on small settlements had started again, each one fast and furious before their ships sailed on in search of other vulnerable villages. Word of Alfred's well-defended burhs had obviously spread and the Danes avoided them like the plague.

Yet again, Alfred realised the necessity of confronting the Norsemen at sea, and his attentions returned to his navy. He spent days visiting his ports, checking on the number of vessels available at each and their suitability for fending off enemy longships. Once home again in May, he had set about designing still more new ships and ordering building work to start immediately.

Ealhswith sank into a chair, weary to the bone and fraught with worry as she recalled the conversation her husband had with Asser in early May, when the raids had started in earnest...

'Beating the Norsemen at sea is the only way we can put an end these attacks. Our ships must become a constant presence in our coastal waters so that the Danes can never be certain they won't suddenly appear as they attempt their cursed raids.'

Asser could only agree with Alfred's reasoning. 'But have we enough suitable ships in our fleet to do that?'

'From what I've seen in recent weeks, not enough to counter a fleet of any size. We currently have nine new vessels under construction, and several more will be built over the coming year. All of them will be of a superior design to anything the Norsemen have.'

Asser gave a tolerant smile. 'In what way will they be su-

Twenty Eight

perior, lord? It seems to me that the design of Norse ships has been successful for generations of men who have sailed far and wide to trade, raid or settle.'

'Indeed, they have, Bishop, but many of the ships belonging to East Anglian or Northumbrian raiders are now old, some having been sailed here during the first invasion by Ivar and Halfdan almost thirty years ago. Most of the ships we captured on the Lea were fit for nothing but burning, and Aethelred said the same of those he captured at Benfleet three years ago.

'As for design, I've come to the conclusion that we need to build our ships much bigger than those of the Danes. Whereas Danish longships are thirty-oar at the most, our new ships will be twice as long at sixty-oar or more. It stands to reason that larger ships with their broader sails will be swifter than smaller vessels at sea. They'll also carry more crew to deal with each raid *and* it will take fewer ships to block estuaries or creeks into which Danish ships have sailed.

'In fact, Lord Asser, the new ships will be bigger all round, with a deeper draught so their hulls ride high in the water, making enemy boarding during encounters almost impossible. Whereas, our men will be able to leap aboard their ships with ease.'

'Then all I can say, lord, is that I hope your new designs bring the success you crave against these Norse pirates. We certainly need to put an end to their wicked pagan raids, but I'll withhold my judgement of your newly designed vessels until they've been fully tried and tested.'

Alfred grinned. 'O ye of little faith…'

Ealhswith mulled the conversation over and sincerely

hoped that Asser's lack of faith in her husband's designs would not prove to be justified and Alfred would feel compelled to start redesigning all over again. His health would not take the strain.

*

Alfred received the message on a balmy day in the last week of August as he prepared to move his court to Wantage for the autumn. But it seemed the court would not be moving anywhere just yet.

'Six of them, you say? In which direction were they heading?'

'Definitely six, lord, and definitely Norsemen. Word is they're East Anglian, but no one knows for certain.' Raulf's face held a thoughtful expression that momentarily threw Alfred. The new, Hampshire ealdorman looked so like his father, Radulf, Alfred's dearest counsellor and confidant who passed away two years ago. 'They sailed along the south coast from the east, raiding a few settlements between Dover and Folkestone before sailing on to raid along the Dorset coast, then turning back to attack villages around the Isle of Wight.'

Raulf ran his fingers through his dark hair, again reminding Alfred of Radulf. 'They were heading back east along the Sussex coast when we left. The portreeve sent a couple of ships out this morning to alert your new fleet. Last we heard they were patrolling the Dorset shoreline after returning from the north coast of Devon. It's a pity they weren't there a week earlier.'

'You're right, and I'm hoping to have at least three fleets

Twenty Eight

patrolling our shores before long, but until then, we make do with just one. I'm certain our nine ships will be more than enough to deal with six Norsemen. With the wind in their sails they'll be on the enemy's tail before long.'

He realised he sounded smug, but the pride he felt in his new ships was not something he could easily conceal. 'Once you and your men have rested and had some refreshments, Raulf, ride back to Southampton and give Eadgar my thanks for his swift actions. I'll be in the port around noon tomorrow.'

*

'What news have we?' Alfred asked after he'd greeted Eadgar in the early afternoon of the following day. The stocky Southampton portreeve had been a great asset to Wessex over the years and an efficient overseer of the building and testing of Alfred's fleet from the beginning of his plans.

'Our fleet was spotted crossing the Solent and rounding Selsey early this morning. They were moving apace, I'm told, with the westerly behind them.'

Alfred's chest swelled. 'They've made good time then. What of the Danes? Have we had sightings of them?'

'We know they raided around Littlehampton then sailed on east, but we've heard nothing since. It's too early in the day for them to have moored in some creek for the night, but they could well be raiding along one of the estuaries – you know how many there are along that stretch of coast.'

Alfred nodded. 'I'm hoping our ships won't sail past and miss them altogether. But there's nothing we can do but wait and hope the next news we get is what we want to hear.'

No further news came in until two days later. Alfred paced the quayside for want of something better to do, idly watching the comings and goings of the fishing vessels as his bodyguard of a dozen played tabula or knucklebones. It was late afternoon and the sun was gradually sinking to the western horizon after an overly warm, late-August day. The stench of raw fish and seaweed drifted across the quayside on the incoming breeze and Alfred peeled his eyes in the hope of sighting something other than fishing craft.

Then, on the distant horizon, he caught sight of what appeared to be no more than small dark dots at first, gradually growing in size as they drew closer. The realisation that they were his nine ships almost took his breath away.

Little was said as crewmen disembarked and filed into the port and Alfred wondered why no jubilant grins of victory could be seen. Close to five hundred men followed him and his guards back towards Eadgar's hall and the open meadow beyond. Here, the mixed crew of Saxons and Frisians sat on the grass and drank the ale that was carried out to them by Eadgar's servants and shipbuilders alike.

'Is anyone able to give account of your conflict with the Danes?' Alfred yelled to those close enough to hear.

'There is, lord. I can explain exactly what happened.'

'Uhtric!' Alfred's voice left little doubt of his surprise at seeing Radulf's younger son as one of his crew. After all, it had been Eadgar who had recruited them all. 'Come forward, if you will, and we can speak while the rest of the men rest out here.'

Once seated in Eadgar's hall with a mug of ale, Uhtric

Twenty Eight

described events along the Sussex coast.

'You're saying the design of our new ships was not an advantage during the encounter?' Alfred could barely swallow down his disappointment.

'Lord, your ships were excellent in the deep, open waters away from the coast: fast and sleek, with huge sails that picked up every breath of wind. In close combat out there, we could have out-run the Norsemen, lashed them to us and boarded them with ease. But, as you know, out in the open is not where most clashes with Norsemen occur.'

Alfred could not disagree with anything Uhtric said and it shamed him to admit it, even to himself. When raiding, Norse vessels clung to the coast as they scanned for villages, or the mouths of rivers along which settlements could flourish.

'In the shallow coastal waters, the deep draughts put us at a disadvantage and were the cause of the Danes almost escaping us,' Uhtric continued, his brow furrowing in thought. 'But before I explain how that came about you need to know how the entire encounter went, so I'll start at the beginning.'

Alfred nodded, hoping to hear no further criticism of his ships.

'Although we can say the battle was an overall victory for us, lord, many of us felt that things could have been better. To start with, we came upon the Danes a little upstream in a narrow estuary. Three of their vessels were already ashore and empty, and we guessed their crews would be either raiding or foraging inland. Our ships moved into position across the estuary, successfully blocking their escape out to sea, and the other three Danes immediately tried to break through.'

Alfred stayed mute, though he knew his face would convey his disappointment in what he had hoped to be a resounding victory.

'We boarded two of the three and killed their crews, and although the third ship got past us, we'd killed all but five of the men, so they wouldn't have fared well at sea once the wind dropped. The only reason it escaped us at all was because our own ships were suddenly grounded with the outgoing tide, three of us landing close to the three beached Danes. I was on one of those ships, and I can tell you, lord, there was nothing we could have done to stop that happening. Our other six were stranded on the opposite side of the estuary.

'The crews from the three beached Norsemen suddenly returned and charged straight at us, screaming and swinging those cursed battle axes like men possessed. The fighting was fierce and the narrow strip of shore was soon thick with corpses, the stomach-churning stench of blood and gore enough to make the hardest of warriors throw up. Yet, despite us having twice as many men as the Danes, the battle seemed to go on for ever and I prayed to God to end this slaughter.'

'And did it... end soon, I mean?'

'It did, lord. Although equal numbers of men had fallen on both sides, our larger forces were enough to see us eventually prevail. But then the tide came in, and with their shallow draughts the three Danish ships were freed some time before ours could move. Survivors rowed out of the estuary, but having lost so many of their crew, they had difficulty getting out to sea. Two of the vessels were hurled back against the rocky Sussex coast and stranded on the beach, so only one managed

Twenty Eight

to sail off, back to wherever it had come from.

'All in all, King Alfred, we can count the day as ours, but I urge you to concentrate on building lighter-weight vessels in future. We need ships with shallow draughts to counter coastal raiders with any success. Norsemen pride themselves on the speed and manoeuvrability of their craft in shallow waters.'

Alfred stared at the fair-headed, slightly-built young man, impressed by the words of wisdom spewing from his mouth. 'Would becoming the master of my fleet be of interest to you, Uhtric? I have shipbuilders working constantly for me under Eadgar in Southampton, and others in Rochester and a few other ports around our coasts. Co-ordinating of all of them, and checking regularly on their progress, would be of great value to me, not least in relieving me of that role. You would also be responsible for manning and leading the fleet out from Southampton when enemy vessels are sighted off our coasts and alerting portreeves elsewhere as the need arises.'

Uhtric's face lit up, and Alfred grinned back, realising he'd said the right thing. 'I confess, I relied heavily on your father for so many such roles when he was alive. And you are so like Radulf in logic and intellect, if not in colouring and build, I feel I must ensnare you before other roles in life take you away.'

'Lord, I would be honoured to be master of your fleet. Ships and the sea have been my passion since I was young, and Radulf would be proud to know I gained your favour in this.'

Alfred downed a swig of ale. 'We'll make the appointment official once I return to Winchester, but for now we deal with the rest of today. How many men lost, would you say?'

'Sixty-two of ours, lord, but the Danes lost around a hundred and twenty.'

'Those sixty-two will be sadly mourned,' Alfred murmured, momentarily overcome with sadness. 'Even victory in battle can sometimes seem like loss. You took the shipwrecked Danes from the two dashed ships captive?'

'We did. There are thirty-five of them, trussed up like chickens in our ships.'

Alfred's lips curved into a grim smile. 'Pirates deserve no better. It will be a spectacular hanging.'

Twenty Nine

Elston, East Mercia: early-September 896

If Eadwulf had thought he'd be sailing to Mercia in his own knarr, Bjorn's apparent affront at not being asked to accompany him soon put an end to that idea.

'After all the fun we've had together, you think because I'm getting old you can leave me at home beside the fire pit, snoring my days away?' The twinkle in Bjorn's green eyes allayed any suggestion of him being serious, and Eadwulf laughed out loud, the infectious sound causing the occupants of his household to laugh with him. 'Kata thinks I'm too old for sailing further than Hedeby these days, but our trip to Cordoba proved her wrong about that.'

'I'm sorry for not asking you,' Eadwulf said, not for the first time thinking how well Bjorn carried his sixty-three years. Only a few grey wisps brushed his temples and here and there a hint of silver striped his flowing, red locks. Nor had Bjorn yet developed a 'paunch to match' Ragnar's, as he'd predicted he would, many years ago. He still looked strong and well-toned. 'I simply thought that having only been back from al-Andalus for a few weeks, you might prefer to stay at home for a while.'

Bjorn huffed at that. 'I could say the same thing to you. In case it had slipped your mind, we all went to Cordoba…'

Eadwulf smiled to himself as he thought of their bickering now, inhaling deeply as the *Sea Eagle* moored along the Trent in the early afternoon on a bright September day. Just over a mile across the meadows was the Elston hall, where Aethelnoth and Odella still lived with their youngest son, Durwyn, the older three having married and moved away. Eadwulf's son would also be there, and his daughter, Leofwynn, was only a few miles away with her husband and their children. It was twelve years since Eadwulf was last in Elston, and although Aethelnoth and Aethelred were expecting him with Freydis and Thora, they had no idea that Bjorn would be with them.

Leaving six of the crew with the ship, Eadwulf led them from the riverbank, crossing the Fosse Way and continuing over the meadows. Scents of late-flowering blooms hung on the air, reminding him of the times he'd picked bunches of them for Leoflaed with Aethelred and Leofwynn when they were young. It suddenly seemed like yesterday.

Barking dogs heralded their arrival as the crew headed to the hay-barn where they would sleep at night, in accordance with the rota for guarding the ship. Aethelnoth had assured Eadwulf in his letter that Odella would insist that all the crew came to the hall for meals.

The hall door was suddenly flung open and Aethelnoth eyed the four visitors, his arms open wide and his face beaming. 'You're a sight for sore eyes,' he said, grasping Eadwulf in a bear-hug embrace. 'It's ten years since we met at Aethelred's wedding, and look at you… fit and healthy as ever and hardly a grey hair in sight.'

Eadwulf grinned back. 'I could say the same about you. I daresay age will catch up with us soon enough.'

Freydis and Thora received the same hugs from Aethelnoth, though in a gentler fashion, and the big man turned to Bjorn

Twenty Nine

who was standing to one side while the two old friends were reunited. 'I should've known you wouldn't let Eadwulf loose on the seas without you. I know you'd have come to Aethelred's wedding if King Alfred hadn't been there.'

Bjorn laughed as he and Aethelnoth greeted each other with hugs and back-slaps. 'My presence at the wedding could have been a little awkward after Alfred's dealings with my three brothers. They weren't exactly Alfred's favourite people. More recently, of course, my cousin, Hastein, has been causing trouble for him.'

'Hastein's been causing trouble for most of his life, as I recall,' Aethelnoth said, grinning at the thought. 'When I was his father's thrall in Ribe, it was always Hastein who couldn't wait for spring so he could be out raiding again.'

'I was little different myself in the early days,' Bjorn admitted. 'But my raiding days have long been over. Hastein claims the same and swears he's enjoying a quiet life with his family in Ribe. He'll be spending the Yule with us this year, so we'll know more about his plans then.'

'In my experience, Hastein makes lots of plans to live a quiet life, but rarely keeps to them. But that's Hastein, and I don't suppose anyone will ever change him.'

Aethelnoth's attention swung to Eadwulf. 'Aethelred's eager to see you all, though he'll be surprised to see Bjorn. He's been here six days already and needs to be back in Lundenburh in another week or so. And now you're here, I'll let Leofwynn know so she can arrange to come through. She'll get a surprise when she sees who else is with you.'

'Aethelnoth, are you going to stop talking and invite us in?'

Eadwulf's serious face made Aethelnoth laugh. 'Point taken, and I think it's your turn to be surprised when you see who else is staying with us.'

The first thing Eadwulf noticed on entering the hall was that little had changed since he and Leoflaed had lived here. The large, central firepit with the cauldron of pottage suspended over it looked just the same, as did the positions of the looms along the wall at the opposite end of the room with the trestle close by where the women did their needlework. The second thing he noticed was that Aethelred wasn't in the room.

'Welcome back,' Odella called, putting down the ale mugs she was carrying and scuttling over to hug each of them. To Eadwulf, the cheery, hard-working woman looked little different to how he remembered when he first came to Elston over thirty years ago, give or take a line or two around her eyes and a wisp of grey peeping from under her head veil. She smiled down at Thora, her head cocked to one side. 'With hair that colour, I'm guessing you must be Eadwulf and Freydis' daughter. You look about the right age, from what we've been told.'

'Yes, my lady. I am Thora and I'm eleven. And my hair is the same colour as Papa's –

and my Uncle Bjorn's. And I know that Papa has a son with hair like mine, but I can't see him.'

'There's no need to call me "my lady", Thora, Odella is fine. And Aethelred's just popped to his bedchamber and will be back shortly.'

Seated around a trestle, they brought each other up to date with events since they'd been together at Aethelred and Aethelflaed's wedding. Eadwulf noticed that Thora was listening

Twenty Nine

with interest as she drank her buttermilk. He also noticed that her attention kept straying to the door leading to the bedchambers. He knew how impatient she was to meet Aethelred and wondered what could be keeping him.

The door eventually swung open and Aethelred came in, a big grin on his face as he hurried over to greet the four of them. 'You have no idea how long I've been wanting to see you all,' he said, seating himself next to Eadwulf, 'and having you here, Bjorn, is an added bonus. It's ten years since I saw my father but I can't even remember the last time I saw you. I must have been quite young at the time.'

'If I remember rightly, you were about nine when I came here to bring Eadwulf and Jorund back to Aros with Beorhtwulf, Ameena and Hamid after we'd to been to Cordoba.'

'That was twenty-five years ago!' Aethelred shook his head. 'That makes me feel so *old*.'

Everyone laughed, including Thora, and Eadwulf could see that Aethelred had already impressed her. They chatted on for a while, until the door to the bedchambers opened again and all heads turned that way. Eadwulf jumped to his feet, instantly recognising Aethelflaed and his young grandaughter.

'Lady Aethelflaed, and Aelfwynn… What a nice surprise. My devious son forgot to mention that you would be here as well.'

'I confess, that isn't Aethelred's fault, Eadwulf,' Aethelflaed said, taking her daughter's hand and coming to stand by the trestle. 'We'd decided that Aelfwynn and I would stay with my parents in Winchester while Aethelred came here. But knowing our kingdom is now safe from raiders, I persuaded him it would be a chance for our daughter to meet her father's family. I already knew Aethelnoth and Odella from our wedding and hoped they wouldn't mind us staying here, and I can say they've been gracious hosts.'

Aethelflaed cast her eyes over the guests, her gaze coming to rest on Bjorn. 'From all the stories I've heard about a certain Dane, I'm guessing you are Bjorn?'

Bjorn stood and bowed his head as Aethelflaed and Aelfwynn sat down beside Aethelred, opposite to him. 'I am, my lady, but now I'm wondering just what you've heard about me. I hope nothing bad was said, or I might just die of shame.'

Aethelflaed joined in with the chuckles. 'Well, most sources said you had a good sense of humour, so I think they were right in that. But it seems that if provoked into losing your temper, people had better stay out of your way. I'll say no more about tempers since I've had the same thing said about me, quite unjustifiably, in my opinion.'

'It's true!' Aethelred put in, pretending to rub an assaulted upper arm.

Once the laughter had died down, Aethelflaed continued, 'Everything else I've heard about you tells me you're an honourable man, Bjorn: a well-loved jarl, and a loving husband, father and brother.' She glanced up and shared a wide smile with Freydis. 'Other than that, I've heard that you've been a fearless seaman and raider in your time *and* that you are much more trustworthy than your duplicitous cousin, whom I had the misfortune to meet.'

Before Bjorn could reply in Hastein's defence, Aethelflaed added, 'You also look uncannily like Eadwulf, who has passed

Twenty Nine

those looks on to my husband.'

'And me!' Thora piped up, holding out a lock of red hair.

Aethelflaed beamed at the young girl. 'It's a wonderful hair colour and we all love it. In fact, I'm a little jealous I don't have red hair myself.'

'One of Leofwynn's two lads has red hair.' Everyone turned to face Aethelnoth. 'Just saying, in case you didn't know. So it seems you handed your red hair on to one of your grandchildren, Eadwulf.'

The following days passed happily as everyone enjoyed each other's company and dreaded the time when they'd all be parted again. Thora and Aelfwynn became almost inseparable, though they allowed Leofwynn and Oswin's sons, thirteen-year-old Kenrick and the red-headed, eleven-year-old Sweyn, to join in with their games when they were present.

'I wish you didn't have to go away again.' Leofwynn pulled back from her father's embrace, sweeping the tears from her cheeks as he prepared to take his leave. 'We've seen so little of you since you moved to Aros.'

Eadwulf's own heart was heavy at leaving again, but his home was across the sea and he knew that nothing would change that now. 'We'll try to visit next spring, once the seas are calm. But don't forget, you are always welcome in Aros. If you can't find passage across the Northern Sea, send messengers to let me know and I'll come for you in the knarr.'

'We might just do that, one day,' Aethelred said, putting his arm around his sister. 'And if we do, you can be certain that Aethelnoth and Odella will come with us.'

Thirty

Winchester, Wessex: late May 897

For the past sixteen months, Alfred's kingdom had been free of invaders bent on conquest, and the benefits were felt across the Anglo-Saxon lands. Minor raids, however, continued around his coasts, despite the constant presence of his new fleets. Alfred had learned much from the encounter in the Sussex estuary last September and, once again, he had designed more ships to replicate those of the raiders. Yet the Danes still evaded them, striking at settlements with whirlwind speed before disappearing along some estuary or sheltered creek.

Such thoughts did little for Alfred's temper, especially when he considered the better design and lighter weight of his newest ships. But the marauders had the uncanny ability to melt into obscurity, carrying their sleek vessels to be hidden in the undergrowth inland, invisible to ships at sea.

'All we can do is rely on our fleets and portreeves to deal with them,' Alfred said to his elder son as they rode back to Winchester after spending a few days with Aethelred and Aethelflaed in Lundenburh. It was a slow journey as the half-dozen covered wagons carrying their families trundled behind surrounded by mounted warriors. 'There are more pressing needs for us to concentrate on at present, including continuing the building work across the kingdom and ensuring the ongoing training of our standing armies.'

Edward nodded. 'If not for the defensive measures you set

Thirty

in place after Guthrum's defeat, Hastein and the Appledore Danes would have been calling our kingdom theirs by now. You have every reason to be proud of your foresight in that.'

Alfred caressed Pegasus' white neck and the old stallion snickered in response. 'Yes, I am proud of that,' he admitted, twisting in the saddle to face his son, 'but I'm even prouder that my eldest son is well prepared to continue the work when I am gone. You will be a great king, Edward. The men already hold you in high esteem and you proved yourself a capable warrior and leader at Farnham. *And* you've already sired a son to succeed you. Babe he might be now, but if his lusty voice is anything to go by, Aethelstan will grow to be tall and strong.'

Alfred felt his anxiety rising and took a steadying breath. 'But Edward, I beg you to beware of your cousins. As sons of my elder brother, Aethelhelm and Aethelbold will undoubtedly declare their right to kingship to be greater than yours. Pray God, the situation will not end in outright revolt.'

'I'll do everything I can to appease my cousins, Father, but if it's warfare they're after, I'll make sure our armies are prepared. I'll also ensure our kingdom continues to expand as well as prosper, and Aethelstan will be raised to know he must do the same.'

'With that in mind I shall die a contented man.'

They rode in companionable silence for some moments, and Alfred savoured the warmth of the May sunshine on his cheeks as he thought. At length, he said, 'I'm also very proud of our ealdormen. Their swift actions saved us from defeat by several bands of Danes while I dealt with those raiding in

Devon. Each of them proved to be a loyal and capable leader, but Aethelred's quick thinking and responses to so many threats particularly stand out. I am truly grateful to him, and knowing how well the two of you work together, I know I'll be leaving our beloved kingdom in good hands. It's also good to know that Aethelflaed's marriage is a happy one.

'Now, enough said about all that. We should be back in Winchester before dusk, and tomorrow I have several documents I need to attend to. I also need to discuss a few things with Asser regarding the book he's writing about my life. He tells me he's almost up to the present, and needs to know more about recent raids, including those at sea.' He laughed. 'What he intends to do with this book after I've gone, I have no idea.'

*

Winchester, Wessex: Mid-July 898

Ealhswith swept into the hall, setting her sights on her husband. As was his norm, Alfred was hunched over a wad of old documents in his working corner, scanning them in earnest with Grimbald and two other scholars while the quill in his hand scribbled on a parchment alongside. Her exasperated thoughts were instantly dispelled by an incoming wave of anxiety. Alfred was working himself into the ground and nothing she could do or say would make him change his ways.

She hurried over, yet again intent on persuading him to take some rest. His old illness had struck so many times since

Thirty

Christmastide, taking him off his feet for three or four days each time. But as soon as he'd managed to rise from his bed, he'd immediately returned to his corner.

'You've been sitting here working since early morning, Alfred,' she said, looking down on his stone-grey hair and laying a hand on his shoulder. 'Don't you think some fresh air and sunshine would benefit you, freshen your mind for later on? You need to focus on something other than your translations for a while and allow your body to recover from the last bout of sickness. Why don't we take a stroll along the Itchen after the morning meal?'

Alfred smiled up at her, as he always did, and stroked her hand. 'I'm not working on translation today. I'm finishing off my design notes for a batch of reading pointers I intend to have made to put inside each copy of my translation of Pope Gregory's *Pastoral Care*. I thought the scroll and pointer together would make a splendid gift to present to nobles and clerics who have earned them in our service, especially at gift-giving ceremonies.'

Despite her anxiety, Ealhswith was intrigued. Alfred had been working for many months on his translation of this treasured book, but until now she hadn't known of his plans regarding the pointers.

'The craftsmen I've hired to create them are extremely skilled, but the design is intricate and the materials were costly, so my instructions need to be clear. Work will begin tomorrow. I've also sent messengers to recipients of the first batch to be in Winchester on the twelfth day of October, when I intend to present a scroll and pointer to some of our most hard-working clerics, mostly bishops and abbots.'

Ealhswith grasped her husband's arm. 'Does that mean Aethelgifu will be coming? You are including abbesses in this?'

'I am, although Aethelgifu is the only abbess on this occasion. We haven't seen our daughter for almost four years and, I confess, I am to blame for that. I warned her not to leave the abbey while the Danes were rampaging. I know I don't need to tell you what could have happened to her and her companions if their convoy had been attacked. Christian nuns are fair game to pagans.'

Ealhswith felt the ripple of revulsion she always felt when Alfred spoke of such things. 'I'm so thankful for the fortifications you insisted on building into Shaftesbury Abbey, Alfred, especially that high outer wall. And knowing that a company of our standing army is close by gives me even greater comfort.'

'And she'll be much safer travelling now, although there are always bandits and suchlike about.'

Ealhswith absently nodded, her thoughts still troubled. 'Aethelgifu's attendance will also depend upon her being well enough, of course. I've a feeling her letters have concealed from us how fragile she's actually become over the past year or two, and I can't help worrying about her.'

'I'll send a company of my men to escort her cavalcade here and back,' Alfred said, the look on his face telling Ealhswith of his own concerns for his abbess daughter.

*

Thirty

Winchester, Wessex: Early October 898

Alfred smiled round at his many guests, his family members amongst them, invited to witness the ceremony that meant so much to him. All but Aelfthryth and her husband, Baldwin of Flanders – the son of Alfred's stepmother, Judith – had been unable to undertake the journey, due to affairs of state. He was proud to note that all his family had taken great care with their attire. Ealhswith looked every inch the gracious wife of a king in her crimson, velvet robe as she waited at his side for the ceremony to begin. Then she would retreat to stand with their children and friends.

The variously dyed robes of the dozen bishops, five abbots and his devoted mass priest, Grimbald, swept the sweet-smelling rushes of the floor as they chatted with each other while waiting for the gift-giving ceremony to start. Alfred was pleased to see that his friend, Plegmund, the revered Archbishop of Canterbury, outshone his bishops with his bright gold pallium over a shimmering linen alb of paler gold. And though all the bishops wore their mitres, Archbishop Plegmund's was more richly adorned with jewels than the rest.

Nonetheless, each bishop's attire was impeccable. Even Alfred's loyal friend and tutor, Asser, Bishop of Sherborne, usually so simply garbed, had excelled himself. Alfred had rarely seen so many decorated chasubles and colourful stoles all in one place. And, like the archbishop, each wore an episcopal ring on the third finger, the purple amethysts set in bands of gold, twinkling in the firelight.

The five abbots had also donned their finery for the occasion, their patterned, multihued copes equalling the bishops' in quality, although they chose to remain bareheaded. By comparison, though neat and simple, Grimbald's plain grey robes of a mass priest looked quite dour. Yet his head was held as high as the rest of today's recipients.

And there amongst them, chatting with Asser and her brother Aethelweard, was Alfred's beloved daughter, Aethelgifu, Abbess of Shaftesbury. For today, Aethelgifu had abandoned her usual dark habit for one of a softer blue, with a white linen head veil in place of the more austere darker one. As a symbol of her office, around her neck hung a pectoral cross garnished with rubies. Alfred had never seen her looking so accomplished, or so at ease amidst a crowd.

A hush fell over the hall as Alfred held up his hand ready to begin, and Ealhswith sidled away to stand with their children.

'Good friends, as I am sure you are all aware, you have been invited here today to celebrate your service to our kingdom in all things spiritual, and for me to express my sincere gratitude to you for doing so. Many of you have also been involved in my efforts to improve learning amongst our people, a desire I hold close to my heart. It has ever been my desire to reward those who help to further the well-being of our kingdom, either by working to increase knowledge and understanding amongst people of all ranks, or by standing beside me against invaders who would subjugate us all and desecrate our lands.'

Alfred lifted one of the scrolls with its attached pointer from the nearby trestle and held it up for all to see. 'In my hand is a copy of my translation of Pope Gregory's *Pastoral Care,* the original of which is only accessible to those with a knowledge of Latin. I freely confess that in my younger days, I was not amongst that group and sorely regretted it.'

He held out his hand, indicating firstly Bishop Asser, then moving it to point out Archbishop Plegmund and finally Alfred's mass priest Grimbald, who was an almost constant presence at Alfred's court. 'I owe my improved status to these three learned friends and counsellors, who were patient enough to teach me to read and write the Latin words that had evaded me for so long. So now Pope Gregory's text can be read by anyone who can read our own Saxon tongue.

'On a different note, I am also indebted to Bishop Asser for undertaking to record the story of my life, intended to inform generations to come of our kingdom's great struggle against the pagans from across the seas. But I'll say more of that on another occasion. Today, I present my gifts to you all, with my heartfelt thanks.'

Edward came to stand beside him to read out the names listed on a scroll, allowing each of them time to come forward and receive their gift. Alfred said a few words of thanks to each, the warmth of his smile reflecting his pleasure in doing so. His pride in his family soared when Aethelgifu stood tall and straight before him, although he could see that the effort was costing her dear. Her ashen face told of ongoing ill-health and he silently prayed that God would watch over her.

As the final recipient returned to his place, Alfred said, 'Inside your scrolls you will have noticed a reading pointer. These were specially made to accompany the scrolls, and I have asked Master Craftsman Alaric to explain briefly how he and his team created them.' He held out his hand to the muscular, dark-headed man who had appeared to stand at his side. 'Perhaps you could all look closely at the pointers as he speaks.'

'Thank you, lord,' Alaric started, his Frankish accent pronounced. 'You will see that the handle of the pointer is an exquisite, tear-shaped jewel, quite tiny at only two and a half inches long and one and a half inches at its widest point. Its outer frame and back are of intricately decorated gold, rounded across the top and tapering at the bottom where the design on thickened gold becomes the head of a ferocious beast. That beast's snout is a short, hollow socket that holds the ivory pointer we've put into its mouth.'

He paused while everyone studied their gifts and waited for the animated buzz of chatter to wind down. 'Look closely at the image at the front enclosed by the gold surround. Interpret it how you will, but I know King Alfred will say a word about what it represents when I am finished. We created it from a transparent piece of rock crystal laid over a decorative piece of enamel, or I should say, a number of small pieces of enamel of vivid blue and green separated by strips of gold wire. It shows a seated figure in a sleeveless green tunic holding two stalks, with what look rather like flowers at their ends. And to finish off the piece, around the sides of the gold we inscribed the words, *Alfred ordered me to be made*. And now, Alaric said, 'King Alfred wants your attention.'

Alfred nodded his thanks to the skilful Francian and addressed the clerics. 'I'm sure you will all agree that these reading pointers are amazing pieces of craftsmanship. Their intricate beauty cannot be denied, but what does the picture mean… if anything at all? Some have suggested the man is a

Thirty

king holding the sceptres symbolic of office – me, perhaps? I can understand that considering the inscription. Others have suggested the pope, or Alexander the Great. Still others have named a number of our saints as possibilities.

'To me, the picture represents Christ, and the wisdom of God Incarnate.' He grinned around at them all. 'No doubt if these precious jewels are still in existence in years to come, people will continue to debate over what the image shows.' He suddenly laughed out loud. 'But, with that inscription, they won't have to think too much about who ordered them to be made.'

*

Winchester, Wessex: almost midnight, October 25 899

Asser, Bishop of Sherborne gazed down at Alfred's gaunt face and sunken eyes, his sallow skin glistening in the light of the flickering beeswax candles. The king had been bed-ridden for over a week, his frail frame supported by numerous thick pillows, and was far too ill to be thinking of anything other than resting and regaining his strength. Physicians had been in constant attendance and his devoted wife, Ealhswith, insisted on nursing him herself. Yet still, Alfred showed no signs of recovery. The gut-wrenching pains and diarrhoea continued to wreak havoc on his body, rendering him barely able to move. But the bishop had been summoned to report on ongoing building works in Alfred's kingdom and he could not have refused.

Asser reached out and swept strands of damp, grey hair from Alfred's brow before seating himself and responding to his query. 'Aethelred tells me that preparations for work on the Lundenburh bridge have now begun and that wagonloads of granite have been arriving from Gwynedd, purchased from King Anarawd,' he said, shuffling his bony frame on the hard, wooden stool. 'A variety of craftsmen will undertake the work, including stone masons who are competent enough divers to repair the foundations of the pillars on the riverbed that will support the five new arches. Aethelred has also hired sculptors to create designs along each side of the stonework of the finished bridge.'

'At last…' Alfred's nod of approval was barely perceptible. 'I've waited so long to hear that. The bridge will take some years to complete, but Edward has vowed that he and Aethelred will ensure the work continues after I've been laid to rest in Winchester Minster.'

Alfred's attempt to lift his hand resulted in no more than a raised forefinger. 'No, Bishop, I don't want to hear assurances that I will soon recover from this cursed illness that has blighted my life. My physicians know that my days on Earth are numbered; I see it in their eyes. I do not intend to dwell on my coming death, nor do I fear it. Grimbald has heard my confession and I am ready to meet my Maker. Much as I might have wanted a few more years to complete the many improvements I long for in my kingdom, I know my heirs will continue to see them through.'

The lengthy speech seemed to drain Alfred's strength and he closed his eyes to allow a degree of recovery. Asser said a

Thirty

silent prayer and waited for the cloudy, amber eyes to open.

'Is there anyone you would like to see now, lord? Your family is still assembled in the hall.'

'They have all been in to see me over the last two days and we've spoken of many things, most of them memories of happy times. And they all know what they will inherit once I've gone. My will was drawn up fifteen years ago, as you know, although a few amendments have been made since then. I pray that Ealhswith will find solace in her Wantage and Lambourn estates. We were always so happy there.'

Alfred's eyelids drooped yet again and Asser watched the slow rise and fall of his chest until they reopened.

'My apologies, Bishop,' Alfred murmured on rousing. 'At times, my body refuses to work. I feel it closing down on me and am afraid that very soon, it won't restart. But we were speaking of my will, I think…?'

'We were, lord, and I can assure you that all is in order. The witan will ensure the bequests of estates, moneys, treasures and livestock are given to those stipulated, including the swords for Aethelred and your young grandson, Aethelstan. And, of course, your wishes for the succession will not be disputed.'

Asser patted Alfred's hand. 'Edward is well aware of your fears regarding your nephews' claims to the throne, but I'm certain your generous bequests will go some way in helping to mollify them.'

'I'm not so sure they will, Bishop, but I trust that Edward and Aethelred can deal with Aethelhelm and Aethelbold, if the need arises. But now, I am weary to the bone and would like to see my wife before I sleep.'

'I am here, Alfred.' Ealhswith emerged from the shadows of the doorway, attempting to stem the flow of tears that had rarely stopped for days and coming to stand at the bedside opposite to Asser. She took her husband's hand and bent to kiss his parched lips. 'You know I'm never far away from you.'

'For which I have thanked God every day for the past thirty-one years. You have been my rock, Ealhswith, and I could not have lasted this long without you. Do not weep, my love, we will be together again, one day...

'And, Lord Asser...' Alfred added, his voice rasping in his throat as the bishop stood and turned away, intent on leaving the couple alone for what he feared would be the king's last moments on God's Earth. 'You have my heartfelt thanks for completing your book and you will be rewarded in my will. The struggle and sacrifices made for our beloved kingdom will never be forgotten.'

Alfred's eyes slowly closed and he seemed to sink deeper into his pillows. His body shuddered as he exhaled what Asser knew would be his last breath and the muscles of his face relaxed, all traces of the pain he'd endured for so long, gone. Midnight had slipped by and it was now the twenty-sixth day of October, just six days before Old Hallows' Day.

Asser stood beside the king's bed and said benedictions for his soul, his voice choked with raw emotion as tears rolled down his cheeks.

'Nor will you be forgotten, King Alfred. Nor will you.'

A Note to the Reader

Thank you for reading *King of the Anglo Saxons: Sons of Kings Book 4*. As the final book in the series, it brings the stories of Alfred of Wessex and Eadwulf of Mercia to a close. If you enjoyed the book, a short review on Amazon, Goodreads, a blog, or any other site you feel is suitable, would be greatly appreciated – a mention on Twitter or Instagram, for example. Reviews help self-published authors immensely and are always gratefully received. A sentence or two is all that is needed.

Reviews of Books 1 – 3

Shadow of the Raven: Sons of Kings 1

"It is rare I find a book so wonderfully constructed that it is capable of transporting me back to another place and time. In the Shadow of the Raven, author Millie Thom has done just that. Rich in detail, full of intrigue, action, deception, romance and revenge, the reader is quickly and effortlessly pulled into the story to experience the trials, tribulations, and development of men who would be leaders and those who would serve them."

"Great characters, a fast-paced storyline, interesting settings, and very intriguing. You will root for the heroes and boo the villains. Overall an excellent read."

"Shadow of the Raven by Millie Thom is truly a remarkable historical fiction. I don't say this lightly either. Whereas Shadow of the Raven is not in my preferred genre of reading, I must admit this one kept me reading and reading, wondering what was going to happen. Millie Thom is an incredibly talented author who writes beautifully. I am looking forward to reading the rest of the series.

Pit of Vipers: Sons of Kings Book 2

"Why is this a five-star read? Millie Thom describes in intricate detail what it was like living in the Dark Ages. The historical details blended with gripping storytelling makes this a must read. I read late into the night on several occasions because I couldn't put it down."

"An excellent historical novel and I am awaiting the follow-up with eager anticipation. If you like Bernard Cornwell's Uhtred series you'll like this series, which shows the clashes between the Wessex Saxons and the Danes."

"…There is also a great supporting cast of other characters, some endearing, many detestable but all fascinating. Ivar in particular is a most odious individual. Ms Thom surely knows her history but also has the ability to make that history interesting. Two books down and I shall be reading the third in this trilogy to see what happens next. I have no hesitation in recommending this second book. A worthy Five star read."

Wyvern of Wessex: Sons of Kings Book 3

"This is book three in the Sons of Kings trilogy and I must say, it's my favorite. The historical details are so intricate, so spot on, it was like I was right there. Lush descriptive narration brings a tumultuous time period to life."

"A very well written and researched book series. I thoroughly enjoyed it and can't praise the author enough. The Amazing journey from book 1 to book 3 just keeps you reading."

"I have read all of Millie Thom's 'Sons of Kings' series and enjoyed them all. Millie has obviously studied the period meticulously and brings it to life… I was engrossed by the story which relates the time that Alfred spent on the Isle of Athelney and his later victory over Guthrum, the Viking leader at the Battle of Edington."

"I have fallen in love with the characters in this book. Ms. Thom breathes life into these great people from our past. The different cultures coming together at this pivotal point in history is fascinating."

About Millie Thom

Millie Thom is the author of the four books in the *Sons of Kings* Series: *Shadow of the Raven*, *Pit of Vipers*, *Wyvern of Wessex* and *King of the Anglo Saxons*. The books are historical fiction, set during the second half of the ninth century in the Anglos Saxon and Danish lands during the lifetime of King Alfred. Millie has also published *A Dash of Flash*, an eclectic mix of 85 flash fiction pieces and short stories, and intends to complete *A Second Dash of Flash* in the near future. She is also planning another historical fiction, although this one is not set during Anglo Saxon times.

As a former history and geography teacher with a degree in geology and an enduring love of the past – including the evolution of the Earth and all who have lived on it – reading and writing historical novels was a natural extension of Millie's interests.

Millie and her husband have six grown up children and live in a small village in Nottinghamshire, midway between the old city of Lincoln and the equally old town of Newark-on-Trent. When not writing, Millie loves swimming, travelling, collecting fossils and taking long walks in the countryside.

The Alfred Jewel

As briefly described in the final chapter of this book, the Alfred Jewel is a magnificent piece of filigreed gold enclosing a tear-shaped slice of clear quartz over a cloisonné* enamel plaque of green and blue. It is about 2.5 inches long and 1.2 inches wide, its purpose being to hold a pointer that could be attached to a page of a manuscript and moved down to facilitate reading of the text. Such implements were referred to *aestels* in Anglo-Saxon times.

The image on the plaque is of a man with prominent eyes, holding two floriate stems. It could be a picture of Alfred himself, the pope, one of the saints, a figure of Sentient Man or Christ Incarnate. Modern thought favours the last two.

The back of the enclosing gold is flattened for smooth sliding over a page and is decorated with an intricate design, thought to represent the Tree of Life. The gold thickens at the base of the 'tear-drop' to become a dragon-like head. Inside the creature's mouth is a cylindrical socket/hollow tube designed to hold a pointer. Most pointers were of wood but other materials were also used, notably ivory. The pointer was held in place by a rivet. Around the edge of the jewel is the inscription, ALFRED MEC HEHT GEWYRCAN, which means 'Alfred ordered me to be made'.

The jewel was ploughed up in a field on land owned by Sir Thomas Wroth at North Pemberton in Somerset in 1693. The site is a mere eight miles from Athelney, where Alfred built his stronghold in order to defend his kingdom from Guthrum, and his invading Danes in 878 (Sons of Kings, Book 3, *Wyvern of Wessex*). The jewel was bequeathed to Oxford University by Sir Colonel Nathaniel Palmer (1661-1718) and today it is housed in the Ashmolean Museum in Oxford, where it has been described as 'a matchless piece of goldsmith's work' by the British Archaeology Collection.

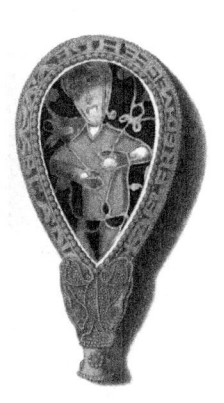

*Cloisonné is decorative work in which pieces of enamel, glass or gemstones are separated by strips of flattened wire placed edgeways on a metal body.

471

Printed in Great Britain
by Amazon